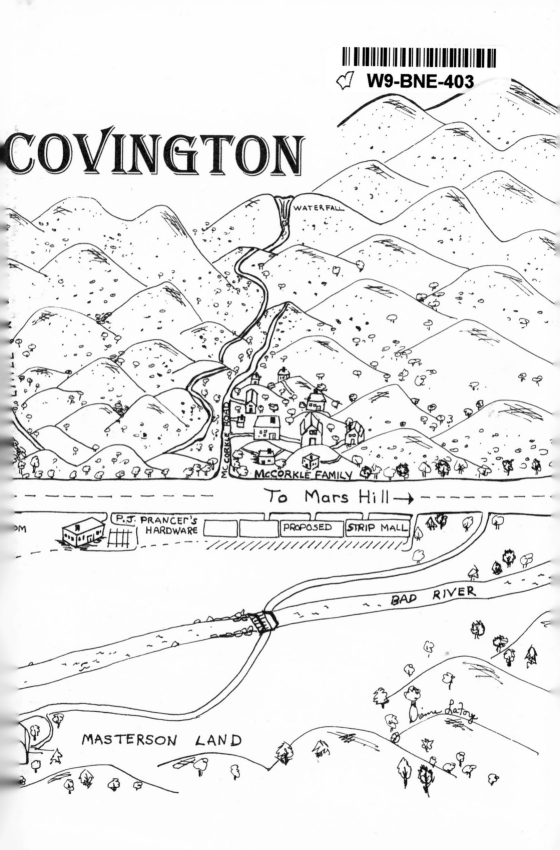

The Gardens of

Covington

Also by Joan Medlicott

The Ladies of Covington Send Their Love

The Gardens of
Covington

A Novel

Joan Medlicott

Thomas Dunne Books
St. Martin's Press ≈ New York

To contact the author or for information about her
Tea on the Porch Workshops:
P.O. Box 355, Barnardsville, NC 28709
jmedlicott@mindspring.com

THOMAS DUNNE BOOKS.
An imprint of St. Martin's Press.

Endpaper map of Covington by Dianne LaForge

Library of Congress Cataloging-in-Publication Data

Medlicott, Joan A. (Joan Avna).
    Gardens of Covington : a ladies of Covington novel / Joan Medlicott.—
1st ed.
        p.   cm
    ISBN 0-312-27555-2
    1. Real estate development—Fiction. 2. Female Friendship—Fiction.
3. North Carolina—Fiction. 4. Neighborhood—Fiction. 5. Aged women—
Fiction. 6. Retirees—Fiction. I. Title.

PS3563.E246 G3 2001
813'.54—dc21

                                                            2001019149

First Edition: May 2001

10 9 8 7 6 5 4 3 2 1

To friends

*Penny Honeychurch Billingham, Mary Lil Colvin, Cass Erickson,
Penny Aylor Freeman, Sydelle Golub, Dianne LaForge, Bobbie Lauren,
Mary Mahon, Anna Miller, Maureen O'Malley, Sylvia Rothstein,
Carmen Sayers, Dorothy Wilkins*

Acknowledgments

The members of my writing group, the Plotters, wended their way through this book with me. They have been, and continue to be, supportive, insightful, and critical in the most positive ways. Thanks to John Alford, Mona Booth, Celia Miles, Bob Reynolds, and Bett Sanders.

It has been a pleasure to work with my editor, Melissa Jacobs, whose sensitivity and skill at editing have made working on this book a pleasant and satisfying experience.

How lucky I am to have Nancy Coffey as my agent, experienced guide, and advocate.

I thank Dianne LaForge, creative friend and artist, for drawing the map of Covington.

Thanks to Karen Bennett, who raises Arucana chickens, for the information she provided me.

My deepest thanks and appreciation to Karen Cragnolin, executive director of the exciting and vital preservation and park development project River Link, for her time and for all the information about River Link that she so generously shared with me.

The Gardens of

Covington

1

The Ladies of Covington Take Tea
on the Porch

Carrying a silver platter brimming with dainty tea sandwiches, and another piled high with her famous, especially thin sugar cookies, Grace Singleton shoved open the screen door with her hip and stepped out onto the front porch of the farmhouse. "Hannah, Amelia," she called lightly over her shoulder, "the ladybugs are back in droves." Orange ladybugs with black dots hugged the porch wall and had begun to stipple the ceiling. Grace set the platters on a low wicker table in front of three rocking chairs.

The door swung wide again. Nearly six feet tall with short, thick, salt-and-pepper hair, Hannah steadied the heavy silver tea tray and service against her middle. She paused as Amelia stepped ahead of her to hold open the door.

"Ugh! ladybugs. *Je les deteste.*" Amelia grimaced as she helped set the tea tray on the table. "They leave such a foul smell on my hands."

"Amelia Declose, don't be so squeamish. Just don't touch them. Harmless creatures. They come for warmth. Few weeks they'll be gone. Good example of a sound environmental concept gone sour." Hannah settled into her rocking chair. "Now, let's have tea."

Every afternoon at four-thirty, weather and schedules permitting, Hannah, Grace, and Amelia came together to sit in their white wicker rockers on the front porch of their farmhouse at 70 Cove Road, to enjoy a genuine old-fashioned English tea, and to share the happenings of their day.

This was their second summer in Covington, and September of 1998 was delivering a record punch of high temperatures. This afternoon, the sun-blasted blacktop of Cove Road shimmered with waves of translucent heat. Across the road, lining the long driveway into Maxwell's Dairy Farm, the leaves on the dogwoods were beginning to tinge a color that Hannah termed maroon, Amelia described as burgundy, and Grace regarded as plum. Whatever the color, it signaled autumn.

Grace's round, smooth face and warm, brown eyes were serene as she poured their tea. As was their wont, other than the clink of a spoon, and the light touch of a cup returned to its saucer, they finished their first cup in companionable silence. "You know the old Masterson place off of Elk Road that we pass every day?" Grace said. "Well, Lurina Masterson, she's eighty-one, fell in her parlor, and Wayne Reynolds and his grandfather, Old Man, found her lying on the floor when they stopped there this morning to visit her. Wayne came dashing over, and asked me to go back with him to check her out. I went, of course."

"Is she all right?" Hannah asked.

"A bit shaken, but nothing broken."

"What's she like?" Amelia asked, leaning forward. Earlier in the summer, Amelia had cut her snow white hair, having decided that she no longer wanted to wear it pulled back in a bun or French twist. Now, soft waves curled about her pale face, setting off her amazingly blue eyes, and she brushed back her hair and reached for yet another cucumber sandwich.

"Well, she's short and thin, and has lots of wrinkles. When I got there, she was lying on her couch propped up by pillows. Her hair's white, and she braids it and winds it about her head like a crown." Grace laughed lightly. "She looked as if she were holding court with Old Man in attendance, bringing her tea, adjusting pillows. She's quite a character. She'd been canning beans in the kitchen, thought she heard a noise out front, and in her haste to get to the front door, she fell over what must be the oldest, most threadbare Oriental rug I've ever seen. In fact everything in that farmhouse is old."

"Antiques?" Amelia asked.

"Some of it, probably. She was born in that house. Never married, took care of her father. Wayne told me that her father, Grover Masterson, left all that property to the state for a park, after Lurina dies, that is." Grace gave her rocking chair a shove. "Oh, and you'll never guess what Old Man's real name is. Go ahead, guess." Her eyes danced. Guessing was a game Amelia had devised for fun.

"Ebenezer," Amelia said.

"Nope. You guess, Hannah."

"Abraham? No, Ezekiel."

Grace shook her head. "Joseph Elisha Reynolds. What do you think of that?"

"See why they call him Old Man." Hannah chuckled.

Grace continued. "Lurina's as concerned about what's happened to Loring Valley, as we are." Grace's brow furrowed. "She sat there and watched it all happen. I think she's lonely. I'm going to take her over some sugar cookies."

"Speaking of Loring Valley," Amelia said. "Brenda Tate called. There's a meeting tonight about that. She insisted we come to the church hall by seven this evening."

Loring Valley was on everyone's mind these days. It lay but a five-minute drive from their farmhouse, off of Elk Road. It had been a lovely valley. People had picnicked there, men and boys had hunted rabbits there, and some had even foraged, illegally, for ginseng on its forested hillsides. No more. Developers from Georgia had moved in on the pristine river valley. Even before the snow melted on the high mountains, construction had begun. All through spring and into summer trucks roared along Elk Road, until the floodplain of Little River, which ran through the valley, had been gobbled up by villas. Hastily constructed condominiums scrambled up mountainsides stripped of vegetation. It had happened so fast, while the people of Covington stood helpless, stunned, and heavyhearted.

Grace slowed her rocker with the toes of her shoes and leaned forward. Distracted, she pinched a dead bloom off of a purple verbena plant that trailed from one of the planter boxes secured to the porch railing. In June, she and Hannah prepared and planted the flower boxes with Day-Glo orange zinnias and bright purple verbenas. "Thank God we live on Cove Road," Grace said. "It's so peaceful here, and so beautiful."

Amelia set her rocker moving. "Indeed, and how lucky we are that Cousin Arthur left me this property, and we had the gumption to move here together. It seems as if we've always lived in Covington, doesn't it? And here it is only a year and five months since we came."

"Indeed it does," Hannah said.

"You'd hardly think that at sixty-nine I'd consider this past year the best year of my life, but I do," Grace said. "I've had more energy than I've had in years. I feel younger. It's been great."

Grace looked across the road at the Maxwell's well-kept, traditional two-story farmhouse, and beyond their hay barn, their red dairy barn, their weathered tobacco barn, and past the windmill and rolling acres of pastureland to the hills, some as round as loaves of bread, and others, mountains, towers of stone cloaked in moss, stretched and thrust upward to crest at the four-thousand-foot peak known as Snowman's Cap. Grace could count eight ridges of mountains this afternoon. Then she said, "Every day, I thank God for good health, for your friendship, for Bob." She waved her hand to indicate the sky and land. "And this incredible view."

But for the creak of their chairs, and the intermittent warbling of a bird and its mate, they rocked in silence.

Grace then spoke. "I've been thinking, let's have a buffet luncheon, perhaps on a Sunday and invite the six other families on Cove Road, and Pastor Johnson."

"Why?" Amelia asked.

"It seems the neighborly thing to do," Grace replied.

"If they'll come," Amelia said.

"Why wouldn't they come?"

"Everyone's friendly, but haven't you noticed they keep you at a distance?" Amelia asked.

Hannah agreed. "They don't take to newcomers easily."

"They visited when you had your hip replacement surgery just after we moved here," Grace reminded Hannah.

"Ever occur to you that courtesy or maybe curiosity prompted an initial visit?"

"You really think that's why they came?" Grace asked.

"Certainly. It was the right thing to do."

"The neighborly thing," Grace said as if suddenly understanding. "They're cautious about newcomers. But we're not newcomers any longer. The Tates are our friends. We've been to their home; they've come here."

"Want to be everybody's bosom buddy?" Hannah asked.

"No, just neighborly." You catch more flies with honey had been a favorite saying of her mother's. It applied now, Grace thought.

"Think about it, Grace," Amelia said. "Harold and Brenda Tate were Cousin Arthur's friends. Remember when we first came to inspect the place, Harold told us how he missed Arthur, how they used to go fishing together, and they'd sit on the porch and swap stories?" Her chin tilted up. "Well, I think, with me being Arthur's cousin and inheriting the place, they simply took us in."

They were unanimous in their gratitude to the Tates. The old farmhouse had seemed hostile in its weatherworn, dilapidated condition, and their hearts hung low that morning when Harold Tate met them on Cove Road and welcomed them to Covington. Ushering them across buckling floorboards, he identified the odd rustling noises as intruding possums, and cautioned them about the broken fifth step on the staircase. He had supplied them with the names of reliable carpenters, painters, plumbers, and electricians; introduced them to his wife, Brenda; and generally watched over them like a protective relative. Grace and Hannah now volunteered at the elementary school where Brenda was the principal.

"I think our neighbors will come, most of them, anyway," Grace responded. "Let's at least ask them."

"Okay." Amelia nodded. "I like a party. How about you, Hannah?"

"What's to lose? They come, fine. They don't come, fine," Hannah said. "We'll freeze leftovers. What date did you have in mind?"

"October eleventh after church."

"You're a cool one asking us," Hannah teased. "You were going to do it anyway no matter what we said."

"I, well." Grace's face flushed. "It just seems right, that's all."

"We'll help." Amelia stopped rocking long enough to reach for another cucumber finger sandwich.

Grace was off and running. "I'll make things I think they'll like: a big pot of pumpkin soup, ham, fried chicken, collard greens, squash casserole, and my special Vienna cake for dessert." Grace ticked off each item on her fingers.

"The one with the colored layers? Oh, that's good cake," Hannah said.

"It'll keep you busy cooking for a week. *Mon Dieu*," Amelia quipped. "I'd simply die if I had to be in the kitchen that long."

"Given a choice, Amelia, you wouldn't go into the kitchen at all," Hannah said with good humor.

"Bob will help me clean up."

Hannah tapped the arm of Grace's chair. "We'll all help."

A cooling wind stirred. Leaves skittered across the front lawn and halted, caught in the thorny stems of rosebushes planted by Hannah along the driveway from their house to Cove Road. Yesterday, Hannah had filled a vase with fragrant, tall-stemmed Chrysler Imperial red roses snipped from those bushes—the last roses before winter. In the stillness, they could hear the muffled sound of a car going by on Elk Road.

"What are you thinking, Hannah Parrish? You look so pensive all of a sudden," Grace asked.

"About how I fretted and worried that you'd marry Bob Richardson and move out of our farmhouse."

Grace chuckled. Bob Richardson had indeed wanted marriage. Back in Dentry, Ohio, her hometown, she had been surrogate grandmother to neighbors' and friends' children, supplying them with cookies and cakes and generally being cautious, conventional, compliant, and eager to satisfy the expectations of others. Without exposure to the more worldly Hannah and Amelia, she would never have envisioned an alternative to remarriage. Having discovered the pleasure and ease of sharing a home with friends, Grace had vacillated for months before deciding against it—not easy, given her background. Expecting a traditional response to his proposal, Bob had been flabbergasted when she said no. "Remember the night I told you we'd *done it?*" Grace asked her friends.

"And I asked you, when's the wedding?" Hannah said. "And you said, 'No wedding. We don't have to be married or live together to have a relationship.' I never expected that."

Grace brought her rocker to a halt and reached for her teacup. "It's worked out well, hasn't it? I mean with Bob and me." She sipped her tea, then set the cup down and started the rocker.

"Bob loves you, and he's wonderfully helpful and kind to all of us," Hannah said.

"I love the way we live together," Amelia said, "coming and going with our own lives, yet being supportive of one another. There's always a listening ear, a helping hand."

The low autumn sun ceased splashing the front porch of the farmhouse with its fierce dazzle and slipped behind the hills. The ladies rocked in comfortable silence and watched the heavens turn flame and gold above a line of pale green sky that reminded Grace of lime sherbet. She licked her lips, tasting the sweetness, feeling the coolness, thinking how the brilliance excited and the green soothed. Day tiptoed into evening, and dusk shuffled across the mountains and slid down into the valley.

Finally, Amelia said, "Something smells great in the kitchen."

Grace nodded. "An old recipe I forgot I had. Baked chicken smothered in apricot sauce."

"Sounds marvelous!"

"Think you still have room for dinner before we go to the meeting?"

"Just try us," Hannah said.

2

The Meeting at Cove Road
Church Hall

🌿 The social hall at the church was plain, its walls painted white, its only ornament a simple wooden cross that filled the space on the back wall between two windows. Men and women wedged shoulder to shoulder on chairs that stretched from a center aisle to both walls. Men of all ages wore their Sunday best, as did the women: older women with deeply lined faces, middle-aged women, most of them round about the middle, and young women, a few carrying babies.

Sitting on the aisle near the door was Velma Herrill, mother of Roger Herrill, known as "Buddy," the young fellow who managed the general store and single-pump gas station on Elk Road, the only road into Covington.

"How you doing?" Velma asked, reaching for Amelia's hand. "That's a right nice picture of the church you made for Pastor Johnson. I saw it in his office just the other day."

Amelia turned her full attention to Velma, a pleasant, plump woman in her mid-fifties. "Glad you like that picture. If you want, I'll come on down and take one of your house," she said. "With all those roses still blooming along the railing of your porch, it would make a lovely color photograph."

"Well." Velma's face turned ruddy with pleasure. "I sure would like that."

"Consider it done. I'll come on Saturday if that suits you, weather permitting."

"Saturday'd be just fine."

"What time?"

"Two o'clock okay with you?" Velma asked.

"I'll be there," Amelia said, touching the other woman's shoulder lightly. Then she moved on to join the others.

Halfway down the aisle, Brenda Tate half rose from her chair and beckoned them to join her. It had been while tutoring the then seven-year-old Tyler Richardson at Brenda's Caster Elementary School that Grace had met Tyler's father, Russell, and his grandfather Bob Richardson. Not only had she and Bob become friends, and she blushed to think of it, they had become lovers, and soon they would be business partners in a tearoom that they were having built on leased land on Elk Road.

"Sorry. Excuse me. Sorry," Grace, Hannah, and Amelia murmured as they squeezed past knees and avoided stepping on the toes of those already seated in the row where Brenda held chairs open for them. People nodded and said hello.

Moments later, Harold Tate walked with a sure stride to the un-adorned oak podium that stood to one side of the cross. "Many thanks to Pastor Johnson for openin' the hall tonight for this meetin'."

From the front row, the tall, round-shouldered, gray-haired pastor raised a hand in acknowledgment.

The room grew still. Harold's deeply lined face flushed. He ran his palms across the top of his brush cut, cleared his throat, and looked at his wife. Brenda smiled encouragement at him. Harold began. "Well, y'all know there's not a darned thing we coulda done to stop all that rippin' and tearin' and bulldozin' and buildin' over yonder in Loring Valley."

"They've destroyed that right pretty valley," a woman said softly.

A refrain of "Destroyed it" echoed through the room. Feet shuffled. A man called, "What we gonna do, Harold?"

"Nothin' we can do about what's already been done, but we can stop it happenin' on Cove Road."

"Cove Road?" Heads turned. Whispers rippled into corners.

"I hear tell." Harold raised his arms. "Now, don't none of you ask me where I heard it. I can't tell you."

As if of one mind and body, the audience waited now, silent, leaning slightly forward.

"I hear tell those developers are lookin' for more land. There's

McCorkle Creek, but that's too narrow and steep, and when old Miss Lurina passes away Masterson's land's going to the state for a park. So, that leaves Cove Road what with all the pastureland and views we've got."

Murmurs rose. Heads wagged.

Harold lifted his arm for silence and continued. "Seems like they're gonna be sendin' us all a letter sweet-talkin' us, wantin' to buy our land."

An electric shock sluiced through the room. Men and women turned or tapped their friends and neighbors on the shoulders, whispered to one another. Voices escalated, whisper to din, din to babble, babble to clamor. The news was confounding. If any of them sold, it would ruin this good earth, their paradise, Cove Road.

Goose bumps clumped on Hannah's arms. Reaching over she squeezed Grace's hand, which was as cold as her own. She remembered something that Harold had said to her recently. "One of them McCorkle fellas with fancy ideas married him a flatlander girl from South Georgia. Betcha he told these developers about Loring Valley."

And the librarian at Caster Elementary had told Grace that she'd heard that the powers that be in Madison County encouraged development. "We're not a wealthy county, you know," she'd said. "Our population doesn't reach twenty thousand. Housing for retirees from out of state's a clean industry, you might say, and it brings in taxes and encourages small businesses. Not a bad idea, really." She had looked at Grace sheepishly. "Unless, of course, the development's in your backyard."

Harold's raised hand folded into a fist and dropped heavily onto the podium. The room grew quiet. "Come an offer, I just want y'all to know that us Tates, and our family, the Lunds, and the Craines aren't gonna sell. I'm askin' y'all to stand with us. We gotta be together in this. None of us sell out, or this valley's done for."

❦

As Hannah drove the short distance home to the farmhouse in her station wagon, the ladies were silent, each lost in her own thoughts. From the backseat Grace studied Amelia's and Hannah's head and neck. Pixie-like, Amelia's shortened hair capped her small, round head. Her neck was swathed in the ubiquitous scarf with which she hid the burn scars that dated back several years to the car crash that had killed her husband, Thomas. Thick graying hair fluffed out in disarray topped Hannah's tall, slender neck. Instinctively Grace smoothed back her hair from her face. We're a good team, Grace thought. Bob had dubbed her the heart of their home, Hannah the head. And Amelia?

"She's sometimes fey, sometimes capricious, sometimes solid and dependable. Why, Amelia's the spirit of our home," Grace had said.

The three ladies had worked out systems, roles, which sprang from their interests and skills. Hannah repaired leaking toilets, changed air filters, oiled creaky doors, unstuck windows, and tended the garden. Grace did most of the food shopping, happily cooked and baked, and sang off-key. Amelia filled the house with flowers and music, and vacuuming and dusting gave her a sense of satisfaction, except when ladybugs returned, as they did each spring and fall, to inhabit the ceilings. Grace sat back. So much had happened since they moved to Covington, and from it all they had become more tolerant, patient, and accepting of one another.

The crunch of gravel under tires brought Grace back to the present. Moments later they were on the porch, and Hannah held open the front door and stood aside to let Grace and Amelia into the entrance hall. From the living room to their left, a tall lamp on a timer cast a soft welcoming glow on the new Kerman Oriental rug with its soft colors and silky look that covered most of the foyer floor.

"I'm absolutely appalled at the idea that Cove Road could be threatened with development." Amelia covered her forehead with her hand. *"Mon Dieu,* I'm too tired to think or talk about it now." She started up the stairs at the end of the hall.

"Same for me," Grace said, and she and Hannah followed Amelia up the carpeted stairs, each to her own bedroom.

Two hours later, lights peeped from beneath their respective doors. Grace was first down to the kitchen. Her yellow-and-white-striped pajamas and yellow socks matched the cheerful yellow walls of the spacious modern kitchen, where white Formica cabinets had replaced splitting wood cabinets, new appliances took the place of rusty ancient ones, and lumpy floors were supplanted by laminate wood floors.

Grace had barely filled the kettle and set it on the stove when Amelia appeared in the doorway in a pink silk peignoir and mules, followed by Hannah, straight and solid as a lighthouse in her gray terry-cloth bathrobe with red lapel and belt and ragged terry-cloth slippers.

"Couldn't sleep," Hannah said, pulling out a chair at the kitchen table.

"Neither could I," Amelia said. "Ah, cookies." She reached for the plate of cookies on top of the refrigerator and deposited it in the center of the table.

"What if someone sells out to those developers?" Grace brought her knife down hard into the lemon she was quartering. From a cabinet above the sink she lifted a compartmentalized wooden box filled with a variety of teas and positioned it on the table facing Hannah. Amelia set the table with small plates, cups for herself and Grace, Hannah's favorite mug, spoons, sugar bowl, creamer, and the quartered lemon. Soon the kettle whistled, and Grace poured the steaming water into the cups and mug. "Well," she said, taking a seat across from Hannah, "we know the Tates won't sell, nor their daughter, Molly, and her husband, Ted Lund. They have just above a hundred acres."

"The Craines own a lot of land, and they're Harold's cousins. Their land's quite steep, though," Amelia said.

Grace opened the wooden box of tea and offered it around. "They'd never sell. They like to tell people how their ancestors, the Covingtons, first settled this valley and gave the area its name."

Bending over the tea box, Hannah considered and rejected mint, Earl Grey, orange and cinnamon, chamomile, and Tetley tea, then pulled out a bag. "Darjeeling." Hannah dangled the bag above her mug, dropped it in, and watched the water curl about it before soaking it through.

Grace's mind was elsewhere. "Beside the parsonage, there are seven families on Cove Road." She counted them off on her fingers. "Us, the Craines, the Tates, the Lunds, the Ansons, the Herrills, and the Maxwells across the road."

"Developers wouldn't be interested in the church's land. That's only about thirty-five acres, nor our twenty-eight acres," Amelia said.

"Maxwells and Ansons are the big property owners, over five hundred acres each, Harold told me." Hannah fished out the tea bag with a spoon and set it on the plate on which her mug sat.

Grace's head jerked up. Anxiety clouded her clear, brown eyes. "Oh, please, God, don't let the Maxwells sell their land."

"Stop this." Hannah tapped the side of her pink mug, which read in bold red script, GARDENERS MAKE THE BEST LOVERS. It was a gift for her seventy-third birthday from her grandson, Philip. "We can't make ourselves crazy. We haven't gotten any letter. Maybe this whole thing is nothing but a rumor."

"Would Harold have called a meeting? Would everyone have shown up for a rumor?" Grace frowned. "The Maxwells didn't come."

"Don't frown, Grace," Hannah said. "You'll get wrinkles, which you're lucky enough not to have."

Grace ran her hand across her brow as if to smooth the lines. "Better?"

"Not much," Hannah replied. "Got to stop worrying, all of us."

"How?" Amelia asked.

"By looking at the facts. First, we're not sure of anything. Two. We don't know that anyone on Cove Road would sell land passed down to them by their forefathers. Three. There's not a darn thing we can do about it, especially not tonight. Enough talk now, let's go on up to bed."

Grace raised her hands. "Tried that. Once I got into bed, I couldn't shut off my head."

"Tell you what," Hannah suggested. "Let's get out the Chinese checkers. Help distract us."

Grace removed the plate of cookies from the table, covered it, and placed it atop the refrigerator. An hour later, when the kitchen clock read one A.M., they put away the game, ready to try their beds again.

"Now remember," Hannah said from her bedroom door, "read, listen to music, breathe deep, whatever helps you get to sleep. Thinking serious thoughts is forbidden, right?"

They retreated into the privacy of their respective rooms.

From light cast by the lamp near Grace's bed, the peach-colored walls glowed warmly, and on a shelf of her floor-to-ceiling bookcase the seven clowns in her collection somersaulted, waved, and grinned with their exaggeratedly painted mouths.

Shutting off serious thoughts was not easy for Grace. Being told not to think of something guaranteed that it was all she could think about. She opened her window, and her eyes searched the dark night for the stream, nearly fifty feet to the east. The security light, on its tall pole in front of the Maxwells' barn, cast long shadows across the road. George and Bella Maxwell. Grace knew their names, but not the people. She couldn't put a clear face to either of them. They waved driving by, yet remained distant. They would send their son, Zachary, over with fresh apples from their orchard, or a fresh baked apple pie, but they had never invited any of them into their home, or dropped in on the ladies. They seemed disconnected from the other families on Cove Road, yet had been conspicuous by their absence at the meeting tonight. Grace's heart plunged. Of all the landowners, if anyone, were they most likely to sell out?

Grace hit the side of her head gently with her palm. Stop thinking. You know nothing about the Maxwells. Pulling a chair to the window, she rested her head against its low sill and listened to the soothing gush and gurgle of the nearby stream. She loved water yet had never been swimming at a beach, never seen the ocean or even the Great Lakes, though she had lived a lifetime in Ohio. Unbelievable. She, with all her books and dreams of faraway lands, had hardly stirred from Dentry.

Something small and hard hit her hand. A ladybug, fallen perhaps from a minute crack in the window frame. She studied its spots, started to count them, and remembered reading somewhere that in a French vineyard a ladybug is a sign of good weather. Pushing open the screen a bit, Grace flicked the ladybug outside. Did it fly away or fall to the ground? In the darkness she could not tell. Raindrops pelted her fingers, and when she drew her hand in, it was wet.

Grace's mind drifted back through the years to Dentry. Like a cloud, she floated above her small hometown and scanned its familiar streets and places: Main Street, Western Ohio Bank, Trinity Church at the end of Livermore Avenue, Barker Elementary, where Roger cried so pitifully that first day of school that she felt her heart would break. She lingered over tree-shaded Park Road, circled her redbrick ranch house and the river of yellow tulips that spring faithfully ushered in each year along both sides of her front walk.

Sitting at her window, the rush of the stream outside seemed to grow louder, and as she listened to its music she mused about her deceased husband, Ted, a good, hardworking man, not given to words or to overt expressions of affection.

"You know me well enough to know what I'm thinking," he'd say when she asked his opinion on things. He must have said he loved her before they married, but she couldn't remember him saying the words in all the years that followed. "Do you love me?" she would ask.

"Why else would I be here?" was his standard reply.

Did she really know what he thought or felt, or even who he was? She shook her head. Did it matter anymore? After Ted died, her life had flipped, flopped, and come to rest in Covington with Hannah, and Amelia, and now, dear, lovable, warm, and expressive Bob. If she could, she would order time to stand still. No changes, she thought, dear God, no more changes.

3

The Buyout Offer

Grace awakened to soft light flowing through her bedroom windows. She stretched, then rolled over and hugged her pillow. She loved this room, this house, this land. If she followed the stream around the farmhouse, through the pasture, and past the apple orchard, she could climb a hill and enter miles of woods crisscrossed with creeks and congregations of wildflowers. If she hiked, as she sometimes did, to the crest of their land, she could see through the bare winter limbs of shagbark hickory, locust, oak, ash, and poplar, to softly humped mountain ranges that vanished in the distance behind a soft bluish gray haze. The Blue Ridge Mountains. Aptly named.

Grace turned from the world of nature to a consideration of practical matters. Today at lunch, she and Hannah would meet Emily Hammer, the young woman that Bob's son, Russell, was enamored with. It had been more than two years since Russell's wife, and Tyler's mother, Amy, had been killed in that dreadful car accident, and now Russell had met a young woman named Emily Hammer, the daughter of new residents of Loring Valley.

Having spent an hour last night deciding what to wear for this luncheon meeting, Grace had chosen a simple blue skirt, a pale-blue long-sleeved shirt, and a vest embroidered down the front with bright yellow and rose flowers. Now, twisting and turning, she inspected herself in the mirror. At times like this, it would be nice to be thinner and more sophisticated. She shrugged. Oh well. When she needed a boost, Grace reread the note Bob had given her, and which she had taped in a prominent place on her mirror.

The beauty of a woman is not in the clothes she wears, the figure she carries, or the way she combs her hair.
The beauty of a woman must be seen in her eyes because that is the doorway to her heart, the place where love resides.
The beauty of a woman is not in a facial mole, but the true beauty of a woman is reflected in her soul. It is the caring that she lovingly gives, the passion that she shows.
And the beauty of a woman, with passing years, only grows!

It came in an e-mail Bob got. "Sort of a chain e-mail letter" was the best he could tell Grace when she asked where he had gotten it and who wrote it.

Thanks to the anonymous sender, whoever it was. Dear Bob. Lucky me. She thought, then, of Lurina Masterson alone in her rambling old house. Meeting Lurina was a happening that had quite caught Grace up. Having noticed the quick twist of the older woman's head, the brightening of her blue eyes, when she, or Old Man, or Wayne spoke, and the slump of Lurina's shoulders when Grace said good-bye, she was certain that Lurina was lonely. Had she no family? Why, at her advanced age, did she live alone in that weather-beaten old farmhouse? Grace determined to take her cookies and tell her about the church hall meeting.

But now Grace needed to focus on Russell and Emily, and where this relationship might lead, and its effect on nine-year-old Tyler, who had become her surrogate grandson, and whom she loved as if he were her very own. Grace smoothed her hair and looked into her own direct, warm brown eyes.

The beauty of a woman must be seen in her eyes. . . .

If the compliments paid her eyes over the years were true, then she must judge herself beautiful. Nonsense. Her father's often used phrase, "Pride cometh before the fall," kicked at her mind. Still, feeling a bit beautiful helped when you were nervous about meeting new people. Grace pinched her cheeks for color and applied a pale rose lipstick. She inserted simple pearl studs in her ears. Below, the doorbell rang. "Get it, will you, Amelia," Grace called from her bedroom door. "I'm almost ready. It's probably the Richardsons come to take Hannah and myself to lunch at the Hammers."

Grace heard the front door open and close, but not the sound of Bob's, or Russell's, or Tyler's voices. What she did hear was Amelia's muffled scream.

Clasping her purse in one hand, Grace grasped the railing and followed Hannah down the stairs. Since hip replacement surgery last year, Hannah handled steps with careful deliberation.

In the center of the Kerman Oriental, among the arabesque designs of the new carpet, Amelia sat cross-legged clutching something white with blue trim to her bosom. The front door stood slightly ajar, allowing the cool October air to chill the foyer.

"It's come," she said, her lovely blue eyes huge.

"What's come?"

"The letter from the developers."

Hannah reached for the envelope, but it was as if Amelia and the Federal Express she had just signed for were fused like wet fingers to a frozen ice tray. Amelia's eyes were blank.

Hannah tugged at the envelope.

Slowly, reluctantly, Amelia released the missive. "Don't open it."

Avoidance and denial, Grace thought. Typical of how Amelia reacts when something threatens the routine and security of her life, Grace's heart softened. Perhaps Amelia's need to hold things firmly in place, to not trust life, resulted from the trauma of having lost her nine-year-old child, Caroline, to some rare parasite, and then her husband in that horrible car accident.

"Let me see it," Hannah said. "The Richardsons'll be here any minute now."

"I'm not going with you to meet those people in Loring Valley. Things are getting complicated since they came," Amelia said.

Grace offered Amelia her hand, and helped her to her feet. Amelia's hand was small, her fingers slim yet strong and dexterous, Grace knew, for she had seen Amelia speedily change camera bodies, and lenses, and set up her tripod with alacrity. "We know that. Don't you remember, you agreed to baby-sit Tyler?"

Outside, car doors slammed. A child's feet hammered the steps and pummeled the porch floor. The front door opened, admitting a freckle-faced, red-haired boy of nine. He stopped, reared back on his heels, and stared at Amelia, then turned to Grace. "What's wrong, Granny Grace?"

From their first meeting, when Grace sat precariously on a child-sized chair in the hall outside of Tyler's classroom tutoring him in reading, he had called her Mrs. Grace. Then last December, he had announced to his grandfather, "I love Mrs. Grace. She loves me. You love Mrs. Grace, don't you?"

"Sure do," Bob replied from the sofa where he lay reading.

With a jump, Tyler landed atop his grandfather's chest, straddled him, and, bending, rubbed his nose against Bob's. "Well, you're my grandpa. We both love her, so Mrs. Grace can be my grandma."

His grandfather rubbed Tyler's nose back and did not disagree. Tyler went on. "Granny Grace is what I'm going to call her."

"Don't you think you ought to ask her first?"

"Nah! She'll say yes. She'll be glad, I know." Tyler had run his fingers across his grandfather's eyebrows and eyed him coyly. "She doesn't have any grandchildren." Tyler's smile lit his face. "She really loves me." And so it was.

Standing in the foyer, Amelia's face was pink, her eyes teary. "You sad?" the child asked her.

Brushing her arm across her face, Amelia smiled at him. "No, *mon petit chou.* I was surprised about something. I'm fine now." She held out her hand to him. "Come, let's get out the Chinese checkers."

A quick nod from Grace assured Tyler that it was all right, and he took Amelia's hand. They headed into the kitchen, from where Amelia's voice sounded a bit too high-pitched as she offered him a choice of Rocky Road, cherry vanilla, or butter pecan ice cream. Earlier, she had promised Tyler that they would play his favorite board game, Chinese checkers. The marble game, he called it.

Bob and Russell appeared in the doorway. They hardly looked like father and son: Bob tall with a shock of thick white hair, Russell short, a bit stocky, slightly balding. "Ready ladies?" Russell asked. His voice was tight, nervous. He fidgeted, shifting weight from one leg to the other.

Hannah had torn open the missive and retreated to the stairs, where she hunched on the bottom step reading the offer from the developers, Bracken and Woodward Corporation, to buy any and all land on Cove Road. Her voice was hard. "They start with a pitch about how beautiful, how environmentally sound, how fast they've sold all of their one hundred condos and villas in Loring Valley. They use the words 'community,' and 'ideal,' and 'growth' a time too much for me." She looked from one to the other of them.

"It's true, then. Harold was right," Grace said.

"I guess they're pitching everyone on Cove Road, and touting the benefits of a strip mall. A food market, pharmacy, beauty parlor, Hallmark store, and a golf shop have already committed to the land along Elk Road that Grover Masterson set aside for commercial use, they say."

"Guess we can expect a phone call about another meeting at the church hall," Grace said. It was appallingly real; development would mean that Cove Road would change and drastically. Suddenly, she felt powerless in the face of it all. She did not want to meet the Hammers and their daughter, Emily, didn't want to meet any of the new residents of Loring Valley, people from Florida, Washington, Chicago, wherever. Grace looked at Bob. He was waiting, holding her jacket. It meant a great deal to him to meet this woman Russell had known for only a month and who had so captivated his son. Unease wrapped itself uncomfortably around Grace like a hot towel on a summer day. Why Emily? Why now? Tyler did not need a change like this. Smiling at Bob, Grace fought back apprehension. "Could we sit a minute and talk about this letter?" she asked.

Russell looked at his watch, once, twice. He collected antique clocks and watches, elegant machines that kept time to the minute, all but one. "We're invited for eleven-thirty. I'll need to call and let them know." He headed for the kitchen.

Grace stopped him. "No. Let's just go. We can talk about this later."

From the kitchen came Tyler's, and then Amelia's, laughter, and Tyler's voice. "I'm getting good at this, Aunt Amelia, ain't I?"

"Ain't is very poor use of our language," Amelia said.

"All the kids at school say ain't."

"Anyone in your home say ain't?"

"Nope," Tyler said.

Hannah started out of the door. "I deluded myself that there would be no letter," she muttered.

Outside, the winds, at seventeen miles an hour, added to the chill of the day, and Grace was glad for her fleece jacket. "Someone on

21

this road will want to sell. I feel it. I just pray it's not the Maxwells," she said.

Head high, eyes dilated with anger, Hannah stopped and looked back at Grace. "If anyone does, I'm going to fight it. Don't know how, yet. But I'm not going to sit back and just let this happen."

Bob looked at Hannah intently. "Any help you need, let me know." Bob loved Cove Road, loved its quiet pastoral, as well as its powerful mountain views. Several times, of late, he toyed with the idea of asking the women to lease him a small piece of land up in their hills where he could build a cottage. Only his concern about tipping the balance of relationships stopped him. Grace was adamant about not marrying, about not moving out of the farmhouse she shared with Amelia and Hannah. That had taken getting used to, but he'd come to terms with her need for independence and appreciated their way of life, the way they seemed to understand and care for one another, even as he envied the support system the ladies provided each other. There was something special about the way women could do this. But still, at times he wished he had Grace to come home to, wished he had her all to himself.

Hannah started down the porch steps and stopped. "You all go. Give my regards to your Emily, Russell, and to her folks. I need to make some phone calls, see what's happening."

4

Meeting the Hammers

Emily Hammer opened the wood door with the leaded glass pane in the center and extended her hand in welcome. Emily was in her early thirties, petite, with soft blue eyes fringed with long lashes, and the firm, quick handshake of a busy professional, which indeed she was, for Emily had a private law practice in Ocala, Florida. She was smartly dressed in dark blue slacks and a pinstriped vest, out of which a lush cream-colored silk blouse spilled. Her no-nonsense Rolex watch contrasted with a decidedly feminine pearl ring designed as a cluster of grapes. Grace could not imagine Emily settling down to the unsophisticated lifestyle of rural Madison County.

Russell introduced his father and Grace to Emily, who smiled broadly at them. "Grace, Bob," Emily said cheerfully, "meet my parents, Ginger and Martin Hammer."

Martin welcomed Grace with a bear hug and Bob with a hearty slap on the back while Ginger held out a hand to them both. Drinks were served on the back patio of the Victorian-style three-bedroom villa. From the edge of the flagstone patio, the lawn rolled gently to the bank of Little River, to a tumble of boulders that hid the water from view. They're meant to be a dike, Grace thought. The builders know that after heavy rains rivers in this area, large and small, overflow their banks. I wonder if the Hammers know this?

Grace watched Russell and Emily saunter away to sit on a boulder by the river. Emily's head reached a trifle above Russell's shoulder, and when she tilted it slightly, as she did now, her head fit easily into the curve of his shoulder. Grace turned her attention to Ginger Hammer.

Grace hated being judged, and did not usually judge others by their appearance. But there was absolutely nothing warm or appealing about Ginger Hammer. She struck Grace instantly as a deliberately theatrical woman whose plum lipstick matched her fingernail polish and her enormous hoop earrings. She had a way of flinging back her head, seeming to address the sky or the ceiling even while talking to you. Grace endured. She listened to Ginger evaluate her home in terms of price. "It was terribly overpriced, but I told Martin . . ." Ginger nodded toward her husband. ". . . if we didn't have a riverfront villa, I wouldn't put my foot in Loring Valley." She gave Grace a smooth, calculating stare. "There are only twenty-eight villas on the river, you know."

Grace was aware of a woman's shadow passing behind the shades of the glass-sliding patio door. Ginger saw the shadow also and rose, then clapped her hands. The couple by the river abandoned their boulder seat and walked slowly to the patio. "Lunch," Ginger said.

It was a relief when they were finally ushered into the dining room. Decorated in prints and solids in all shades of apricot, the dining room was pleasing to the eye. Grace finally relaxed and watched Russell devour Emily with his eyes. Over lunch, Emily spoke about the sprawling growth taking place in central Florida, and the hot summers, and told them how much she loved to bicycle and hike. Grace changed her mind. Maybe Emily could make a life here. She proceeded then to create in her mind a scenario in which Emily and Russell married, and Emily opened a law practice in Mars Hill. She was busy blessing them with children, a boy and a girl or even twins that she could grandmother, when Ginger's voice interrupted.

"Emily tells me you volunteer at an elementary school nearby."

Grace stopped cutting her chicken Florentine, and placed her knife on the edge of her plate. "Yes. Caster Elementary. I work with second graders on their reading."

Ginger's fingers toyed with the stem of her wineglass. "I was A Number One in real estate sales in New York and in Florida. Of course, years ago . . ." She waved her hand. "My degree was in education. I never taught." Ginger leaned toward Grace, half covered her full, plum-daubed mouth with her palm, and spoke softly, though she needn't have, for the men were engrossed in conversation. "Martin picked this place." She rolled her eyes. "Why, I'll never fathom. He's got to go to Weaverville, or Asheville to play golf." Ginger's eyes narrowed. One long plum fingernail tapped the table. "He was tough, one hell of an investment banker. He adored the rat race, New York. Before his heart attack, that is. After we moved to Florida, Martin really slowed down." Brushing back strands of curly dark hair, Ginger raised an impeccably plucked eyebrow.

"Real estate" Grace pondered. Would she go back to selling real estate, resales in Loring Valley? Grace would never use her as a realtor.

"Look at him. He's gotten so old," Ginger was saying, and she shivered slightly. Into Grace's imagination walked the final portrait of Dorian Gray. "Oh, well." Ginger raised the wine to her lips and drank deeply, leaving behind on the crystal goblet the pale plum shape of her lips.

A maid in a crisp blue uniform cleared the table, served coffee and pecan pie for dessert. Martin sat at the head, or foot, of the table with Bob to his right. Then came Grace, and across from her, Emily and Russell, their chairs squished together, their eyes warm, their conversation animated, but only with each other. Ginger at the foot, or head, smiled benignly and nodded her head toward them. "Cute couple, aren't they? He's well established here, is he?"

"Russell's a computer network consultant. He's very busy."

"Oh, well." Ginger sighed. "Young people today. They change careers, change locations, marry, divorce, remarry, try to blend families. Russell has a child, Emily tells me." She splashed a dash of cream into her coffee.

"Tyler. Red hair, freckles." Like his mom, Grace almost said. "He's nine now. Very dear to me."

"So," Ginger said, done with Tyler. "What's with you and Bob? Emily says you're not married. Are you planning to be?"

Whooh! Grace thought. You don't waste much time before snooping into other people's lives, do you? Her face heated, but she smiled. "We have no plans." She looked at the men, hoping for a lull in their conversation, hoping to catch Bob's eye, wishing they had decided on a signal, hoping he would recognize her need to leave, as soon as politely possible.

When Ginger spoke again, there was in her voice a challenge and not a hint of resignation. "Well, if I'm stuck here, I'm going to have to find something to keep me busy."

Relax, Grace warned herself. Take a breath. The woman is all pretense. It was hard for Grace to like someone like Ginger, and that bothered her. "The hospitals and the three museums at Pack Place in Asheville have strong volunteer programs."

"Three museums?" Ginger asked.

"The art museum, the children's museum, the gem and mineral museum. A really fine complex."

"Yes, that might be better than trying to fit into some provincial school out here."

Ginger's cool words did not surprise Grace. She glanced at Bob. He and Martin had pushed back coffee cups and dessert plates and were gesticulating enthusiastically. Russell was focused on Emily. Grace tried again with Ginger. "Do you have hobbies like gardening, sewing, bridge?"

"Scrabble," Ginger replied, her eyes suddenly interested. "I compete nationally in Scrabble contests."

Suddenly Grace felt sorry for Ginger. She and Hannah and Amelia lived in Covington out of love and choice. To use a gardening metaphor, this woman's roots had been rudely yanked from the soil, and no new hole lovingly dug, watered, fertilized for her to grow in. She studied the hard lines of Ginger's face and found no trace of the softness visible in Emily's face. Ginger's round hazel eyes were her best feature, and in those eyes, fleetingly, Grace detected pain. She felt a stab of empathy. "I didn't know they had Scrabble contests."

"Oh, yes. People gather from all over the country. There are international competitions too, but I haven't gone overseas. Martin won't travel, so . . ." She shrugged. The light in her eyes faded.

Martin would not travel, so Ginger did not go, but set aside an activity she felt so passionate about. This touched a chord in Grace that sent her shooting back in time to Ted, who, in his own quiet way, had controlled her life. Imagine, all those years, never driving far from Dentry, what with Ted's fear of highways and flying, and her father's crushing and limited vision of the world. She thought it was their generation, hers, and Amelia's, and Hannah's, who gave over control of their lives to their husbands, but here was Ginger, ten, maybe fifteen years younger than she, or Amelia, or Hannah, and still giving over control to her husband.

She blessed Hannah, who had been on her own for so many years. Hannah had pushed and prodded Grace, and offered her new ways of being and thinking. Hannah had challenged Grace to be spontaneous, adventurous, creative, and brave, ah, yes, brave. Grace felt braver than she ever had in her life. It takes gumption to question ingrained beliefs about how things ought to be, how a person ought to act, and then to dispute one's expectations, and she had done that.

"You're ripe and ready for change," Hannah had said.

Ginger was another matter. Grace had no sense that, miserable as she seemed, Emily's mother was aware that there was anything she needed to change. She seemed locked in the armor of her attitudes and beliefs. Mind your own business, Grace said to herself.

"You can't fix anyone's life but your own," Hannah was forever preaching, and, of course, she was right.

※

Streetlights were not a part of Covington's nightscape, and without a moon, the grassy shoulders melded into the dark road, making it essential to focus on driving. Several times the tires on the right side of Russell's car slipped off the road, jarring them. Obviously, Russell's mind was elsewhere. He talked of nothing but Emily. "Isn't she beautiful? I love her laugh, don't you? She's smart, very smart. She doesn't do divorce in her practice," and on and on.

"Her eyes are beautiful, such long lashes," Grace concurred.

"They're incredible," Russell said.

"Watch the road, son."

"Yes, sir." Russell slowed the car.

"If there's no car coming, use your brights. You won't find yourself on the shoulder if you focus on the white line in the middle," Bob advised.

Russell complied. "Did you like her, Dad?"

"Why, yes, I did. Seems a fine, intelligent young woman," his father said as his hand flew to the dashboard. "Just take it slow around that curve."

"When did you get to be such a backseat driver?" From the backseat, Grace nudged Bob's shoulder.

"Russell's distracted, and he's not paying any attention to where he's driving."

"She's leaving next week," Russell said.

"So, will you go to Florida, see her in her own environment?" Bob asked. "Could she live here is a big question."

"If you love someone you can live anywhere," Russell replied.

Spoken with the love-struck heart of a forty-year-old teenager, Grace thought. But she felt great empathy for Russell. When Amy died in that car crash, he had nearly stopped functioning. It had been a hard two years, and Grace was glad that Russell seemed ready to start a new life. It was Tyler she worried about.

"Go slow," Bob said, and this time he did not refer to Russell's driving.

"I am," Russell said. "I'm only driving twenty miles an hour."

"What your dad means is give your relationship with Emily some time. Tyler will have to meet her. He'll need to get used to seeing you with a woman."

"Tyler will love her," Russell replied with absolute assurance.

A dreamer, Grace thought, and she directed her attention to Bob. "You liked Martin, then?"

"Martin's interesting," Bob said. "He's signed up for my January class or World War Two at the Center for Creative Retirement at the university. The man knows those war years as well as he knows the lines on his face. He'll keep me on my toes."

Grace decided this was not the time to tell them that she hoped never to see Ginger Hammer again.

5

Was It an Apple or a Mango?

A plate of sugar cookies in one hand, her purse tucked under her arm, Grace walked up the unpainted, slightly tilting steps to the porch of Lurina Masterson's farmhouse. The old lady opened the front door slowly, her eyes squeezed to the crack, then wider, smiling broadly.

"Well if it ain't Grace. Come on in and sit a bit."

"I've brought you my homemade sugar cookies."

"Well, ain't that nice."

Grace followed Lurina into the kitchen at the back of the house. The floor was covered by old green linoleum worn bare in places. The rear door stood ajar, and Grace heard the cackling of chickens. "You keep chickens?"

"Special chickens." Lurina opened the refrigerator door and pulled out a dish filled with eggs ranging in color from olive blue to turquoise. She laughed. "Surprised at the color? One day I'll take you out back and introduce you to 'em."

That said, Lurina returned the bowl to the refrigerator and reached for a cookie. "Good," she said. "Old-time-like, thin, not too sweet. Just right for dunkin'. Your ma hand you down this recipe?"

"My mother didn't like to cook. She had no special recipes. All of mine came from friends, their family recipes."

"Imagine that." Lurina took Grace's arm and propelled her into the room she called the front parlor. On an old velvet couch sat a large

Bible whose pages had yellowed with age. Lurina eased herself onto the couch alongside the good book, took it into her lap, and tapped the open page with a finger. "Read the Bible, Grace?"

"I have. Long ago."

"I been readin' real careful like, that part about Adam and Eve livin' in the Garden of Eden." She patted the page. "Now it says here that Adam and Eve were naked. The Garden of Eden must have been in a warm climate, tropical like, wouldn't you say?"

Grace nodded. She respected other people's religious beliefs. This was only her second visit with Lurina, but Lurina seemed not to care, and proceeded as if they were lifelong friends. She's lonely, Grace thought, and settled down to listen.

Lurina continued. "Well, I reckon, apple trees don't grow in the tropics." She grinned, excited now, and leaned forward. "So, I come to think that Eve couldn't have picked an apple." She fell silent and waited. Grace said nothing. "What Eve picked and gave to Adam was a tropical fruit. I figure it was a mango." Lurina squinted up at Grace with such intensity that it made Grace uncomfortable. "A mango," Lurina repeated. "Ate one once, right sweet it was."

Grace waited, expecting more, but Lurina had finished. She closed the Bible, seemingly satisfied with her interpretation. "I gotta talk to Pastor Johnson 'bout this."

They chatted a bit. "I seen too many changes in my lifetime," Lurina said. "I used to walk behind Pa's plow settin' potatoes. Times are, I wake up at night from dreamin', and think I feel the cold mud of that field oozin' through my toes. I cried a pint when Pa stowed our old buggy, and turned the old horse to pasture, and got him one of those new Fords. Telephone, radio, television, big old stores you can't find anything in." She shook her head, and the braids atop her head bobbed. Her eyes grew sad. "I done watched 'em rip and tear hills and all over in Loring Valley." She shook her head. "Glad I'm old. Too much change. I hear tell they've called another meetin' at the church hall tonight. You goin'?"

"Yes. We are."

Lurina's brows knitted. "Tell me, Grace, you get a letter about sellin' your property?"

"Everyone on Cove Road got a letter. I could come by tomorrow, if you'd like, and tell you what happened at tonight's meeting."

"That'd be right nice of you."

Grace shared Lurina's concerns about the development of Loring Valley, but now she asked Lurina how she felt after her recent fall, and in reply, Lurina launched into a description of her family's solid history of good health. "We Mastersons die of old age, sometimes more than a hundred, like my pa. We never get operated on, never have strokes, nothin' like that. We just lie in bed, and when the Lord calls we go, and that ain't early on. He ain't in no hurry for us Mastersons. We're an ornery bunch."

Lurina launched into a story about her father's death, the first of many death stories that she would tell Grace. "Pa, he wasn't sick or nothin'. Just took to his bed one July afternoon. Lordy me, it was hot that day. 'Lurrie,' he said. That's what he called me, Lurrie. 'Come sit in this here chair next my bed.' Time was he could heft him a calf under each arm and walk a mile. Well, that afternoon, he raised up his arms a ways, and they just plopped back on the bed. 'Strength's gone,' he said, 'time to go.' Then he heaved hisself a big sigh, turned his head to the window. 'Look at all that light. Ain't it fine, Lurrie?' is what he said." At that Lurina fell silent. She stared down at her gnarled and wrinkled hands.

A heavy stillness filled the room, much like the stillness in the doctor's office the day when he had told Grace and her husband that Ted's cancer was inoperable. At that moment, Lurina lifted her head, and her eyes sought Grace's.

"Pa, he seen a light. I ain't seen no light." She sighed. "Well, he got him the most peaceful look in those old eyes of his." Lurina flicked her wrist. "Quick as a lamb can twitch its tail, he was gone." Her mood changed, lifted. "Mighty fine way to go, wouldn't you say?" She laughed.

If I closed my eyes and heard that laugh, Grace thought, I'd think she was a much younger woman. Grace's moment of melancholy lifted, and she laughed lightly with Lurina. It was a mighty fine way to go. Then Grace helped Lurina from the couch, took the older woman's arm, and they ambled out to the front porch, where Lurina settled herself in her weatherworn and creaky rocking chair.

"Won't you come with us to this meeting, Lurina. We'd pick you up and bring you home. You've seen what's happened to Loring Valley firsthand. You could tell them."

Lurina stiffened. "I told you, I don't go out at night."

"Yes, you did. I'm sorry," Grace said, preparing to leave. "Well, I'll see you."

"Come back soon."

When Grace reached her car, she turned and called to Lurina, "I'll bring Hannah and Amelia to meet you." And thus began a friendship between Grace Singleton and Lurina Masterson that led, in time, to Grace's ongoing involvement in Lurina's life.

6

Hannah Steps to the Podium

🌿 Tired and frazzled, Harold leaned on the podium. His shirt bunched above his belt, and his tie hung loose and limp. Using a gavel, Harold silenced the crowd. "Everyone get a letter?"

This second church hall gathering to discuss the offer from the developers took place on a Sunday evening. The hall was packed, standing room only. Once again, the ladies sat with Brenda while Russell and Bob, who had accompanied them tonight, stood with others at the rear of the room.

Hands, holding letters, shot up. Everyone yammered. Harold slammed the gavel hard. "Raise your hands, and I'll call you to this podium, and you can all have your say."

Hands fell, rose, some fell again. "Charlie Herrill, get on up here," Harold said, and stepped aside to accommodate the husky farmer, in overalls and a baseball cap, who strode from the back of the hall. The crowd parted for him, several of the men stood as he passed them and congenially slapped his back. "You tell 'em, Charlie," someone yelled.

Charlie grinned, pulled out a big checkered handkerchief—it reminded Grace of her own bandanna—and wiped his face. "Folks. We've got us a peck of trouble. These here folks"—he waved his letter—"they know how to sweet-talk. Me and my kin been in this valley nigh onto ninety years." He smoothed his letter on the podium, then lifted it high in the air. "Here's the Herrills' answer." Huge hands tore the letter in two, then in four. The pieces seesawed to the floor. Cheers and claps exploded. Low murmurs and objections followed.

Charlie Herrill, smiling and pleased with himself, left the podium, stomped down the aisle, and stood behind the chair at the back of the room, where his wife, Velma, sat.

Harold recognized Jake Anson, patriarch of the Anson clan, and waved him forward. An Ichabod Crane type, gangly, slightly stooped, with an Adam's apple that bobbed even when he wasn't talking or swallowing, Jake rose from the second row and ambled up to the podium.

"I reckon I don't see it like old Charlie here does. Times are changin'. My girl, Louise, you know, she ain't so good, got the cancer, and we carry her to the hospital every couple of weeks for treatments. My boy Timmie's wantin' to open him up a mechanic shop over in West Asheville. Our oldest gal Susan's married and lives over yonder off Patton Avenue in West Asheville. Maggie and I been wonderin' what's the sense to stay out here." He paused.

Everyone in that meeting hall collectively held their breath.

Jake continued. "We ain't gettin' younger, my missus and me. We could use a little ease." His eyes scanned the room, and for a long moment Jake hesitated. Then he stepped away from the podium and straightened his shoulders. "I'm sorry, folks. I know a lot of you gonna be darn mad, but a person's gotta do what he's gotta do."

The neighbors of Jake Anson turned in slow motion and watched as he plodded down the aisle, took the arms of his son and wife. Linked together they walked slowly, heavily from the church hall. Then, the room exploded. "Just what you'd expect from a man whose kin fought with the Union," someone yelled.

Grace looked quizzically at Brenda, who bent and whispered in her ear. "Anson's family goes back a real long time. They settled over in Walnut, only it was called Jewell Hill back then. It's common knowledge the Anson men fought with the Union; their womenfolk hid deserters. Story is Jake's granny buried her own Bible and a handkerchief with her initials embroidered on it with a Union soldier."

That the Civil War had divided Madison County families, friends, and neighbors, Grace knew, but this information about the Ansons concretized what she suspected. In this mountain fastness, old feuds and angers faded but never disappeared.

"Turncoat," another voice called. "Selling out on us. Just like your kin." The words struck the walls, jounced here and there about the room, piercing minds and hearts, stirring old angers. Then came silence.

Finally Harold said, "Well, what do you know about that?"

The jam-packed room smoldered with a jumble of body heat and heightened emotions. Driblets of perspiration tickled Grace's skin under her arm. She pressed her cotton shirt against her skin, just as a purl of protest came from the front row. Beside her, Amelia fanned herself with a Japanese fan hand painted with lotus blossoms. It was one of several fans she had collected on her world travels, and that now decorated the wall above Amelia's dressing table. She turned her head, hoping to catch a draft from Amelia's fan.

Harold touched the gavel to the podium. "Y'all know Hannah Parrish. She'd like to say a few words."

Hannah rose. No crowd parted for her as she made her way, with many "excuse me's" and "pardon me's," to where Harold waited. She made a mental note of two young men who stuck out a hand and edged a foot toward her indicating that if they could, they would bar her way. She noticed Zachary, the Maxwells' son, sitting third in the second row eyeing her sheepishly.

"Let the lady pass," Harold said firmly.

Relieved, Hannah reached the podium. "Jake Anson's got troubles, illness," Hannah began. "I'm sorry. But, I ask you all to think what happens to this valley if one owner sells. Everything changes. Anson's land sweeps the curve, a huge tract that greedy developers will ruin with hundreds of houses and condominiums." Hannah waited a moment. Then her voice rose. "First there'll be bulldozers and blasting, then there'll be huge trucks delivering cement, and gravel, and lumber, then cars, two at least for every family. Imagine the traffic, the dust, the noise on Cove Road."

Voices buzzed and muttered. Harold wiped his forehead with his handkerchief, stepped closer to Hannah, and lowered the gavel on the podium.

Even with the noise, Hannah seemed unflustered, cool, and sure of herself. "Kids won't be able to play ball in the road on Sundays, as they do now. Then there's the pollution. Runoff from the construction will pollute our streams and creeks."

Whispers seeped like mist through the room. Harold silenced them once again with his gavel. He looked worn-out, Grace thought, almost defeated, standing there behind Hannah.

"What makes Cove Road so unique," Hannah continued, "is that all of us, you, me, we all love its quiet beauty. We enjoy sitting out on our porches. It's a comfort visiting with passersby, and relaxing. Isn't that so?"

Heads nodded.

"The way it is now, we can set our clocks by when folks drive past. Charlie Herrill, there." She pointed at Charlie. "He drives his big blue truck past our place at nine o'clock sharp six days a week. If he didn't, I'd call Velma to inquire if he was sick. Brenda Tate leaves for her school at seven-thirty in the morning. If she drives by before seven, I know she's got a meeting, and when I see her, I ask, "How'd the meeting go the other morning, Brenda?""

It was true. The whole room knew it, and laughed lightly.

"And Molly Lund. Every afternoon at five-thirty when she comes home she waves, whether she can see any of us or not. Even if we're inside, one or the other of us sees her. She brightens our day, makes us feel connected. All that will change with the development of our valley."

"It's not your valley," a disgruntled voice said. "Jake's got a right to sell."

"True, he does, but I'm suggesting there might be a way to buy his land and find another use for it other than housing."

"You're makin' a mountain out of a molehill."

"No, I'm not," she replied. "Development, so-called progress, will eliminate the very things you hold dear."

"What we got that it'll eliminate?" a voice called.

Hannah lifted her chin. "What folks all over America crave: a sense of belonging, of knowing your neighbors, of people caring what happens to others." She gestured with both hands, intending to encompass everyone in the room. "You come to church; you know everyone. Someone's sick, you bring food. When there's a death, you visit and comfort, at a birth you celebrate. Community." The word came out reverentially in almost a whisper, and she repeated louder, "Community, that's what people crave."

Sitting in the front row, a woman blew her nose. Someone coughed. Someone else asked roughly. "Whadda you know about us?"

36

"I know you're hardworking people, religious, close to your families. Grace, Amelia, and I feel some small part of your community because some of you, Harold and Brenda Tate, Pastor Johnson, the Lunds, the Herrills, have opened your hearts to us, and we thank you for that." Hannah's voice cracked. "Community. Belonging. My God, I believe that's worth saving."

"Who are you to talk? You moved here," someone called from the back of the room.

"We moved into a house that was already here and repaired it. We didn't tear it down to build a modern glass and stone house. Go on over to Loring Valley and take a good long look at what they've done there. They've built right on the floodplain of Little River. They've cut trees, torn up the hillsides. Just stand in front of Anson's land and look at the size of it, picture the houses, condos, denuded hillsides." Hannah ticked off on her fingers. "And after the construction we'll have the traffic from homeowners, their families and guests, from garbage trucks and delivery vans, from gas trucks and meter readers. It will not stop." She paused, and waited for a moment, and heard the shuffling of feet, a cough, a whisper, but no outpouring of protest. "We like to sit out at night and watch the stars. Do you?"

Hands went up around the room.

"Development means lights: houselights, safety lights, streetlights, lights on the golf course and tennis courts at night." Hannah shook her head. A murmur rose mainly from the women, who nodded agreement. Hannah leaned forward. Slowly her eyes moved across the room meeting misty eyes, worried eyes, defiant and angry eyes. "Well," she said, "one sure thing. We can say good-bye to the stars. Light pollution'll see to that."

There was clapping when Hannah stepped from the podium.

Her place was taken by one of Velma Herrill's sons, an accountant at the county courthouse. "You're all aware how taxes are going up every year. It's gettin' harder for a man to hold on to his land. We ought to be thinkin' about ways to stop tax increases, or there'll be more folks than Jake Anson lookin' to sell their land."

One after the other, Harold recognized those whose hands were raised. John Stokes, a grandson of the Craines', ambled up the aisle. He had his say in favor of Anson selling. "We got to make sure we're free to do what we want with our property," he finished. All the cheers and whistles caused Harold to pound on the podium for silence. Shortly after, he brought the meeting to a close.

Although many people patted her back and shook her hand as she left the church, Hannah felt frustrated that she had not come to the meeting anticipating that someone would want to sell, and had offered no solution.

"Good talk. You laid it out for them," Bob said as they walked the quarter of a mile back to the farmhouse.

"What use was it without offering a concrete next step? I didn't have a plan."

Russell fell into step alongside Hannah. "Don't blame yourself. You had no idea Jake Anson was going to announce he's intending to sell."

"I should have anticipated that someone might."

"You stirred them up, got them thinking, Hannah," Russell said.

"I watched their faces," Amelia added. "People were visibly moved."

Hannah did not want to be consoled or coddled. Many in that audience had been in the palm of her hand, and she'd turned them loose without a follow-up meeting, without a plan. She felt duty bound to stop Anson from selling to the developers, but how?

Gusts of chill wind beat at their backs, and they drew their jackets about them and walked more briskly. Overhead a fringe of black cloud dangled like a windblown toupee atop a half-full moon. Ahead of them loomed the farmhouse, porch lights glowing. Home. Hannah loved coming home. She was putting down roots here, as were Amelia and Grace. She looked at Grace swinging along like a teenager, her hand fastened in Bob's, and Amelia, chatting with Russell, tossing her head, walking lightly as if she trod on clouds.

Hannah wondered if any of them felt the apprehension, the sense of urgency she felt. Deep in thought, she strode past them. It wouldn't be easy, she knew that, but when had something difficult ever stopped Hannah Parrish? She must, she would find a way to preserve the beauty, the quiet, the integrity of Cove Road. Her spirits lifted, fired by the idea that important work, perhaps the most important work of her life, lay before her.

7

The Tearoom

"Should we postpone the opening of the tearoom so we can help Hannah?" Grace asked as they hefted themselves up into Bob's Jeep.

"I think not. Hannah's got plenty of work to do first. She'll let us know when she needs us."

They turned right onto Cove Road from the farmhouse driveway and then left onto Elk Road, which at this juncture was heavily wooded on both sides.

"It's almost as if old Grover Masterson had a premonition," Grace said.

"A premonition about what?"

"About growth, here in Covington. Maybe he sensed that even in this remote area change would come, and people, and they'd want stores closer than Mars Hill. So he set aside this strip of his land for commercial use."

Bob nodded. They passed the run-down gas station, after which the trees dwindled away, leaving open patches through which one could see fields and Bad River bisecting Lurina's land, and beyond the river to more fields and the old farmhouse. About a mile further, Bob turned the Jeep into the parking lot neighboring a delightful cottage perched just off the road.

"Funny," Grace said, "that our tearoom will be the first new business to open."

Following their shadows, his long and lean, hers short and round,

Grace and Bob walked across the freshly paved parking area. Hand in hand they moved along the curving brick pathway that led to three porch steps. Every last nail had been hammered, every last wall painted or papered, every last shutter hung.

Bob gave her hand a squeeze. "It's perfect." He pointed to the oval sign hanging from the peaked roof just above their heads. It read, COTTAGE TEAROOM.

Even at fifteen hundred square feet inside, and with an extra-wide front porch, the tearoom appeared every bit the charming country cottage they had initially visualized: double-hung eight-pane windows, cheerful rose-colored shutters and front door, white clapboard siding, intricate fretwork above the porch. Grace pictured pink roses climbing in and out of slats on the porch railing by next May. They had planned the tearoom, its size, the position of its windows, mainly west and south for light and air. And after dreaming it for months, here it was bright and fresh, its kitchen ready to go, chairs and tables due tomorrow. Grace sighed as they walked to the front door. The finger sandwiches, the pastries, the cookies she would make, the exotic variety of teas from around the world, the cozy, comfortable ambience would assure success, so she told herself in those clammy, heart-racing moments when doubt pried her from sleep.

In the weeks prior to construction, they had studied the architect's plans for hours at the farmhouse kitchen table with Amelia or Hannah hovering, making suggestions, or at Russell's dining room table. Smiling, they listened attentively to everyone's input: buy round tables, buy square tables. They take up less room. The kitchen should be larger. The floors must be carpeted. Tile or vinyl would hold up better. Then, alone in Bob's Jeep, the plans spread out between them, they finalized their decisions according to their own likes and dislikes.

Tom Findley, the young carpenter who had handled the renovation of the farmhouse for the ladies, now operated his own construction company. He had been infinitely patient with Grace and Bob as they decided, undecided, changed this or that. How much space needed for how many tables, or should there be booths also? They visited restaurants, evaluated space, and Bob made templates of round and square tables and chairs before they chose round for the aesthetic of it. They considered flow to and from the kitchen. Equipment for the kitchen opened a new world for them as they pored over magazines and visited commercial salesrooms. Here Bob had to restrain Grace's culinary enthusiasm.

"A bigger oven," she kept saying, or, "Don't we need another sink?"

"It's not a restaurant, darling," he reminded her. "It's a tearoom, pastries and finger sandwiches. Knowing you, you'll probably do most of the preparation at home."

The tearoom had been her idea. "But, what if we decide to serve lunches, salads, soufflés?" she asked.

"Grace." Soberly Bob had placed his hands on her shoulders and turned her to look at him. "Please focus. This is a tearoom, open from two to five in the afternoons. We planned it that way."

"I know that's what we said, but what if people want lunch?"

"Let them eat in the new restaurant they're building in Loring Valley at their clubhouse. If we serve lunch, we won't own our lives." He kissed her nose.

On the porch, they leaned against the railing and looked up and down the street. She relished this delay. Once inside she would face reality. She wondered if Bob worried too. Down the road to their left, the shabby gas station was out of their line of sight, and about two miles down Elk Road to the right, the red tin roof of P. J. Prancer's hardware store loomed above a line of mature oaks whose leaves had turned a copper color. Beyond the hardware store, the unseen walls of a strip mall mushroomed from the red clay soil. No denying the convenience of shopping close by, even if it came courtesy of Loring Valley. Even if another house or condo was never built in its environs, Covington, Grace knew, had already changed, and like it or not, there was an excitement in that fact. Who were they, these new residents? Where had they come from? Why had they chosen this remote, rural area? How would their being here affect the lives of those entrenched in Covington?

Two large sedans, one blue, the other gray, drove slowly by. Someone in the gray sedan waved from behind closed windows. Grace waved back and thought of something her new friend, Lurina Masterson, had said to her just yesterday as they visited and drank much-too-sweet iced tea on Lurina's porch.

"I been countin' them cars, Grace. Must be a thousand new ones comin' and goin' day and night. In all my years I ain't never seen nothin' like it."

Grace patted her hand. "I hate change too."

Lurina had squeezed Grace's fingers hard, and they had sat in silent understanding for a time.

Now, Grace turned to Bob. "I'd like to invite Lurina Masterson to our tearoom opening."

Bob smiled at her. "Of course."

"I'll deliver the invitation to her personally."

Another car passed. A zing of excitement swept through Grace. The Hammers were the only residents in Loring Valley that she had met. Maybe, with the tearoom, she would meet more likable people. A thought crossed her mind. Maybe this desire for a tearoom sprang from her unspoken wish to prove that she too could work out in the world. Was it also fueled by a desire to meet the newcomers, to be part of the change, and to be recognized in the orb of their small world? It all got jumbled in her mind when she lay in bed at night and tried to sort it out.

Bob rummaged in the pocket of his slacks, pulled out two rings of shiny new keys. He handed her one set. Grace slipped the keys into her purse, even as her doubts intensified. Be optimistic, she told herself. It's going to be just fine. Bob and I are equal partners. Remember how powerful and confident you felt writing your check at the bank?

The funds from her share of the sale of her home in Dentry, wisely invested in a Fidelity account, had yielded a 23 percent profit. Feeling financially independent for the first time in her life, Grace had used some of these funds for this investment. But now, having the shiny keys, symbols of responsibility and liability in her purse, her stomach lurched. Would she like running a business? Already she could see it would tie her down, interfere with her volunteer work at Caster Elementary, the time she would have to spend with Hannah and Amelia.

An October sun, low in the heavens, spilled golden light across the porch. Grace forced her attention to matters of the moment. It was hot out here. Would it be too hot to sit and drink tea outside in summer? Bob had suggested fans, and she had pooh-poohed them. Perhaps they *would* need awnings, and fans. Grace looked at Bob unlocking the front door. Her heart swelled with love remembering

42

the feel of his broad back beneath her hands, the way his thick, white hair parted under her fingers. How wonderful to lie in his strong arms. She marveled that, at seventy-one, he was so virile. Then she smiled. She wasn't so bad herself. I am lucky, Grace thought. Stepping forward, she slipped her arms about his waist and leaned into his back. Turning, he held her close, her face against his chest, low, between his ribs. The steady beat of his heart reassured her. Had she loved Ted like this? She must have, once, when they were young. She just couldn't remember.

"A new phase in our lives, darling," he said, swinging wide the door. "Our own business."

A disturbing thought struck Grace. Was his enthusiasm for the tearoom Bob's way of capturing most of her time? She brushed the idea away, stepped into the room, and was immediately overcome by a sense of pride, as if seeing the pleasant friendliness of the tearoom for the first time. The room seemed enormous, yet softened and warmed by nostalgic floral wallpaper. Tom and his wife, Marie, had hung the rods, and gossamer cream-colored curtains. Bob opened the windows, inviting the last of the day's sunlight to sneak in and play cat and mouse on the polished wood floors, and the wind to flutter the curtains.

"Now, Grace," Bob said, as if reading her mind. "Remember, we laid it all out on paper. Once the tables, and chairs, and the credenzas arrive tomorrow, it's going to look just right, believe me."

She smiled at him, and nodded. She was scared. If she spoke, at that moment, she might not be able to control a trembling chin, or even tears. Gaining control, she tugged at his arm. "Maybe this is a mistake. Aren't you scared? Suppose we've wasted our money, made a huge mistake?"

"Darling, I'm not scared. A trifle nervous, and excited, but I don't believe in mistakes," he said, his face and eyes serious. "They're blips on a screen, a challenge, a learning experience."

"And I suppose you believe you can rebuild bridges you've burned?" she asked, jesting, but he looked at her, and his eyes grew serious. He was silent for several seconds. "Yes, I think I do believe that. As long as we're alive, it's possible, I think, to mend fences, rebuild bridges to places, relationships."

"How optimistic that is. I wish someone had suggested such a possibility to me years ago. I've spent most of my life afraid to leave

43

my cocoon." Grace frowned. "When Amelia and Hannah first knew me, I was afraid to take risks." She made a quick pass of her hand through the air. "But you know all that." Snuggling against him, she took his arm.

"It's going to be fine, sweetheart." He pulled her close, bent to lift her face, smoothed back the light brown hair that fell in soft waves just below her ears. "Such wonderful eyes," he said. "Kind, gentle. Did I ever tell you it was your eyes that first drew me to you?" And with that he kissed her softly.

8

Lunch Beneath the Great Oak

On Saturday, the day prior to Grace's big lunch beneath the great oak, the ladies sat on their porch. Hannah said, "I need your creative input." She picked up her pad. "I've been over to the county seat in Marshall. There's a preponderant attitude that a man's land is his domain. I could not persuade the powers that be to intervene to prevent Cove Road from going the way of Loring Valley. One of the commissioners asked me what we needed another park for, since the Mastersons left the state a whole chunk of land. Looks like funding will have to come from elsewhere if we ever hope to buy that land from Anson. We need a name for the project so we can rally people around this cause. Any ideas?"

"Cove Road Project," Grace threw out.

"Sounds like road construction," Amelia said. She nibbled on a fingernail. "How about Cove Road Preserve Coalition?"

At that moment, Mike's car crunched the gravel of the driveway and Amelia sprang to her feet. "We're going over into Jackson County today, near Sylva. The terrain there's spectacular, rugged." Amelia's eyes filled with enthusiasm. "Mike's a terrific photography instructor, seems there's always something more to learn. We're doing low-light photography these days." And with a wave of her hand, she trotted down the steps and was gone.

"Working on another book, she tells me," Hannah said.

"Black-and-white photos, this time. It's a lot of work. I never re-

45

alized how many rolls of film a photographer has to shoot to get a few great pictures."

"Doesn't seem to bother her. She's enjoying herself," Hannah said.

Hannah looked at her pad. She had written *Cove Road Preserve Coalition*. "Sounds as if hundreds of people are behind this project."

"And maybe they will be," Grace said.

It was the second Sunday in October, and merely a hint of fall in the air. By one o'clock in the afternoon only the Richardsons and Mike had arrived for lunch. Under the great oak, four tables stood decorated with centerpieces of multicolored gourds and various-sized pumpkins on festive orange tablecloths.

"It's totally, utterly wonderful," Mike said, and the Richardsons agreed.

At the Tates' farmhouse, Brenda stopped to look in the hall mirror and fuss with her hair. Harold and Pastor Johnson were waiting near the front door. "Come on, Brenda, it's gettin' late. Ladies are waitin' dinner for us," Harold said.

"Dinner, lunch, what difference does it make what you call it?" Brenda smoothed her cotton shirtwaist dress and walked toward the men. "Maggie Anson's made a big issue of it when she said she wouldn't be going today, and it wasn't because of Hannah's speech at the church hall." She mimicked Maggie. " 'Folks from the North can't even learn to call a meal by its right name. Dinner's noontime and supper's the evenin' meal, we all know that, except those Yankees.' God, that woman exasperates me."

"Put it out of your head now, Brenda," her husband said.

Molly Lund, the Tates' daughter, her husband, Ted, and their sons, ages five and six, headed the parade of three cars that lined up behind Bob's Jeep in the ladies' driveway. Pastor Johnson rode with the Tates. Representing Brenda's cousins from the Craine family were Alma and Frank, their daughter, Claudia, and their ten-year-old granddaughter, Paulette.

Grace counted eleven, plus seven already there, and wondered how she could eliminate several of the tables. Then she saw that Bob and Russell were in the process of joining two of them into one long one. Grace moved toward the guests, a wide smile on her face. "Welcome. I'm so glad you came." Having worried that no one would show up, she was delighted to see those who had.

"Velma Herrill wanted to come real bad, but Charlie's got a fright-ful bad cough and fever, can't hardly breathe," Brenda said as they hugged. "The Ansons." She shrugged. "Well, you know, and the Max-wells don't come out for anything." She spoke rapidly, nervously. "Still, Maxwell sends help when anyone has a problem, like when the Herrills' barn burned, and when we had that mother of all storms, winter of '93. Snow piled halfway up our front door. His plows came and opened Cove Road and plowed everyone's driveways. But"—she shook her head—"they don't socialize." Brenda slipped an arm about Grace's shoulder and kissed her cheek. "Never you mind. We'll have us the best old time." She looked toward the brightly decorated ta-bles. "Isn't this just so festive."

The farmhouse door slammed. Hannah stepped onto the porch with a pitcher in each hand. At the top of the steps she halted.

"How about you give me a pitcher to carry, Hannah?" Brenda has-tened toward her.

"Come see the house," Grace said and moments later, Alma Craine, her daughter, Claudia Prinze, and Molly Lund followed Grace up the steps. Tubs of ferns and pots of orange impatiens clus-tered at either end of the porch. In one conversational grouping, a hanging swing shifted lightly in the breeze. Facing the swing were two high-backed white wicker chairs. At the side of the porch nearest the great oak, three white wicker rockers were positioned in a semi-circle around a low table. "We have tea out here every afternoon, weather permitting." Grace gestured toward the rockers.

Alma touched an orange impatiens in a tub near the door. "My impatiens took the cold we had the other night and died."

"They're protected up here on the porch," Grace replied. "The western sun warms them."

That settled, Alma moved cautiously, slowly behind the others. She was dressed for church in a blue shirtwaist dress with silver buttons marching from neck to waist, and midheel shoes with clip-on silver buckles. The buttons of her dress strained, and the material puck-ered, revealing bits of pink slip. Grace fell back to walk beside her.

47

"This kitchen," she said, "was a mess. The floor had rotted in places. We tore out everything and started over."

"Mighty nice." Alma stood near the doorway. She clasped her arms about her ample chest and looked as if she would bolt any minute.

Grace showed them the powder room tucked under the stairs.

"Frank would never fit in here." Alma giggled, then her hand flew to cover her mouth, and she looked embarrassed.

"It's small, I know, but this way we don't have to be running upstairs all the time," Grace replied, shutting the door.

In the dining room, Molly said, "This is such nice wallpaper. Toile's perfect in here."

"Amelia says the color rose soothes her. She chose the wallpaper," Grace said.

In the living room, the two younger women admired the antique pine mantel around the fireplace. Grace explained, "This mantel was a complete shambles when Tom and Marie Findley, who did the repairs for us, found it at a yard sale. They refinished it."

Standing there with her mouth slightly agape, Alma's eyes traveled the floor-to-ceiling bookcases framing the fireplace. "So many books." It sounded more a condemnation than a compliment, as if the space might be better used for something else.

"Did you know," Molly asked, "the Herrills used to own this whole side of the valley?"

Grace looked at her with interest. "I didn't know that."

"They came after the railroad, when the main industry of Madison County was lumber, timbering. Their land was owned, then, by a family named Owens, and they'd overtimbered. Herrill's grandpa bought it off Owens for a shotgun, a wagon, a set of pots and pans, and a pair of mules. Later, Charlie Herrill's pa sold a piece to Alma's father-in-law, and later, these twenty-eight acres to Arthur Furrior."

"Hannah and Amelia will be interested to hear that."

Claudia stood below Amelia's prizewinning black-and-white photograph that hung above the mantel. "It's wonderful. It must take so much patience to get a shot like that."

"A good eye. Patience, yes, and luck. Amelia just happened to be on that street at the moment the little girl tumbled off her tricycle. See how the child's mouth is puckered, getting ready to cry?"

"I can see why it won first prize for Amelia," Claudia said.

No one moved or spoke for several seconds, then Grace said, "Well, why don't we go out and get ourselves some lunch."

Outside, under the great oak, a bountiful buffet filled a table end to end. Grace lifted the ceramic head off of the chicken-shaped tureen. "Pumpkin soup. Please, help yourselves."

"Not for me." Tyler rolled his eyes.

"Not for me." Paulette followed suit, as did the Lund boys. Against the protests of their parents, the children piled fried chicken legs on their plates, skinned up their noses at everything else, and trotted pell-mell to sit under the great oak and eat.

Pastor Johnson said grace. "Bless this food and the friends who share it." Moments later, he turned appreciative eyes to Grace. "I've never had such delicious pumpkin soup."

"Grace is a wonderful cook," Amelia said. "Now, Pastor, you be sure and leave room for the rest of lunch. We've got ham, fried chicken, and all kinds of salads."

Grace smiled at Pastor Johnson. "I'll fix you a nice big container of soup to take home for dinner."

At the table, talk centered for a time on this year's low price for the tobacco crop, the growing of an alternative crop like soybeans, the health of Hannah's new apple trees, which had put on thirteen inches of growth in one season. No one seemed eager to speak of the developer's offer. Just as well, Grace thought. It'll only get Hannah riled up, and Grace knew that there would be no stopping Hannah in her determination to preserve Cove Road from development. At that moment she heard Hannah saying, "Yes, Wayne Reynolds has green hands, not just green thumbs."

"Lord, remember last year Fourth of July at the park when he knocked into your chair and sent you sprawling?" Harold asked.

"Inauspicious start," Hannah replied, "followed by an encore when I toppled over Wayne's legs in P. J. Prancer's."

"Quite amazing, you two working together now." Brenda laughed.

"Since Wayne's running Hannah's greenhouse, he's become like family," Grace said. Grace liked Wayne. She was glad he had agreed to purchase Hannah's greenhouse. It had become too much work for her friend, and Hannah was teaching Wayne the marketing and book-keeping aspects of selling ornamental plants. She was also grateful to Wayne for the way he had helped Hannah after the fire that destroyed the apple orchard. Wayne had prevailed on Hannah to accompany him to the Reynolds' homestead up in the northernmost mountains of Madison County, where he and Old Man had generously plied her with sufficient sapling trees to replant the orchard.

Grace's musing was interrupted by Harold rising to return to the buffet table for seconds. Amelia joined him. "Let's move these platters over on our table, and just pass them," she said.

With Harold's help, platters of ham, squash casserole, fried chicken, potato salad, and corn pudding were soon making the rounds.

In almost no time at all, Tyler and Paulette shoved plates of chicken bones at their parents and raced off to the stream, followed by Molly's two boys, futilely yelling, "Wait on up, wait on up."

The talk turned to ladybugs, which, as the days grew chillier, peppered the ceilings and windowsills of everyone's homes. "Stinky things. I can't stand them," Amelia said. "No matter how we seal the windows, they still get in."

"Useless to even try to hold 'em out." Harold rocked back on his chair. "Little critters squeeze through the tiniest crack, even attic vents." He shrugged. "Takes gettin' used to, but they don't harm none." Harold brought his chair upright and poured Brenda and then himself another glass of apple cider from a ceramic jug. "Fact is they feed on aphids, good for the garden."

"Isn't there some kind of insecticide or spray I could use around the doors and windows to kill them, or on the ceilings inside? I tried wasp spray. It killed them, all right. In the meantime I thought I'd choke." Amelia's hand fastened about the bright blue scarf at her neck.

"You'll poison yourself if you keep sprayin' in the house. Just you brush 'em off the ceilin', scoop 'em up, and dump 'em back outside," Harold said. "Ladybugs you save today may be the very ones eatin' the aphids off your plants next season."

Amelia shuddered. "Put them outside? *Mais non.* There are enough of them out there already." She brushed her hands together as if she had just discarded a handful of ladybugs. "Even after I vacuum, the smell is everywhere."

"Harmonia axyrdidis," Hannah chimed in. "Brought in as a natural pest control, and now they're out of control."

"Do what with a harmonica?" Pastor Johnson asked.

"That's the name of the ladybugs, or in popular usage they're called Southern Lady Beetle, or Multicolored Asian Lady Beetle," Hannah said.

Harold set his glass down and leaned forward, elbows on the table. "I hear tell they have 'em as far north as Canada."

A cloud meandered across the bold face of the sun, creating a long shadow that swept across the table and changed the mood. Talk turned from ladybugs to the meeting at the church hall, and the future of Cove Road. Harold shook his head. "I was right and everyone called me an alarmist. Never been called that in my life." He shrugged.

Brenda patted her husband's arm. "No sense to go on about this. Nothin' you can do. Too nice a day."

Hannah slammed one fist into the palm of her other hand. "I don't believe that. If we band together we can do a lot, even if the local government's not interested."

"Anson wants a peck of money. We folks can't raise a million dollars," Harold said. "It's too big a project for us."

"We can't from our own pockets, Harold, but tracts of land are saved all the time because ordinary people join together. They get out there and march on city hall. They get the press interested, and hopefully some land trust or conservation group gets interested."

"Who cares about little old Covington, anyhow?" Ted Lund asked.

Molly poked his arm.

Hannah's face flushed, and her eyes widened and grew increasingly intense. "Maybe some private conservation organization, like the Nature Conservancy."

"What's that?" Ted asked.

"They raise funds specifically to save land. Sometimes they sell the land to other agencies or the government; sometimes they hold on to it. They own about thirteen hundred preserves worldwide right now. They operate the largest private system of nature sanctuaries in the world. Cove Road Preserve Coalition will turn to them first."

Amelia clapped her hands. "You used the name I picked."

Hannah nodded. "For starters, however, if we could get on Anson's land, if we could find one species, a bird, flower, animal that's endangered, we could ask for a moratorium on the sale, which would give us time."

"Well, I'll be darned." Harold shook his head and chuckled. "Freeze a deal like you'd freeze fresh caught fish."

No one else picked up the conversation, or asked questions. Grace noted the dull glaze that screened Frank's and Alma's eyes, and was glad that Hannah let the issue drop.

Now and then a yellow leaf wafted onto their table. One settled in Grace's hair. "Winter's coming." Bob lifted the leaf from her hair.

Across from Harold, Alma sat like a statue, hands in her lap, ignoring or unaware of the traces of pink slip that oozed from between her silver buttons. Frank reached for another fried chicken leg. A twig snapped high above them. Everyone looked up as a squirrel leaped from one branch to another.

"Squirrel's stockin' up for a cold winter," Pastor Johnson said.

Ted Lund nodded. "Woolly worms got them a thick coat this year." The platter of chicken made its round of the table and returned to Amelia.

The silence felt uncomfortable to Grace, and after a time she said, "I met Lurina Masterson recently."

"Well now, how is she?" Harold took out a pipe and a packet of tobacco from his back pocket and began to pack it. Brenda lay her hand on his arm before he could light it.

"She fell," Grace said. "Wayne and his grandfather found her. She's fine, no broken bones or anything. I invited her, and Old Man, and Wayne today. The Reynoldses had a christening to attend over in Tennessee, and Miss Lurina said no." Lurina would not tolerate Grace calling her Miss Lurina, but when Grace spoke of her to others, she felt compelled, by respect for the woman's age, to add the Miss.

"Miss Lurina ain't left that house since her pa died, couple of years ago. He must of been, what?" Alma Craine spoke for the first time at the table. She looked at Brenda. "About a hundred and two or three, wouldn't you say?"

Pastor Johnson's voice rose. He crossed his hands over his thin chest. "Over a hundred he was. Full church that day. Henry Dobbs up at the funeral home fixed Grover Masterson up real good." He smiled at the others benignly and shifted in his chair. "Old Grover lyin' there in his black jacket, all ruddy-faced. He didn't look near a hundred."

Those who had attended the funeral agreed.

"Church set up a committee for helpin' Miss Lurina. Ladies doin' their Christian duty, visitin' her, takin' her food, cakes or pies, fruits in season," Pastor Johnson said.

Grace was surprised to hear that. "She never speaks of anyone visiting her."

"Old lady Lurina don't like visitors. She's been known to run 'em off with her shotgun." Ted Lund leaned his chair back on two legs and grinned. "Ever seen her totin' that old gun of hers?"

Grace shook her head no. She'd neither seen anyone visiting nor seen food dropped off, and Lurina had certainly never mentioned it. "Folks really take her food?" she asked.

"Well," Alma said, "if they do, they get out of there fast. Old Miss Lurina, she smells bad of mothballs. It could knock you out. Folks just slip round the back and lay the stuff on the kitchen table if the door's unlocked, or by the door outside."

Grace bridled. She'd been aware of the faint odor of mothballs that sometimes issued from Lurina's clothing. Grace felt heat rising, bringing color to her face. "Lurina doesn't always smell of mothballs, only when she wears clothing from the closet where she keeps her best blouses and dresses. She believes that mothballs preserve her clothes."

Ted continued. "Miss Lurina ain't been off that land of hers since her pa died."

"A ranger from the park service comes by regularly to check on her," Grace said. "I get the sense that Miss Lurina worries that if she's not at home when the ranger stops by, they'll start bulldozing her house."

Ted was on a roll. "That old shotgun of Miss Lurina's is about as long as she is tall. I heard she stands on her porch holdin' that shotgun at that ranger fellow. Tells him to get off her land." He laughed. "Ain't no bullets in that gun, but that Yankee ranger fellow don't know that."

"They can't take Miss Lurina's land while she's alive, can they?" Molly Lund turned to her mother.

"No, honey," Brenda said, looking at her daughter. "Not until they're sure she's dead and the proper papers are filed."

"Not leaving her house in years." Molly shook her head. "Someone needs to tell her the truth about that situation. You should tell her, Grace."

Grace nodded. She liked Molly. Lurina would like Molly. Molly taught math at North Buncombe High School in Weaverville. Her husband, Ted, sold used cars over in Asheville, a thirty-five-minute drive from Covington. With Harold's help, they had built a home on land her parents gave to them as a wedding present ten years earlier. Grace looked at Molly. She found the young woman intelligent, bright, and much better educated than her husband. He's too young a man to have such a paunch, and Molly's so trim. Then she caught herself and thought, who am I to talk? I have my own love handles.

"You visit her, Grace?" Brenda asked, drawing Grace out of her musing.

Grace smiled and nodded. "Yes. We sit out on her porch sometimes and swap stories. She tells me about being a girl in Covington, about walking barefoot on dirt roads, helping her father build the barn, delivering calves. I tell her about Dentry, and bring her cookies or sometimes dinner. Miss Lurina finds the idea of stuffing a meatball with a prune both funny and ridiculous."

"Sounds right strange to me too," Alma muttered.

"I took her some, and she actually enjoyed them. She keeps chickens, did you know that?"

Brenda and Molly shook their heads.

"She took me out back and introduced me to her chickens."

"Well, don't tell. Introduced you to a chicken, did she?" Alma rolled her eyes.

"Nine chickens and one rooster. The hens lay blue eggs."

"Blue eggs?" Amelia said. "I never heard of blue eggs."

Grace placed her elbows on the table and leaned forward. "They're called Arucana chickens. Originally from Chile. They're small, and some have furry feet. Miss Lurina says their favorite food's watermelon, so now I bring her watermelon, just for them."

"Must be what we call Easter egg chickens," Brenda said. "I've seen those blue eggs at Easter time."

Having captured the interest of those sitting closest to her at the table, Grace continued. "The chicks were one day old when Miss

Lurina got them. She kept them inside, in the kitchen, for two months for fear of a fox getting them. They became like house pets."

Bob's arm was about Grace's chair, his fingers touching her back. Grace looked at him, noted the look of pride on his face, and was filled with warmth. "She's got a favorite chicken she named Pee-Wee. It comes inside sometimes and sits on Miss Lurina's head just like it did when it was a chick."

Harold slapped his thigh, threw back his head, and laughed. "That must be a sight. That old lady with a chicken sittin' on her head." Others laughed.

Grace felt uncomfortable, as if she'd set Lurina up for ridicule. "I think it's pretty terrific that a woman her age gets out there every day, rain or shine, to feed and tend her chickens. They're like people, like friends to her."

"I didn't mean to mock her." Harold's eyes were apologetic.

"I like her." Grace looked from one face to the other, her eyes serious.

"Miss Lurina and Old Man probably got their schoolin' in a one-room schoolhouse. The one-room schoolhouse was torn down to build the church." Pastor Johnson helped himself to another slice of ham from a platter that Amelia passed.

Frank Craine ran his hands across his thinning hair. "Good to know Old Man's still alive and kickin'."

"Lurina told me his name's actually Joseph Elisha," Grace said.

"If I ever knowed that, I forgot it years ago." Frank chuckled. Heat and sunshine caused his high, bald forehead to glisten. A taciturn man with pockmarked skin rough as the surface of the moon, he had rarely spoken since his brief "Howdy" on arrival.

It was a relief to Grace when Alma Craine suddenly began to prattle about the proposed stores for the new strip mall, the drugstore, the market, but especially the new beauty parlor. She came alive. Her face flushed and her eyes glowed. "Honey," she said, addressing no one in particular, "it sure makes Maggie Anson mad, 'cause everyone goes to her beauty shop, back of her house, now. Wonder how many she's gonna lose when a real beauty parlor opens?"

Suddenly it was as if someone had uncorked the Craines. Frank leaned forward, slapped his hand on the table as if it were a gavel. "I been talkin' to them fellas about a space in that there new shopping center for Billie and me to open us up an auto parts store. Billie," he said, looking at Hannah, who sat directly across from him, "he's my oldest boy. He's gettin' out of the Army next month. They trained him as a mechanic." He beamed with pride.

"How old is Billie?" Hannah asked out of politeness.

"How old's that boy, Alma?" Frank asked.

Alma scratched her brassy red hair. "Let's see. Tim's twenty. He's our young 'un. Junior's twenty-two; that'd make Billie 'bout twenty-four."

Frank turned to Hannah and asked, "What you want to do with Anson's land, Hannah?"

"Preserve the land, hiking maybe, camping, a park."

Frank scratched his head and took the bit of twig he was chewing on from between his teeth. "Dunno why we'd want another park after we've got such a big piece comin' from Masterson."

Amelia's blue eyes danced. "We can never have too many parks."

Mike, who had been eating contentedly for some time, couldn't resist mimicking Amelia's lilting voice. "Never too many parks."

She swatted his shoulder. "Stop it, you monster." They laughed.

Hail falling from the sky on a sunny summer day could not have evoked the degree of shock and grim disapproval that transformed the faces of Frank and Alma Craine. My God, Grace thought, they just figured out that Mike's gay, and gay is definitely not good in their eyes.

"Claudia, call Paulette. We best be goin'," Alma said, poking her daughter's ribs.

Claudia had talked with Mike earlier about taking his beginner's photography class. The ladies knew, from Brenda, that under enormous family pressure, Claudia had quashed her aspirations to study art, taken a computer program at AB Tech, and now worked as office manager for an architect in Asheville. When her husband, a press operator at the Sony plant in Weaverville, left with another woman, Claudia, and her then four-year-old, Paulette, moved home, which probably, Grace thought, accounted for the resigned expression that settled into Claudia's green eyes when she looked at or spoke to her parents.

Alma drew back her shoulders, which further called attention to her ample chest and gaping blouse. Shiny patches of wet, dark against her blue dress, appeared under her arms. Seemingly unaware, she folded her napkin into a neat square and reached for her husband's napkin and did the same. "We gotta go," she said, standing. "Real good dinner." She emphasized *dinner*.

"There's dessert," Grace began, but Hannah's quick look warned her to silence.

Amelia stood. "We're glad you came. It's been nice visiting with you for a bit." She focused on Frank. "And hearing about your plans for an auto parts store. We certainly wish you the best of luck, you and Billie."

As if making a statement to her parents, Claudia hugged Mike good-bye, slipped him a card with her work phone number, then called to Paulette that it was time to go.

Paulette ran to her mother, pouting. "I don't wanna go, Mama. Me and Tyler been catchin' tadpoles outta the stream."

"Grandma's ready to go. You can see Tyler in school."

After the Craines' departure, Harold and the parson strolled off, Harold to smoke his pipe, the parson a cigarette. Brenda rose and began to scrape and stack dishes, but Grace took a dish from her hands and insisted that they sit and relax. Bob slipped his arm about Grace's shoulders just as Russell, who had been very quiet all during the meal, pushed his chair from the table and crossed his legs.

"Russell," Amelia said. "Where is that Emily of yours?"

"In Florida. She has a law practice there."

"I'm sorry. I'd have enjoyed her being here today. You've never even told me how you two met."

"Didn't Grace tell you?"

"That's secondhand." Amelia pouted. "You tell me." She leaned toward him, her elbow on the table, and her chin set firmly on the back of her bent wrist.

"It not a romantic story, Amelia. We were both getting gas at Buddy's station."

Amelia sat back. "No, that's not very romantic."

His eyes twinkled. "What if I told you I knew at first sight that I wanted to marry Emily?"

Amelia clapped her hands. "Much better. Love at first sight. *Comme c'est romantique,* that's marvelous."

"Amelia's incurably romantic," Mike chimed in.

She turned to Mike. "*Chéri!* And you're not?"

Mike threw up his hands. "I am. Yes, I admit I am."

"We're celebrating our two-month anniversary Saturday night. I met Emily on August seventeenth."

"Two months already? What will you do to celebrate?" Amelia asked.

"Not sure yet, I . . ."

"Oh, Russell, take her someplace special with music and soft lights."

"Leave Russell alone, Amelia," Hannah said.

"It's okay, Hannah," Russell said. "Amelia's well intentioned."

"I am indeed." Amelia flipped her head toward Hannah. "Take her to the Poseidon Restaurant in Swannanoa. They have music some nights, and the food is *très bon.*"

Mike nodded. "That's a great idea, Amelia."

Moments later, Harold and Parson Johnson returned smelling of tobacco, and soon a conversation about football developed.

"Want some help?" Bob offered as the women began to stack dishes on trays to transport to the kitchen.

Grace kissed his forehead. "You stay here, love. We're just fine."

Once the dishwasher was loaded, the women settled around the kitchen table and began to do a postmortem of the afternoon. "Alma, the old gossip, was dying to go upstairs," Molly said.

"How could you tell? She seemed uninterested," Grace said.

"She was interested all right, her eyes were everywhere at once."

"If I'd sensed she wanted to, we could have gone up."

"Not into my bedroom." Hannah crossed her arms. "I don't want gossips like Alma prowling about my bedroom."

"Well, Alma can't say the table wasn't beautiful, or the food wasn't wonderful. You did so much work. The decor, the tables, the food, perfect."

Grace smiled. "Thank's Brenda. We all did it. I'm just sorry more of our neighbors didn't come, like the Maxwells."

Brenda studied her fingernails for a moment. "Bella Maxwell, well, she doesn't bother much with folks." Her eyebrows arched sharply. "Always ailin', you know the type. One child. Spoiled that boy, Zachary, right proper."

Molly had taught Zachary in school, and found him to be shy, withdrawn, into art. She liked the boy, but had found his parents distant, though cooperative. She changed the subject. "I love what you ladies have done with this old farmhouse. Years ago I came here with Dad to visit Mr. Furrior. We sat on springy old chairs in the living room, and the dust flew up. I couldn't see out the windows for the grime on them. Something, I thought it was a rat, ran across the floor, and Dad and Mr. Furrior ignored it, even when I yelled. Dad said, 'Hush you up, Molly,' and I did, but I sure was glad when we left."

"There were possums in the house when we first got here." The ladies laughed, remembering. "Seems like we've lived here always." Hannah's eyes roamed about the kitchen and met Grace's and then Amelia's. They nodded and smiled at her.

"Seems so to me, too," Molly said. "Mom talks all the time about the work you ladies do at her school." She looked at Hannah, into whose thick hair bits of tiny leaves had infiltrated. "Your gardening program's the envy of other elementary schools around here, and, Grace, Mom's always bragging about how you helped Tyler after his mother died in that awful car accident, and how great you are with all the children you tutor."

Suddenly, Amelia said. "Now, wouldn't it be nice if Russell married Emily?"

"I don't know." Brenda's brows drew together. "Tyler's just settlin' down to life without his mother. It might take some hard gettin' used to if things changed now. Be better a year down the road when he's more adjusted and a little older. New woman takin' his mother's place could send him into a tailspin."

"Well, he has Grace, his adopted grandma," Amelia said.

But Grace agreed with Brenda. She knew how hard change was, and Tyler's coping mechanism after his mother's death had been to sullenly withdraw.

9

A Map of Covington

Two nights after the lunch under the great oak, Grace and Bob returned from seeing a movie in Asheville to find the light still on in the kitchen. "Hi there," Grace called.

"Come on in here a minute," Hannah called back.

Hanging their coats in the hall closet, Grace headed for the kitchen with Bob towering behind her, his thick white hair windblown. Warm October days had bowed to forty-degree nights. A small fire glowed in the glass front of the blue ceramic-coated wood-burning iron stove in the corner of the room. Harold Tate had suggested they might need such a stove should a winter ice storm bring down power lines and leave them without electricity. A moist multilayered Vienna cake, one of Grace's specialties, baked mostly for special occasions, sat on the counter under a clear glass dome. Grace had had a yen for it, and made it earlier. A delicate whisper of vanilla remained in the kitchen.

Hannah and Amelia sat at the kitchen table hunched over maps, both flat and topographical, and loose white paper, and colored markers strewn helter-skelter across the tabletop, leaving not an inch of room for a mug or a glass.

"What are you two doing?" Grace asked.

The mandarin neck of a kelly green pajama top stuck out above the lapels of Hannah's homey gray bathrobe.

Momentarily distracted, Grace asked, "New pajamas?"

"From Miranda. Came earlier this evening by UPS with a letter that said, 'Do not wait for Christmas, use them now,' so . . ." She spread her arms wide. "You can assure my daughter when she calls that I'm using them." Hannah wiggled her shoulders. "They're silk pajamas. Prefer flannel. Don't tell Miranda. Nice letter, though. Here, let me read you some of it."

She fished her daughter's letter from the pocket of her robe and began.

"What fun it was visiting with you and Grace and Amelia. Some special kind of companionable serenity seems to flow between you three ladies. It drew me in, made me welcome. You're all so involved in life and busy, busy, busy. When do you ladies ever stop?"

Hannah released the letter into her lap. "Never while life lasts," she murmured in response to Miranda's question. Then she said thoughtfully, "After all these years of estrangement, it's good to feel cared about, appreciated by my daughter."

Grace understood. It had been the same with her son, Roger. After too many years of separation and chilly, rare comings together, Grace's planned move to Covington had precipitated angry exchanges, explanations, apologies, and forgiveness for which she was grateful. And now Miranda and her husband, Paul, and Roger and his longtime companion, Charles, were business partners in Branston.

"I remember," Amelia's voice cut in, as if she were reading Grace's mind, "when both your children opposed your moving to Covington from Pennsylvania. For days I worried you would change your minds. Imagine, if we'd gone on living at Olive Pruitt's dreary boarding-house." She waved her forefinger at the others, and grimaced as she mimicked their former landlady's raspy voice. "For older ladies in good health, only."

"When we lived at Olive's place life seemed stalled, a dead end. How different things are now." Grace chuckled, then grew serious. "Imagine," she said, looking at Hannah, "if we'd let our children dictate our lives."

"Here's a part about you, Amelia." Hannah fished Miranda's letter from her lap and read aloud.

"Amelia amazes me, beginning a new career in her late sixties. I've framed the photograph of hers I bought, and her lovely book's on my coffee table."

"She's so right, Amelia. You uncovered a latent talent. Look how successful you've been," Hannah said.

Praise from Hannah came rarely, and Amelia beamed with pleasure.

As if embarrassed, Hannah looked down. "Miranda covers a bit of everything in this letter. Says she's glad I sold the greenhouse to Wayne." She paused to scan the letter, then continued. "Listen to this."

"I'm glad you're volunteering at Caster Elementary School. You're teaching a whole new generation of youngsters to garden, and to value and be caretakers of the earth."

"And it's not just the kids you're teaching," Grace said. "There's Wayne and all he needs to learn to run a plant business successfully."

"Wayne's getting the hang of the business," Hannah said. She smiled. "Such a character. Never on time, but. . . ." She shrugged. "He gets things done, in his own time. And perhaps, someday, one of those young people from Caster Elementary will say to someone, 'Hannah Parrish taught me about plants, started me thinking about a career in environmental education or horticulture.' "

"Or one of them might become a senator from North Carolina who'll fight for the environment," Amelia said.

"Read the rest of it, will you, Grace?" Hannah handed Grace the letter. From the evening that Roger deposited his sad-eyed mother at Olive's boardinghouse, Hannah had liked Grace, felt that Grace was a good and honest person, a trustworthy person, and she had been right, and Hannah enjoyed the melodic, soothing quality of Grace's voice, liked to hear her read.

Grace reached for Miranda's letter and began.

"When I got home from work the other night, I found a message on my machine from Laura. Said she and Captain Marvin are sailing his boat south, to the Caribbean. She said that she plans to phone you before they leave."

"Well, she hasn't." Hannah sighed and stared into space. "So different, my girls. Laura's a good person. Handful to raise, though. Frightfully rebellious and independent."

"Wonder where she got that from?" Grace smiled at Hannah, then read on.

"We've been nothing but busy since the Gracious Entertainment Shop opened. People have plenty of money and no time these days. They delegate, and we plan their parties for them."

"Charles and Roger came up with this idea at just the right time, didn't they?" Grace turned to Hannah. "Who would have imagined that your daughter, and my Roger, and his Charles would go into business together? They didn't even know one another before we came to Covington that first time, and a few months later they were going into business."

"It seems to have turned out well," Amelia said.

"Your son, my daughter, in business. It makes us like a family," Hannah said, unwittingly lassoing Grace's meandering mind.

Grace noticed Hannah's broad, stub-nailed fingers curled lightly over the arm of her chair. Gently, she touched the taut, blue-veined skin of her hand. "Chosen family," she said.

With that, a wide grin spread across Hannah's angular face.

Hannah's almost beautiful when she smiles and her eyes light up, Grace thought. They're not the deep blue like Amelia's eyes, but blue enough.

Amelia's knuckles rapped the table. "Me too, I'm family."

"That you are, Amelia," Grace said. Reaching out, she touched both their hands. "Chosen family. The best kind, often better than flesh and blood relations." Saying that, she flashed back to how much Roger, her only child, had hurt her. After his father's death, and after her "little" heart attack, he had dashed in from his life in Saudi Arabia to insist that she sell her furniture, rent her home in Dentry, Ohio, and move to Olive Pruitt's boardinghouse in Pennsylvania. Upon his return from Saudi Arabia, he had pressed her to sell her home in Dentry so that he and Charles might invest in a new business. For the same reason, and at the same time, Miranda harangued Hannah to sell Hannah's former plant nursery, which Miranda ran, and in which her mother retained a financial and emotional interest.

Grace and Hannah had both capitulated. In hindsight it seemed that, young and old, they had all been reaching for new lives that year. Providentially, their dreams had materialized. Their children's business was successful, as were Amelia, Hannah, and herself, each in her own way, here, in rural North Carolina.

"One more sentence," Grace said.

"Well, this is all for now, Mother. My love to you three ladies of Covington. Miranda."

Grace folded and handed the letter back to Hannah, who shoved it back into her pocket. It had set Grace thinking about her son and Charles. "I'd like to see Roger and Charles. Charles is like a son to me. I worry about him so much since the diagnosis." She sighed. "Even if he's lucky and never gets AIDS, the threat's always there."

Charles had been diagnosed nearly five years ago.

"If I were Charles, I'd be frantic. I'd never sleep," Amelia said.

"At least, so far, his T cell count's high, well up over nine hundred, so that's good," Hannah said. They all nodded, then spoke no more of Charles.

She turned back to the plastic topographic map and squinted at its configurations.

"What are you doing?" Grace asked again.

"I've been trying to find Covington."

"Before we came down here we couldn't find Covington on any map." Tracings marked the sheet of paper Grace picked up. She turned it this way and that and studied it.

"I'm trying to rough out a map of Covington," Hannah said. "There is none." She nodded at the heavy-ridged map. "So many mountains and hills, and the French Broad River runs right through the county."

"A map of Covington." Amelia spread wide her fingers. "It somewhat resembles a hand without a thumb, the valleys would be the space between my fingers." She wiggled her hand.

"Show me."

With a black marker, Amelia traced the outline of her hand on a blank sheet of paper. With a green marker, she filled in the three valleys between her fingers: Cove Road, Loring Valley, McCorkle Creek. Using a brown marker, Amelia scribbled in the spaces where her fingers had been. "These are the mountains that separate the valleys."

Grace inspected it. "I think you're right, Covington does resemble a palm."

Hannah looked and nodded. "I think, you've got it. This will help the graphic artist I've hired to get a map made."

Amelia rose, turned toward the refrigerator, and pulled out a baked ham wrapped snug in heavy tinfoil. Amelia set it on the sink counter, and as the ham was presliced, she eased off a slice with her fingers. "Anyone want a ham sandwich?" She tossed her head and laughed. "I'll use a fork and knife." No one did. Amelia helped herself to another slice of ham, ate it, then resealed the heavy foil. "I don't know what I want to eat. That didn't do it."

Turning to Hannah, Grace asked, "Why do you want a map, Hannah?"

"Need a map so people can see what we're talking about, to explain to interested parties why they should join the Cove Road Preserve Coalition."

"Who may these interested parties be?" Amelia asked.

"Audubon Society, Sierra Club, hiking groups, other concerned citizens, private funding sources. I've got addresses for the Sierra Clubs in Buncombe, Madison, and Yancey Counties. Flyer being printed to send out. When they come will you help me address them?"

"Of course," Grace said. Amelia, whose mouth was full, nodded yes.

"I'd be glad to help, too, Hannah," Bob, who had been silent, said.

"Did you have a good time tonight?" Grace asked Amelia.

"Mike and I went to Be Here Now, a club in Asheville. I felt old enough to be everyone's grandmother." She flung back her head and laughed. "A young man with tattoos on both arms asked me to dance. Mike glowered at him, and he nearly tripped in his hurry to get away." Amelia returned the ham to the refrigerator, peered inside, shuffled things around, and took out an English muffin and red raspberry jam. "Cake's too sweet this time of night. Maybe a muffin."

Hannah's eyes followed Amelia. "You have neat handwriting. Print 'Masterson Land,' 'Elk Road,' 'Loring Valley,' and 'McCorkle Creek' on this paper, and make a little house with a cross to designate Cove Road Church, will you, Amelia?"

"And little houses for the seven farmhouses on Cove Road, and their owners' names," Grace said. "And be sure to put in Maxwell's windmill, and show how the hills drift away one after the other, the way they look in the evening. You can do that, can't you?"

Pop went the toaster. Amelia removed the English muffin. "I can try, but I'm no artist."

Bob studied the very rough sketch. He reached for a blue marker and drew a curving line across the area to represent Masterson's land. "Bad River," he said. "What a name. Why Bad River?"

"Lurina told me that years ago it flooded so high that all the crops were destroyed, animals drowned, and the house was nearly dragged off its foundation," Grace said.

Hannah's brows knitted as she pulled the sketch toward her. She added a straight brown line across where the knuckles on the hand would be. "And this would be Elk Road." She looked at it carefully, then, using a marker, she thickened Elk Road. "Grover Masterson set aside this five-mile strip, three hundred feet deep along Elk Road for commercial use." She brown-marked it in.

"Soon to be home to a strip mall, as well as P. J. Prancer's and the old gas station," Amelia said.

"And our tearoom," Bob added.

Amelia slathered jam on her muffin and picked up her cup. She yawned. "Leave it on the table, Hannah. I promise, early tomorrow I'll print in the names. Now, I'm off to bed. *Bonne nuit.*"

"See you tomorrow." With Amelia gone, Grace shoved the fledgling map toward Hannah. "You do it. You can print small. At least do Cove Road, Loring Valley, and McCorkle Creek."

Hannah rummaged among the pencils and paper and found a fine-tipped pen. Carefully she printed McCORKLE CREEK.

"The McCorkles are Scotch-Irish," Grace said. "Hardy folk, with strong family and religious ties. Did you know this area's famous for its authentic folk music and that Madison County's noted for its excellent folk musicians?"

"How do you know all of that?" Bob asked.

"Librarian at Caster Elementary," Grace replied. "I ask questions. Jane, the librarian, loaned me a spiral-bound book published in 1974 to mark the bicentennial of the Declaration of Independence. It's called *This Is Madison County*. It tells all about the county, its geography, where the settlers came from and when, the ups and downs of the economy, about the music and songs from the old country that have been kept pure here.

"There's a chapter on floods: 1876, 1916 . . ." She hesitated, tapped her forehead with a finger. "1928, 1940. People still argue about which was the absolute worst."

"How can you remember all those dates, Grace?" Hannah asked.

"I wonder myself. I can't remember the names of new people to save my soul, and I forget the grocery list, but . . ." She shrugged. "Maybe I remember what interests me. You know I'm a history buff."

The fire in the woodstove had died down to a mere glow, but the room was warm, and Bob removed his sweater. He made no move to leave. If he didn't feel like driving home, he was welcome here and would spend the night either with Grace or in the guest room. He and Grace would decide that later.

Hannah stacked the maps and papers and topped them with the topographic map and sat them on the floor beside her chair. Only the budding map of Covington lay on the table. "Cove Road's the shortest valley, like a pinkie," Hannah said. "Shortest valley. Farthest one in along Elk Road."

"Who were the Covingtons?" Bob asked.

"Harold's family. Covingtons settled here in 1871. Covington's named for them," Grace said. "Harold says when they came it was still dense forest with patches of grassland. They tried growing cotton but gave it up for tobacco. The Mastersons arrived in 1875, then the McCorkles."

"Loring Valley may be the widest valley, but Cove Road's the most beautiful," Bob said.

"And those confounded developers built villas no more than fifty feet back from Little River, right on the floodplain in Loring Valley. Piled rocks at the river's edge, as if that'll hold back rampaging water," Hannah said.

Grace felt the hair rise on her arms. They hadn't had a really heavy rain since they'd arrived here, but she remembered Harold's saying they had sixty-five to seventy inches of rain most years, and flooding happened if the rain was intense and frequent enough. Heavy rains, he warned them, had been known to propel their small stream over its banks. Luckily their house was built on a foundation three feet above the ground, and their land sloped gently toward Cove Road. Grace tried to recall if the Hammers' villa was raised or set on a slab, and couldn't remember, then she was distracted by the creaking of Hannah's chair. Hannah sat back, drew her robe tight about her, and knotted the red belt.

Red belt. Green pajamas. Christmas was coming. Grace smiled. Having taken advantage of after-Christmas sales last January, she had only to wrap her presents when the time came.

Night sounds wafted through the half-open window: leaves rustling, a car passing, an acorn, perhaps, from the great oak pinging onto the porch roof. Hannah said, "Every time I think of Loring Valley my blood boils." She knotted her fists.

Grace remembered. The noise of construction had reverberated between sky-scraping mountains, poured from Loring Valley, and hurled shivers of sound along Elk Road, into McCorkle Creek, over Masterson land, and down Cove Road. Grace covered her ears. "I'll never forget the sounds of it. Miss Lurina says she's sure the blasting made her deaf."

Hannah handed the fledgling map to Grace, who changed several lines in the sketch of McCorkle Creek. "McCorkle Creek's very narrow except for the flat area close to the entrance, and that's jammed with McCorkle farms and houses." She held up the drawing. "When McCorkle children and grandchildren marry, they build a house, share the barns and farm machinery. Laura Hill, our librarian, told me that she camped up on Beef Mountain once. She could look right down on that valley. She says the McCorkle complex resembles Brigadoon at night; by day it's a dowdy collection of weathered buildings. And the street names: McCorkle Ditch, Lone Pasture Lane, Plant and Pick Road, Old Horse Lane, Fall Down Corner, and so on, and they're all no wider than the width of a truck." Grace stood, covered the Vienna cake, and put it on top of the refrigerator.

Bob closed his eyes and drew a deep breath. "Being in this kitchen always makes me feel warm inside and happy. My mother's kitchen smelled of vanilla."

Grace ran her finger along his cheek. For several minutes, the only sounds in the room came from Bob's chair as he shifted his weight, and the intermittent whistles from the kettle that was about to boil again. A tiny mouse scurried across the floor. Amelia would have screamed and stood on a chair, Grace thought, as she watched the tiny critter disappear behind the refrigerator. She wondered how many mice raised families behind their walls.

Bob's voice cut into her thoughts. "McCorkle Creek's got a splendid waterfall."

"Ever walk to that waterfall? Exacting terrain along that stream, like someone took tons of jagged boulders and tossed them helter-skelter." Hannah shook her head. "But Loring Valley." Her eyes grew speculative. "How could it happen that Bracken and Woodward Corporation out of South Georgia found this out-of-the-way place? One morning we woke up to the roar of their equipment charging along Elk Road and into Loring Valley. If we can't stop them, Cove Road is next."

10

Lance Lundquist

"They've closed the Blue Ridge Parkway, Amelia. The fog's too heavy," Mike said on the phone. "But it should be gorgeous with all that fog drifting about and skirting trees in the forest. What say we meet at Ingle's, off New Stock Road in Weaverville, and go on up Reems Creek Road to Ox Bow? We'll head up the mountain. Even if we get only a little way, it should be glorious for photography."

The house was quiet. Hannah had gone to Hendersonville with Wayne to check out a potential retail outlet for the ornamental flowering plants they grew in the greenhouse out back, and to talk to a graphic artist about her map.

This being the last week of October, the fall foliage was at its peak, and Grace, Bob, Russell, and Emily were off to Jonesborough, a quaint and charming town in Tennessee where a storytelling festival was held every year. Amelia didn't like being alone in the farmhouse. Noises, barely audible when the others were there, frightened her. Was it really old boards contracting as they cooled or warmed, or was it the light steps of a thief on the stairs? Or a ghost? It was, after all, an old house. Or was it a small animal trapped indoors? Thank goodness Mike had called.

"I'd love to go," she said. Pulling aside the curtain at the kitchen window, Amelia peered into the mist. Fog blanketed everything within her sight, even the windmill at the Maxwell farm was invisible, and it was ten in the morning. She felt momentary panic at the idea of being on the road in this pea soup. Silly. She could do it. She'd just crawl along getting to Weaverville. "It's foggy out here. I may be late," she said to Mike.

"You're never late, but considering the fog, I'll wait, do some grocery shopping. If I'm not in the van when you get here, look for me in the Fresh Market."

"Will do." She hung up, checked the front and back doors to be sure they were locked, walked away, then returned and propped a chair against the kitchen doorknob. Showering when she was alone in the house invariably stirred memories of Hitchcock's movie *Psycho*. Pity she'd ever seen it. Well, she'd showered yesterday. Amelia sniffed at her underarm. Smelled of violets from her cologne. She wouldn't shower after all.

The ceiling of the foyer resembled a medieval battlefield of confused ladybugs unsure of procedures on the field of battle. The living room ceiling brought the same image to mind. Amelia resisted the urge to shwoosh at them with a broom, dash them to the floor. No, she'd get up on a sturdy chair and vacuum them. Amelia started upstairs, turned, came back down, and speculated again about the ladybugs. Why bother now? They'd only come back in droves. Was she becoming resigned to ladybugs? Heaven forbid. Someone in this household had to fight the good fight, or the little creatures would inundate them. But later. They would be there later and so would she.

*

It was ten-thirty in the morning when Amelia, encased in plastic rainwear, slid into her Taurus and snapped fast her seat belt. The strap pressing against her chest bothered her. Nervous, and overcautious, Amelia scanned the road right and left a minimum of three times prior to turning from the driveway onto Cove Road. Signs indicating a curve ahead brought her to a crawl. Railroad crossings with their lights off and their railings raised brought her to a dead halt. On entering or exiting ramps on or off of Highway 19–23, the four-lane into Asheville, Amelia held her breath and drove much too slowly.

Years ago, after the big sedan with darkened windows ran a stop sign and plowed into their car, killing Thomas and leaving her with horrid burn scars about her neck and shoulder, she swore she would never own a car again, much less drive one. So much for vows. Living in the country, depending on a ride from others every time she needed a jar of rejuvenating night cream for her face, or film, or notepaper, anything, had grown unbearable. With Grace's and Hannah's encouragement, she had asked Harold Tate to help her select a car. They chose a Taurus, not too big, not too small, just right for a person five feet three and slight of build.

Amelia inched the Taurus down the driveway and stopped at Cove Road. The Maxwells' farmhouse was barely visible in the resolute, opalescent pall that lay thick upon the land. No oncoming headlights honeycombed the furlongs of yawning fog to left or right. Amelia considered fog fickle and unpredictable, at time dense and unyielding, at times pliant and tensile, at times peripheral, hugging roadsides, or floating in patches over dips in the road. There were times she could see her way on one street, turn a corner, and have to pull off the road and wait for a car or truck to pass her, then follow those taillights, tiny red gleams in the murk.

Amelia turned right on Cove Road. Visibility was perhaps fifty feet. The first twenty-five-mile-an-hour speed limit sign that she passed lay bent and twisted at an angle. It had been that way for months. The second, though erect, bore the pitted scars of bullets. Too many teenagers had guns, and target practice on street signs was standard entertainment. Relieved that no car appeared in her rearview mirror, Amelia drove at ten miles an hour.

At Elk Road she stopped, waited, then turned left. She looked for markers: the entrance to Loring Valley Road, then she would pass McCorkle Creek Road. Beyond Elk Road, the two-lane to Mars Hill was wider and considerably less foggy than these roads in Covington. Something, Harold Tate said, about this area being lower and enclosed by hills and with several rivers. Once she was out of Covington, visibility would improve, and Amelia planned to increase her speed to thirty-five, maybe even forty miles an hour.

Trees overhanging Elk Road formed a charming bower on sunny days, but dank and fog-banked as it was today, they created a sinister and brooding feel. The fog thickened. Visibility dropped to near zero. Sensing something, Amelia slammed on her brakes.

When the smack and the grinding crunch struck her rear fender, the seat belt squeezed against her chest and waist, and her neck snapped back. I should be screaming, she thought. They say I screamed and screamed when Thomas and I were hit. But no sound came from her lips. Amelia closed her eyes. Mike would worry when she did not show up. He would come. He would find her here. "Mike?" she said in response to the banging on her car door. "Mike?"

"No." The voice was deeper than Mike's. "It's Lance, Lance Lundquist."

Amelia opened her eyes to the cheerless grayness beyond her windshield. What had happened? The windshield remained intact. Amelia tried the door. It opened easily. Her arms moved normally, and her legs, though gone to rubber, moved. Her neck ached, as did her chest, bruised as it was by the seat belt. There was no fire, as there had been on that fateful day when Thomas died. "I'm not hurt?" she whispered.

Tall and stocky as a bear, a man stood in the open door of her car. He extended a hand swathed in shaggy brown gloves that reminded her of bear's paws. A bear that talked? Ridiculous. Amelia blinked, rubbed her eyes. In the flare of headlights from an oncoming vehicle, she noted blond hair turning to silver, a white shirt peeping from a heavy brown jacket. Fumbling with her safety belt, she felt it go slack.

"Are you hurt? Can you move your legs, arms? Can you turn, rotate your head?" the man asked.

Slowly, Amelia rotated her head.

"Give me your hand." When she did not move, he repeated calmly. "Let me have your hand. I'll help you out. It's a rear-end collision, my fault. Thank goodness we were both going slow. My front fender's damaged, and your rear fender. I am totally at fault. You had the right of way. I didn't see you when I turned onto Elk Road. My insurance'll handle it." He stood there, filling all the space. "They need a light here, one we can see in fog like this."

His voice was directive and authoritative. Amelia pictured him striding up to the mayor's office in Marshall, demanding a stoplight, one that glowed in the fog, and the next day four men and two trucks hastening to install the light.

"Miss? Mrs.?" he asked.

"Mrs. Declose," she replied. "Amelia Declose."

"May I help you out of the car, Mrs. Declose?"

Unwittingly, as if instructed by a schoolteacher to raise her hand, she placed hers in his and stepped onto the road alongside the stranger.

"That's better," he said. "Now, who is Mike? I'll do my best to locate him for you and notify him of our accident."

He made it sound so neat and personal—our accident.

The large truck coming toward them stopped. A door slammed. Muffled footsteps approached. A bulky form materialized. "Howdy folks. Need help?"

It was George Maxwell, the dairy farmer from across Cove Road.

"Mr. Maxwell," Amelia said, relieved. "My car. I've had an accident. Can you give me a ride home?"

A tall man, thick-muscled, sharp-featured, with keen dark eyes and graying brown hair that hung lank in the fog, Max, as he was called, moved cautiously around both cars. "Got you a fender bender," he said. "I'll help get your bumpers unstuck, and you can probably drive it home yourself, ma'am."

Tears rushed to Amelia's eyes. "I can't. I just can't."

"The lady's terribly upset," the stranger, Lance, said.

"I have eyes, just like you," Maxwell said. "Well, we need to push her car off the road before someone crashes into it, again."

Dampness from the road oozed through the soles of Amelia's shoes. The chill of a thousand foggy days slithered up her light wool pants and hugged her legs and thighs. She stood there shivering, watching through mist as the two men disengaged the bumpers one from the other, then shoved her car onto the soggy shoulder, a safe distance off the road. This freed Lance's car, a Buick Regal, to be driven.

"Come on, I'll take you home," Maxwell said with a nod toward his truck.

Amelia hesitated. Lance, whatever his name was, had been kind. She owed him the courtesy of a thank you, but before she could speak, Lance took her arm and walked her to Maxwell's big truck.

Once she was safely inside the tuck, the stranger motioned for her to roll down the window and asked for her phone number and address. "I'll drop by later, when the fog clears, to get the information I'll need for my insurance company."

"Thank you, Mr.?" She hesitated. The cab of Maxwell's truck was warm and smelled of dogs, and tobacco.

"Lance," he said.

75

His intense gray-blue eyes met hers and held them. "Lance," she said. "Thank you for your help." She wondered if he heard her above the din of Maxwell revving his engine. Then they were off.

"Why would you thank that fellow? He hit you."

It was true, why had she thanked him?

"Which one of the ladies are you?"

"I'm Amelia, Amelia Declose." She reached out her hand to shake his, but he leaned into the steering wheel, gripped it with both hands, and squinted into the gloom.

"Dangerous drivin' in this kind of weather," Maxwell mumbled. "Lucky he wasn't comin' at you head-on."

Amelia shivered.

Having stripped off her scarf and coat, Amelia paced from the foyer to the living room and back, the portable phone in hand, giving ladybugs threatening looks while she waited for the manager of the market to page Mike. Please let him still be in the store, she prayed. When the doorbell rang, relief swept through her. Mike, she thought. He's here. Grabbing up her blue cashmere scarf, she flung it about her neck and threw wide the door.

Lance Lundquist, hat in bulky, brown-gloved hands, stood in the doorway. Gray-blue eyes fixed hers from under wild eyebrows. They were thick and bushy with fugitive white hairs curling toward his forehead and others straggling like vines off to the sides. Amelia ignored the urge to get out her scissors and trim the vagrant eyebrows into conformity. She wondered about his age; he looked about sixty, younger than she was, surely.

Realizing that she was staring, Amelia drew back and motioned him inside. "Excuse me a moment," she said, hearing a sound on the portable phone in her hand. "Mike? Is that you? I'm so glad I got you. I had an accident. No. I'm not hurt." She listened, all the while waving Lance into the kitchen, which seemed the place to bring a strange man. "Just the rear fender. The man who bumped into me is here now. What's his name? Lance?" She looked at Lance with raised brows.

"Lundquist," he said.

"Lance Lundquist," Amelia relayed to Mike. She looked at the stranger, who was removing his coat and draping it, along with the shaggy brown gloves, over a chair. Then he drew out a chair and sat, waiting, his hands crossed on the table, his eyes glued to her face. "Mike wants you to wait until he gets here."

"Certainly." He smiled for the first time, and Amelia noted that several of his front teeth overlapped one another.

She relayed his full name again to Mike and hung up, then stood in the doorway watching him uneasily. He raised his hands. "No weapons." He smiled. "Maybe while we wait, we could go over the insurance information, your driver's license number, insurance policy."

Amelia left the kitchen and returned a moment later, rummaged in her purse, and extracted a billfold with all the information needed. Lance copied it in a meticulous print into a small blue book he then tucked into his tweed jacket pocket. Then he asked, "How long have you lived here?"

"A year and five months." Amelia slipped into a chair across from him. "Would you like a cup of coffee? A cookie? My housemate, Grace, makes incredible cookies."

"I'd love a cup of coffee. No cookies. Mike's your husband?"

"*Mon Dieu,* no." She chuckled. "Mike's taught me all I know about photography. He's a very dear friend. I was on my way to meet him. We were going to shoot pictures of the forest in the fog. You can get some spectacular shots in the fog."

Amelia poured coffee into a mug and brought sugar and cream to the table. She had let a strange man into her home, but he seemed so pleasant, had been so apologetic about the accident, and she was glad not to be alone. "So, you live in Loring Valley?"

He took a long drink of coffee and held the mug in both hands, as if to warm them. "Yes, for two months now. I'm originally from Nevada. I'm an architect, retired, but I had my own architectural firm in Denver for years. Last year I sold out, got into my car, and traveled for four months."

He's larger than life, Amelia thought. He fills the chair, the whole kitchen it seems. Her heart did a strange unaccustomed flip-flop.

Lance set his mug on the table. "After Denver, I wanted someplace with mountains, but warmer. Picked up a brochure on Loring Valley at one of the welcome stations, and came up to have a look." He leaned a bit toward her. She straightened and leaned away.

"How do you like the area?"

"The scenery's great, but I expected Asheville to be more cosmopolitan." He shrugged. "Maybe I'm judging it too soon."

"It's not cosmopolitan, in the sense that we don't get Broadway musicals or opera with full sets. Asheville's . . ." She thought a moment. ". . . less homogeneous than some other cities in the South. There's been a lot of migration into the area from everywhere in the United States." She bit her lip, looked thoughtful. Should she tell him that Asheville hosted a large gay and lesbian community? And he must recognize all the adult hippies sporting gray beards, long hair, and wearing sandals, and the women with trailing hair and skirts. He must know about all the new retirement communities being built in Weaverville and Asheville, and the golf courses. "There's art here, and lots of fine crafts, and theater, more summer stock than Broadway."

"But no flashy musicals straight off of Broadway, eh?"

"One can go to Greenville in South Carolina or down to Charlotte for theater, but I don't think there's a stage large enough here to accommodate a huge cast and sets. We keep hoping they'll build a cultural center with a fine theater, not a multipurpose arena, but I guess we're years away from that."

"Perhaps the infusion of outsiders will bring the money and interest sooner rather than later," he said.

She wondered if Lance was one of those rich, interested newcomers. "Perhaps. That would be wonderful."

A car door slammed. Hurried steps crossed the porch announced Mike's arrival, and moments later he called from the hall, "Amelia, where are you?"

Lance sat stiffly. He straightened his tie.

Amelia half rose from her chair. "In here, Mike."

Mike lighted in the doorway, strands of long brown hair adrift from his ponytail, his dark, sensitive eyes wide and worried. Then, tearing off his cashmere scarf, a gift from Amelia, he rushed to her and flung his arms about her. "I was frantic. Horrid fog. It's my fault for asking you to come out on a day like this. It's terrible in your valley." He spoke in quick sentences, all the while unzipping and removing his windbreaker and draping it over the chair he pulled out next to Amelia. He took her hand in both of his and held it securely, possessively.

"I love this woman," he said to Lance, a huge grin on his wind-reddened face. "She's incredible, and such a talent. Have you seen her work, her book? Glorious."

"Stop it, Mike." Amelia blushed, but she liked it that Mike tooted her horn, letting Lance know that she was a woman to be respected.

"I haven't," Lance said, "but, I'd like to." His eyes sought Amelia's, and a shiver of—what? excitement?—whipped through her. His eyes were filled with greater interest now, and curiosity, Amelia thought.

"I'll get her book," Mike said, releasing Amelia's hand. He returned moments later with the coffee table book of photographs, *Memories and Mist: Mornings on the Blue Ridge,* and opened it on the table facing Lance. "See what splendid work she's done?"

Lance turned the pages, slowly perusing the photographs. "The light in your photographs is marvelous. You have quite a talent."

Mike stood behind Lance as he turned the pages. "A real talent. I love this woman," Mike repeated. His eyes shone with affection as he looked at Amelia.

"And, I love you, Mike," she replied softly, then added, "you're such a good friend."

11

Lance and Amelia Meet Again

With her camera dangling from one shoulder, her camera bag filled with lenses dragging down the other shoulder, and her tripod teetering under her arm, Amelia struggled to lock the front door of the farmhouse behind her.

"Here, let me help you."

Shivers raced along Amelia's arm and neck. She had not heard his car or his footsteps, but she would know Lance's deep, resonant voice anywhere. "Hi." Stepping aside, she allowed him access to the door, which he pulled firmly shut, then locked the dead bolt with the key she handed to him. "Thanks."

"It's a fine, sunny day today, so I thought I'd drop by and see how you were, after yesterday's jolt. See if you needed a ride, with your car in the shop and all."

"I'm fine. I have Hannah's station wagon. I was just on my way to shoot my neighbor's roses. Want to come? It's just down the road."

"Sure." Without asking, he slipped the heavy camera bag from her shoulder and the tripod from under her arm. "I'll be your caddy."

"You don't have to."

"I do have to. Besides, I want to."

In silence they drove the short distance past the church, to Velma Herrill's house with its wraparound porch. Velma was sweeping her front steps. She stopped and waved. "Had to get it spick-and-span before you started takin' pictures."

"It looks fine," she said as she slid from her car. "Velma, this is Lance Lundquist, one of the new residents over in Loring Valley. Lance, my neighbor, Velma Herrill. She waved her hand toward the roses, luscious, pink clusters twining in and about the porch railing. "Just smell them. They're marvelous." Amelia lifted a heavily laden branch and bent to inhale the sweet odor.

"Old world, heritage roses," Velma said. "They're the hardiest, and smell the best. They've bred the smell out of most of the hybrid teas."

"I know. That's why Hannah used only red Chrysler Imperial roses along our drive. They're among those hybrid teas that retain their smell, and it's delicious, like these." She bent to take another whiff. "Only your roses smell, well, more delicate, lighter, and they bloom longer." Amelia motioned Lance to smell them, then she stepped back. "A hedge of rambling roses, absolutely lovely." Amelia knew she was rambling, nervous with Lance there.

Setting up her tripod, Amelia screwed her camera onto it. Without stretching, or straining, or bending, her eye fit right over the viewer. First she would get a wide shot of the front porch, then she would focus on the roses. She asked Velma to bring out a large bowl, partly filled with water, the kind she would use on her dining room table. When Velma complied, Amelia instructed her to cut roses to fill the bowl. Velma leaned way over the railing, and as she did, Amelia shot frame after frame, then reloaded her camera before Velma moved to the front steps, sat, and began to place the roses in the bowl. So absorbed was Velma in arranging the roses that she seemed to forget Amelia, who soon forgot that Lance was leaning against the car watching her work.

Later, when he drove Amelia to Mars Hill to turn in the film to be developed, Lance said, "I was impressed. You're incredible, how you got her to relax and forget you were there."

"You get the best shots that way."

"You love this work?"

"I certainly do. I never worked before I found photography."

"Why not?"

"I had a husband with big dreams and big projects who wanted me at his side in attendance constantly."

"Maybe he needed your help."

"Maybe Thomas did. I'll never know."

"Men need women, especially someone as lovely as you are," he said. "A man is enhanced when he walks into a room with a beautiful woman on his arm. I understand your husband's desire to have you by his side. You're fresh and lovely as a sunrise."

Amelia flushed bright red. Enhanced. What an odd word to use. Lance seemed so self-assured, why would he need any woman in order to feel enhanced? Still, she had enjoyed it when men and women looked, not at Thomas, but at her when they walked into a room. She'd forgotten.

"I'd like to take you for dinner. I've heard there's a lovely restaurant and dancing down at Lake Lure. Would you go?"

"I'd love to go."

"Saturday night, then? I'll pick you up about six."

"Fine. Thank you."

"No, lovely lady, I thank you."

Suddenly, Lance swerved to avoid a car. "Damned idiot." He looked behind, and Amelia noted for the first, but not the last time, the cold gray that banished the blue from his eyes.

Later that night, Amelia sat at the kitchen table with Hannah and Grace, addressing flyers to members of the Sierra Club. "Lance came by," Amelia said. "He went with me to shoot Velma's roses. Then he drove me to Mars Hill. He's asked me to go for dinner and dancing Saturday night at Lake Lure."

"Lake Lure, eh? Long drive up a mountain and down with so many nice places right here and in Asheville," Hannah said.

"Of course there are nice places here, but the lake and all, and the moon's nearly full, it'll be gorgeous, and so romantic, don't you think? It's been so long, I've forgotten what it's like getting all dressed up and walking into a room on the arm of a stunning man. It'll be fun."

"Well, you just go and have a grand time." Grace wrote the zip code numbers on the last of the flyers on the table near her, and reached for another pile.

It was Grace who Amelia awakened late at night when she returned from her first date with Lance Lundquist. "I have to talk, Grace. I'm so excited."

"You had a good time?" Grace rubbed her eyes and propped herself up in her bed. Amelia took the rocking chair by the window. She wore a pale yellow, ankle-length chiffon dress that hugged her slim body.

"You look beautiful," Grace said, "fresh as a daisy even after a night out dancing. Did you have fun? Did he kiss you?"

"Goodness no. Never on a first date." She was on the edge of the chair now. "Oh, Grace. It was so exciting."

"So tell me, what's he like?"

"Great fun. A terrific dancer. Gracious, well mannered, polished, stunning, you've seen him. Isn't he gorgeous? His eyes are blue-gray, remember? And when he's happy they're blue, but when he gets upset they change to gray, and go all steely."

Grace shivered. "I wouldn't like that."

"At least I know how he's feeling."

"So tell me about him. Does he have children, grandchildren? Where do they live?"

Amelia frowned, and the light faded from her lovely eyes. Uh-oh, Grace thought, trouble. "What is it, Amelia?"

Amelia slipped off her high heels and rubbed her toes. "When we had that accident, Lance said he'd lived in Denver, been an architect, sold his firm, and retired here. I don't know one other thing about him, where he was born, if he has any family, nothing. He doesn't talk about his past. Tonight at dinner, when I pressed him, his eyes turned gray and his mouth got that firm set. So, I backed off."

"I seem to recall a time when you were pretty private, not telling anyone about your past, about Thomas, your burns, Caroline."

"That's true." She tossed her head, scooped up her shoes, and stood. "Maybe he just needs time to get to know me, trust me." She departed with a flourish, leaving Grace sitting in bed and wide awake.

12

A Tale of Dying and Burial

October slipped into November. Leaves spilled from trees, and trails through the woods became clearly visible. Under the great oak, banks of fallen and decaying leaves released their dank and heavy odor. Clear and brilliant, constellations accompanied by myriad hand-maiden stars traversed the heavens. Orion's Belt sailed smoothly across the southern sky. Grace's weekly visits with Lurina became routine. Sometimes Amelia joined them, sometimes Hannah. Lurina came alive when their cars drove across the bridge.

"Lurina Masterson would be a marvelous subject to photograph, Grace," Amelia said as they drove into Mars Hill one morning to pick up prints of photographs she had shot. "Black and white I think." When Grace did not reply, Amelia said, "I'll have to get to know Miss Lurina better, of course, before I ask her, unless you'd do it for me."

"I think you should get to know her better."

"You care for her deeply, don't you? I'm jealous." Amelia laughed.

"I guess I love her, and you, Hannah, Bob, and so many others. Love stretches like a rubber band to encompass many people."

"A rubber band stretched too far will snap and break," Amelia said.

"Think of it as a very thick and long rubber band, then."

Amelia shrugged.

"I'd wait until you know Miss Lurina better before you ask her." Grace's hand slipped from the steering wheel to cover Amelia's. She gave a slight squeeze. "I don't own Miss Lurina. You do whatever you want. Maybe she'd be willing." Grace doubted that, but you never knew, and Lurina seemed to like Amelia, had even given her tea in her best china cup.

They drove in silence through the fall landscape, past hillsides decked in pastel shades of rose, salmon, peach, and apricot, intermingled with yellows and rust. In these mountains, the fall lacked the vibrant reds and purples of states further to the north. Grace did not pine for what she did not have. She relished autumn's soft loveliness, but Amelia did not.

"I hate it that our fall is so pale. I miss the reds," she complained. "Every year, I promise I'm going up into Pennsylvania to see more color. I haven't done it yet."

"So just relax, and try to enjoy what we have here."

Rebuked, Amelia sat silent for a time, then she said, "I'd like to invite Lance to the opening of the tearoom."

"You don't have to ask. Any friend of yours is welcome."

"Why do I think Hannah doesn't like Lance?"

"We've only met him twice when he came to pick you up. You like him, that's what matters." Grace slowed the car and pulled onto the grassy shoulder of the road to allow a pickup and a sedan to pass them. "You've seen a lot of him."

"We go to dinner, or a movie, sometimes we go dancing."

"You used to do those things with Mike."

"Not the dancing. Mike doesn't like to dance. He understands."

"Tell me more about Lance," Grace said.

"You know he's gorgeous. The second time we went dancing, down at this great club in Hendersonville, he said we made a great team."

"But, what's he like?"

Amelia shifted so that she could look at Grace, who kept her own eyes glued on the road. "He's generous, takes me to the best restaurants. He's very complimentary, tells me I'm beautiful, things like that."

"So he spends money, and he flatters you, and he's a good dancer. Is he kind, sensitive, gentle, pushy, selfish?"

"I don't go around analyzing people."

Grace tried a different tact. "What do you talk about?"

"I prattle about everything, where I grew up, my travels with Thomas, my photography. He won't talk about himself at all." She grew serious, her voice dropped. "Once, when we were driving, I pressed him, and he said in a really angry voice, 'That's enough, Amelia.' I wanted to cry."

Grace looked over at her quizzically. "What did he do then?"

Amelia made light of it. "He saw how upset I was, so he stopped the car and apologized. He held me. He was so sweet, how could I be mad at him?"

"So what was the outcome?"

"I don't ask about his past, and we're just fine. Fine and happy."

Grace tried again. "What do you talk about, when you have dinner?"

"The news, local events, politics. He likes to talk about politics."

"Politics bores you, Amelia."

Amelia leaned away from Grace, toward her door. She tossed her head. "I'm having more fun than I've had in years. I'm being escorted by a stunning man, and he's attentive. I don't give a hoot what he talks about. Thomas taught me that if I didn't understand or wasn't interested in what people were talking about, all I had to do was smile and look interested. 'Look up at them with those gorgeous eyes of yours and just smile,' he'd say." She flipped her head. "It always works."

They rounded a curve, and the solid redbrick buildings of Mars Hill College rose before them.

Later, Grace sat with Hannah in their living room making lists. Hannah's included the courthouse, the library, the Rock Café, the firehouse, and stores in Marshall. Bob would tack up posters wherever they would let him. The posters were a call to arms for environmentalists and included a new phone number for the line Hannah had installed in the farmhouse. Grace's list focused on Mars Hill, on places she thought might be amenable to their cause: Margaret Olsen's Hillside Bed and Breakfast, the drugstore, the deli on Main Street, the flower shop, the herb shop, the college cafeteria.

Grace slid her list toward Hannah. "I've got to get over to Miss Lurina's. Take her an invitation to our opening."

"Think she'll come?"

"I hope so. I've explained that the government cannot legally walk in and take her land while she's alive, so, hopefully, she's more comfortable now about leaving her property."

"Amelia's asking Lance?"

"Yes." Grace sank back into her chair. "Amelia's totally enamored of him. She's having a great time. But he takes up more and more of her nonworking time these days."

Hannah folded her hands across a stack of flyers. "And her working time. Mike was over. He says Amelia's not showing up for shoots they plan, so it's more than just her social time that Lance is taking up."

"I didn't know that."

"I feel uneasy about him. Only met him twice." Hannah slapped her thigh. "God, I'm suspicious. Judge too fast."

"And I tend to be too accepting." She chose not to tell Hannah about Lance refusing to talk about himself with Amelia and how gruff he had been with her. Grace pushed back her chair. "Well, I'm off to Miss Lurina's now," she said.

"Say hello to her for me."

Grace had explained, clearly she hoped, that Lurina could safely leave her house unattended. "Legally, no one can walk in and do anything to your land. No one can touch one blade of grass or one scoop of dirt on this property until you've been declared dead, and you're properly buried, and papers have been filed with the courts."

"How long after I pass?" Lurina had asked.

"Weeks or maybe months."

That pleased Lurina. She smiled, then laughed. "Got 'em," she said with enthusiasm. "Betcha Ranger Billingham, the young fella that comes here regular, don't know that." It had surprised Grace that Lurina knew his name considering that she met him with her shotgun when he visited. Lurina clapped her hands, and her eyes grew mischievous. When she laughed, Grace laughed with her, and soon they had doubled over, holding their middles.

Today, Grace found Lurina huddled in a bulky wool shawl, sitting in her creaky rocker on the porch. It was cool, in the fifties. The old lady was shivering, yet here she was sitting out of doors. "Air clears my head," she explained to Grace. "I can think clear outside. Inside, I get muddled sometimes."

Still, Grace helped Lurina from the rocker, and they ambled into the front parlor. Dark, heavy drapes cast a pall on a Victorian sofa long past its prime. Several straight-backed chairs felt as if they were stuffed with horsehair. A long mahogany sideboard peppered with bric-a-brac was overhung by a wide mirror in a gilt frame, and large ornately framed portraits of ancestors stared solemnly down from high on every wall. Lurina patted to a spot on the sofa beside her, and Grace ignored the broken spring poking her rear end. A film of dust lay on every tabletop.

Lurina launched into a tale of her grandparents' death and burial. The story seemed to come out of nowhere, or had Lurina been ruminating on this since their conversation about the government not taking her land until she was dead for months?

"You can go to our family cemetery up on the hill a piece." Lurina pointed to the rear of the house. "You can see 'em for yourself. Old wood crosses still a-standin', and still got their names and dates carved in 'em." She slapped her thighs. "Old horse, he done dropped dead while he was a-haulin' their buggy. Buggy pitched into a ditch an' rolled on 'em, killed 'em dead." Her face grew serious, as if it had happened, not seventy-some years ago, but yesterday. "Ain't no funeral parlors, then, to make 'em all fine like they done Pa. Laid 'em out on plain wood boards till they got the caskets hammered up. Rough they was." She held up a hand and showed Grace a small calloused area. "Got me a right deep splinter in here runnin' my hand over that wood."

Lurina resumed her exposition on country funerals. "Buried Granny and Grandpa the next day after they passed. People comin' and goin' all day and night, and singin' and prayin'. I was little, but I remember people stayin' the night. I asked someone why, and an old woman told me, 'We's sittin' up with th' corpses.'" Lurina slapped her thighs again and laughed that light, young laugh, and Grace laughed with her, seeing beyond the image of two caskets set on tables to the room crowded with people, and among the bustle and hustle of it all, a little girl with a splinter in her aching hand.

"Next day," Lurina was saying, "they carried them there wood coffins to the church in a wagon hauled by steers, and when we got near the church the bell started ringin' and ringin' 'cause they used to ring it one time for every year, and there was two of 'em they was ringin' for. And then the organ playin'."

Grace kept her eyes on Lurina's face and listened intently although the odor of mothballs was stronger today than usual, and the smell irritated the membranes in Grace's nostrils. Her eyes stung. Grace blinked again and again.

"They was old," Lurina said, "so the service went on and on with

89

everyone gettin' up and sayin' somethin'. My bottom was numb from sittin', and I got a good slap from Ma for squirmin'. Those times, the family viewed the corpses last, after all the congregation. Pa lifted me up and carried me up to where the coffins sat open, and he said, 'There's your grandpa. There's your grandma,' and I started wailin', so he carried me out." She stopped. Lines fell in deep vertical slats between her eyes. The grooves down her cheeks seemed to darken. "Friends dug the graves. It was considered an honor. Seems to me these days folks don't have the kind of feelin's they had for others back then."

She sat back, looking satisfied. The room grew heavy with the silence. All Grace could think about was the mothballs. She knew that this dress had been selected from among Lurina's best, for Grace herself. Still, a good airing in the sunshine would help. Grace determined to ask Lurina if she would like her to hang and sun her dresses now that she was getting more company: herself, Amelia, Hannah, Old Man, whom she knew came fairly often, and Wayne, and soon Lurina would meet Bob.

They were quiet for so long that Grace decided Lurina had finished her story. "I came to bring you an invitation to a fete we're having to open our tearoom. It's a pre-opening party." She held out the blue envelope with LURINA MASTERSON written large in graceful calligraphy. Every time she looked at one of these envelopes, Grace imagined monks in damp, candlelit cells hunched over tables, dipping their quill pens in ink.

Lurina studied the envelope. She held it close to her squinty eyes. She turned it over. "Mighty fancy." She smiled at Grace. "Pretty. Blue's my favorite color."

"Wayne and Old Man will bring you to our tearoom," Grace said. "You like a good cup of tea. It'll just be friends like you, and Wayne, and Old Man, and Hannah and Amelia, and the Tates."

"The Tates?" Lurina's eyes brightened as she looked into the past. "I remember the day Harold married that nice little Jones girl from over in Caster."

"Brenda," Grace said. "She's principal of Caster Elementary School. I told you, that's where I volunteer tutoring children. The Tates have been very good to us since we moved down here."

Lurina straightened her shoulders. "Good people the Tates. First to come to this valley, just 'afore my people."

Grace waited, wondering if Lurina had a story to tell about the early settlers, the Covingtons, and her own family, the Mastersons. Grace wondered if the two families had intermarried, but was afraid that if she asked now, a long tale might follow, and Bob was waiting. She started up from the sofa. "You'll come, yes?"

Lurina stared in silence at nothing. "You gotta phone the government, from here, and let 'em tell me how they can't take my land till I'm six feet under."

"I'll be glad to do that."

"You do that, and I'll come a-singin'."

After making a phone call to the county ranger's office, Grace helped Lurina to her feet. Lurina might be physically frail, but she was tough inside and resilient, and Grace adjusted her steps and walked slowly with the old woman to the front porch.

"It's chilly. Gimme that there old coat of Pa's. I'll just sit out a bit."

Grace stepped back inside, lifted the scratchy, heavy wool coat from the rack, carried it out, and slipped it about Lurina's shoulders. Burdened by the weight of the coat, Lurina sank into her rocker. "Maybe that Billingham boy'll show up, and I won't hold my shotgun on him." She laughed happily. "That ought to set him spinnin'."

The grass in front of the old farmhouse was high as the belly of a young calf. Supposedly, once a month, a Madison County road crew roared in on cyclopean machines to mow the pasture between Elk Road and Bad River. Too heavy to cross the bridge, the machines sat puffing steam across the river, waiting patiently, like a bear for salmon, while a half dozen men scattered about the pasture close to the house with weed-wackers. It was obvious that they had not been here in months, but then with winter on them, perhaps they intended to allow the tall grass to die and topple over. Lurina, Grace thought, is alone without an advocate, so they take advantage. She felt both guilty and lucky that she, and Amelia, and Hannah had committed to caring for one another in health and in illness.

Having settled Lurina on the porch, Grace bent and kissed her elderly friend's wrinkled cheek. Moments later, when she turned from her car in the driveway to wave good-bye, she saw that Lurina's hand was plastered across the spot where she had kissed her, and there was a look of wonder and quiet pleasure on the old woman's face.

13

The Fete at the Tearoom

The day was bleak, with hovering, overcast skies. Dark, damp, bare branches hung low, seeming to grieve the loss of their leafy clothing. Inside the tearoom, it was summer. On each round table, on pale yellow tablecloths, sat clay pots brimming with out-of-season flowering pink dwarf crape myrtle brought to peak bloom by Hannah and Wayne. On either side of the buffet table, which ran along one wall, morning glories in huge pots had been trained onto tall stakes in columns of blue. A row of velvety magenta gloxinias bloomed in pots set among platters of food on the buffet table. White candles added sparkle and romance. A section of the room had been reserved for dancing, and a rented jukebox had been programmed with forties and fifties melodies.

The guests numbered thirty-five and included the Tates and family, P. J. Prancer and members of his staff, the Herrills, Jane, the librarian from Caster Elementary, Emily and her parents, Mike, Lance, Lurina, Old Man, and Wayne and others.

Nervous, eager to please, Grace moved among the guests with platters of sweets and sandwiches. At one point she approached Ginger Hammer, who lingered outside on the porch. Ginger dripped pink: pink slacks, blouse, jacket, lipstick, pink fingernails, handbag, and shoes.

"My dear, Grace." Ginger accepted a flower-shaped tea sandwich from the platter Grace extended to her.

Grace bridled. Even the tone of Emily's mother's voice annoyed her. In her trim white pinafore apron worn over her dress Grace felt put down, and although Bob had reminded her that she, Grace, could take control and allow Ginger's tone and comments to roll off her back, she could not help but feel diminished. Ginger flung back her head and waved her arm. "You. This place. These cute sandwiches, all so adorable, really."

Grace retreated, leaving Ginger leaning against a porch column. Ginger eyed Amelia, who waited at the top of the steps, a veritable one-woman committee welcoming their guests. Lance Lundquist stood alongside Amelia, looking as though he were lord of the manor. Ginger's throat tightened as she appraised Lance. Then she approached Amelia. "You, and Grace, and Hannah live together. I should think it would be quite dull only women in the house."

"I assure you it is not dull," Amelia replied brightly. She arranged her scarf securely about her neck and shoulders. Her shimmering silk scarf matched the sapphire of her eyes. At that moment, Wayne's pickup turned into the parking area, and moments later he and Old Man were out and reaching up to assist Lurina from the cab. Amelia barely heard Ginger say, "Quaint, a regular *ménage à trois*," or saw her arched eyebrows raise higher with a questioning look as Lurina's feet touched the ground. "What an oddity." Ginger nodded toward the parking lot.

Amelia heard that comment and, fuming inside, drew away from the pink-clad woman and nearly crashed into Grace. Together they hastened down the steps to meet the threesome slowly making their way toward the tearoom. "Miss Lurina, how wonderful to see you, and don't you look splendid," Grace said.

Beneath a short lace-edged jacket, Lurina's dress, a lightweight print challis that came to her ankles smelled, not of mothballs, but of cedar. Lurina smiled a shy, closedmouthed smile. "They was right good fellas, these two. They come and get me, and waited for me to finish fixin' up for your party, Grace." Lurina's single braid was wound three times around and crowned her head, pulling her forehead tight, and widening her eyes. They must have been pretty eyes, and flirtatious, Grace thought. Why had Lurina never married? There was a story someday perhaps Lurina would tell her.

The years had eroded Old Man's height, bent his shoulders, and bowed his knees. His dark blue suit, baggy over his shoes and shiny at the elbows, suggested attending a funeral, not a celebration. But his eyes twinkled, and he stayed close to Lurina. With protracted steps, they made their way to the porch, where Bob offered his arm and escorted Lurina Masterson, as if she were a queen, into the dining room to a round table where Brenda and Harold Tate sat with Molly and Ted Lund, Claudia Craine Prinze, her daughter, Paulette, and of course glued to Paulette's side, Tyler, who appeared to have forgotten all else, so taken was he with twelve-year-old Paulette.

Everyone at the table rose to welcome Lurina and Old Man. Wayne drifted away to the punch bar set up in one corner of the room. Immediately the natives of Cove Road began to chat about their neighbors: who had moved to Asheville or beyond, about new babies, about illnesses and recoveries. Ignoring his toothless gums, Lurina passed Old Man crustless egg salad sandwiches, and seemed bewildered when the platter was empty. At a sign from Brenda, Tyler ran into the kitchen and returned with a plate heaped with tiny sandwiches, some on brown, some on white bread, some shaped as hearts, others as flowers. Lurina graced him with a pleased smile. "Why, ain't you a right nice boy."

Eventually, as it nearly always did this time of year, the talk turned to the ladybug infestation. "You want to save them, at first," Molly said, "so you scoop them up and deposit them outside, but by the third day, your empathy for them disappears, and you go from irritation to sheer disgust, and you hate them."

"They'll go away when real cold sets in," Brenda said, looking for Harold out of the corner of her eye. He had excused himself from their table to chat with Martin Hammer and Bob near the kitchen door. He looked content.

"I kind of like sittin' and watchin' ladybugs. They fall down and die, and after some days they shrivel up and disappear." Lurina looked from one face to the other and settled on Tyler's. "Kind of ladybug round about here's got nineteen spots. Ever count 'em, boy?"

"No, ma'am," Tyler replied. He poked Paulette in the ribs, and they giggled.

"I've found the best way to handle them is to turn on a light in one corner," Brenda said. "Ladybugs migrate to light, chunk all together in a corner of the ceilin', so they're easier to vacuum." She helped herself to a cheese puff and a cucumber sandwich.

"I like the little critters." Old Man nodded approvingly at Lurina. Then they sat in silence for a time sipping tea and devouring Grace's sandwiches.

Lurina's eagle eyes roamed the room. "Who's the good-lookin' couple over yonder seem all caught up in each other?" Lurina asked.

Tyler skinned up his nose. "That's my dad, and his new friend, Emily. Her folks live over in Loring Valley." He and Paulette giggled.

"They sweethearts?" Lurina asked.

"Nah! Just friends. Dad's too busy with me, and Grandpa, and Granny Grace to have a sweetheart." He and Paulette giggled hard and doubled over.

Just then Russell took Emily's hand and they walked over to the table. "Miss Lurina?"

"That's me."

"Grace has spoken of you often. I'm Tyler's father, and Bob Richardson is my father. I'm pleased to meet you. This is Emily Hammer. Her folks live in Loring Valley." He reached for a table napkin and wiped Tyler's chin. "Now, what's going on here, young man?" He turned to Brenda. "If Tyler gets raucous, disturbs any of you, just give me an eye, will you? He'll spend the rest of the afternoon sitting out on the steps." He eyed Paulette. "Alone."

"Leave 'em be." Lurina waved both hands as if to shoo Russell away. "He's a good boy, just likes to laugh." She looked coyly at Old Man and nudged his arm.

"Any trouble, just let me know." Russell reached for Emily's hand, and the pair drifted away into the crowd.

"Ain't sweethearts, eh?" Lurina whispered to Old Man, and they laughed and nodded yes to the pitcher of punch Wayne brought to their table.

"Don't you get yourself drunk, Old Man," he admonished his grandfather. Wayne winked at Lurina. "Or I'm gonna have to put you to sleep it off on Miss Lurina's couch."

Their shoulders touched and the two old people laughed and shooed Wayne away. "Git you gone, boy," Lurina said.

"Git you gone, Dad," Tyler whispered, waving his hand at his father's back. Paulette heard, and again they burst into giggles.

Moments later, Hannah came to the table. "Miss Lurina," she said. "Welcome. I see you're in the best of company." She smiled warmly at Brenda and Molly and tousled Tyler's red hair, then pulled up a chair and sat with them for a time, chatting about the table decorations and how nice the place was.

✒

Out on the porch, Ginger noticed Lance standing alone. A quick look assured her that Martin, and Bob, and Harold were engrossed in conversation at a small table near the kitchen door. Unselfconsciously, Ginger sidled up to Lance and without a word squeezed the biceps of his right arm. "Work out a lot?" she asked.

"Some."

"Where?"

"I have a home gym." He stepped back.

Ginger moved into his personal space. "And where, pray tell, do you live?"

"Loring Valley." He backed away from her.

Her eyes grew seductive. She tipped her head. "We're neighbors."

Unnoticed, Amelia watched this interchange from inside. Lance had been courting her with flowers, phone calls, gifts, and special treats. He had taken her to see a Broadway musical, *Smokey Joe's Cafe,* at the Peace Center in Greenville, South Carolina. He had spared no expense, and had even hired a limo to transport them to and from Greenville. She loved being with him, and was very upset when suddenly he had announced that he must go out of town, and then refused to say where to or why. Amelia's happiness had been jolted. When he returned she'd asked, "How was your trip?"

"Tiring. Same as every trip. I go every month."

Amelia was dismayed. "Where did you go?"

His eyes went gray. "I do not discuss personal business, Amelia. Please get that into your pretty little head." He looked deep into her eyes then, and his eyes were blue again. "How beautiful you are. You have the loveliest eyes I've ever seen." And she had melted. Later, his whispered endearments made it easy for her to set aside her doubts.

Now, Ginger flirting with him infuriated her. Quickly, Amelia joined them on the porch, and slipping her arm through Lance's, she gave him her most innocent big-blue-eyes look. "Lance, we need you to pop the champagne."

Ginger swept ahead of them into the tearoom and stopped, exclaiming, "Well, this beats all."

A circle of guests, their eyes shining with appreciation and approval, watched as Old Man led Lurina Masterson in a slow waltz. It mattered not at all that they missed some of the beats, that they danced haltingly, or that they were old and bent and wrinkled. At that moment, they were simply beautiful.

It was seven o'clock and dark when the last vehicle pulled out of the parking lot, and Bob put his arm about Grace and led her to a table near a window far from the kitchen. "You sit. You've been on your feet enough today." He stroked her hair. "I'll get Russell, and Emily, Tyler, and Paulette can help, and we'll clean up and fill the dishwasher."

"Where is Tyler?" Grace asked.

"With Paulette playing Go Fish on the porch. We'll drop her off at home when we leave here tonight."

"Isn't it too chilly for them outside?"

"Kids don't feel chilly, haven't you noticed?"

Grace's day had begun at five A.M. when she woke to prepare three tall and beautifully iced Vienna cakes that were devoured within the first half hour. The recipe had been a friend's grandmother's, and over the years Grace had changed it. She mixed each layer separately and colored each layer with egg coloring, which produced moist layers in rose, yellow, green, and pink. All day long she had cooked: sheet after sheet of cookies, and endless platters of finger sandwiches and French pastries. Now, Grace's feet, legs, arms, back, and shoulders groaned for rest. Grace leaned back in the armchair, slipped off her shoes, and stretched her feet. Within moments Hannah joined her, pulled up two chairs, sat in one, slipped off her shoes, and set her feet on the padded seat.

"What a relief to be unshod," she said.

"Your flowers are just magnificent, Hannah. Thank you." Grace pushed the flowerpot with its pink blossoms to one side of the table so that she could see Hannah's face.

"The food was sumptuous. A huge success, Grace." Hannah patted her stomach. "I'm stuffed."

"It went well, didn't it?" Grace brushed back hair from her eyes and set her elbows on the table. "Elbows off the table" was what her mother would say when she was a girl, and even later. There was no one, now, to nag her about sitting up straight, or to slap her arms and elbows, so she left them there, and in time lowered her arms and rested her head on them. She felt Hannah's fingers pass lightly across her hair, and heard her say, "Poor dear, tired, tired, tired."

Comforted, Grace nodded, though she wondered, yet again, if the tearoom wasn't too much at this moment in her life, what with all her other interests and commitments.

"Maybe this is a mistake," she said softly not looking up.

"The tearoom?" Hannah asked.

"Yes."

"Like my greenhouse? What did you tell me then, Grace?"

"That it would be too much for you."

"It was," Hannah said.

"And I suggested you sell it," Grace said.

"So," Hannah continued. "I suggest that you build up the tearoom for a few months, then sell it to one of the newcomers in Loring Valley. There's got to be some advantage to these people living here. There'll be someone who's always dreamed of having her own business just down the road." Grace nodded, smiled weakly, and let her head fall into the crook of her arm.

Hannah touched Grace's head lightly with her hand. It had been a long day. Where's it going to end? Hannah wondered. She thought of Bob and Russell, then of Tyler, who had reportedly thrown a fit when he heard that his father would be taking Emily to the tearoom party. She had heard him telling everyone at his table that his dad was too busy to have a sweetheart.

And then, just yesterday, on one of the rare occasions when Amelia was home for several hours, Amelia had raised another issue. "If Russell marries Emily, Bob'll move out. He'll put pressure on Grace to move in with him again."

"Grace won't move out." Hannah had dismissed the idea with a wave of her hand, but it hung there in the back of her mind, nagging at her. "And Tyler's not the first child with a stepmother he started out disliking."

14

Tyler

At seven A.M. on the morning following the party at the tearoom, nine-year-old Tyler let out a howl of pain that reached from his home into Grace's bedroom at the moment her phone rang.

"Forgive me for waking you. I don't know what to do with Tyler. He's hysterical. Can you come over?" Bob's voice was tight.

Instantly awake, Grace tossed three pillows behind her and sat up in her bed. As she listened to Bob, Grace began to unbutton the top of her purple-flowered pajamas. The small bone button came off in her hand, and she took comfort in fingering it, turning it over and over, feeling its smooth ridges as she tried to think how she could help.

"Russell brought Emily home last night," Bob was saying. "Strolled up the walk holding hands, kissed right in front of Tyler. How was he supposed to feel? They haven't prepared him."

A thin slant of sunshine pierced the crack between the wood frame of her bedroom window and the closed mini blind and for a moment struck her eyes. Grace shifted to avoid the direct glare. "What happened?"

"Tyler started to cry, and next thing he ran his head like a battering ram into Russell. Emily almost fell. She was holding on to Russell's arm. You can imagine how upset she was."

"My God," Grace said softly.

"Then Russell lost it. He spanked Tyler in front of Emily. God-damned stupid thing to do. He's an adult; Tyler's a child."

Grace felt empathy for Tyler and anger at Russell. Russell had been dating Emily for only a few months. She was to leave for Ocala again, and would be returning in three days. Grace and Bob had suggested to Russell, in the very beginning, that he bring Emily slowly into their lives, have a picnic, play games, take Tyler to McDonald's, anything to further the boy's contact with Emily. At the time, Russell kept insisting that Tyler wasn't ready, and instead he was subjecting his son to this trial by fire. That made no sense. Perhaps, Grace thought, it's Russell who isn't ready to face Tyler's reaction.

A solid, dependable man and devoted father, Russell had, under the influence of this wild, irrational love, lost all sense of rationality. Perfectly sensible people came unhinged under the chimera that was love's insanity, and now, for a moment, as she listened to Bob, Grace recalled how she had gone absolutely nuts when, early on in their relationship, she thought that she had lost Bob to Amelia.

"I warned him," Bob was saying. "I suggested we all go someplace, IHOP maybe, so Tyler could be with Emily under relaxed circumstances. But, no. And then last night Russell brings her home, and kisses her in front of Tyler." Bob paused, and Grace knew he was fuming. "Tyler's face. Damn it, Grace, you should have seen his little face."

The tears in his voice tore at Grace's heart. Her stomach tightened, and she pulled her knees snug against her chest with her free arm. In the silence on the phone she heard Bob trying to regain control.

"And then?" she asked softly.

"Tyler was sent to bed. He cried for a long time. Russell took Emily home, and didn't return until very late, so he and I haven't talked. Damn it."

"And this morning?"

"No change. Can you come?"

"Give me time to dress, grab a bite, and I'm on my way."

"Drive carefully, honey." Then he said, "You know this isn't like Tyler. He doesn't throw tantrums, doesn't even argue."

"That's right," she replied, "he withdraws. Like he did after Amy died." She was out of bed, dressing even as she talked on the phone.

"What can we do?" Bob asked.

"Love him, listen to him."

"We'll reassure him we're here for him. We're not going anywhere," Bob said.

Did Bob hear himself? Hadn't he recently mentioned to her that if Russell and Emily married, he would feel obliged to move out? He had even suggested to Grace that she, and Amelia, and Hannah rent or sell him a small piece of their land up in the woods where he could build a cottage. Focused as she had been on the opening of the tearoom, and because she didn't want to deal with it, Grace had not told Amelia and Hannah.

Grace ran a brush through her hair and grimaced at herself in the mirror. The brush was a birthday gift, last November 24, from Bob, and had a smooth, lovely tortoiseshell back and thick bristles. Her thoughts turned to Tyler, and the shock, and grief, and sense of betrayal, and pain he must be feeling. She loved the child, loved his red hair that wouldn't lie flat, his blackberry eyes, his too-large ears, his high-pitched laughter, his firm arms flung about her when he hugged her. He was the grandson her own son, Roger, would never give her, and she considered herself blessed in loving Tyler.

"I'm on my way. I'm hanging up now, Bob."

It was Sunday. Hannah and Amelia slept late on Sunday. She slipped a note for them under a dog magnet on the fridge, grabbed a glass of orange juice, and ran.

The thermometer on the porch read forty-two degrees. Grace needed a heavier coat and went back inside for it. Back outside, she thought how her legs would freeze while the car warmed up, while the world warmed up. She thought of Hannah, who wore tights under her slacks every winter morning.

"They can easily be removed in any bathroom, anywhere, when they get uncomfortable," she had once told Grace.

Grace would consider tights, but hated their snugness and worried about what she would do with the tights after removing them—sling them over her shoulder?

"Get a tote bag," Hannah said.

A tote bag and tights. Today she wished she had listened to Hannah.

✦

Russell Richardson's home nestled in a grove of pine trees at the end of a cul-de-sac. It was one of a dozen brick-and-wood ranch houses in a one-street development located between Covington and Caster that the builder had, unimaginatively, named the Circle. The fifteen-minute drive to the Circle paralleled a wide, shallow river spanned intermittently by wooden bridges the width of one car. Brenda had told Grace that several years ago spring rains had turned the languid river into a torrent, washing out underpinnings and dashing bridges into the rampaging water.

From then on, Grace pictured the easygoing river as Dr. Jekyll, and the rampaging river as Mr. Hyde. Now, rebuilt and reinforced with high guardrails, the bridges seemed to say "stay out," and this notion whetted Grace's curiosity about the people who lived across the river, across deep green fields, in homes tucked high in the woods.

"Who lives over there across the river?" Grace had asked Brenda.

"Wealthy locals, and some folks from out of state. The land was owned by one family, the Colemans. They sold it in large parcels with the restriction that it could never be subdivided."

Ah, Grace thought, no developer will torture these hillsides with condos.

Immediately, as Bob met Grace at the door of the house, he put his arms about her. "Tyler hid in his room until his father drove out this morning."

"We go to IHOP?" Grace asked.

Bob nodded.

"Hey, Tyler, love," Grace called as she headed down the bedroom hallway.

Flinging wide his door, Tyler met Grace halfway. Pitching his little body against her fullness, he attached like a barnacle. "Granny Grace." Huge teary eyes looked pleadingly at her. "Daddy brought that stupid, ugly Emily home last night. Can I come live with you and the ladies? Please, please, Granny Grace."

"We'll see," she said. "So it's ugly, stupid Emily, eh?" Grace half hauled Tyler down the hall to where Bob waited.

"Ugly, yes."

"You sure about that?"

"Well," he admitted grudgingly, "maybe she's not ugly, but I don't like her."

This conversation would get them nowhere. Grace rubbed her tummy. "Grandpa and I feel like waffles at IHOP. What about you?"

Tyler rubbed his tummy. A tiny smile etched the corners of his mouth. His eyes were big and teary. "I'm hungry."

"What are we waiting for then? Let's hit the road." Bob stood at the end of the hall, their coats in hand, and moments later they were cruising the back roads, heading for Highway 19–23 to Asheville, and Grace trying to lift Tyler's spirits by singing, *Mares eat oats, and does eat oats, and little lambs eat ivy,* off-key.

That night Grace and Bob baby-sat Tyler. After a light dinner of chicken salad and fruit, after Tyler had been told a story by Grace, reassured of their love, cuddled, and kissed good night, they sat on the blue corduroy love seat in the den. A cheery fire warmed the room. Grace's head fell onto Bob's shoulder. Bob smoothed hair from her forehead. The hairy knuckles of his hands, and the tiny ripple of freckles across his nose, were the first things Grace had noticed when she met him, and his eyes, of course, his honest, kind eyes. He was tall; she short, a regular Mutt and Jeff, but so compatible.

"You helped Tyler so much after Amy's death. You brought him back to us," Bob said. "If anyone can talk to him, help him now, you can."

Grace stirred. "I'm no therapist. I tried to talk to him back at the restaurant, when you had to wait in line at the cashier. We went outside, remember?"

He nodded.

"He wouldn't talk about Emily or his dad, just clammed up, like he did about his mother."

"Maybe you could get him to draw pictures again, like he did then."

"Art therapy. Amelia told me about it. She'd seen it used very effectively with children who lost families after an earthquake in Mexico."

"Well, it worked for Tyler."

"He's older now. I feel so sorry for what he's going through. I know how shattering change can be. Why wouldn't Tyler be upset?" Grace snuggled tight against Bob's chest. "Maybe there's some kind of guilt thing going on for Tyler. If he loves or even likes Emily, he's betrayed his mother."

"Tough on the little fellow, losing his mother. You're so wise, Grace."

They sat quietly for a moment, then Bob changed the subject. "Have you spoken to Hannah and Amelia yet about my idea?"

Grace tried not to tighten her shoulders. Things with herself and Bob had been going along so well. Russell and Emily's involvement was changing more than Tyler's life. "When have I had the time? We had an opening at the tearoom, remember?"

"Don't get upset; it's just a question."

She felt a tightening of his chest and shoulders.

"I'm sorry Bob. I'm tired, and I'm worried about Tyler. I will talk to them, soon." She nuzzled his neck. His lemony aftershave pleased her. Such a clean, neat man, she thought, then wondered, if they lived together would he fall into patterns like Ted had? Would he expect meals, perhaps even lunch every day at a certain time? She cooked dinner most nights, but for breakfast and lunches the ladies were on their own. Would he leave socks and underwear on the floor for her to pick up? Would her time still be her own? She doubted that. Soon she'd be apologizing and feeling guilty just going to a movie with Hannah.

A clock bonged, deep and resonant. Russell collected clocks. The sound came from his 1885, ornate, iron-fronted, mother-of-pearl-inlaid clock on the mantel. Suddenly it was competing with Russell's prized nine-foot-tall grandfather clock that dated back to 1745, which stood against one wall and bonged nine times.

"It's ten o'clock," Bob said, checking his wristwatch. "That clock's never right."

Grace's mind remained fastened on his request to buy or lease land from them to build a cottage for himself. If he did that, would he expect to eat with them every night? Would he show up at the door any old time? Would he intrude on their teatime? Even if he did not, would she, Grace, feel obliged or anxious thinking she ought to invite him to join them at tea? Men, the best of them, by their very presence, changed the tone of women's exchanges, inhibited the essence of their conversations. "I'll talk to the others, I promise." Grace dropped her head back onto his chest, for fear he would see the concern in her eyes.

"If you all agree," he said, "I'd build out of sight of the farmhouse. Don't want to be looking down on you ladies wondering what you're doing." He squeezed her shoulder, kissed the top of her head. He laughed. "Seriously, I'd try to be unobtrusive."

As he talked and the clocks ticked, she realized how serious he was about this cottage, and Grace hated herself for the irritation she felt at his asking.

15

What About Bob?

Monday dawned exceptionally warm, and since Lance was away, again, and the tearoom had closed early, Amelia and Grace joined Hannah for tea on the porch.

"Probably the last time this winter we'll have a day as warm as this," Hannah said. "Look what that hard freeze last week did to our planter boxes. Everything's shriveled and brown."

As usual, they sipped their first cup of tea in silence. Then Grace told them about Tyler's crisis.

"Russell's fault," Hannah said unequivocally. "Just because he's enamored with Emily, he can't expect the boy to feel the same."

"Poor little fellow." Amelia looked worried. "What will happen now?"

"And on top of that," Grace blurted out, unable to put it off longer, "Bob expects them to marry, and he's planning to move out. And . . ." She hesitated a moment. ". . . he's asked if we'd sell or lease him a piece of our land so he can build a cottage to live in."

Surprise registered in Hannah's eyes and her brow furrowed. "So, Bob wants to live here." She said it without affect, not pleased or disapproving.

Immediately, Amelia ceased rocking and began to examine, and then push back, the cuticle at the base of her fingernail.

Hannah drew a small pair of clippers from the pocket of the smock she wore over her clothing when she worked in the yard, and snipped away a brown and crumpled trail of verbena hanging from the planter box.

Grace remembered an old jingle advertising tea from years ago: one line, *take tea and see what a difference,* went round and round like a carousel in her mind. Grace held her cup with both hands, appreciated its warmth, sipped her tea, and waited. Drinking tea calmed and soothed her and offered time to gather one's thoughts, as when a man lights a pipe, slow and deliberate. "Bob says if we'll let him he'll build out of sight." She wanted to give Bob a fair hearing, but it was obvious that his request stunned Amelia and Hannah, as it had her. Then her eyes sought Hannah's. "He says he intends to stay out of our way."

"How, if he's living up on our hill?" Amelia asked softly.

"Start popping in whenever he wants," Hannah said. But he did that now, Hannah reminded herself. He complemented their lives like butter on toast, was good company, helpful, like when the pump stopped working last winter. It was Bob whose fingers turned blue fixing it. Yet, living right here, on the hill behind their house, that was different. He would be—she struggled in her mind for the appropriate word—ubiquitous.

"I was taken aback when he proposed it," Grace said. "I should have handled it, said no right away."

"Why didn't you?" Hannah asked, more in speculation than in annoyance.

A dreamy look came over Amelia's face. "It's hard to say no to a man you love."

It was hard, and it tore at Grace's heart imagining Bob sitting alone in a cottage up on their hillside somewhere watching the sunset, or standing disconsolately in his kitchen opening a can of tuna while they enjoyed their dinner, or being alone with his TV, while they shared their home and each other's company. Would the lights of his cottage twinkle between tree branches in winter when the leaves had fallen? Would his aloneness lure her to abjure the quiet comfort, the independence she relished, sharing a home with Hannah and Amelia, and go to him? Grace looked toward each familiar face. "Say something, Hannah, Amelia, please."

But they were silent. And in that silence, her mind raced. Had she met Bob a year after Ted's death, she would have danced naked in delight in the privacy of her own home. She would have married him and resumed doing, giving, pleasing. Before meeting Hannah, especially, she would never have envisioned that life without a husband could be so utterly satisfying. She loved Bob, yet she relished coming home to her own room, to control of her time, to privacy.

"A ruse. He wants you living with him," Hannah blurted.

Grace pushed her chair vigorously with her toes. She and Bob had been all over this, and living with or marrying him was a moot issue. Grace's fingers curled involuntarily into loose fists. Good God, she didn't want to relinquish her independence. If she did, in time, anger and resentment would tarnish, might even destroy what they had. Butterflies played leapfrog in her stomach. Say something, she wanted to yell, say no, straight out.

Hannah stretched her arms, making an arc. "All of Madison County, and he wants to live here."

"*Mon Dieu.* This is a problem."

They were angry; suddenly Grace felt the need to defend Bob. "He loves this area. He thinks Cove Road's the loveliest part of Madison County." So why did she resent his asking? She loved him. He loved her.

Amelia clapped her hands as if to get their attention. "Bob's been nothing but considerate to all of us, still . . ." Her gaze shifted to some spot off in the distance.

"Living so close," Hannah muttered. Why was she feeling so territorial? Twenty-eight acres could accommodate one more person, especially if he were out of sight, and there were parameters. But would Grace be able to set parameters?

"Bob's here a great deal, and he's never a trouble, but when he goes home, he's out of sight, out of mind, if I may use a cliché," Hannah said. She wanted to say a firm no, but how could she when they owned the land together. Major decisions like this must be unanimous, and how could Grace refuse Bob? She could see it all clearly. Grace would feel obliged to have Bob for dinner every night, or take dinner to him. Then she would stay the night, the weekend, and pretty soon it would be weeks, and she'd be packing to move.

Their lifestyle, even with Amelia going through this thing with Lance (which she was sure would come to no good), suited Hannah perfectly. Last year, the thought of Grace marrying and moving out had distressed her deeply and forced her to acknowledge her own jealousy. Grace was the best, the only real friend she'd had in more years than she could remember, and it had been a huge relief when Grace decided not to marry. Confound it. Why hadn't Grace simply said no to Bob now? Didn't she realize how Bob living in their back-yard would change her life? Change Hannah's life. Waves of anxiety, possessiveness, and guilt for wanting to hold things static, for her lack of consideration of Grace's needs, washed over Hannah. Grace was the glue that held their home together. She was tolerant where Hannah was not. Grace radiated sunshine. She filled their home with warmth and love. Enough self-centeredness. Hannah looked intently at Grace. "Will you be able to sleep nights knowing Bob's up there alone?"

"You speak as if he's there already. Don't you understand. I don't want this. I just didn't know how not to hurt Bob. When Russell remarries, Bob'll be alone again, like he was in Florida, before Amy's death brought him here. I feel selfish."

Amelia, lost in her own thoughts, simply stared into space. The click-clack sound of her rocker on the uneven boards of the porch floor suddenly irritated Hannah. She wanted to reach across Grace and stop Amelia from rocking. "It's got to be your decision." Hannah began to gather up the tea things. "Let's go inside. It's getting dark."

"But, I don't want it to be my decision."

"Does this decision have to be made now? Can't we all think about this for a few days?" Amelia asked, slowing her rocking chair. Her teeth grazed the top of her lip.

Grace stacked saucers on the tray. "Help me find a way to say no without making him feel rejected." Her eyes misted.

They were silent. Amelia rose, and held the door open for them. Hannah picked up the tray and started inside with Grace following.

The kitchen was warm and cozy, one of their favorite gathering places. Recently, Grace had bought thick new cushions in a rich purple and white stripe for the chair backs and seats. Purple com-plemented the yellow walls and seemed to complete the decor. Han-nah set the tray on the counter and began to load the dishwasher. "One damn tough decision after the other. That's what life's about, it seems to me."

"At least Bob's not pressuring me to get married," Grace said.

Hannah wondered how long that would last, and she stifled her growing exasperation with Bob for creating this situation in the first place.

Amelia's face was capable of amazingly quick changes of expression, and now it went from consternation to consideration to soft and caring. "This is hard on you, Grace, I know. Sleep on it."

"Fine," Grace agreed, "I'll sleep on it." And Grace wondered if some divine providence were testing her newfound independence. She had seen retired couples in the mall, in restaurants, in markets, their faces masks of frustration, or boredom, or indifference, or resignation. There were, thank God, spaces in her and Bob's togetherness. What they did together, they thoroughly enjoyed. An idea formed and nagged at her. Was the tearoom, and now Bob wanting to live on their land, a ruse, as Hannah had put it, to seduce her into living with him?

16

Tyler Speaks of Moving Out

Facing south, the long galley kitchen in Russell Richardson's home was both bright and functional. At one end the room widened into a bay window, and every Sunday morning in this sun-drenched dining alcove Russell cooked and served a special brunch of grilled ham over baked scalloped potatoes—recipe courtesy of Grace—to family and friends. Sometimes Grace and Hannah joined them, and Emily, once. Rather a silent meal that was. Amelia never came for breakfast.

"Mike and I always take Sunday brunch in Asheville," she had explained to Tyler, who wondered, since they *took* lunch, why they didn't just stay in Covington instead of packing a picnic and taking it into Asheville. Someday he'd ask. But today it was just Tyler and his father and grandfather.

Outside the bay window, on a wide-rimmed bird feeder, a red cardinal, its wings whirring, pecked, pushed, and chased other birds away. Territoriality, Bob thought, and possessiveness. He identified with the cardinal. He wanted Grace to himself. Yet if he stopped to think about it, he knew that he also liked not worrying about having smelly feet after hours on the golf course, or leaving dirty dishes in the sink, or flinging his legs and arms wide on his bed without concern for another's space.

Outside at the feeder, the smaller female cardinal joined her mate. She was not as richly colored as he was. When Bob heard Tyler's voice, he turned his attention from the birds to his grandson. Something was different. Tyler was smiling, and he was not bad-mouthing Emily.

"Maybe Emily's not so bad, Dad," Tyler said as his father spooned a second helping of cheese-topped scalloped potatoes onto his plate.

"Emily's a very nice person, if you'd give her a chance."

Tyler speared a potato slice, blew on it to cool it, and popped it into his mouth. He chewed vigorously. "Hmm," he said. "This tastes as good as when Granny Grace makes it." Tyler was a connoisseur of Grace's food. He loved every morsel of anything she cooked, even meatballs and prunes. They tasted great, he thought, with the rice and gravy Grace served them with.

"That's a compliment, Tyler. Thanks," his dad replied.

The clock on the wall of the dining alcove, another of Russell's treasures, seemed to tick louder as they sat and ate in silence and watched the cardinals at the bird feeder. After a time, Tyler downed another glass of juice, after which he turned to his father. "You planning to hitch Emily, Dad?"

Russell nearly choked on a piece of ham. He coughed and reached for his water.

Bob patted his back. "You okay, son?"

Russell nodded. He looked at Tyler. "Hitch her? Where'd you get that expression?"

Tyler shrugged, raised his arms a bit, and opened his palms in a "you know" kind of gesture. He grinned. "Old cowboy movies. They hitch their horses to posts outside saloons, and they get hitched to ladies." He shrugged again. "That's what they did in the old West. Hitched," he said. "Funny word." Tyler chortled, and bent double until his face reddened and his eyes watered.

Bob glanced at Russell, then at his grandson. He patted Tyler's arm. "Tyler, eat up, now. We can't keep Grace waiting." He looked at his watch.

Tyler frowned and studied his watch, a smaller version of Bob's, that Grace had given him on his ninth birthday. "It's not eleven yet, Grandpa." But he set to work finishing his potatoes and ham.

"We don't open on Sundays, generally, but today we have two buses coming in to the tearoom from Maggie Valley at two this afternoon," Bob said "They've ordered special. Tyler's going to help us make sandwiches."

"Think we'll get to make that green mushy stuff?" Tyler asked.

"Avocado dip?"

Tyler nodded.

"Isn't that a bit spicy?" Russell asked, suddenly aware that he was taking large mouthfuls, guzzling his food as if he were in a race with them. Deliberately he set his fork on his plate and sat back. A hush fell over the room, broken only by the clink of forks on china plates.

Then Tyler said, "Yes, avocado dip. But Dad, Granny Grace's recipe's sweet."

"Sweet?" Russell looked at his father.

"Sweet. A Grace special with crushed pineapple, and a touch of orange brandy."

"It's good, Dad. Want us to bring you home some?"

"Thanks, but, no thanks. I like my guacamole piquant."

Tyler's freckled face grew serious. "Piquant?"

"Spicy, Mexican-style," his father replied.

"Piquant," Tyler repeated, folding his napkin and placing his knife and fork on the plate side by side, pointing inward. Grace had taught him that in restaurants this indicated to waiters that you were finished. He shook his head. "We never serve older folks spicy food, Dad. Their stomachs can't handle it, Granny Grace says."

Bob laughed. "Grace's natural sweet tooth has a lot to do with the menu."

They cleared the table and set plates and utensils in the dishwasher. As they were filing from the kitchen, Tyler tugged on his father's hand. "It's okay if you get hitched to Emily. I'm going to live with Granny Grace." He stopped, turned, and studied his grandfather. "What about you, Grandpa? They only have one extra bedroom at the ladies' farmhouse, and that's mine." He scowled, and put his hands on his hips. "Dad, where's Grandpa going to live?"

Neither adult replied. Several weeks earlier, anticipating that Russell might marry Emily, Bob had told Russell his idea about building himself a small cottage on the ladies' land, if they'd sell or rent him a piece.

Russell had strongly advised against it. "Good Lord, Dad, what are you trying to do?" he asked. "Remember how you pressured Grace to get married last year? Nothing's changed. She likes it this way, and you seem content. Separate living quarters seem to work just fine for you two."

"We'd still be separate, but maybe you're right, my boy." Bob's arm had circled his son. "The way it is with Grace and me, now, is just fine."

"You're welcome to live with us, Dad. Emily likes you. We'll move to a bigger house, with an apartment for you. It'll be easier on Tyler," Russell said, dropping his eyes.

Bob shook his head. "I've lived with you for a couple of years now. Time I was on my own." He refrained from telling his son how hurt and rejected he felt that after almost two weeks Grace had given him neither a yes nor a no regarding his request. "I'm going to check out a condo over in Loring Valley. There are one or two resales."

"I'd like it if you stayed with us," Russell replied.

Now, as they moved from the kitchen to the front hall to get their sweaters, Tyler kept up a running commentary. "That way, I can teach Aunt Hannah how to use her new computer. She asked me if I would, you know. That's why she got it, 'cause she knew I could teach her how to use the Internet and do e-mail." The sweater he shoved his arms into was made of soft mohair with big blue and yellow checks. Grace knitted it for him for Christmas this year, but he'd had to try it on so many times to get the arms right, she'd given it to him way ahead of time, the moment it was finished—a trifle baggy here, one sleeve a bit longer than the other, but it was Tyler's absolute favorite.

"What did you say?" Russell asked, turning on his heel to face his son.

"I said," Tyler rested his hands on his hips. He reminded Bob of Grace herself. "I'll live with Granny Grace and the ladies, and then I'll be there after school so I can teach Aunt Hannah about her new computer."

"Your home is with me, remember that, son."

Tyler pouted. "You'll have Emily and Grandpa too."

Russell's eyes narrowed. His mouth tightened. Bob put a hand on his son's arm. "Not now, Russell."

Russell relaxed. Tyler tugged at his father's arm. From habit Russell bent for a hug. Tyler squeezed tight. "I love you, Dad," he said. "Please let me live with the ladies. I'll come for brunch every Sunday, and I'll be very nice to Emily. I promise."

17

The Condominium in Loring Valley

For Grace, transforming ingredients into satisfying meals or desserts was a practical activity that usually nurtured her soul. Today, however, as she mixed the batter for coffee cakes, formed tarts, and prepared sandwiches for two busloads of customers from Maggie Valley, she wondered why in heaven's name they had agreed to open on a Sunday afternoon to accommodate these people. She had planned on cleaning out her closet, putting away her summer clothes, and here she was, working, and all because it was business, and she felt she couldn't say no.

The door flung wide, admitting Bob into the kitchen, with Tyler in tow. Tyler's hair looked as if it had not been combed and Bob's face was red.

Bob rubbed his hands together briskly. Tyler followed suit. "Windy out there. A real chill in the air."

"I've come to mash avocados for the dip," Tyler announced. He flung his jacket on a chair.

"No dip today," Grace said, "but you can help me stamp out these sugar cookies. Pick the shapes you'd like." She shoved a low box toward him across the worktable.

Tyler examined the metal forms: angel, butterfly, dog, rabbit, cow, Christmas tree, crescent moon, star, woman, man, train. "It feels like an angel and a butterfly day," he said.

From a yellow bowl, Grace lifted a round lump of dough. "Fine. Bob, you roll out this dough. You've got stronger arms than I do. Make it real thin. Tyler, get the cookies as close together as possible, but not touching."

"I can do that," he said, brandishing the butterfly cutter.

Grace noticed that Tyler looked happier than she had seen him in weeks.

At two o'clock in the afternoon the buses arrived, and soon the tearoom filled with chatter and laughter. The customers seemed happy to be there, and ate with gusto. And when, at three-thirty, right on schedule, the buses pulled away from their parking lot, Grace began pulling off tablecloths. Moments later, Russell arrived to pick up Tyler.

"Do I have to go?" Tyler turned mournful eyes to Grace.

"Your dad's taking you to the Y swimming. It'll be fun."

"Emily going?"

"I don't think so, just you and Dad," Bob said. "Get your jacket on now."

After his son and grandson drove away, Bob switched on the vacuum. Its whir stirred a complementary whir in Grace's mind. She looked about her. Even without the tables set with their crisp, white lace-edged tablecloths, the room was charming. Surely someone would buy this business, relieve her of this responsibility she was feeling more and more.

"Too bad the Athens Restaurant isn't open on Sundays," Grace said. It was a favorite eatery of theirs in Weaverville.

"I've been sneaking goodies all afternoon. Are you hungry?" Bob asked.

"Not really. I'm not in the mood to go home yet."

Grace had stayed up half the night rehearsing how she would tell Bob that she thought it best he find another place to live. She would offer to house or apartment hunt with him and help him furnish it. Also, sooner or later, she must tell him that much as she loved cooking, she hated being tied to baking on demand. He might not understand about a cottage on their land, but he would surely understand her tiredness. Pulling out a chair, Grace flopped into it and stretched out her legs. They ached, so did her back. She wiped the sweat from her face with her bandanna. "Too much," she said softly.

"Too much of everything, baking, cooking, waiting tables, being on our feet," Bob said. "We need to consider getting some help in this place." His car keys jingled as he dug them from his pocket. "Let's get out of here."

Untying her apron, Grace rolled it into a wad, opened the utility room door to dump the apron into the washing machine, and changed her mind. "I'll do this with my things back at the house tonight."

"Let's go," Bob said. "I want to show you something."

"A surprise?" Her face lit up.

He wiped a smudge of flour from her chin and nodded. "I hope you'll like this one." They left the tearoom, and moments later his Cherokee turned into Loring Valley.

"Tell me we're not going to the Hammers'."

He chuckled. "Your favorite people. No, we're not going there."

The road was new and freshly paved, the roadside newly planted with large, mature rhododendrons interspersed with twenty-foot-tall dogwoods. She recognized them by their bark. Hannah was helping her identify trees and shrubs. They must have cost a fortune, Grace thought.

The Victorian motif of the condominiums, of the entire development, was, Grace had to admit, quite attractive. There was none of the boxy sameness one often saw in developments. These structures had been carefully designed, the colors carefully, tastefully chosen. All boasted covered porches dripping with fretwork, and many of the porches were furnished with wicker or wrought-iron chairs, tables, swings.

Still, the natural contour of the land lay ravaged. The hairpin curved road had been gouged from the mountainside, leaving insufficient vegetation to hold the slopes under pressure of a heavy rain, Grace was certain. Bob negotiated one sharp curve after another, and suddenly Grace's negative feelings were overridden by the splendid view that spread below and across the valley. Alongside the river, the villas seemed no more than dollhouses, while across the river, the mountainside—too steep to vanquish—rose pristine in shadowed folds and layers to meet the sky.

Bob pulled the Cherokee into a driveway in front of a closed garage. "Who lives here?" Grace asked.

"You'll see." Rounding the Jeep, he offered her his hand. The height of his Cherokee was forever a challenge to Grace, though it was easier to slide down and out than to clamber up. She placed her hand on his arm, and he slid his other hand about her waist and eased her to the ground. "Thanks," she said, then smoothed her dress. She felt, and probably looked like, a rumpled hen, and he was taking her to meet new people. Rummaging in her purse yielded no comb. Grace smoothed her hair with her hands. "Okay, let's go."

From his pocket Bob fished a set of shiny keys. He opened the front door, swung it wide, stepped back, and waved her in.

"What?" Grace stepped into an entry hall, and then into a lovely, large empty living room graced with a stunning crystal chandelier hanging from the center of a rosette medallion. Deep dental molding joined walls to ceiling. French doors opened to the porch.

"You like it?" Bob asked. His eyes twinkled, and a mischievous grin plastered itself across his face. Opening the French doors, he took her arm and guided her outside. The view was stunning. If she focused only on the pristine mountainside, she could forget what was below. "Lovely, eh?" he asked.

It was cooler up here than in the valley. The air was so clear that when a hawk appeared from a cleft in a rocky outcropping across the valley, and plunged from its perch, free-falling, then extending its wings to soar on billowing currents of air, Grace gasped and clutched Bob's arm. "Did you see that? I thought it was injured or someone had shot it, the way it fell. Amazing, those great powerful wings."

"Like a symphony, wind, and wings, and bird," he said softly, holding her close.

"Yes." She turned to face him. "So, whose place is this?"

Light flickered in his eyes. He smiled. "Mine."

"Yours?" Grace gasped. "But I thought . . ."

"I know, love. It was foolish of me to even suggest living on your land. With your sense of responsibility and you being such a caretaker, it would have confounded your life. Martin Hammer and I played golf one day, and he suggested I look at a condo here. I said no initially, but when he brought me up here, well, you see . . ." He waved an arm. "So, I went ahead and made an offer, and the owners agreed last evening and left the message with Russell."

Grace drew back. "You bought this without telling me, without showing it to me?" All this time she had been fretting and worrying. Stepping out of his arm, she backed away, turned, and started inside.

Bob followed. "Talk to me, Grace."

She stood silent for many moments, her back to him, then she turned. "Why didn't you tell me, Bob?" She was angry. Why? He should be angry with her. She was the one who had rudely ignored his initial request, had not even brought it up to Hannah and Amelia until yesterday. His buying this condo lifted the burden from her shoulders. But, they were a couple, and he hadn't told her. Come off it, Grace, her mind said. Bob knew just how you felt, even if you said not a word. He did this as much for you as for himself. She went to him then, and standing on tiptoe eased her arms about his neck and kissed him. He held her tight, and they did not speak. Love, Grace thought, is both a puzzle and a seesaw. She snuggled close to him, remembering a cozy moment in bed recently, a shared time that had warmed a place deep within her.

"It's beautiful here," she said.

"You're not angry? You like it?"

"Not angry. I do like it. It's lovely inside and out. Show me the rest."

There were two large bedrooms, each with a wall of windows, and there were two baths, one with a double Jacuzzi. The second bedroom was large enough to hold two beds for Tyler and a friend he might invite to sleep over. The kitchen and dining alcove were cheery and light and overlooked the view. What troubled her were the hills directly below them. Eight hundred feet above the river, they had been heavily wooded with pine and deciduous growth that were now gone. The scarred earth would heal, in time, she knew, but would it before the rains that sometimes pounded the area? The condominiums on either side of Bob's, and below his, seemed like mountain climbers clinging to the rock face for dear life. Were they firmly rooted into the bedrock? She did not realize that she was frowning.

"You're thinking they'll do this to Anson's land, aren't you?" Bob asked.

She nodded.

"Not if Hannah has her way, and I think she's going to find a way to stop him."

Below in the valley and on either side of the condo, lights came on. Behind the mountain, a magenta sunset changed, softened to peach and gold. Amazing colors, amazing sky. It would be pleasant to visit here, to stay overnight. Everything would be all right.

He looked at his watch. "It's early. What say we go find me some furniture, a bed at least so I can start moving my things over here."

On the way to the furniture store Bob asked Grace, "Not angry about the condo anymore?"

Grace twisted a hand back and forth in the air. "No. You're the one who ought to be angry. I didn't get back to you about the land and your cottage."

"I pouted," he said, "for a while, but, I got over it. It was a dumb request. You'd end up spending your time worrying about how I was doing, what I was doing, eating, whatever."

With her fingers she traced the white, springy hairs on the knuckles of his hand on the steering wheel. How large and square his hands were, how small hers were, and pale by comparison. "I worried so about it. I couldn't even talk to the others until last night."

"How'd they react?"

"Amelia and Hannah said it was my decision."

"Russell gave me hell." He reached over and grasped her hand. "I got carried away. Truth is I hoped in time you'd come and live with me if I were right there. Forgive me?"

"Nothing to forgive. But, it's good with us like it is, isn't it? Are you unhappy?" Reaching with her free hand she traced the curve of his cheek with her fingers.

"No," he replied. "Not unhappy. Selfish."

She smiled at him. "I adore you."

They spent several hours looking at bedroom sets and big bulky chairs. "I've always liked heavy dark furniture, and I always end up buying something light and with smaller proportions," he said.

"You get whatever it is you like, my dear," Grace said.

They walked about the store slowly and came to rocking chairs, overstuffed chairs with hassocks, and recliners. "I want us each to have a comfortable chair for when we watch TV. This is as good a time as any to select them."

They did just that. Bob chose a green leather recliner, wide and with a deep seat, and Grace settled into a smaller version of his, also green with a shorter seat. "They'll be perfect together," he said, and he gave the salesman the order. It was the fastest, easiest shopping Grace ever saw. But Bob did not select the dark walnut, but rather chose a French country bedroom set made of pine that Grace loved. "It's wonderful," she said. "I love the rounded corners."

She fell in love with a sized-down French country dinette set, which he bought. "We did good," Bob said, squeezing her hand. "Never would have gotten so much done without you."

After a quick dinner in Asheville, they headed back to Covington. The traffic on the highway was heavy. Huge trucks bound for Tennessee and beyond hogged the road and tore past them. "They own the road," Bob said, slowing. "I yield to them."

Finally, they reached the turnoff at Mars Hill, and soon turned the corner into Cove Road. The wind had risen, and the windmill at Maxwell's farm turned steadily. In the near dark several recalcitrant cows, nagged by a blue heeler dog, trudged across a hillside toward the barn. Grace took a deep, satisfied breath, then felt a tingle in her nose. She gasped, her ribs contracted and expanded, and she covered her mouth and sneezed. It was a physical relief, just as it had been knowing that Bob had bought a condo.

"Bless you," Bob said.

"We missed you at dinner," Hannah said, waving her to join them in the kitchen.

"I know. I'm sorry. Wait until I tell you where I've been and what I've been doing." Grace strutted into the kitchen, where Hannah and Amelia sat at the table finishing chef salads. "You have two guesses, one each." Grace stood near the stove waiting.

"You and Bob were making out in the tearoom." Amelia's eyes twinkled.

"Sure. On the tables." Picturing this made Grace laugh.

"A multitude of people arrived at five-thirty," Hannah said.

"No, they left at three-thirty," Grace said.

"Well, chéri, tell us," Amelia said.

The kettle whistled. Grace lifted it from the fire. "Anyone want more tea?"

"Well, tell us," Amelia said.

No one wanted tea. She poured water into a cup and dunked a

chamomile tea bag for herself. "Well, Bob figured that my silence said it all. He bought an apartment." Carrying the cup and saucer, she joined them at the table.

"*C'est loin?* Is it far? Asheville? Fairview, where Mike lives? They have some lovely new places there."

"Loring Valley."

"Loring Valley, what?" Hannah's startled look disconcerted Grace. Hannah hadn't aged at all in the last few years, in fact, since coming to Covington, the lines in her face had softened, but now, tonight, there was a tension about her chin, and tiny lines puckered around her pursed lips.

"Bob's bought a condo in Loring Valley, up on the highest tier, with a stunning view."

The silence in the kitchen seemed enormous, and deep, and cool as the interior of a cavern. Grace's hand shook slightly as she lifted the teacup to her lips. It was too hot, and it spilled when she lowered it abruptly to the saucer. She wiped the tabletop with her bandanna.

"Loring Valley, well," Hannah said.

"He wants to be closer to the tearoom."

"Loring Valley," Hannah repeated.

Grace decided this was not the moment to tell them about the furniture-shopping expedition.

18

Hannah Surfs the Internet

Hannah scrutinized each and every room in the house, seeking a place for her new computer. She considered the kitchen. Too warm, and too busy with Grace baking and cooking. The dining room? No. They enjoyed having people for dinner. The living room? She couldn't usurp the living room; it was used by everyone. The spare bedroom? No. Bob stayed there some nights, or Tyler slept over, or her or Grace's family might come to visit. Finally, she settled for her own room, the largest of the four bedrooms. It simply required a bit of rearranging. She would push her dresser closer to the window, the leather wing chair nearer the door. Soon, her new computer found a home on a table along a wall, with a window on the adjoining wall that afforded a pleasant view of trees and a wide pasture and cast a soft northern light.

There had been horses in that pasture when they first arrived in Covington. She remembered standing at this very window and calling the others to see the mare and colt. The horses were gone now, and the tottering old barn tottered even further, one side nearly touching the ground.

"You picked a good place for your computer," Tyler said. He had come to the farmhouse on the bus directly from school. "Our teacher at school says you need to rest your eyes every two hours. Just turn your chair and look out of this window, remember."

Hannah sat forward in the swivel office chair she had purchased along with the computer. "Okay, let's do it," she said to the boy, who sat in a straight-backed chair she had pulled up to the keyboard. The machine confounded her, intimidated her. The white plastic rectangle with which you clicked here, clicked there, or pushed an arrow about, was called a mouse. Why? Because the arrow scurried? So, why was the arrow called a cursor and not a mouse?

Deftly, Tyler started up the computer. How, Hannah wondered, did little kids learn this technical stuff so fast? "Got to learn how to use this thing." Hannah leaned closer to the monitor.

"It's easy, Aunt Hannah." Tyler touched something. The screen rolled. A tiny slim gray line blinked in a box called Search. "Dad taught me to use Google. It's called a search engine. I click on Google over here in this list on the left. That brings up Google's home page. See the blinking line?"

"I see it."

"Now, you sit here and type in the name of whatever you want information about."

Hannah typed in *N-a-t-u-re C-o-n-s-e-r-v-a-n-cy*. Immediately the screen changed, and a long index appeared. "Now what do you want?" Tyler asked.

"I don't know yet," she replied. "Let me read this list." Her finger ran down the listed items and settled on the word *purpose*. "Purpose. Let's try that."

"Click on purpose then."

Hannah did, and in moments she was reading that the Nature Conservancy sought out natural habitats in danger of being destroyed, and, working closely with communities, individuals, corporations, bought the land. Endangered species, flora, or fauna, seemed to be emphasized. She read out loud. "Membership is only twenty-five dollars a year. The Nature Conservancy's considered the number one conservation organization with regard to accountability and spending practices as listed in the American Institute of Philanthropy's ratings. What do you think of that, Tyler?"

But already, Tyler was busy with his magic game cards. He shrugged.

Hungry for details, and information, Hannah scanned the index, which listed such topics as purchasing power, ecological classification, and law of the land. She pointed to *law of the land* and clicked the mouse. An article appeared. Hannah scanned it.

There is a thirty-five-year-old statute that few have ever heard of. In fact, the Land and Water Conservation Fund just might be the most visionary yet anonymous landscape protection measure ever passed.

For a moment Hannah rejoiced, until she read that today the LWCF, whose funding came from offshore oil drilling royalties, found itself at a turning point. As she scanned the paragraph, hope spiraled down, down into the pit of her stomach. She spoke out loud, then, more to clarify the material for herself than to share it with Tyler. "Over the past few decades the LWCF has been woefully underappropriated, not because the money hasn't existed, but because Congress has siphoned off its funds into other programs."

Tyler lifted his head from his cards for a moment. "It sounds so boring. I could teach you to play my magic game or put a game on your computer."

"Maybe another time." She could not take her eyes from the monitor. It was amazing. An encyclopedia at the touch of a mouse; no turning razor-thin pages or struggling with fine print in heavy volumes, and without having to leave the house for the library. Marvelous. The possibilities of the computer suddenly stretched before her like a field of wheat, ripe and nourishing. Hannah smiled at Tyler. "I could get to like this thing, after all."

"You will, Aunt Hannah. When you're done looking up what you need to, I'll teach you to play games, if you want."

"I'd like that, Tyler," she replied, and went on reading. Royalties, she noted again, levied on offshore oil drilling had funded the LWCF. Good she thought, and continued. These royalties, as high as $900 million in one year, went to federal land acquisition for conservation and recreation, or monies could be turned over to the states in a matching fund program that allowed the states to decide which lands they wanted for new parks, which they wanted to enhance older parks, and which for open space.

Usage. That word leaped at her. What usage could be assigned to Anson's land that would interest the LWCF or the Nature Conservancy, or any other organization dedicated to preservation, or the state, or individuals? As a park? No. Masterson's land was going to be developed as a park. Open land, unspoiled forests, hiking trails? Endangered species, of course. The Nature Conservancy was interested in preserving habitats of endangered flora or fauna. She liked their approach. Surely, there must be something endangered on Anson's land. How could she find out?

Below in the driveway, a horn blew and blew again. "Gotta go," Tyler said. "Want to shut it off yourself when you're done reading, or should we print out copies?"

"Shut it off. Your dad's waiting. You can show me how to print next time." She hugged him, conscious that she was strong and bony, not soft and round like Grace.

He dawdled. "I hope you can stop those builders from tearing up Mr. Anson's land." His eyes were dark and wide and very serious. "They sure cut a lot of trees down where Grandpa's bought his apartment." He lowered his head and she saw that his chin quivered. When he looked up at her, his eyes held tears. "Grandpa's going to move, and I'm going to be all alone with that Emily and my dad."

"That's hardly being alone, Tyler."

"Oh, yes it is. You haven't seen them, Aunt Hannah, always kissing and stupid stuff like that." He was silent, and Hannah didn't know what to say. She'd never been good at talking to children.

"Here's how you shut it off." Tyler clicked the mouse, and the computer screen changed color, rolled, and finally went dark. Then the words *It is safe to turn off your computer now* appeared. Tyler slipped from his chair alongside Hannah, bent, and switched off the red light on the bar on the floor. Without looking at her, he mumbled, "Dad's probably mad at me. We had a meeting with Mrs. Tate and my teacher this afternoon."

"This afternoon?"

"I came here from school on the bus to help you."

"What was the meeting about that you decided to avoid, Tyler?"

"I got an 'F.' Didn't turn in a project." He shrugged. A weak smile curled about his lips.

Hannah gave him her full attention. Seated, she towered over him, but her eyes were gentle and her voice soft. The horn blew again. "What's going on, Tyler? You're very smart. You didn't want to do the project?"

"No." He studied his shoes, and shuffled from one leg to the other.

"Look at me," Hannah said, then reached to draw him to her. "No inquisition, boy. I care about you."

Tears trickled down Tyler's freckled cheeks. Hannah's heart went out to him. She lifted him easily onto her lap, and thought about her two grandsons and how little patience she had had with them when they were Tyler's age. She would try to do better, now, with this child. "Tell me," she said gently and smoothed back his hair with her hand.

"I want to live here with you, and Granny Grace, and Aunt Amelia, and Dad says absolutely not. He's going to marry Emily. Grandpa's going to move out. I'll never see any of you, only Emily and Dad. I hate them both." He stifled a sob.

*

"Damn, where is he?" Russell started to open the door of the car, but Emily's hand on his arm restrained him. "He knew we had a meeting with his teacher, so he gets on the bus and comes over here."

"Russell." Emily's voice was soft. "I'm going home to Ocala for a while."

"You're what?" The nerves in his jaw twitched. "What about us?"

"We can wait. Can't you see it's too soon for Tyler?"

Russell turned to her, but she averted her eyes. The pain in him was palpable. "I love you, Emily. I want us to get married."

"I want that too," she murmured. Leaning into his chest, she hid her trembling chin. "I love you, but how can we be happy if every moment of our lives together causes Tyler so much pain?"

Russell's free hand gripped the steering wheel. He lowered his head until his forehead touched the hard rim. "He's a child, Emily. He'll adjust. Kids adjust. He'll get to know you. He'll love you."

"Maybe in time, he will, but I can't live with his hostility, Russell. I just can't."

*

From outside the horn sounded again. Hannah sensed Tyler's helplessness and anger. She ached for him, for his loss, and now this sweeping change. "Have you explained to your dad how you're feeling?"

"He knows. He doesn't care."

"I don't for a minute believe that." She could feel Tyler stiffen. He stepped away from her. If only Grace and Bob were here. They could sit down, all of them, and talk to Tyler and to Russell. She would talk to Grace about this. But for now, an impatient Russell waited in the driveway, and Tyler was so upset she hated to let him go. "We'll think of something, Granny Grace, and your grandpa, and I."

They walked downstairs slowly, hand in hand. Hannah opened the front door and waved at Russell. "Tyler's been wonderful," she called. "He's so smart. We were shutting down the computer. He's coming. My fault. Sorry." Closing the door, she knelt beside Tyler.

"You're a gutsy kid. Listen to me. Your dad loved your mother very much, but he's lonely. You have us all to love you. Who has he got?"

"Me. Grandpa." Tyler's voice was small, and blue, and defeated.

"Emily's a nice woman. You don't have to love her, only respect and be polite to her."

"Got to go," Tyler said.

Hannah nodded, certain that she had failed him. Grace would have said it all so much better. By speaking favorably of Emily, had she, in Tyler's mind, joined the ranks of the enemy? She prayed not.

He bounded down the porch steps, barely missing Emily, who had dashed from the car, up the steps, and across the porch to where Hannah stood in the doorway of the farmhouse. "May I come in, Miss Hannah?" she asked.

The car door slammed behind Tyler, but the car did not start or drive away. Hannah and Emily stood for a long quivering moment in the foyer. Emily's chin trembled. Then Hannah took the young woman's arm, guided her to the kitchen, pulled out a chair at the table for her. Stalling for time, Hannah set a plate of cookies in the center. "How can I help?" she asked, finally taking the chair across from Emily.

"I'm not sure anyone can." Emily's voice was sad, plaintive, and lonely. "I can't marry a man whose child hates me. I'm going home to Florida."

"Sure this is what you want to do?"

"No," she wailed softly, beginning to weep, then wiped her eyes with her sleeve. "I don't know what else to do. This is a huge change for me. I have a successful practice, and I'm willing to give it up, but not this way. I've tried with Tyler. He won't let me read to him, won't talk to me. When he does say anything, it's 'yes, ma'am' and 'no, ma'am,' and then he looks past me or right through me." She shuddered. "He gives me the willies." Shifting in her chair, Emily leaned toward Hannah and lowered her voice nearly to a whisper. Involuntarily, Hannah leaned closer. "I told Russell, right from the start, that I needed to meet Tyler, that we needed to plan things that included him." Emily's body quivered. Hannah reached over and placed a hand on her arm.

"Time. It's a matter of time, and it helps, I've learned, if you can talk about the things you're feeling."

Emily shook her head. Her eyes, under their long lashes, were sorrowful. "For me and Russell, I think it's too late." She began to cry again, hunched over the table, her face buried in her hands.

"Do you love Russell?" Hannah asked.

She nodded and muttered something indiscernible.

"I don't believe in impossible," Hannah said. Pushing back her chair she walked to the window. "Russell's car's sitting in the driveway."

Emily lifted her head. "Still there?"

"Waiting for you, I imagine. Listen, Emily. Everyone's hurting, you, Russell, Tyler. You must sit down and talk."

"We never do that," she replied. "I don't know why."

Hannah meshed her fingers tight. Interference was not her way. The light in the kitchen seemed suddenly to dim. When Hannah looked out of the window, she saw the low bank of gray clouds that hovered above Snowman's Cap. Weather changed so fast in these mountains. Would it snow? No, it was in the forties, too warm for snow, except, of course on Snowman's Cap. A cap of snow. She brought her mind back to Emily and Tyler.

Butt out, Hannah, she told herself. A counselor you're not. But someone has to try. Hannah laid her hands flat on the table. "I'll talk to Grace and Bob. Between us, we should be able to get you all together to talk about what's going on."

"Oh, would you, Hannah?" Hope flared for a moment in Emily's lovely, sad eyes.

"Sunday," Hannah said, wondering at her concern for this young woman, and where this impetuous desire to help was coming from. "Sunday, you bring Russell and Tyler for lunch. Grace and Bob will be here." A pang of guilt stung Hannah for an instant. Grace did not cook on Sundays. On Sundays they all did their own thing, both in and out of the kitchen. Oh, well, there was always tuna salad. Then Hannah, not given to touching, leaned over and brushed a strand of loose hair back from Emily's forehead. "Up now, my girl, out to the car with you." Side by side, they walked to the door. Hannah's heart raced as she watched Emily move slowly down the steps, hesitate a moment, then open the backseat of the car.

She liked Emily. Why? They had hardly talked until today. Was it because Emily was an attorney, an independent woman? She must love Russell very much to be willing to give up her practice, her life in Florida. Would she, Hannah, have married, had children if she had had a lucrative career? Her record as a wife and mother suggested she would not. Only recently, working with Wayne in the greenhouse, her mind had drifted to Emily, and she found herself comparing her life to Emily's, envying the younger woman, worrying about her. She had absentmindedly transplanted three anthuriums into one pot!

Wayne had asked, "What you got your mind on, Miss Hannah?"

"I'm really out of it today," she'd replied, and they had laughed.

Now, from the car came Russell's voice, hard and loud. "Tyler, get in back."

And from the backseat, firmly, Emily said, "No. Tyler, stay where you are. I'm just fine here."

Moments later they were gone, leaving Hannah wondering what exactly she'd gotten herself into.

19

Doing What Lance Wants

Everything annoyed Amelia today, most of all the repulsive and ubiquitous ladybugs lying dead on the carpet in the living room. They were, she knew, the last of the season, and their kin would succumb to starvation as they had, and tumble from their hiding places. Long after the cold forced them into hibernation, she would find a ladybug on her bedspread, in her shoes, on the sink in the bathroom. When the phone rang, she heard it dimly and ignored it until Hannah called. "Amelia, it's Lance."

Amelia walked briskly with eager steps to the kitchen and lifted the phone from the wall. "Hello, Lance," she said, then, "Sunday?" Her brows drew close, and her eyes clouded. "I can't cancel Sunday brunch with Mike again. Can we do it another day?" She waited, rubbed her forehead, twisted the cord of the phone. "Their last day?" She scratched her head. "It's a problem for me. Can I call you back?"

It was obvious to Hannah, standing in the doorway of the kitchen, that Lance had said no, it was not all right for Amelia to call him back.

Unaware of being watched, Amelia mouthed, "Damn it," then paced the length of the cord, frowned, looked worried. Whatever persuasive argument Lance used, it worked. Amelia stopped pacing, stopped twisting the cord. She stood straighter, looked out the window, tossed her head, and laughed lightly. "You make it hard for me to say no." The husky seductiveness of her voice gave Hannah a clue of what was being said on the other end. The crinkle lines on Amelia's forehead smoothed. She laughed again. "Eleven, then? See you Sunday. Damn," she muttered, as she hung up the phone. Then she saw Hannah.

"Don't like Lance," Hannah said bluntly.

"Well, *mon ami,* I do," Amelia replied with another flip of her head. She looked at Hannah, then away, then back at Hannah. "Why don't you like him?"

Hannah leaned against the kitchen counter. Amelia stood by the door, one hand on the frame as if poised for flight. "He's egocentric," Hannah said. "Selfish. He leads, you follow." She placed a hand on her forehead and shook her head. "I hate self-centered men who smother women."

"No one smothers me." Amelia's eyes dilated and blazed.

"Come on, Amelia. Can't you see that Lance already has you wrapped around his finger?"

"No, he doesn't."

"What do you call canceling brunch with Mike?"

"An exception. Mike will understand."

"Like he did when you canceled your theater date, and the opening of Marty Green's watercolor show? Mike showed up here all upset both times. He's been a true friend, Amelia." Hannah tapped her foot. "What's Lance's thing this time?"

"He's got old friends in; he wants me to meet them."

"Monday or Tuesday disappear from the calendar?"

"Sunday's their last day." Amelia looked away. The words sounded hollow, and Hannah made her feel guilty. She hated that.

"He waits until the last minute, and you're supposed to cancel your plans and do what he wants."

This statement of fact, plain and simple, infuriated Amelia. She struggled not to cry. Her hand on the frame shifted downward slightly. She wanted to yell at Hannah, "Leave me alone."

Hannah stepped toward Amelia. "Guilt's written all over your face. When was the last time you felt guilty, Amelia, tell me, when?"

Amelia pulled back. Her hand flew to her cheek as if Hannah had slapped her.

"I'll tell you when, my friend. When you were having nightmares about Thomas denigrating and destroying your work, remember, before you accepted the fact that you had a right to your own life and success?" Hannah's voice dropped, as did her shoulders. She walked heavily to a chair and sat. "You stopped feeling guilty when you let Thomas go and started to lead your own life. Are you leading your life now or Lance's life? Think about it."

Amelia's eyes misted. It was true. She had been a pale, almost invisible gofer for Thomas in his important work with the International Red Cross. Years after his death she had been unable to shake off her dependence on him and make her own life, and she never would have without the encouragement and support of Hannah, and Grace, and Mike.

"Need I say more?" Hannah asked.

Amelia rallied. Angry at Hannah, she turned in a huff and swung from the room. She hated it that Hannah was right. Mike would be angry and feel betrayed. He didn't deserve this. In the early days, when she felt like a dodo unable to grasp the principles of photography, Mike had encouraged her, focused on the positives in her work, and later, when she began to win prizes, urged her to self-publish her work. It was he who had located a printer, accompanied her to Tennessee, negotiated a contract. Other than Grace and Hannah, Mike was the only advocate she had ever had.

With weighted steps and using her hands one over the other to pull herself along, Amelia mounted the stairs. Once she was in her bedroom, a decidedly feminine room with lacy white curtains and bedspread, the cream-colored walls closed about her.

Her window offered a splendid view of the mountains with Snowman's Cap, the pièce de résistance, in the distance. Amelia stood at the window and considered how her life was changing under the constant pressure of Lance's deadlines. Rushing made her nervous. Nervousness knotted her stomach and sent her trotting to the bathroom. Yet, when he was away she missed Lance's unconstrained spontaneity. So, why did she feel yoked like an ox, rather than light-hearted and happy?

Amelia turned from the window, yanked open a dresser drawer, and slammed it shut. She was sixty-nine, and she ached for someone special, someone male to love. Hannah didn't need a man, and Grace had one. Why shouldn't she? Mike was good company. They enjoyed theater and much more together, but Mike was gay, and occasionally he disappeared for a day or two, probably on some tryst. Bob and Grace. She envied the way Bob wrapped his arm about Grace's shoulder, their kiss good night at the door, envied the loving tone in Bob's voice when he spoke to Grace. She loved Grace, and was happy for them. It was confusing.

Plopping on the side of her bed, Amelia kicked off first one shoe and then the other. Was Hannah right about Lance? Meeting his oldest friends was like being taken home to meet his parents, who were probably dead. Lance never said. You'd think he could say if his parents were deceased. Amelia's hand shook as she pulled her scarf off. It hit the floor and formed a tent over the shoe closest to her bed. She would put it right with Mike. She would meet Lance's friends at noon and then join Mike at the Purple Plum Gallery by three on Sunday afternoon where they would hang her photographs for a show that would open next Wednesday. She'd have dinner with Mike and explain, and he would understand. He had to.

※

On Sunday, Amelia's hair was still wet from her shower when Hannah called up the stairs. "Amelia, Lance is here."

Her bedside clock said ten-forty-five in the morning. Forty-five minutes to get to Asheville. Brunch was at twelve. He was early, again, and hated being kept waiting. Amelia raked a comb through damp hair, pulled on stockings and soft gray wool slacks. The zipper caught. It took moments to work loose. She tucked her mauve silk blouse into her slacks. Over it she buttoned a snug-fitting, handmade vest in shades of violet, and around her neck she wore an amber necklace: both were presents from Lance after his trip.

One side of the vest hung lower than the other. Unbutton. Hurry. Her fingers shook. Button correctly. Hurry. She must go to the bathroom once more. Amelia took several slow, deep breaths, dabbed on lipstick, and grabbed her daytime purse. Sitting on the edge of her bed she dumped the contents on the bedspread, singled out a few items: compact, lipstick, comb, keys, and flung them into a small tan satin clutch. She lost several moments carefully placing her scarf about her neck, covering the burn scars. "I'm coming," she called, and started down the stairs. She tripped on the second step and almost fell. Amelia leaned against the railing, her heart pattering. A fine way to start this date.

Lance paced the foyer. The padded shoulders of his overcoat added to his substantial Nordic frame. His big, brown-gloved hands twisted his hat. Amelia noted the shift in his eyes from annoyance to appreciation as he looked her over, top to bottom. "You look lovely," he said, extending his hand. Then with urgency in his voice, "Come on. We're late. Let's get a move on."

✳

Lance towered over Amelia. Debonair in Armani slacks and sport jacket, a silk ascot hung deliberately about his neck, Lance wore an air of arrogance, as if he were shouting to all the men and women in the room, "Hey, you lesser creatures, look at me, and weep." While they waited for the maître d' to seat them, Lance positioned them conspicuously in the center of the raised foyer, from where they looked down on the closest diners.

Amelia's heart scampered wildly in her chest. I'm Amelia Declose, she reminded herself. I've traveled extensively worldwide, dined with princes, ministers of foreign countries, ambassadors. So, why then did she feel Lilliputian and diminished? The next moment, she was being propelled forward, down several carpeted steps, across a Mexican tile floor through a dimly lit room with the feel of evening, not midday, and she realized that there were no windows. A penguin of a man, seeming out of place in a black tuxedo, led them to a table in a far alcove. Heavy drapes, tied back with thick cords and knotted tassels, isolated the alcove from the rest of the room. A chair at a round, dark table was pulled back, and moments later Amelia was sitting watching Lance shake hands with the men and kiss the women on their upturned cheeks or lips. Two couples. She had expected only one couple, old friends, a warm get-to-know-you chat during which she anticipated learning more about Lance.

She studied the room, noted its high, wood-beamed ceiling, saw that most of the booths were full, the voices subdued, the music low, but the drumbeat distinct. In the corner of a booth, huddled close to a casually dressed woman with gray hair pulled back in a chignon, snuggled a tiny papillon dog with long, silky white hair and large, erect ears that resembled butterfly wings. A dog in a restaurant? Why had she never been to this restaurant before, never heard anyone speak of it? Mike kept abreast of new clubs and restaurants.

Now, everyone at their table was greeting her, reaching out to shake her hand. The women were smartly dressed in bright-colored

139

Adolfo suits reminiscent of Nancy Reagan, or were those button-down jackets Bill Blass? They seemed younger than Amelia, until she noticed the topography of their hands. Thickened blue veins traversed raised swirls of wrinkles. They had had facelifts, and good ones, but hands do not lie.

"Amelia is widely traveled," Lance boasted.

"Oh, where have you been to?" Lucille asked.

"Where haven't I been?" Amelia replied. These effusive well-dressed men and women reminded her of the people Thomas had cultivated: newly rich and philanthropic. Amelia chatted amicably, superficially, knowing she would never see any of them again. "My husband was an executive with the International Red Cross. We lived abroad more years than we lived in America."

The slighter woman, Sonya, had spent a summer after college vacationing, and sailing the Mediterranean coast off the small Italian town of Spezia. Amazingly, Amelia and Thomas had honeymooned there. The women agreed that revisiting Spezia today would only destroy their memories of the quaint seaside village.

Later, over lunch, the men exchanged golf stories and talked of football, the women waxed ebullient about travel and clothes. Amelia wondered which of these couples were Lance's oldest friends. She could distinguish no difference in his interactions with any one of them, in fact she noted no particular camaraderie or familiarity, no inside jokes, none of the quick understanding nods or winks one would expect between old friends. Amelia looked at her watch. "Lance," she said, when she was able to get his attention. "This has been lovely, but I have to get to the Purple Plum Gallery within fifteen minutes. Can we leave?"

"Sure," he said. He shoved back his chair as if to rise and went right on chatting with Henry, to his left.

Amelia stood. She would take a cab. "It's been a pleasure meeting you all. I hope to see you again, but I must go now."

"Must you?" Sonya's hand clung to hers. "We're going to tour your most famous tourist attraction, the Biltmore House. From the pictures it looks like a castle right out of Europe."

"It's a lovely place, the gardens too, but I am sorry." Amelia tugged a bit to get her hand back. "Didn't Lance tell you? We're hanging my photographs at a gallery this afternoon. My show opens Wednesday." She held her purse tight to her waist, and realized that in her haste she had not brought her wallet, not even a quarter to phone Mike. Her mouth went dry. Butterflies beat their wings on the walls of her stomach. Amelia tightened her jaw to keep it from trembling.

"You have a show? What kind of show?" Lucille asked.

"I'm a photographer."

"Big-deal photographer around here. She's even got a book out," Lance said.

He had never told them. What had he said about her?

"Quite nice pictures." Lance stood and swung his arm, possessively, around Amelia's shoulders.

"Lance, you bad boy," Lucille said. "Why didn't you tell us. We could have all gone along and seen Amelia's work."

"But we bought tickets to the Biltmore House," Sonya said.

Lance started to lead Amelia away. "Well, it's been a blast seeing you guys. I'll take a rain check on the Biltmore House. Call when you're in the area again." He stopped for a moment to slip one of the men several folded bills. "Take care of the tab for me, will you?"

They stepped out into cold sunshine. The glare stung her eyes, more so, even, than when coming out of the movies. "They loved you," he whispered to Amelia. "I knew they would."

"How could you tell?"

"I know them all so well."

"Which of the couples are the old, dear friends you wanted me to meet? I couldn't tell." She struggled to keep the edge from her voice.

"Couldn't you? Well, perhaps not. I've known both couples, on and off, for years." He held open the door of his car for her.

Amelia felt tricked. She had hurt Mike and for what? Who was Lance anyway? And who were those people? All she knew was that Lance had been an architect, lived in Denver, and retired to Loring Valley. And he still, at his age—how old was he anyway?—caught every woman's eye, like Ginger Hammer's, at the party at the tearoom. Unwittingly, a wave of pride swept over Amelia, and an almost palpable aura of superiority that Ginger might want him, but she, Amelia, had him. She cast a sideways glance at Lance. Yes, he was egocentric, and he was also gorgeous with his Nordic fair skin, and sexy, and an exquisite dancer. She adored dancing. How young, how bold, how free she felt when they danced.

The sign extended over the sidewalk. Bright purple plums on leafy green vines surrounded the name PURPLE PLUM GALLERY. Lance slowed the car. "Damn it," he muttered. "On a Sunday, you'd think parking would be easy."

"It's never easy parking in downtown Asheville anymore." But Amelia's mind was light-years away, thinking how when Lance had left town the last time she had felt betrayed and bereft.

"I'm not tolerating this kind of treatment," she'd told Grace. "I'm going to end it with him."

But just hearing his voice on the phone when he returned left her weak-kneed. She found him utterly desirable, and that, and the dancing, was his power over her. She was ashamed to admit this to Grace.

The dance club they frequented boasted velvet draperies, raised parquets dotted with small round tables, a highly polished maple dance floor, and crystal chandeliers. A four-piece ensemble of versatile musicians played forties and fifties music: jazz, waltzes, polkas, tangos.

"Ready?" he had asked after their first glass of wine. And Amelia had extended her hand to be led out onto the dance floor. To dance with Lance was a dream come true. Thomas had been a decent dancer, but a novice compared to Lance. With his dancing skills, his graceful, elegant manner, his self-assurance, each step executed with finesse, they had been the center of attention.

Dancing with Lance was like floating on air. Together they were a team, virtuosos of the dance, astounding onlookers with their lithe movements, masterly dips and whirls, and moving effortlessly across the smooth, shining floor.

Once, long ago, in another lifetime, in another era, she had danced the night away with Thomas in a palatial room at the French Embassy in Morocco. And then the dancing had stopped. On Thomas's last mission, Korea, 1954, he had been diagnosed with gout. South Korea was bleak, devastated by war, boring. A young captain, Bob Richardson, strikingly attractive in his uniform and not at all boring, had been assigned as their guide. What a shock it was when he had resurfaced with Grace these many years later.

Suddenly, Lance slammed on the brakes, jarring her. Muttering curses he began to reverse into a newly vacated space a block down from the gallery. She could see Mike standing under the sign, his feet planted firmly, arms akimbo, looking hurt, and here, next to her, was Lance, grim jawed, his eyes an angry gray. Lance, she had come to realize, did not deal with frustration well.

"Just let me out, why don't you?" Amelia started to open the door. "You can still catch up with your friends at the Biltmore House."

Half in, half out of the space, Lance slammed on the brakes. "Okay," he said, ignoring horns blowing.

20

Hannah Intervenes

At the moment that Amelia and Lance left the restaurant, Hannah was presiding over a tuna salad lunch. It takes great courage to face pain directly and with honesty, which is why the conversation during this lunch Hannah had put together dealt with matters of the weather and population. "We're having an unusually warm winter," Russell said. "Hardly any snow. I worry about the reservoirs being too low this summer."

"Mother Nature's hardly acting motherly," Bob said. "She's capricious, mercurial."

"Maybe there's an innate wisdom in nature," Hannah said.

"How so?" Russell asked.

"Overpopulation will probably destroy this planet, unless Mother Nature takes matters in her own hands and makes certain it doesn't happen," Hannah replied.

"Are you referring to Malthus's theory?" Russell asked.

"Yes, Thomas Malthus. In the eighteenth century he projected that population growth would exceed the food supply. Then nature, he believed, would intervene, controlling populations by famine, disease, or war. He's been accurate historically. Recently we've had wars in Yugoslavia, famine in Ethiopia and other places in Africa. For a while, it looked as if we had it licked, what with increases in the food supply due to the use of pesticides, and with birth control, but it's all gone hay wacky. Too many people."

"All this frightening projection," Grace said, "because of a warm winter in western North Carolina, when a cold one was predicted. Can we talk about something else?" She left the dining room and returned with Tyler's favorite dessert, a Vienna cake, moist and rich and with colored layers.

"This is incredible cake, Grace. Do you share recipes?" Emily asked.

"Recipes are meant to share. I'll write it down for you."

It grew quiet in the room except for the tap tap of Bob's fingers on the table. Grace squeezed his hand, and the sound of silence returned, broken only when Tyler patted his tummy and pushed his plate away. "Full. Can I go upstairs and play a game on your computer, Aunt Hannah?"

"Not now, love," she said. She had seated Tyler between herself and Grace. Hannah took his hand in hers. It was cool and dry and she noted that his fingernails needed cutting. Who took care of such matters in their household? "I've asked everyone for lunch today," she told Tyler, "so we can talk."

Tyler squirreled his hand from hers and stared down at the tablecloth. With his fork he raked indentations in the tablecloth. "Nothing to talk about," he muttered.

"Yes, there is. Right now, at this table there are three very unhappy people."

Tyler stopped raking and looked at her. "Three?"

"Three. You, your father, and Emily. They're just as unhappy as you are, Tyler."

"Sure. I believe that," he muttered.

Russell gave him a "Watch yourself, young man" look.

"Emily, why don't you tell Tyler, tell us all, what's been going on for you."

Emily flushed. Her eyes swept over them and stopped at Tyler. "I'm leaving, Tyler. I am going home to Ocala. I know how unhappy you are about your dad and me, and I'm sorrier than you'll ever know." Her chin trembled. She swallowed hard and took a moment to gain control. "I wanted you to like me. I just didn't know how to reach you. I've never been around children. I have no brothers or sisters." She fumbled in her pocket for a tissue and wiped tears from her cheeks. "I love your father, but I can't marry him. You hate me. I sense you want to throw up every time I come into the room."

Tyler made a gesture he had made behind his father's back many times, for the benefit of Emily and Emily alone. He stuck a finger in his mouth and mimicked gagging.

Russell's napkin hit the table, nearly tumbling his glass. Across the table Tyler flinched as if someone had struck him.

Reaching up, Bob grabbed his son's arm. "Now, son. Easy. I know you're angry. That's why we're here. Control yourself. Let's hear Emily out."

"Russell, please," Hannah said. "We're here to talk, to listen to one another. This is how your son feels. Emily's hurt. You're hurting. Emily feels helpless, and perhaps you do also. I know Tyler feels helpless." She fixed Tyler with kind but firm eyes. "You are not helpless, my boy. Emily's planning to leave. You have the power to end this relationship between your dad and Emily." She hesitated then, thinking how precious love was and how easily frayed or lost it was. Her eyes turned to Grace for help.

Grace's arm cradled Tyler's shoulders. She spoke softly. "It's true, Tyler, love. You are so powerful that you can drive Emily out of your lives. She's a gentle woman. She's going to leave, rather than come between you and your father."

Tyler stared at Grace, his mouth open. His eyes filled with pain and tears.

Grace squeezed his hand. "You see, my love, power carries enormous responsibility. Power can hurt, or it can help and heal. It's how you, or anyone, handles power that's important." Grace's heart pattered. "Do you understand?" Grace lifted Tyler's tear-stained face to hers, bent, and kissed his cheeks.

"Mommy's dead. I don't have a dad anymore," Tyler said. His voice was resigned and pained, tears just below the surface.

"I know." Grace hugged him gently. "It's very hard. It's been hard for your father too." She wanted to weep for this little boy.

"No. It's not. Dad's found someone to replace Mommy. I don't matter anymore." He nodded toward Emily. His voice took on a defensive tone. "Dad's got no time for me."

"That's not true," Russell said. "You're my boy. I love you."

Tyler stared at his father. "How do I know, when you drive with Emily, that you aren't holding her hand, or kissing her, and not paying attention to the road? I've heard Grandpa tell you to pay attention to the road. You can get in a car crash and die, like Mommy."

"Is that what this is all about?" Russell let out a breath. He sank back into his chair. A slight quiver at the corners of his mouth added to the look of pain and confusion in his eyes. It was clear he did not know what to say or do. Emily helped him.

"And I didn't do anything right," Emily said. "I didn't take time to be with you, take you to the movies, get to know you. I was scared you wouldn't like me. I didn't know how to talk to a boy your age. I thought when your dad and I got to know each other better, I'd feel more relaxed, and could get to know you more easily. By then of course, it was too late. You'd made up your mind about me, and I didn't know how to bridge the gap."

"And I," Russell said, standing, "did not help." His voice was soft, now, and his eyes loving as he spoke to Tyler. "I didn't explain to you, son, what I was feeling. I loved your mother with all my heart. But she's gone, son." His voice cracked. "She's gone." He lifted his head and cleared his throat. "I never expected to marry again, but then I met Emily. I liked her. I thought you'd like her." He shrugged. "Well, it's too late." He looked at Emily, and the pain in his face was palpable. "She's leaving, going back to Florida."

A long silence followed. Bob jiggled his feet under the table. Grace placed a hand on his leg. The jiggling stopped. Everyone's attention turned to Tyler, who, in a motion that sent his dessert plate spinning, flung his head into his arms on the table and sobbed and sobbed.

Russell raced around the table to his son.

"You don't miss Mommy," Tyler managed between sobs. "You never cried for her."

Russell reached his son and knelt beside him. A moan issued from his throat. "Oh, God, Tyler, son. I cried. How I cried, at night, alone, scared if you saw me, it would just hurt you more. Thank God your grandpa came to be with us." He could see it now. In trying to shield his son from his pain, Russell realized that he had created a wall between them, and it had widened with the passing months. He had sent Tyler two messages: don't cry, and that his dad didn't miss and long for his mother. He realized, then, how infrequently Tyler cried. Withdrawn, yes, stopped functioning at school, yes, but he had hardly cried. How presumptuous to assume that a child would recover fully from the loss of a mother he loved in just a year or two. And who knew what incident, big or small, could trigger grief, again, and yet again. So immersed in his own grief had he been that when Grace came into the picture, he had abnegated many of his responsibilities for Tyler. Russell knew that he had messed up big time.

Russell took the boy's freckled face between his hands and looked deep into the dark, anguished eyes. "I love you, Tyler. With my whole heart, I love you. I never meant to hurt you." He swooped the child into his arms. Tyler's arms fastened about his father's neck, and he clung, sobbing.

There was not a dry eye at the table. Lines from *The Prophet* came to Hannah's mind. *Your pain is the breaking of the shell that encloses your understanding.*

It was close to midnight. Hannah and Grace sat on Grace's bed in their bathrobes talking about the day, as they often did when they were alone in the house at night, which happened more often lately, with Amelia gone so much and often returning quite late. "Do we ever stop grieving for someone we've loved?" Hannah asked. She had confided in Grace about Dan Britton, her great passion, her finest love, found late and lost.

Grace clasped Hannah's hand. "No. I don't think we ever do get over it completely, and things like today surely trigger the memories and open wounds."

"Like a powder keg waiting to ignite."

It had certainly seemed that way at their dining room table that winter afternoon. The sun seemed also to grieve, for it dove behind compact and clotted cirrus clouds, and the temperature dropped, and within the hour a gentle snow had begun to fall.

"Good that Amelia wasn't here. She'd have been a basket case, her daughter, her husband," Grace said.

"Gotta be hell. Left with those burn scars. Probably grieves every time she looks in the mirror." Hannah shifted and straightened her legs, which were cramped under her on the bed. "Your legs go on and on forever, like a stork," her mother used to mock her. She'd been the tallest girl, taller than many boys right through high school, and had hated her height. But like so much in life, you get used to things, learn to live with them.

"What's with Lance?" Grace suddenly asked. "Amelia go off with him and stand up Mike, again?"

"Yes." Hannah shook her head. Her lips drew into a thin line. "I don't like the way Lance controls Amelia, how she thinks, what she wears, everything. Why can't Amelia deal with a man in her life like you do, Grace? You haven't dropped me, Amelia, any of your friends. You maintain a balance."

"Amelia's hungered for a man of her own for a long time," Grace said. "Some women do."

"He's so manipulative. Can't she see that? Disappears for a week, won't say where, comes back bearing gifts like that gorgeous amber necklace, and she forgets she's been angry at him or hurt by him. To me that's sick."

Grace considered this. "She's vain, that's just Amelia. Finally getting the attention she's craved probably muddles her thinking."

A thoughtful quiet settled about them, then Hannah said, "She's walked right back into a situation like she had with Thomas. She's abandoning her work, Mike, hardly has teatime with us anymore. It's all about Lance and pleasing Lance."

"Amelia's not stupid. She's bound to recognize what's going on, eventually." But Grace wasn't sure she really believed that.

"Optimist," Hannah said.

Grace pulled her covers over her feet. "Cold toes all winter."

"Rag socks'll keep your feet warm," Hannah said. Moments later they said good night, and Hannah left Grace's room. Neither of them had heard Amelia come upstairs, or realized that she had stood outside of Grace's room and overheard their conversation.

21

Holding On

Amelia unfastened the amber necklace from about her neck and placed it on her dresser. Then, she pulled a long, flat rosewood box, a gift from Lance, from her top drawer. Inside the box a narrow velvet-lined space lay empty, awaiting the amber necklace. It was as if Lance had made a sketch of the interior of the box, for his gifts. He had to date presented her with a gold charm bracelet with zodiac signs dangling from it, magnificent sterling silver buckles for a pair of plain, black shoes she had bought because he liked them, pearl earrings, a pearl-crusted pin, a strand of onyx beads. All fit the sections. The box was nearly full. Two empty slots for rings remained. What kind of rings would he give her? Her heart skipped a beat.

Amelia slipped her feet into her old, worn, comfortable slippers. Every year she bought a new pair of bedroom slippers intending to give away, or throw away, the old ones. Every year she gave away the new ones. She found it impossible to discard her ragged, comfortable bedroom slippers, just as she found it impossible to discard a threadbare, comfortable chair she never used anymore and had stored in their attic. Impossible to dispose of a chipped, favorite teacup. Impossible to end her relationship with Lance, no matter that at times he made her anxious.

Although Amelia fussed and complained while he was away, Lance's reappearance inevitably galvanized her energy and set her quivering with excitement. Always she hoped, dreamed that he had missed her, and was ready to embrace her and their relationship totally. She loved Mike, treasured his friendship, but Lance needed her, she knew it, felt it. Mike and Lance hated one another, and Amelia hadn't a clue how to weave a bridge she could safely walk between them. Yet she could give up neither man.

Slowly, Amelia undressed and hung up her clothing. The warm flannel nightgown that Hannah had given her last Christmas hung on a knob inside her closet door. She inserted her arms into the long sleeves of the nightgown, then remembered the conversation she had overheard between Hannah and Grace. Yanking her arms out, Amelia threw the gown on the floor. Deciding not to shower or brush her teeth, she climbed into silk pajamas, slipped into bed, and lay there wide-eyed, her mind racing.

Once, long ago, speaking about her growing intimacy with Bob, Grace had said, "It seems to me that relationships follow a logical sequence of change. First you meet someone. If you're both attracted to one another, the dance of courtship begins, revelations take place, intimacy grows, and eventually comes commitment."

If this was true, then something was wrong in her relationship with Lance. They had met and been attracted, and Lance was decidedly romantic in his courting of her. But revelations were not forthcoming, and although being together was fun and exciting, no deepening intimacy occurred. Someone, Amelia decided, had hurt Lance terribly. She was determined to prove her love by her sweetness, consideration, cooperation, even if his demands on her time sometimes overwhelmed her. Once he knew and trusted her, he would relax and open himself to her. Surely he would not shower her with gifts, court her with such intensity if he did not care deeply, even if he never said, "I love you."

There was a positive side to the lack of intimacy, however. Lance never pressured her to go all the way sexually, until recently, and that was fine with Amelia. Famished as she was for the affection of a man, she instinctively resisted his increasingly intense sexual advances, and, suddenly, lying there in the dark, she knew why. With Lance it was one long courtship. By not revealing himself, he froze intimacy. It wasn't her scars, or her sixty-nine-year-old body that held her back. It was a lack of trust. If she trusted Lance, master of evocative compliments and enticing endearments, Amelia would, long ago, have placed her yearning body, all her senses, in his hands. And then, the other night, Lance had said, "I love the chase, but for how long? We're not teenagers." He's ready to go all the way, Amelia thought. She needed someone to talk to about all this, yet pride barred her from sharing her confusion with Grace. She certainly couldn't with Hannah or Mike.

At breakfast the following morning, Hannah said, "Mike called. He's coming over. Says he needs to talk to you."

"I haven't much time." Amelia looked anxiously out of the kitchen window. "Lance will be here any minute."

Hannah rested her hands on her hips. "Heaven, Amelia. You've been out with Lance every day and every night this week."

"Just to a movie, lunch, dinner, the theater." Amelia turned exasperated eyes to Hannah. "Grace understands. I wish you did."

"Understand what? You behave like a foolish schoolgirl the second Lance's car pulls into our drive."

Amelia's jaw tightened. Hannah was neither her mother nor a jail warden. She wouldn't let Hannah intimidate her. "He makes me feel young. It's flattering to be told you're charming, interesting. . . ." She looked at her hands. "Pretty. It's been a long time, and besides," she said, with a toss of the head, "I'm having fun." She looked Hannah up and down. "And where are you going?"

Bundled in a dark green down jacket and wearing wool pants and high boots, Hannah looked as if she were about to climb a mountain. "To meet with a woman named Karla Margolin," she replied.

"Dressed like that?"

"It's cold out there. Not going above thirty-five today."

"Who's Karla Margolin?"

"An environmentalist. Woman who's made the French Broad River her cause. She's working to clean up the river and turn the area around it into green space and parks."

Amelia snorted. "There's nothing down there but old factories and junkyards."

"Wrong. They've created a lovely park over on the west side of the river off of Amboy Road. It takes a person with fire in her soul to change things. Karla Margolin's got that fire."

153

"And I suppose you think you do."

The crunch of tires on the gravel driveway sent Hannah and Amelia to the window. "Ah, there's Wayne," Hannah said.

Amelia didn't care.

Hannah hurried to the door.

Wayne wore creased and dusty knee-high boots. Below the sleeves of his blue flannel shirt, winter underwear hugged his arms and wrists. A worn leather jacket hung loose about his shoulders. "I'm gonna get onto Anson's up high, through Lund's. Probably take me all day," he said.

"Grace packed you a lunch and cookies, lots of them, and drinks." Hannah handed him a brown paper bag.

Wayne took the bag she held out to him. "Appreciate that. I dropped Old Man at Miss Lurina's. They been seein' a lot of one another since the party over at the tearoom." He shrugged. "Ain't many of their generation left. Guess they talk about old times."

Hannah pulled a red knit hat over her hair and worked her hands into soft blue gloves. Her clothes were often mismatched. She lacked style in clothes. She knew that, and didn't care. "Bye, Amelia. See you later."

At that moment, Grace ambled down the stairs just as the phone rang. Lance would be late. Relief flooded Amelia. I can talk with Grace alone, she thought.

🙢

Sometimes crying, sometimes laughing, brows furrowed, eyes intense, Amelia shared with Grace her fears of losing Lance, and of losing Mike. "Mike's on his way over here. What shall I tell him?"

"What can you tell him? You've known Lance a few months, and look what's happened to your photography, and your relationships with your friends. Make time for your work and for Mike, I'd say."

"Mike hates Lance and vice versa. It was awful last night. Lance came to the gallery. I was to have dinner with Mike. What could I do? I couldn't ask Lance to join Mike and I, so I asked Mike to forgive me and went with Lance. I felt like such a heel, Grace. The anger and disappointment in Mike's eyes, and the resignation." She shivered. "That was the worst."

"What troubles me in all this," Grace said, "is you throwing away a friendship that's important to you. Lance can't be jealous of Mike. It makes me wonder who's next on Lance's list. Hannah, me?"

Amelia's head ached. Her stomach knotted. She rubbed her temples. Lance seemed so self-assured. Didn't anyone understand that he needed her?

"What did Lance think of the work you chose for the gallery?" Grace asked.

Amelia studied her fingernails. "He didn't really look at them." She hastened to add, "He was in a hurry. It was late."

"I see."

Quiet enveloped the room, only to be broken by the sound of heavy vehicles, rudely intrusive as they roared by on Cove Road. The house seemed to shiver. Amelia started. Somewhere a dog barked, and then another. Then the house grew still again. Amelia spoke. "Last night, when I came home, I heard you and Hannah talking about me and Lance."

"I'm sorry you heard. We worry about you, Amelia. What's going on with Lance seems to be a repeat of your relationship with Thomas."

Amelia bridled. "I don't care what either of you think. Lance excites me. He makes me feel like a real woman." Amelia's face seemed to crumble, showing the ravages of a sleepless night, shadows beneath her eyes, lips turned down, trembling. Her eyes felt gritty. She rubbed them with balled fists. "Hannah thinks I'm a silly fool."

"Hannah worries that Lance is manipulating you." Grace stood up, moved to the sink, and washed sticky jam she had smeared on toast off her hands.

Amelia's shoulders slumped. "Lance is like Thomas, and he's not. Thomas was all business, and not at all romantic. He worried all the time about appearances, how things looked, what other people thought of him, of me." Amelia's eyes suddenly lit up. "Lance doesn't give a hoot what anyone thinks. Oh, Grace, I feel so alive when Lance touches me, when we dance. Isn't it like that for you with Bob?"

"Yes, to some extent, but with a quieter passion."

"I can see the way you two are together. Don't I deserve that also?"

Another noisy vehicle rumbled down their road. Grace stifled the urge to peer out the window and stayed focused on Amelia. Drying her hands, she returned to the table. "Of course you do. Have you tried setting parameters with Lance, say you have two nights a week, or two days a week to yourself when he's in town?"

"I can't do that. He needs me." Amelia averted her eyes.

"I doubt that Lance needs anyone," Grace blurted. She cared deeply for Amelia and was increasingly disturbed by her unhappiness when Lance went away, and Amelia's willingness to forgive everything when he returned. Grace wondered what kind of hold the man had on her friend, and worried that Amelia could be so tunnel-visioned.

"What does he do when he's away?" Amelia's voice cracked; tears gathered behind her lower lids. A sad silence followed, before Amelia collected herself. Then she asked, "Tell me, what's it like to, you know, be with a man again. It's been so many years."

"You haven't gone to bed with him?"

Amelia wished she had never asked the question. She lowered her head into her hands. "Not yet." She lifted her chin. "But I'm going to."

Grace went to Amelia and put her arm about her. "Don't worry, Amelia. It'll come naturally. The feelings come back, and it just happens."

"You didn't worry about being older?"

"Of course I did. I was a mess thinking about it, but when it happened, it was the most natural thing in the world."

"You and Bob love one another," Amelia said.

"Would you go to bed with someone you didn't love or who you felt didn't love you?"

Amelia wrung her hands. "I don't know." No one spoke. Amelia walked to the blue woodstove. Embers, the remains of a fire, glowed. She added kindling. A flame shot up. "I'm cold," she said, "aren't you?"

Grace rubbed her arms rapidly with her hands. "Yes, I am, as a matter of fact. Thanks."

"Sometimes," Amelia confided in a low voice, "I think Lance loves me, sometimes not. He certainly excites me." Strands of hair hung about her face. Amelia brushed them back as she moved slowly to the table and leaned on it. "More tea, Grace?"

"That would be nice."

A car's tires stirred the gravel in the driveway. "Mike," Amelia said distractedly. "Talk to him while I run up and finish making up, will you, Grace?" Amelia headed for the stairs.

"Hey there," Grace said. "Where's the spring in your step, Mike?"

"I walk like I feel," Mike said. "I'm not someone who can put on an act."

True enough, starting early in his life, Mike had never been a closet gay, and life had blessed him with unconditional love from a family who recognized early on that he was gay and accepted him. Secure with whom he was, Mike was easygoing, creative, and helpful, a loyal friend. He fit right into the surrogate family the ladies had unwittingly put together. Grace believed that if any of them needed him, rain, snow, or shine, Mike would be there, and this, she knew, compounded Amelia's guilt.

"She'll be right down. Sit. Let me get you coffee. You like hazelnut, right?"

He nodded. His shoulder-length brown ponytail was combed back in a careless manner. Yanking off his jacket and gloves Mike stood holding them as if he were a stranger in the house. "Cold out there," he muttered.

"Hang your things in the hall, then come sit with me," Grace said.

He needed no further urging, and did as told. Mike had no permanent companion like her Roger had Charles, and Grace prayed that in his occasional affairs Mike was extra careful. Charles strayed from Roger once, only once, and had gotten HIV. That's all it took, one time. Mike looked terrible, dark under his eyes, his skin pale and dry. He was thinner. He loved Amelia as a sister, and Grace understood how much he depended on Amelia's companionship and friendship. Now it was being snatched away, and Mike was understandably hurt.

Bright as sunshine, smiling, wearing yellow, Amelia floated into the kitchen. Makeup almost hid the effects of sleeplessness. "Mike." She hugged him and kissed his cheek.

Mike beamed, then his eyes clouded. "Amelia . . ."

Grace set his coffee on the table, along with a plate of brownies. "I'll leave you two alone."

"Oh, Grace," Amelia said. "You don't have to go."

"Yes, please stay, Grace," Mike said. He fixed his hands snugly around the mug of coffee. "Amelia, I understand that you want someone who can give you more than I can, but many married people have business partners, and lives, and friends outside their marriages. There's no room for me in your life anymore."

Amelia wept softly. "I'm sorry, Mike. I do love you. You're the best friend in the world. There is room for you in my life."

He looked deep into her eyes. "Amelia, your work's suffering."

A chill sent rapid fingers flying across her arms and neck. Her work. Her beloved work. He was right. Rush, hustle, dash, that's how she spent her days when Lance was here, and when he was gone, scrambling to catch up with a million little things. "I'll work it out," Amelia said. "I'm going to start saying no to Lance."

The phone rang again; Amelia stiffened, then rose to answer it. "He's coming, Mike. I'll take care of it. I promise."

22

The Conservation Roller Coaster

As she drove to Asheville, Hannah reviewed what she had accomplished to date. Phone calls to the national office of the Nature Conservancy in Virginia led to referral to their North Carolina field office in Raleigh, who suggested she contact the North Carolina Department of Environmental and Natural Resources. They in turn directed her to the North Carolina Natural Heritage Program, where, they said, a biologist would explain the protocol for surveying land to identify endangered species. They did supply her with a list of active inventories of threatened sites, already priorities of the state. Days later no biologist had returned her call. A hopeless tangle of red tape and time, more time, probably, than she had, for just yesterday she had seen surveyors' vans on Cove Road, heading north. If Wayne found a ruin it could provide a stay of execution. Karla Margolin, Hannah anticipated, with her years of experience fighting to preserve the river, must have uncovered funding sources that might help Hannah.

She met Karla Margolin for lunch in a restaurant filled with people who leaned over their tables and spoke in controlled low voices. Karla was a forty-something woman with ash blond hair that came almost to her shoulders. Her eyes were brown, soft, and intelligent, her gaze direct and open. Hannah liked her instantly. "We began in 1987," Karla explained, "with a planning committee to study and create a plan of action for public uses for the French Broad River's waterfront.

There are," she said, "one hundred and seventeen miles of river running through four counties. It's a wonderful river, gentle in places with wide river valleys, narrow in others, rapids, some quite dangerous."

"Four counties. I didn't know that," Hannah said.

"It starts in Transylvania County near a town called Rosman and flows north through Brevard, Buncombe, and Madison Counties and into Tennessee. You get strong, at times dangerous, rapids in Madison County where you live, but in some places sections of the river have been used as a dump."

Hannah was embarrassed that she had never visited the river. She'd seen it of course at Biltmore Estate flowing wide and clean and gentle along a section of that property. She had seen it on various visits to the town of Marshall, the seat of government for Madison County. The river ran wide there and shallow with boulders visible at low tide. Grace had once suggested a picnic at Hot Springs further down the river, at a place where river-rafting trips began, but they had never done it.

"How are you funded, if I may ask?" Hannah said.

"A variety of sources. Unless the project's put together by the Nature Conservancy or some other state or national organization with clout, and they undertake to write grants and push papers, it takes multi-sources, local, private, government."

They fell silent when the waitress brought their salads. Karla smiled across the table at Hannah. "We do a great deal of fund-raising ourselves now. We own several of the buildings, the old cotton mill, and the warehouse studios where our offices are, and we rent space in both to artists and craftspeople."

"I've heard of events sponsored by River Link, river trips, cleanups, tours."

"We're active and busy," Karla said. "We offer monthly bus tours of the riverfront. We help prepare wildflower beds. We help monitor water quality, publish a quarterly newsletter called *Water Mark*. We work closely with many organizations planning fund-raising events: river races, parades, bridge parties, French Broad Cabaret."

"I'm impressed," Hannah said. "I've been to the park you built on the west side of the river. It's quiet and pleasant."

"We hope it'll serve as a model for a series of parks along the length of the French Broad." Karla's eyes flashed with enthusiasm. Hannah could tell that ten years had not dampened her passion for this huge undertaking.

"What's your dream for this project?" Hannah asked.

"A wonderful, vital waterfront, with restaurants, clubs, and other entertainment, development on hillsides overlooking River Road, greenways, bike and walking paths, water activities, trips on the river. Chicken Hill," Karla said. She stopped to sip her iced coffee. "It's the hill behind the old cotton mill. Four builders have bought it with plans for mixed housing, small and large homes, apartments, restoration of what's there in some cases."

They finished eating and sat chatting for a time. The restaurant emptied. A young waitress apologized for running a carpet sweeper. Finally, Hannah told Karla about Loring Valley, her concerns about flooding and mudslides, and about the developers' interest in Cove Road, and that Jake Anson was determined to sell his land. "I know he has a right to do what he chooses with his land, but development will destroy the quality of life on Cove Road for the rest of us."

"It's hard to locate just the right source of funds for that sort of thing," Karla said. "It takes a great deal of time."

"Which I haven't much of." Hannah rubbed her forehead and sighed. "I've contacted the Carolina Mountain Land Conservancy. They work with cooperative landowners. The Land Trust Alliance promotes *voluntary* land conservation. The Trust for Public Lands has a wonderful mission statement: protect land for the well-being of people, for recreation and spiritual nourishment. But, again, it works with community groups, and I haven't got one, or willing landowners, or government agencies that exhibit interest.

"On the Net I found the National Religious Partnership for the Environment. They're concerned with advocacy, and with teaching the care of all creation. It made for interesting reading. Catholic Bishops in the Pacific Northwest sending a pastoral letter advocating for the Columbia River, "Redwood Rabbis" working to protect the redwoods, evangelical Christians lobbying Newt Gingrich against the rollback of the Endangered Species Act and citing God's covenant with all living creatures. Turns out they were quite instrumental in saving that piece of legislation."

With a heavy heart, Hannah drove back to Covington. Her project differed so from River Link, which was a vital community project. North Carolina abounded with national forests, state forests, and parks making Anson's land redundant to potential funders.

Then she thought of the Maxwells and began to wonder if perhaps she could enlist their interest, their help. They were reputed to be the wealthiest landowners on Cove Road. Huge trucks purveyed milk to processing plants from Maxwell's Dairy Farm three days a week. Several times a month, the fat round rumps of cows crowded into wood-slatted trucks were shipped off to the stockyard. But the most lucrative business the Maxwells operated, according to Harold, was a stud farm, and there were days, when the wind was right, that she, and Amelia, and Grace could hear the calls and laughter coming from the fenced pasture used for this purpose behind the barn. George Maxwell, known as Max, had given Amelia a ride home after her accident in the fog. Amelia said he was pleasant and seemed concerned about her. It was time to visit the Maxwells, maybe they could at least point a direction.

23

Bella Maxwell

Walking briskly, Hannah crossed Cove Road, passed between open iron gates, and proceeded up the winding drive to the Maxwells' beautifully maintained two-story farmhouse. She climbed the steps to the front porch, which were built with six-inch risers, making them easy to ascend. Spanning the entire front of the first floor and wrapping one side was a wide porch furnished with rocking chairs, tables, and huge clay pots, bare now of greenery. In summer she had seen red geraniums spilling from them. Above, off the second floor, a matching roofed porch ran the length of the house.

A section of the wraparound first-floor porch was glassed in, and one end had been curtained in green-and-white-striped broadcloth. There was plenty of room for the long pine table, painted apple green, and eight matching chairs that occupied the center. A dark green hutch trimmed in mustard yellow flowers, with open shelves on top and drawers below, stood against the white clapboard wall. It housed a collection of crockery plates and platters, mugs, and tumblers.

Hannah let the front doorbell chime and chime again before the door was opened by a stout, olive-skinned woman with dark springy hair. "Missy no home," she said in broken English.

Not expecting a housekeeper, Hannah was surprised. The Maxwells obviously exceeded their neighbors financially. Perhaps that was why there was such a skinning up of noses and all the snide comments whenever their name was mentioned. They seemed alien, strange folk to the others on Cove Road. Hannah wondered who did the shunning. Only Zachary had attended that first meeting at the church hall, and she had assumed he represented his family.

"Mr. Maxwell, then," Hannah said.

The woman shook her head and shrugged. "Mister no at home."

Beyond and above the solid body of the little woman, a highly polished railing and stairs curved up to the second floor landing. "Thank you." Hannah turned from the door.

It was another of those unexpectedly warm December days. A slight breeze caused a rocker close by to stir slightly, inviting Hannah to sit. She did. Across Cove Road their farmhouse looked small but cheerful, with its bright yellow windows and front door. Next May, red roses would explode in color, drawing the admiration of everyone on Cove Road.

It was so peaceful that Hannah had no idea how long she sat before the blue truck turned into the drive. When it drew up to the front steps to discharge its passenger, a slim-hipped, long-legged woman with graying hair waved off her husband's help as she eased slowly from the cab. Hannah saw that the truck bed was piled high with bales of hay. "Max" Maxwell tipped his baseball cap at her and mouthed "Howdy," then shifted into gear and drove toward the first barn. Hannah stood and waited, uncertain what to do, as Bella Maxwell grasped the railing and hesitantly, one uncertain, painstakingly slow step at a time, climbed to the porch. She stood grasping the railing with both hands and took long, uneven breaths. She isn't well, Hannah thought.

Bella Maxwell shuffled haltingly toward Hannah, smiling. "Are you Amelia?" she asked, as she folded like a fan into a rocking chair. She was pretty and as frail as one of Amelia's treasured fans.

"I'm Hannah. Hannah Parrish."

"How nice to meet you." The lightness of her Southern accent indicated that she was not from these parts, or that she had lived, or been educated, elsewhere, and Hannah wondered that they could have lived across from one another for a year and a half and never met, and that no one, not even Brenda Tate, had told them anything of consequence about the Maxwells, other than that they had money and were not disposed to welcome visitors. Bella, however, seemed genuinely glad to see her.

"You okay, Bella darlin'?" A loud, blustering voice came from the end of the porch where it curved to wrap the house. Maxwell rounded the corner. He wore overalls and mud-caked boots with thick soles. He stood a moment, hands in his pockets, surveying the two women through worried, dark eyes set firmly above thick pouches in his grave, weathered face. Then he clomped over to where they sat.

"I'm fine, Max, dear, just fine." Hannah noticed then that Bella's hand, the hand she extended to her husband, the hand he clasped in both his big, thick hands, trembled, a fine slight tremor, as did her other hand and her head.

"Next time we have a doctor's appointment, let me know ahead. That dern old truck's the last thing you oughta be ridin' in."

"You just go on back to your barn. I know you're busy, honey. Hannah from across the road's come to visit. She'll see me inside, won't you, Hannah?" She turned to Hannah, who nodded. Bella's eyes were golden brown, and shot through with resignation. Her oval face was marred by sprays of spiderweb lines, and her sweet smile gave way to signs of discomfort. Hannah's heart went out to her.

"I'll do whatever you need me to do," Hannah said.

They sat awhile, rocked gently, and did not speak. Cars rolled past on Cove Road. Molly Lund, Frank Craine, Ted Lund, Brenda Tate. Grace's car turned into the ladies' driveway and moments later Grace emerged, her arms filled with packages.

"Which one of the ladies is that?" Bella Maxwell asked.

"That's Grace."

"I hear she's a fine cook, well known for her cookies and some exotic dish she makes with meat and prunes." Bella said it simply, seeming not to need a response from Hannah. Silence closed about them again, and when she spoke it was to say, "My name is Arabella. Max prefers Bella."

Hannah's head spun with questions. Where are you from? With what are you ill? Why are you so isolated from the other residents of Cove Road? She remained silent, allowing the gentle, sad-faced woman to decide when they would talk and what about. Wisps of white clouds drifted past. One moment the air seemed warm, then breezes cooled it, and then it died down and grew warm again. Across the street, Grace slammed the front door and returned to the car for yet another package.

Brown, curled oak leaves chased one another along the floor of the porch, making a rattling sound. "I hate it when winter comes. For me in December the world goes bleak," Bella said in almost a whisper. She shuddered slightly. "I guess I should go in, but it's so nice sitting here visiting with you."

Hannah was surprised as they had hardly spoken, and yet Bella considered that they were visiting. Perhaps she had little or no company. In their year and more in Covington, they had never seen this woman in her yard, or out walking, or sitting on this porch, or driving a car. A pang of guilt struck Hannah. They had simply listened to others, and had never paid a call on their closest neighbor.

"I'd like to say, 'I'm fine, Hannah,' and that I'll manage to navigate into the house by myself. But the truth is, I've been sittin' here hopin' and prayin' for the energy to pry myself from this rocker. Will you help me?"

"Certainly," Hannah said, glad for something to do.

"To get me up, you need to stand in front of me, then bend over and hook your arms under my arms and pull." Her voice had a sing-song quality. "Can you do it? It won't hurt your back will it? Are you all right? You did have surgery on, what was it, your hip, last year?"

"Hip," Hannah said, wondering how Bella knew this. The woman was light, wispy and easy to lift. She can't weigh a hundred pounds, Hannah thought. Moments later, supported by Hannah, Bella shambled to the door and into the house.

"Ah, Anna, my dear." Bella spoke to the stout, dark-haired woman who hurried toward them, her face filled with worry. "This is Miss Hannah from across the road. She's going to help me to my room."

"I take Missy Bella," Anna said, reaching out, but Hannah shook her head. "Just tell me where."

"Just a follow me, Miss Hannah," Anna said.

Bella's pale skin was cool, thin, and dry, papery to the touch. Supporting her, Hannah moved tentatively across the foyer, following Anna, who kept turning, Hannah was sure, to make certain that Bella was all right. She led the way into what must have been the original dining room of the big house. A high tray ceiling rose above a fine old mahogany bed. A wall of windows looked out onto the porch and across Cove Road to their farmhouse and the hills behind. Faces east. She cannot see the spectacular sunsets here, Hannah thought. A pity. And Hannah wondered if she would ever sit with Amelia and Grace on their porch again without thinking of this woman lying in her mahogany bed, perhaps watching them?

166

Hannah eased Bella onto the bed. With one deft hand, Anna fluffed pillows, and with the other, mounded them to support Bella's back. Gently, Anna lifted Bella's legs and slipped additional pillows under her knees. "She make more comfortable like this," Anna said. "I bring soup, now, yes?"

"Yes. Thank you, Anna," Bella said. "Would you like fresh home-made vegetable soup?" she asked Hannah. "I prefer chicken soup, but this is what Anna does best. It's quite good."

"No, thanks." Hannah had forgotten completely what she came to the Maxwells' home for. In the face of whatever affliction Bella had, it didn't matter.

Bella sighed, and reached for Hannah's hand. Hannah grasped it in both of hers and felt the tremble of the soft palm and the fine, thin bones of her fingers. "I heard you're trying to stop Anson from selling out. He's a fool." She shook her head. The muscles of her neck and throat seemed to possess a life of their own, for they continued to quiver, when Hannah knew that Bella wanted them to stop. "Thank you, Hannah Parrish, for helping me. Will you come again? Bring the others?"

"I'll come, and I'll bring the others," Hannah replied. "I hope you feel better." Then she turned and walked quickly through the foyer and let herself onto the porch. She grasped the post at the top of the steps. The farmhouse across the road, and the women who lived there with her, had never seemed as precious.

24

Wishing Will Make It So

Grace could not get Tyler out of her mind. At Hannah's lunch he had seemed to grasp the idea that he could change the course of his father's and Emily's lives. Yet, from what Bob told her, Emily had nonetheless returned to Florida with no intention of returning.

With Russell's permission, Grace picked Tyler up after school one day. She was able to get away because, after many discussions about it, they had decided to hire help at the tearoom. The young woman, a college student named Sybil, seemed to be getting the hang of things, though she would never be clean or neat enough to satisfy Grace. Still, having her there gave Grace more flexibility.

Tyler raced down the school steps beaming. "Granny Grace." He scrambled into the car and hugged her tight before fastening his seat belt. "It's good you came for me. Dad doesn't talk anymore, he grunts or snarls."

"Your father's unhappy, Tyler, and I think you know why."

He looked sheepishly at her. "I drove Emily away."

They were on the highway now, heading south toward Weaverville. "I'm afraid you did. How do you feel about that?"

His eyes misted. "Not so good."

"Do you want to do something about it?"

He shook his head. "Can't."

"Why?"

"I wished her gone."

A huge truck came up beside them. Grace clutched the wheel and slowed down. The truck zoomed past with a roar. Grace relaxed. "You what?"

"I wished Emily would go away."

Somehow, Grace was not surprised, and they were silent until they reached the Burger King in Weaverville. "You want to go in or eat in the car?" Grace asked.

"Eat in the car."

They ordered, then Grace parked the car in a spot that faced the mountains in the parking lot of the Weaverville Shopping Plaza. One thing she loved about the area was that almost anywhere you went, you could see mountains.

"All right," Grace said when they had almost finished their burgers. "What's this business about wishing Emily gone?"

Tyler blushed. "Since Dad met Emily, every time I saw a falling star, or an eyelash of mine came out and I blew it away, or I broke a wishbone, I wished that Emily would go back to Florida."

Waiting for more, she handed him another napkin, and after wiping his hands he looked earnestly at Grace. "You know, Granny Grace, wishes are real. They fly away to heaven and get written in a book, and when you send enough wishes about something, it happens."

"Who told you that?"

He shrugged. "Can't remember, but wishes came true in *Pinocchio*."

"You wanted Emily gone so badly, you made this wish again and again?"

"I did, Granny Grace, and now it's too late. I can't take it back."

Grace hugged him to her. She could feel his ribs. The boy had gotten thinner. "What happened to that appetite of yours, Tyler?"

"It's gone too."

"Your dad not feeding you?"

"It's not Dad. He tries to cook. He's not good at it. Mom was a great cook, and Grandpa cooked before he started moving his things over to his new apartment. But, it's not the food. I'm just not hungry."

Grace considered this. She offered a silent prayer for wisdom, for insight and the right words to help Tyler sort out what must surely be a mass of mixed emotions. "So, we have a problem here. I wonder what would happen if you reversed your wish, changed it to wishing that Emily would return, that she and your dad would be reunited? What do you think?"

"I never thought of that."

"Well, you think about it." She placed an arm about him. He unfastened his seat belt and snuggled against her. "I don't believe you really hate Emily, Tyler, love." When he did not argue, she continued. "You loved your mommy so very much, how could you like, maybe even love, someone else?"

He began to cry. "I want Mommy back."

"I know you do. I wanted my husband, Ted, back after he died, and yet, in time, I met your grandpa. If I hadn't accepted that Ted was gone, how could I love your grandpa?"

"So, you forgot about your husband, Ted?"

"No. I didn't forget. I think of him often and with love, but he's not in this world to talk to me, to comfort me, or be my friend, and I had to accept that, and go on with my life. Ted would want me to."

"You think my mommy wants me to . . . to like . . . someone else?"

She nodded. "When we truly love someone, we want the best for them. Your mommy loved you with her whole heart and soul. Yes, I think she would want you to go on with your life, to care for other people, even someone your dad cares for."

"You think Dad still loves Mommy?"

"I do. I'm sure he'll love and remember her all his life. But just like all of us do, you, me, Grandpa, he needs people he can touch and talk to, don't you think?"

Tyler turned a tear-stained, smiling face to Grace. "You think I can wish Emily back?"

"I most certainly do." She looked down at his hand. "See, there's an eyelash of yours. You can start right now."

Tyler lowered the window, lifted his hand, and blew hard. The lash disappeared into the air. "I did it."

Grace laughed lightly. "Another five or six wishes and you'll have wished Emily right back into yours and your dad's life."

Grace would have been proud of Tyler had she been at their home that evening when the phone rang. Russell dashed to get it, and Tyler watched his face change, soften, his eyes glow. Russell took the portable and walked from the room.

Emily, Tyler thought. He followed his dad into the kitchen. "Is it Emily, Dad?"

Russell glared at Tyler, then he nodded and his look softened a bit.

"Dad, please, can I talk to her?"

Russell placed his hand over the mouthpiece. "Why?"

"I want to tell her I'm sorry."

Russell stared at him, and slowly he lowered his hand and said to Emily, "Tyler wants to speak to you." Handing Tyler the portable, Russell sat heavily in a chair he pulled from the table.

"Hi, Emily," Tyler said. "How you doing?" He looked anxiously at his father and wished he had talked to Granny Grace about this. She would have told him exactly what to say, and they could have put it on a piece of paper. "I'm fine. School's good."

"I thought you were going to apologize," Russell whispered.

Tyler covered the phone with his hand. "I am, Dad. I am. I'm looking for the right words." Then he spoke into the phone. "Emily, I'd like it if you came home." She must have asked what home he meant, for he replied, "This one, here, with us."

Then Tyler handed his father the phone and dashed from the room.

25

Mike's Consternation

Hannah had been engrossed in transplanting in the greenhouse, and she did not see Mike's car parked behind Grace's in their drive until she decided she'd had enough on her feet for one day and came into the kitchen. Grace sat at the kitchen table. Mike was there and he paced, every now and then stopping to right a can of beans or corn that had spilled from a tipped-over brown paper bag on the counter near the sink. Hannah had the feeling he had helped Grace carry in the groceries and was somehow responsible for the tipped bag. For a few moments, Hannah stood in the doorway looking from one of them to the other, unnoticed by both.

"We were fine for two days," Mike said. "Amelia actually shot film. She seemed happy, too." From a plate on the table Mike took a cookie, then rounded the table to the sink and filled a glass with water. After taking a sip he set the glass on the counter so hard some of the water spilled, wetting the paper bag. He grabbed a paper towel to blot up the spill. "When one person consumes another person's life so they have no time for themselves, or old friends, or other interests, or work, it cannot be healthy."

"No," said Hannah, walking into the room, "it's not healthy."

"Hannah, how are you?" He turned to her. "You understand what I'm saying? Amelia's so talented. I feel so frustrated and helpless."

Hannah strode over to him and grasped his shoulders firmly. "Mike. Come. Take a seat." She maneuvered him to a chair. "We all dislike this Lance, but he's not doing this alone. Amelia makes choices. She goes along."

"I think she's afraid if she opposes him, she'll lose him," Grace said.

"But he's so bad for her," Mike said. "Doesn't she see what he's doing?"

"Maybe she does, some of the time," Grace said. "When you're in love, or think you're in love, you get a little crazy."

"A lot crazy," Hannah said. She began to put the canned goods in the cabinet over the counter. "Amelia can be quite vain. Even if she sees what's happening, her pride may be preventing her from doing anything about it."

Mike reached for another cookie. "Amelia's regressed."

Grace looked at him sharply. "How has she regressed?"

"It's like all the confidence she developed over the past year has faded."

Hannah's eyebrows shot up. "True enough. Amelia's in the process of giving herself over to this Lance. Never had much respect for women who lose themselves in a man, who let him decide how she will live, by what rules, when to do what, and with whom."

"Stop!" Grace hit the table with the flat of her palm. "It's Amelia we're talking about, not any woman. We know she's vain and proud and all that, and we love her anyhow. I'm worried about her. Like you, Mike, I'm frustrated."

"Point well taken," Hannah said. "You're right, of course. What Amelia's got is like a sickness. Hopefully, her inner strength will make her able to persevere. This Lance thing will run its course, and hopefully she won't be too badly hurt."

Mike looked at them shyly. "I ran off with a pretty face when I was eighteen, wouldn't go to college. My folks took the attitude that I'd come to my senses. I did. But I think one has more resilience when one's young. I just hope Amelia comes out of this unscathed."

"We're talking as if Amelia's headed for doomsday. Aren't we being a bit melodramatic?"

Mike helped himself to another cookie. "Maybe, Grace. But it feels as if Amelia's soul's in danger from the Prince of Evil."

"I bet on Amelia," Grace said. "She's going to come out of this and be fine."

"With or without Lance?" Hannah asked.

"Hopefully without," Grace said. "Or if he's still around, it'll be with a new set of rules. Maybe Amelia's right, and he's been deeply hurt and is needy. If he starts trusting her, he may open up and be a different person."

"Optimist." Hannah turned to Mike. "Planning to eat yourself to death? I'm surprised you don't have diabetes, all the sweets you eat." Hannah patted his shoulder.

He withdrew his outstretched hand from the plate of cookies. "Didn't even realize I was devouring so many." He shook his head. "Meanwhile, I have a dilemma. We advertised a workshop. Twelve people signed up for our Florida Everglades trip in January, and now Amelia tells me to find someone else to help lead the group." He ran his fingers through his hair, dislocating his ponytail.

"Mike. Listen to me. Wait this out," Grace said slowly, emphasizing each word.

"Wait it out?" Mike's voice rose octaves above its normal range. His eyes widened in dismay.

"I think Lance will blow it way before January."

"Grace is right, Mike. Wait it out," Hannah said firmly. "And while you're waiting find someone else to help lead that January workshop. Life does go on, with or without Amelia."

"You're such good friends." Mike reached for Grace's hand, and then Hannah's, and looked hopefully from one to the other. "You think Amelia will see the light, so to speak?"

They nodded.

"When?"

Hannah shrugged. "Eventually, she'll see Lance as the self-serving bounder and controller we think he is. Amelia may be capricious, but she's never deliberately cruel. Be patient."

He lifted his shoulders and raised his hands. "What else can I do? Do you know she never came to her own show last Wednesday?"

They were surprised.

"We sold half of what we usually do. It's Amelia they want. They adore her charm and her flair. Everyone wants to talk to her. They like it when she signs a work for them." He scowled. "Wait it out. How?"

"Stay busy," Grace said. "Don't fight with her about Lance."

Mike nodded. He took another cookie. "Comfort food," he muttered.

"You have the recipe. I framed it for you last Christmas, remember?"

"Of course, and I make cookies, but these days . . ." He wrung his hands. "I'm not myself. Last batch I made burned up in the oven." He looked exhausted.

"Mike." Grace squeezed his shoulder. "Don't drive all the way back to Fairview now. Go on upstairs and rest. There's a small TV and some nice travel books in the guest room."

"Take a shower if you want, or a bath," Hannah said. "There's a clean terry robe behind the bathroom door. Use it."

A wisp of a smile tugged at Mike's mouth. He sighed. "I love you both. You've saved my life. I'll take you up on your kind offer."

They waited as Mike mounted the stairs until they heard the guest room door close lightly. Then Grace said, "Whew! This thing with Amelia's getting worse."

"Grace, I went across the road. I met Bella Maxwell. She's not a well woman," Hannah said. "Is it warm enough do you think to sit out on the porch?"

"With jackets, I think. Let's give it a try."

"I've got a lot to tell you."

Minutes later they were on the porch and Hannah told Grace, first, why she went to the Maxwells, then about the wraparound porch and its furnishings, then her surprise about Anna, and heartwrenching visit with Bella Maxwell. "She knew about my hip surgery, that you're a great cook, she even knew about your meatballs and prunes. Someone's keeping her informed. Go with me to visit her?"

"Certainly. Is it Parkinson's, Hannah?"

"Perhaps, or something like it. It's odd," Hannah said, suddenly remembering. "I was about to leave when out of the blue Bella said that Anson was a fool for selling. Swear, I never mentioned the man's name."

"Odd," Grace said.

"I'll never bring that subject up to them," Hannah said. "They've got enough to worry about." Then Hannah told Grace about her lunch with Karla Margolin. "I like her. She knows her stuff," she said.

Grace had news of her own for Hannah. She had found Old Man and Lurina seated side by side on the old springy couch, going through picture albums. "He brought his pictures, and she must have dug out at least seven of her albums. Bet it took them hours to get around to them all. I heard a bit of it: every snapshot led to a long discussion about what happened to this person, that person, who they married, when they died, if they were dead. Most are. Quite a pair, those two," Grace said. "Maybe they'll get hitched, as Tyler would say."

"Well, that's a dream. Who gets married at their age?" Hannah laughed. How free and easy this friendship with Grace is, Hannah thought. Three people living together can be difficult. We've managed pretty well, but two is just easier.

26

A Time for Planting Daffodils

Mercurial and unpredictable, weather in the Blue Ridge Mountains of North Carolina often defied the best efforts of local TV weathermen. A forecast of snow might liquefy to rain, and conversely, a mild prediction often turned dark with hoary skies. December, this year, fluctuated from lows in the forties to highs in the sixties and even the seventies. Today was in the sixties, clear and sunny as Grace and Hannah walked across the road to Bella Maxwell's home.

Anna served lunch on the screened porch. They ate on yellow plates set on purple place mats on a green table. "Anna loves bright colors," Bella said. "And why not? They liven things up." She leaned heavily on Hannah's arm as they moved slowly down the length of the porch.

Anna had prepared chicken and rice, Spanish-style. The rice was golden, with tiny pieces of black olives and bits of red pimento, but was not too spicy. "You take more," Anna urged Grace. "You like, I give recipe." She waved her hand toward the kitchen. "Chicken come from back of house. Jose, he chop heads. I cook." The image was not appealing, but Anna stood there proud as a queen. The women assured her that lunch was delicious, and it was.

"I've seen you working in your yard, Hannah. Do you think it's too late to plant daffodil bulbs?" Bella asked. "Zachary brought me a bag of fifty. He says they're early bloomers." Her voice trailed. "Early bloomers, March, I hope."

"Tell us where you want them. Grace and I'll help you plant them."

"Would you do that?" She brought both hands together as if to clap them, then squeezed them as if in prayer.

"Of course."

"That would be heaven," Bella said. "Of all the things I've had to give up, I miss gardening the most, and my art. I paint, you know, watercolors."

"How wonderful. I'd love to see your work," Grace said.

"Upstairs, in my studio. I don't go upstairs anymore." Tears filled her amber eyes.

"No problem," Hannah said. "I'll carry you up the steps."

"But your hip?"

"That's why I had surgery. Fitter now than before."

Grace worried about Hannah's bravado, but then Bella seemed light as a summer breeze.

After a time, Anna cleared the table, and Bella said, "Anna, could you find a nice thick blanket and spread it on the ground under that tree?" She pointed to a spot about fifty feet from the porch. "Then, I could see them from my bed when they bloom."

Anna looked at her blankly.

"The ladies are going to help me plant the bulbs Zachary brought."

"You no can walk there, Missy Bella."

"We'll get her over there," Hannah said, and a smile suffused Anna's broad face.

"What first?" Hannah asked Bella. "Planting bulbs, or see the paintings?"

"Bulbs. Anna, please bring the bulbs, and ask Jose for that tool he uses to dig holes for planting bulbs, and oh yes, fertilizer, a jar of fertilizer, the one where the numbers are the same, ten-ten-ten, you know what I mean."

Anna nodded and hurried away. A door slammed shut. "She's not good at closing doors gently," Bella said. She stood shakily, and Hannah slipped her arm about her waist, and they began their slow pilgrimage to the steps. Bella spoke of Anna and how the woman had come to work for them. "She came with her husband, Jose, Max's foreman, from Ecuador, and after she spent three months of walking about the place mumbling to herself in Spanish, Jose begged Max to hire her inside the house, said she was a good cook. She was driving

Jose crazy. Not enough to do. And what a boon she's been, especially since I became ill. She's an angel in disguise."

Grace and Hannah wafted Bella down the steps and across the lawn to where Anna had spread a thick blanket. Gently, they set the frail woman down beneath the sycamore tree. "They'll bloom here, won't they?" Bella looked worried.

"They'll bloom. Long before the leaves of this tree come on," Hannah said.

"Good." Bella folded her hands in her lap.

A door slammed. Anna came toward them carrying a stack of thick pillows. These she propped behind and about Bella. Satisfied, Anna marched away and moments later a door slammed again, and then slammed again, as Anna returned with all that Bella had asked for.

Hannah bored six-inch holes. Grace opened the bag and handed the bulbs to Bella, who leaned forward to drop them into the holes. When her arm could stretch no further, Grace took over, helping Hannah to fertilize and press the earth firmly above them.

"They'll be magnificent, I know it," Bella whispered. Her eyes glowed soft and gentle. "Thank you. You've gifted me with a most joyful day. It's like a ceremony for me."

Grace wondered if Bella had spotted them that moonlit night last fall, when they paraded to the rear of the farmhouse carrying a box, a time capsule filled with remembrances of their lives. With great ceremony, they had buried it in their backyard.

Bella extended both her hands to them. For many moments they sat silent, until a bedeviling wind chilled their faces and arms. The sun vanished behind a cloud. Almost simultaneously, Bella's face clouded and she looked exhausted.

"Let's go in," Grace said.

"You'll come again?"

"Certainly, and next time we'd love to see your paintings."

Bella smoothed her slacks. She smiled, a soft, sweet smile, nodded, and lifted her arms to Hannah.

27

Art, and Life's Passages

Hannah visited the *Citizen Times Newspaper* in Asheville and managed to interest a young reporter in doing a story on Loring Valley. Her tour of Loring Valley stressed the environmental damage done there. Then Hannah realized they could look at but could not enter Anson's land, nor could she really show it to anyone else who might support her cause, or poke around on it to search for an endangered species of bird or animal.

The reporter wrote about Loring Valley, then went on to tell about the Masterson park-in-waiting, all four hundred acres of it, and questioned the need for preserving another large tract of land in Covington. Bitterly disappointed, Hannah cried when she read his article.

Time was running out. Wayne had stumbled upon several dilapidated wooden buildings, a shed, a still for making corn liquor, unused for years, but no stone or brick chimney or foundation suggesting that it was of historic value or could be dated to over one hundred years. He would, he promised, sneak onto the land again on Wednesday, when he brought Old Man to visit Miss Lurina. There was a twinkle in his eye at the mention of his grandfather and Miss Lurina, but Hannah's mind was fastened on other matters, and she let it pass.

"We need to visit Bella," Grace said several days later. "I saw an ambulance drive in there earlier."

"An ambulance?"

"It seemed to be delivering something and went off without a passenger."

Goose bumps raised on Hannah's arms. "Let's go now. Could use a break from worrying about Anson's land. That biologist in Raleigh finally called. He has to have permission from the owner to survey for endangered species. I suggested he sneak on, like Wayne does. He said they don't do business that way."

Carefully, Hannah lifted Bella from her bed, and moments later she and Grace were following Anna, all aflutter and anxious about her patient, up the stairs and down a long hall to a large room with north-facing windows and pale blue walls hung with framed watercolors. Bella melted into the oversized chair in the corner and watched with anxious eyes as Grace and Hannah made their way around her private art gallery.

Bella painted landscapes. There were paintings of a stream bordered by daylilies. Another of children wading in a winter river, their faces screwed tight as icy cold water whirled about their ankles. One of a river at flood stage. There were scenes of hillsides with grazing cows and windmills. A copper sunset played off mountaintops. Grace and Hannah each stopped when they saw that Bella had painted their farmhouse, not once, but three times. The woman with the wide straw hat kneeling below the porch planting flowers could only be Hannah. Behind her, purple clematis twined about porch railings. In another, three women sat in rocking chairs on a porch, their porch, and in yet a third painting someone, Amelia, crouched near their stream with her camera held to her eye. In the manner of the impressionists, the lines and form of the house and of the great oak were carefully blurred.

"You did these last year?" Hannah asked.

A faint yes from deep in the chair.

"They're wonderful," Grace said.

"You were sad when you did them?" Hannah asked.

"Lonely, and yes, sad." Bella raised a thin arm. "You don't like them?"

"I like them very much."

"Look, over there."

Neither of them had seen the painting she was pointing to until this moment. More intense in color, the brushstrokes were bolder than any of the others. It took several moments before Hannah realized she was looking at Anson's old farmhouse and land. Tinged gold by sunset, the hills behind the house swooped and soared in a great amphitheater. Light smeared the rusty roof of his house copper.

"Have you noticed how the sunset colors Jake Anson's land?" Bella asked. "I tried for years to paint it, but never could get it right. Did I get it this time, do you think?" She turned her face away. "I may never have another chance to paint it."

"It's more than right. It's perfect," Grace said.

Hannah studied the painting. Beautiful land threatened by development. "I'm trying to create a coalition to find funding so we can save it from development."

"I know you are, and every night I pray that you can do that. Zachary told me how splendid you were, stirred everyone up at the church meeting. I would have liked to have been there." Her voice was small and tired.

Hannah wondered why such lovely works of art were shuttered away, rather than being exhibited. She did not ask. A pang of regret, the sense of something special found and lost, saddened Hannah. If only she had visited Bella sooner.

"Would you like to come over for tea some afternoon? We'd have to have it in the living room. I'll come get you, or Max could bring you."

Bella smiled. "How I would like that."

When Anna opened the door the following afternoon, she stood there twisting the edge of her apron and shaking her head. Her eyes were red from crying. "Missy Bella, she no can get out of the bed."

"Did we tire her excessively? Can I go in? I won't stay long."

Anna wrung her hands. "Missy Bella sleeping. Ambulance come early, bring oxygen. After you go, doctor come. He give big needle."

"What's wrong with Miss Bella?" Hannah asked.

Anna shrugged and continued to block the doorway. "You ask Mister Maxwell. He in barn."

"Thanks, Anna."

Hannah moved around to the window of Bella's bedroom and leaned into the glass with both hands, shading her face in an effort to see inside. The shades were down. No sound issued from the room. She circled the house to the barn. Every building, every shed, was freshly painted, every machine and tool sparkled clean, every animal stall freshened with a thick layer of straw. George Maxwell was nowhere to be seen. Hannah walked down their drive and returned home.

The next time she and Grace would see Bella would be at her funeral in the little church on Cove Road, with Arabella Maxwell laid out on blue satin in a burnished copper coffin, as pale and sweet-faced as in life.

The church was less than half full. Hannah recognized several of the Herrill boys sitting close about Zachary, and their parents, Charlie and Velma. Jose and Anna and several other Spanish-looking people sat in the row behind Zachary. The Lunds and Tates were there, and a dozen other people that neither she nor Grace recognized. Hannah's soul pinched with regret for not having known Bella sooner. Silently, tears inched along the ridges of Hannah's face. Next to her, Grace wept.

George Maxwell gave the eulogy for his wife. He stood tall in a dark gray suit and tie and quoted from, he said, Madame De Stael: "We understand death for the first time when he puts his hand upon one whom we love." He spoke of Bella's gentleness, told how she had abandoned a budding career in art to marry him, praised her devotion to himself and their son, spoke of the gardens she tended, the poetry she wrote. "She was an introvert," he said, almost apologetically.

Pastor Johnson spoke and assured the assembled that Arabella Maxwell rested in God's bosom and would be waiting for her husband and son in heaven.

Later, in the subdued gathering in the church hall, Maxwell approached Hannah. "Thanks for comin', Hannah Parrish. Bella never stopped talkin' about you. Liked you right well."

"I, too, liked her a great deal." Hannah had to know. "Mr. Maxwell, I must ask, what did she pass away from?"

"Max, my friends call me Max."

Hannah nodded.

"Damn doctors never made a clear diagnosis, looked like Parkinson's but wasn't. Some rare, incurable thing I can't pronounce. A long ailin', then downhill fast." His voice trembled.

"I'm so very sorry." A red-faced, swollen-eyed Zachary approached them. Maxwell put his arm about his son. Someone else stopped to talk to them. Hannah slipped her arm through Grace's, and they stepped into the cold December day and turned away from home and north toward Anson's land.

Two surveyors' vehicles were parked in the driveway of the derelict farmhouse. Rust had clearly established itself as the major color on the old tin roof. Hannah imagined it bathed in golden light, the way it looked in Bella's painting. Silently, the women studied the horseshoe of rolling land rising to rounded hills, then to higher mountains. Hannah thought of a baseball stadium, rows of seats, up and up and up, and the seats became houses and condos. Her throat constricted. Grace tugged at her arm. "We'd best be going."

Two men stepped from the farmhouse and headed for one of the vans. Jake Anson, a bulky jacket held snug to his chest, grinned and waved at the men from his front steps. Ignoring the women, he went inside and slammed the door behind him.

Grace fidgeted. Hannah surveyed the outbuildings: a tobacco barn, an old kiln half covered with vines yet identifiable by stone walls and chimney and small vents just above ground level. Hannah saw the smokehouse Harold had described to her. It was falling to one side. Harold had also said that Anson's grandpa used to operate a water-powered sawmill back up the valley behind the house, but Anson was too lazy to keep it or anything else up. Hannah felt a small thrill of hope remembering that. She would ask Wayne to try to find it. But would it meet the criterion of being of historical value? and who would determine that?

Burdened with sadness, Hannah walked home alongside Grace. The biologist had finally called her back, but he would not come. Had he taken her for a babbling old fool? Bureaucrats from one office had merely referred her to bureaucrats in other offices, in and out of the state. They had their priorities—wetlands, barrier islands, a tiny endangered, unheard of reptile in a forest in Avery County—to preserve. Grace met someone at the tearoom who suggested that Hannah contact a philanthropic organization, the George Aracson Foundation. Hannah wrote them, but they were not interested.

Grace tried to comfort her. "Don't give up, Hannah. Something will happen." But Hannah was becoming discouraged.

"This is nice, the three of us," Amelia said.

Outside, rain spattered from the roof onto the edges of the porch. Battleship gray clouds shrouded the mountains. It had been weeks since they sat together, unhurried and relaxed, and a week since Bella's funeral. How ironic that this dreary day, Hannah thought, could be pleasant, actually, with the three of us together for a change.

Amelia sorted pictures. Grace bent over accumulated items that needed mending. Hannah tried to concentrate on a novel. But the memory of Bella haunted her. The funeral, Max's eulogy, confirmed for her that Bella, involved in her own private projects, had been a shy loner, not hostile to the community. What was it Voltaire said? "The happiest of all lives is a busy solitude." Was it, really? In her brief encounter with Bella Maxwell, Hannah sensed within her a yearning for companionship.

"I'm sorry you didn't have a chance to meet Bella, Amelia," she said.

"I was always going to go over there tomorrow."

"And tomorrow never came."

"I'm glad we're alone today," Amelia said, changing the subject. "I've missed our times together."

Grace pulled thread from a spool and held the needle to the light to rethread it. She jumped as a clap of thunder sounded close by. The thread slipped past the needle, missing the opening. She lowered the needle and thread into her lap.

Hannah said, "I remember a song about thunder Miranda used to sing to the boys when they were little. How did that go?" She tapped her forehead. "Come on, mind, remember. Oh, yes. 'Who's afraid of thunder? Thunder's just a lot of noise.'" She stopped.

"What's the rest of it?" Grace asked.

"I don't remember."

"Lightning scares me. I can handle thunder, usually," Amelia said, as she straightened the box of photographs on her lap.

"Where's Lance?" Grace asked.

Amelia's eyes clouded. "Gone again, twice this month. He never says where."

Hannah folded a flap of the cover into the book to mark her place and set it on the table. "Have you asked him?"

There was a long pause, so long that Hannah reached for her book, and Grace lifted her needle. This time the thread slipped through its eye.

"Of course I ask him, or used to. I've learned not to probe."

"That would annoy the hell out of me." Hannah closed her book with a slam.

"You think it doesn't bother me?" Amelia tossed her head. "Well, at least with Lance away, I can spend time with Mike."

Hannah wanted to scream, Can't you see Lance for what he is? A liar, deceptive, secretive, controlling? Instead, she clamped her lips tight and silently blessed Grace for changing the subject.

"You're never going to believe this," Grace said.

"What? Want us to guess?" Amelia leaned forward. Guessing had become a game with them. Their guesses were invariably off the mark, but they laughed.

"You'll never guess."

"Oh, let's try," Amelia pressed.

"All right," Grace said. "You go first."

Amelia rubbed her hands together. "They're opening a four-star restaurant and a massage parlor in the shopping strip on Elk Road."

Grace shook her head. No matter how silly the guesses, she loved the game. When Amelia had suggested such a game several months ago, she had considered it foolish, but it was fun and made them laugh. Today, however, it wasn't a game Hannah wanted to play. Nevertheless, she sighed and went along. "All the schoolkids in Mrs. Bennet's first-grade class came for tea at the tearoom."

"No, silly," Grace replied laughing. "But they'd be more fun than some of the people who do come in."

"So, tell us," Amelia urged. Like Miss Muffit on her tuffet, Amelia sat on the hassock, her hands dangling loosely over the edge of the box of photographs.

Grace slipped the needle into a lapel of the pajama top bundled in her lap. Her eyes twinkled. They would be speechless when she told them.

"That call I took earlier. It was Lurina. She and Old Man have decided to get married."

"No," Hannah said. "Impossible." The book fell from her lap. "Old Lurina and Old Man. Scamp Wayne's said not a word."

"Lurina and Old Man haven't told anyone but me, not even Wayne. They're concerned about family interference. Old Man's telling him tonight, Lurina said, so she felt she could tell me." She laughed lightly. "I'm to be her matron of honor. She wants to be married in a 'right proper white wedding dress,' and I'm to help her find it."

"Eighty-one and she wants to be married in white?" Amelia snickered.

"First time for her. Virgin bride," Grace replied.

"No," Hannah said.

"Bet one of those magazine shows would like to get their hands on that story." Amelia waved her hand across an imaginary marquee. "Ninety-one-year-old mountain man takes eighty-one-year-old virgin bride." Throwing back her head, Amelia laughed. The box on her lap bounced, sending photos spilling onto the carpet.

"Not funny. Don't you go calling one of those shows," Hannah said.

Amelia shrugged. "Just an idea."

"All we need's a gaggle of reporters and cameras all over Covington."

"The publicity might help with Anson's place." Amelia raised her eyebrows.

Grace leaned toward Hannah. "Amelia may have a point. What if we could convince them to include something about the Cove Road Preserve Coalition? Maybe a conservationist-minded philanthropist would see it, and bingo." She snapped her fingers. "Land saved."

"A pipe dream." But for a moment such a prospect set Hannah's heart skittering.

"I'm chilly." Grace got up, knelt before the hearth, and turned a knob. The gas fire leaped between fixed logs. Grace missed the crackle of a wood-burning fireplace, but not the mess of ashes or creosote in the flue.

"Good," Hannah said. "I don't even realize this old house is chilling until I find myself rubbing my arms."

Amelia asked, "What interference are Lurina and Old Man concerned with?"

"Jealousies maybe, or inheritance. She wasn't specific. I imagine in time I'll hear, whatever it is."

"Marriage. At their ages. Imagine." Amelia laughed. "Why not just move in together?"

"Not proper. Their heads are in the 1940s, when decent people didn't do that," Grace said.

"When's this wedding going to happen?" Hannah asked. "And where?"

"Cove Road Church, of course. July. Lurina says she must be married in summer. Says she's not wearing a satin wedding gown out in the cold."

Hannah interrupted, "Do you realize Christmas is two weeks away? Where's our tree, Grace?"

"The Richardsons will bring one fresh off a farm over by Little Switzerland this weekend."

"Good." Hannah cleared her throat. "Jose and Anna are going to Ecuador for the holidays. I want to ask George Maxwell for Christmas dinner, and Zachary of course, if he's back."

"Where is he?" Grace asked.

"On some kind of an Outward Bound program he'd signed up for months before his mother died. His father urged him to go, thought it would be good for him."

"How thoughtful of you," Amelia said. "And you hardly know Maxwell. He gave me a ride home that dreadful night of the accident with Lance. Maybe, *I* should ask him."

"I know Maxwell enough to invite him," Hannah said sharply.

"Well." Amelia's eyebrows shot up. "Okay with me. I've asked Lance, if he's here, and Mike, of course, and Grace has Bob and family. "Looks like we'll all have dates." Amelia's laugh sounded false.

Hannah wanted to choke her. "Max is a neighbor who's just lost his wife, not a date."

Grace raised her hand. "Let's count heads, see if we need another table? With Emily, Lance, and Maxwell, that's ten. We'll be fine with two leaves added."

The phone rang. Amelia scrambled from the hassock. More photos landed on the carpet. She picked up the phone. "Oh, *bonjour,* Rus-

191

sell, how are you? Fine, just fine, thanks. Hold on." She handed Grace the phone. "Russell."

"Hi," Grace said. As Russell talked, Grace's face grew brighter. "Oh, I'm so happy for you, Russell. I'm so pleased with Tyler. Hug him for me. Tell him I'm terribly proud of him. When's Emily coming? Maybe we can all go to IHOP together." When she hung up, she said, "Looks like we're going to have another wedding. Tyler's come around, at last. He asked Emily to come back."

"So," Hannah said, "Tyler changed his mind. Must have been hard for him, he was so adamant."

"I think he actually got to like Emily, but couldn't extricate himself from his position. Thanks to you, Hannah, for bringing the issue to a head, getting everyone to talk. I'm sure Tyler's change of heart started there, so we'll have Emily for Christmas too."

28

Tyler as Hero

Russell and Tyler leaned against the glass pane of the waiting area. Their eyes followed Emily's plane as it turned and slowly made its way back to the terminal.

It seemed a long wait, but then Emily came toward them, her arms opened wide, and Russell rushed to embrace her. Tyler hung back. Then Emily was on her knees beside the boy. "Tyler, I'm so glad to see you."

She hesitated, then hugged him. He returned her hug, then, suddenly, shy, hung back while they identified Emily's bags, three big ones, and stowed them in the car, and then they went to the cafeteria near the airport. Tyler was so nervous he selected only Jell-O and mashed potatoes.

"That's no supper, Tyler," Emily said.

For a moment Tyler was sorry she had come back. Now he'd have someone else telling him what to do, but she was looking at him with such warmth that his heart melted. She was kind, and she was pretty, not as pretty as his mom, but he could see why his father liked her so much. Tyler added cake to his tray, and she did not make a fuss. Good!

The next morning, Emily took Tyler Christmas shopping. "Help me find the perfect gift for your dad, your grandpa. . . ."

"And Granny Grace."

"Of course, Granny Grace, and I think it would be nice to get something for Miss Hannah."

"The best present for Aunt Hannah is computer paper, lots of it. You never saw anyone use so much paper." He rolled his eyes. "She's always making mistakes and printing things over and over."

Ten days before Christmas the mall was manic, bristling with teenagers dashing about in groups, worried-looking adults rushing by, their arms loaded with packages and trying to avoid the teenagers. It took them four hours, but in the end they got everything. They picked up a screen saver for Russell's computer, one of those things he talked about getting and never did, and cashmere sweaters for Bob, and Russell, and Tyler, all in the same red color. "You'll look like triplets," Emily said.

"A sweater for Granny Grace in blue, and one for you too, in blue. You look nice in blue." Tyler held out a roll of bills his grandpa had given him for this purpose.

"Get those two ladies of ours something real special," Grandpa had said.

Of course gifts had to be bought for Emily's parents, and something for the house, and for the ladies' house, and they were loaded with packages when they wearily wended their way back to the car.

The lot was crowded. Dad's Toyota, which Emily had borrowed, looked like every other white car, and they wandered a bit until Tyler recognized it by the bumper sticker, I HAVE A GREAT KID AT CASTER ELEMENTARY SCHOOL, and he ran toward it. Tyler had just reached the car when he heard Emily scream. He turned and froze. A man wearing a black wool cap pulled low on his face was yanking at Emily's purse.

When Emily tried to fight him off her packages flew helter-skelter. "No," she screamed, then, "help me." Emily fell to the ground, and the thief grasping her purse began to run in Tyler's direction toward a van with dark windows and its motor going.

Emily lay crumpled on the ground, and Tyler was certain that the man had killed her. Pain sliced his heart. The thief ran past him, and as he did, something snapped in Tyler. The dark van pulled close, and when the man opened its door, Tyler lunged, grabbed the man's leg, and sunk his teeth into his calf.

The man yelled in pain and kicked at Tyler with his other leg. Tyler fell back, clutching his stomach, and passed out. Tyler did not see the van pull away, nor the van and the thief being apprehended by the police.

When he opened his eyes, Emily was bending over him, holding him, calling him, and crying. They had died, both of them, he thought, and gone to heaven, but then Tyler saw policemen pressing back people, who seemed to be leaning toward them. Some of the people were crying, others looked stunned, and when Tyler attempted to sit up, he fell back holding his ribs and they cheered, and he heard people say, "Brave little fellow" and "Slowed them down so the cops could get them."

Tyler clung to Emily, and hid his face in her shoulder. All he wanted was to go home and be with his father.

Grace wept when Bob phoned to tell her what had happened outside the mall.

"Don't cry," Bob said. "Our little hero's couple of broken ribs will heal fast." There was pride in Bob's voice; Grace felt only concern for Tyler. "Little fellow slowed the bastard down, so the cops could get him."

Grace imagined the scene, and how Tyler must have felt, and that awful man kicking her baby. She wanted to go to the jail and wring the man's neck, or as Hannah would say, "Kick him good, you know where."

"We're real proud of him," Bob said. "Didn't know he had the spunk to do something like that."

Men, Grace thought, and their heroics. "Tyler could have been killed."

"But he wasn't, and he saved the day, remember. The newspapers are going to do a story about it."

"How's Emily?"

"Quite shaken. Bruised, but she'll be fine."

"We'll have to do something special for him for Christmas."

"Just bake Tyler a Vienna cake, and let him eat it all himself. He'd love that."

But there was so much to celebrate this Christmas. Yes, she would bake Tyler's favorite cake, and she, and Hannah, and Amelia would plan something for Tyler, something that would express their pride in him, and their gratitude that neither he nor Emily had been seriously injured or killed.

29

Roger and Charles

Grace spoke to Roger and Charles every week, sometimes only a quick hello. It was Charles who updated her on their lives with little notes dashed off in his fine calligraphy: sales were brilliant, doubled in a year, Miranda was a love to work with, Miranda's younger son, Philip, a great help in the shop during the holidays. Charles sent her an article from their local Sunday paper raving about the Gracious Entertainment Shop. He was sure, he wrote, that her name in the title brought them good luck.

Charles also kept Grace abreast of their health—Roger had a cold, Roger was better, Charles was feeling fine, he and Roger were walking an hour and a half every day—and about their lives. They had bought a lorry, a truck, he explained, when she asked what a lorry was. They had recently entertained at home, and he had prepared her meatballs and prunes. Everyone raved, wanted the recipe. Could he pass it along to friends? Would she write it out for him?

"Of course, I will," she assured him.

Grace appreciated Charles staying in touch and his willingness to share their lives with her.

Her talks with Roger were more perfunctory and brief. She would tell him all the latest news from Covington. "Yes, our tree's up. We decorated it last night, Russell, Bob, Tyler, Mike, same as last year. Oh, and Emily too." She told Roger about the purse snatcher and what Tyler had done. "Our Tyler was very brave," she ended her story.

"Brave, yes, and foolish, really. That man could have smashed the boy's head in," Roger declared, sounding concerned.

Grace agreed wholeheartedly, but had been trying to see it from Bob's vantage point and to give Tyler credit. He was a gentle child, and his behavior had taken her totally aback. He had told her that all he could think was that he had lost his second mom, and he didn't care if the bad man hurt him.

Then Grace told Roger about Lurina and Old Man.

"Well, that's something." Roger laughed.

Was she the only one who did not think this wedding was funny? Lurina would have a family, and not live in that rambling old house of hers alone.

"I imagine we'll have two weddings next year, Russell and Emily too."

She listened then to her son explain, unnecessarily, that they would not be able to come for Christmas. She hadn't expected them to come. It was their busiest time of year. "I do understand. We'll miss you," Grace said.

Then Charles picked up the extension, and she had to repeat all about Emily coming, and Tyler's act of bravery, and the two upcoming weddings, although Russell and Emily had not announced officially as yet.

"Poor little guy. I hope he's well enough to come to you for Christmas."

"He'll be here. How are you, Charles?"

"Good. We hired help. I'm not knackered at night like I used to be."

When Roger first brought Charles to Dentry to meet his parents, Grace found Charles's English accent strange and had to ask him, sometimes, to repeat himself. Now, she was quite used to his referring to the hood of a car as a bonnet, the trunk as a boot, to a line as a queue, or a bathroom as a loo. Over the years, Charles had endeared himself to Grace, and she worried about him no less than about Roger. Last year, the news that he was HIV positive had devastated her, but so far he remained healthy and careful with his health.

Then Charles told her about a recent event in nearby Philadelphia at which Prince Charles of England was the guest of honor. "It was brilliant, brilliant. You should have been there. The Prince is much warmer in person than on the telly. Some people just are, you know."

She could picture her Charles's round pleasant face, flushed and happy.

"The Prince was brilliant," Charles was saying. "Came over to thank us. When I spoke, straightaway he asked where I was from 'at home' and about my family. You should have seen me, Mother Singleton. My legs went weak, thought I'd faint."

Grace imagined them standing there trying to appear cool and confident, Charles, short, compact, graying, beaming with pride, trying to maintain his dignity, and Roger, tall, blond, handsome, smug. "How nice of the Prince," Grace said. "And I'm sure you deserved every bit of his praise."

Charles turned chatty. "So, Russell's going to marry his Emily? Wait a sec." She heard him calling to Roger, who had hung up his phone. "Pick up in the kitchen."

Roger came back on the line. "Russell's getting married next year. When they set the date, what say we block out the time, toddle on down there, and do their wedding? We could make it a smash, brilliant. A present from you, and me, and Mother Singleton."

Grace pictured him standing there, one hand on his chest, his eyes aglow, a huge smile on his face. "Can you really do that, get away, come here?" Then her enthusiasm faded. How would this play with Queen Ginger, as the ladies referred to her among themselves.

On the line, Roger was silent. "Roger?" his mother asked. "Are you there?"

"Here, Mother."

"What do you think?"

"Well." He hesitated.

Charles's voice came over their extension. "Come on now, Roger. Once we have a date we can straightaway mark off those dates. We'll write the trip off as business. It'll be fun. We can spare two weeks."

"Well, okay." Roger sounded cautious. "First we have to clear it with Miranda and Paul."

"Of course. Of course," Charles said. Moments later they said good-bye.

"Have a happy holiday. Talk to you Christmas Eve," Grace said.

"Late night for us," Roger said.

"Christmas Day, then."

Grace returned the phone to its cradle and sat immobile in her rocker. Outside the stream gushed and swished. For several weeks now, rain, though intermittent, had been consistently upon them. Rivers, creeks, and streams ran high, near to cresting. Her eyes swept the room, her room, everything in it chosen by her for her own comfort. Her bed, low to the floor, so that when she sat her feet lay flat on the carpet. The peach-apricot walls, so warm and pleasing. By her bed, on a wooden stand, sat a glorious fan, a gift from Amelia last Christmas, from Amelia's fan collection.

Such a lovely collection it was: fans from Europe, one whose painted facade bore in great detail the ruins of Pompeii, an Edwardian-era fan that advertised corsets, a Brise fan whose sticks, Amelia explained, simulated the arches of the Cathedral at Chartres.

Grace's fan gave her pleasure every time she looked at it. "It's a copy of an eighteenth-century European fan," Amelia had said. In vivid color and minute detail it depicted a ballroom scene from the era of Louis XIV. Grace could almost hear the minuet playing, the swish of satin skirts, and the gay laughter.

And there were her clowns. Bob had started her on a clown collection, and last Christmas gave her two clowns, one somersaulting, one sitting on the ground cross-legged petting a small dog. She loved them. I'm happy, Grace thought, and saw Tyler's bright little freckled face in her mind. So much to be grateful for. Then Grace remembered that Lurina was waiting for her. They were to go over some of the plans for Lurina's wedding.

30

A Tale of Death and Burial

Lurina opened the front door of her farmhouse and grinned at Grace. "I been waitin' to show you somethin'." Her eyes twinkled. Her bony hand grasped Grace's solid fingers, and she led her into what had once been a pleasant dining room and now was cluttered with grocery store boxes stamped CAMPBELL'S SOUP and busting with heaven only knew what. Grace never asked. One day perhaps Lurina would tell her. The original table had long been supplanted by a small, round oak pedestal table, and its grainy finish was now burdened with stacks of photo albums.

"Sit you down," Lurina said. She patted Grace on the back and pulled out a cane-backed chair. Opening one album, she pointed to a faded picture of an old couple. "Found me this here picture." She tapped the heads in the picture. "Aunt Emma and Uncle Elvin. Passed too young, fifty-nine, and he done caused it."

Lurina shook her head. "Day clear as today. Aunt Emma cut her foot on a piece of rusty roof tin. Doctor was thirteen miles, and one mule to carry 'em. What'd Elvin do?" She eyed Grace seriously, challenging her to guess, knowing she'd never get it right.

"He put her on the mule and led her to the doctor?"

Lurina flung back her head and laughed so heartily she nearly toppled the chair. "Well that there's a good one. What he done is get him a pot of hot bacon grease and pour it on that there cut. Aunt Emma screamed so loud you coulda heard her a mile down the road, 'cept nobody lived a mile down the road." Her forehead furrowed above thin white eyebrows. Lurina shook her head again. "A no-gooder, that Elvin. Spent his days gommin' and piddlin'."

"What's gommin' and piddlin'?" Grace asked.

"Loafin'. He was real fine at loafin'." She uttered a sigh of resignation. "Before you know it, she took to her bed and plain old died, while her lazy drunk husband was a-jawin' with hired help out by the pigsty."

"Why'd he put hot grease on it?" Grace asked.

"People tell 'bout hot grease curin' everything on the outside of your body, and corn whiskey takin' care of what's inside." She laughed lightly, then deeply, and Grace laughed with her. She couldn't help laughing with Lurina. It was one of those things that drew her to the woman. Grace always left the Masterson farmhouse with a spring in her step and laughter on her lips.

Grace studied the photo. Elvin's lean, pinched face was lined and hostile. Fifty-nine-year-old Aunt Emma looked seventy-five, her face gaunt, and her eyes preached resignation. They peered at Grace from the grayness of time.

"I don't like his face," Grace said.

"Nobody did. That's probably why the lawman carried him off. They said he killed her. Pa gave Aunt Emma a right proper burial."

"Lurina," Grace asked, changing the subject. "When do you want to go hunt a wedding dress?"

"I ain't goin', honey. I want for you to go lookin' and when you find what you like, you just bring it here, and it's done."

"I can't choose your wedding dress."

"Ain't nobody else I trust to be pickin' me a dress. You knows me best of all the folks around here."

How was that possible? Grace wondered. Where was community and caring? She found it hard to believe that Cove Road folks didn't pay much attention to Lurina.

"We'll measure me up and you can tell 'em at the shop." She stood, holding to the table. Years of damp had penetrated the faded striped wallpaper of the dining room, and sections curled while other strips hung loose near the ceiling. Family pictures of Lurina's stern-faced parents bore jagged water stains on their mattings. The original crystal chandelier hung above them, coated with dust. There were no windows in the room, only a door into the hall, and another to the

202

living room. Once started, Grace could not stop sneezing. Lurina seemed unfazed by damp and dust.

"I guess you're about a size six." Grace measured her, then jotted numbers on a small pad and rose to leave. "Bob's waiting for me at the tearoom."

Lurina tucked the tape into her apron pocket, which already held a small paperweight, chunks of balled papers, hairpins, and a small comb. To this mélange, Lurina added the tattered tape, then she tottered after Grace to the door. "You best be off. Rain's comin' agin." And then one last admonition, "Now mind you, I don't want to show no shoulder, and no bosom."

"I'm sure they'll let me bring several gowns so you can choose."

"Fancy a shop that'd do that?"

"Sure they will."

Lurina clapped her hands like a child and laughed. Her eyes vanished among wrinkles. Grace hugged her good-bye.

Grace went straight from Lurina's to the tearoom, which was fast becoming a popular watering hole. Tea came with a platter of French pastries, Danish pastries, tiny crustless sandwiches, and sugar cookies. People always said her sugar cookies were great for dunking.

Sybil, their new employee, hovered at a large table of mostly older women, probably retirees living in Loring Valley, taking their orders. Voices rose and fell. Bob stood behind a counter taking credit cards. There were several people in line.

Along the back wall, a fire flickered cheerily in the fireplace. With its floral wallpapered walls and soft curtains, the room was warm and welcoming. Grace admired the room. Were she a customer, she would enjoy taking tea here.

Later, in the kitchen, Bob turned from arranging another platter of sweets Grace had prepared last night. "Missed you," he said.

She kissed his cheek, then wiped where her lipstick had smeared.

"Don't wipe it off," he kidded. "Makes the women wild with jealousy."

She kissed him again and left the smear. "Roger and Charles offered to come down here and do Emily and Russell's wedding, when they announce their date. What do you think?"

"I think it's great, but I'm not the one to ask."

"I know." Her shoulders fell. "Ginger."

He shrugged. "She might consider it fashionable. What'll they charge her?"

"It's a wedding present from them."

"Well, she just might go for that deal. That's real generous of the boys."

"I agree, and I'm pleased." Grace tied an apron over her skirt, turned on the oven, then reached into the refrigerator, where a tray of unbaked croissants waited. "Hannah found this recipe on the Internet. Did you know croissants were not originally French?"

"Really?"

"They're Viennese. In 1863 Vienna was under siege by the Turks. Bakers working at night heard noises underground. Turks digging a tunnel under the city. They reported it, and the army wiped out the Turks. To celebrate, they designed these crescent rolls, shape taken from the crescent in the Turkish flag. Imagine, all that information came with the recipe on the Internet, straight from a bakery in Vienna."

"When we reprint our menu again, let's put that story in a box to the side," Bob said.

"Good idea." A ping from the oven indicated 350 degrees had been reached, and Grace slipped the tray onto the center rack.

"Please, will you ask Russell what their plans are?"

31

Lance Insists

"We'll use my frequent flier miles," Lance said. "Rome would be nice, or Vienna? Or maybe the Côte d'Azur and Italy."

Amelia set down her wineglass. Rome? Vienna? France? A long plane trip, swollen ankles, cramped seats, jet lag. She'd done it all for years with Thomas. She had not the slightest desire to return to any of those places, not even with Lance. His suggesting travel at this time was a clear indication that he did not value her time, or respect her work. It occurred to Amelia then that she had set this whole thing up. Why should Lance take her commitment to photography seriously when she had canceled field trip after field trip, and had even canceled the Florida workshop with Mike in January, just to accommodate him.

Amelia sighed. If a time was ever right to say no to Lance, this was it, here, in a busy crowded restaurant that was overdecorated for Christmas. Blaring music made it hard to talk. Already her blood beat like a drum in her temples. She preferred quiet, preferably French restaurants. Lance sought out crowded, loud eateries. Amelia endured them. She hesitated. If she opposed him, would he explode in anger? Ignore her? Reject her?

Lance leaned forward and stroked her fingers. Amelia's resolve melted. Lance's power over her, she realized, was his sensuality. The prospect of someday sleeping with him enthralled her. She dreamed of it. Only her lack of trust in him, and her fear of sexually transmitted diseases, held her back. She couldn't ask about his relations with other women, she knew that, so how would she ever dare to bring up the subject of HIV testing?

"So?" Lance set down his knife and fork and leaned back against the tufted leather booth.

He's gorgeous, Amelia thought, and accustomed to having his own way.

The music grew suddenly quieter, or had it been supplanted by the crash of breaking glass from somewhere behind a partition? A muffled curse followed. Someone in the booth behind them laughed. Someone clapped. Behind the partition, feet shuffled.

Amelia waited and when the hubbub receded, she lied. "I'd love to go with you, but . . ."

"But?" He leaned forward. The movement was abrupt and nearly sent his wine spilling.

"But, I have work . . ."

"Are you saying you'd rather spend time in a smelly, stuffy dark-room?"

"I have a show coming up, and I'm behind by five photographs. I have to shoot dozens to get five good enough to exhibit."

He scowled and shook his head.

She tried another tack. "Lance, dear. You're always welcome to come with me on a shoot, like you did that day we went to Velma Herrill's."

"Well," he said pulling back. His eyes were gray. "Guess you prefer that fag's company to mine."

Amelia raged inside. Don't let him get away with disparaging Mike. Sliding to the edge of the booth, she hesitated a moment, remembering where she was. I can't confront him here. She sat silent, stewing. A wave of disgust swept over her. Drawing on every ounce of courage she possessed, Amelia slid from the booth. "I have to go now. I don't feel well." Grabbing her jacket, she fled toward the lobby of the restaurant. She could hear his voice, calling loudly, "Waitress. Check."

He caught up with her on the sidewalk. "I'll take you home," he said grasping her arm.

"I'll get a cab." She shrugged him off and walked faster. The lamp-posts were decorated with lanterns etched in tiny white lights. Amelia's new high heels, shoes she bought because Lance liked her in high heels, pinched her toes. Tears scoured her cheeks. She could hardly see the pavement. Her scarf loosened and trailed behind her. Through her unbuttoned coat she felt no cold, although the temperature was in the thirties. "Oh, God," she prayed aloud, "please, send a cab."

Miraculously, a taxi cruised by. Amelia waved it down and offered the reluctant driver a twenty-five-dollar tip to take her to Covington. Inside the cab, she lay her head against the seat and pressed her fists against her temples. The throbbing persisted. Ripping off her shoes, Amelia opened her window and tossed, first one, then the other, into the street.

"They got a litter law, you know," the driver said.

"Expensive shoes are hardly litter," she replied and closed her eyes.

From the kitchen window, Grace, who was having a bout of insomnia, watched Amelia stagger from the taxi. She's ill, Grace thought. Hurriedly wiping her hands on a kitchen towel, she hastened to open the door for her friend, only to find Amelia barefoot.

A hysterical Amelia fell into Grace's arms, sobbing. Grace led her into the living room, where tiny white lights on the Christmas tree— Grace liked them on day and night—blinked cheerily, and softened the black-and-white photograph of an older couple on a park bench feeding the pigeons that Amelia had taken from her motel window on a field trip to Savannah. (B. L. Mike called it—before Lance.)

"Now, tell me what's happened," Grace said.

Pride, regret, shame, a deep sense of loss mixed like soil and water and stuck like mud in Amelia's throat. She could only heave low, gasping sobs.

Grace handed Amelia her bandanna. "What's happened, Amelia?"

Outside, rain fell. A scrim of water hid the Maxwells' house and barns and landed with a pinging sound on the edge of the porch floor. Grace asked, "It's Lance, isn't it?"

Amelia nodded, covered her face with her hands. Her shoulders shook.

"I'm sorry," Grace whispered. "Would talking help?"

"If you swear you won't tell Hannah," Amelia muttered from between her fingers.

"That serious?"

"Yes."

"Hannah isn't one to gloat. She'd be sorry whatever it is."

"She hates Lance."

"Hannah loves you. She doesn't like the way Lance treats you."

"It's hard, so hard," Amelia said, and her sobbing continued.

"I'll guess," Grace said. In the dark night with rain cascading and the bitter cold beyond their walls, time seemed to stand still. The lights flickered. Grace wondered if the storm would plunge them into darkness. She looked about her. Where were those flashlights? Hannah had put one in every room.

Amelia wiped her eyes. As if the bandanna were a precious object, she held it scrunched tight in her hand. "Okay," she said, "guess."

Grace set aside her concern about the lights going out. By making it into a guessing game, she would ease Amelia's tension. Amelia could defer telling, and would only have to nod, yes or no.

Amelia curled her legs beneath her and snuggled into the cushions. Her chin quivered. She grabbed a pillow and hid her face. "I'm waiting." Her words were muffled by the pillow.

"Let's see." Grace tapped her cheek, made funny noises with her teeth, and clapped once, as if indicating, let's get the show rolling. "Lance wants you to give up photography."

Amelia shook her head, but she knew he would prefer she packed away her camera. "Guess again."

"How many guesses do I have?"

Amelia's eyes narrowed as she considered the question. Then she raised a hand and spread apart her fingers.

"Five," Grace said. Seconds passed. Amelia squirmed.

"Lance wants you to move in with him?"

"No." In the beginning, she had hoped and prayed he would invite her, and in those early days she had experienced nothing but excitement, and never considered the consequences of moving out, of splitting up their household. "No," she said again, firmly.

"Lance proposed?" Grace asked.

Amelia snickered. "No."

"That's three. I'm not doing well, am I?"

"Don't give up." The game diverted Amelia, and prolonged the inevitable telling.

Grace pushed up from the sofa. "I think better on my feet." Crossing the room, she straightened a lamp shade she herself had tipped for reading. In front of Hannah's armchair, the hassock was askew. With her foot, Grace pushed it straight and closer to the chair. Then she bent and retrieved from the carpet a small rose-colored button she had lost the other day, and then she opened several table drawers seeking a flashlight.

Amelia scrunched in the corner of the sofa, defeat masking her face, her shoulders slumped, her head low, an uncharacteristic pose for the graceful Amelia.

"Lance doesn't want to be with us for Christmas; he wants you to go off with him somewhere," Grace said.

"Christmas isn't involved in this." Or was it? Lance didn't like Hannah any more than she liked him. He abhorred Mike, tolerated Grace, and considered Tyler too rambunctious.

"Undisciplined child," he'd said with contempt. "I've no patience with children. Never have."

Did he have children? She never knew. "You have one more guess." Amelia sat a bit straighter and stretched out her legs on the couch.

"My last guess." Grace set her hands on her hips and looked down at Amelia. "Lance demands you do whatever he wants, that's what I really think it is. Sorry."

Amelia sighed, and tipped her chin up. "It is, and it isn't." Her reserve broke. She told Grace how Lance was making travel plans without consulting her, of his denigrating her work, his reviling Mike, and her walking out of the restaurant.

Grace felt a momentary pride in Amelia. She had actually walked out of that restaurant and come home without Lance.

Amelia was speaking. "When he attacked Mike, something snapped in me." She longed to admit to Grace how desperately she wanted Lance sexually, and how afraid she was to sleep with him, and why. But sex was something one didn't talk about. Once, only once, when she was married a year, she'd complained to her mother about the infrequency with Thomas.

"Take a cold shower, and be glad you don't have a man who's all over you," her mother had replied. "And, Amelia, don't tell people about your private life. It'll just drive them away." She made a tish-tish sound between her teeth. "Lousy for your husband's career." She peered at Amelia over her glasses. "One more thing. Don't trust so called girlfriends."

Stupid advice, Amelia reflected. It may have served her mother, but it had never served her well. Life in this farmhouse, with these two women, was good, and it was safe. She trusted Grace and Hannah. Hadn't she transferred the deed for the farmhouse into all their names? And she trusted them to attend to her last wishes; her living will gave them authority. Amelia's fists tightened. She uncurled, pushed up from the couch, walked to Grace, and hugged her. The need to confess all her longings and fears hammered at her chest. Tell Grace. If you can't trust Grace, the closest friend you've ever had, then who?

Amelia hesitated. She must find the right words, so that she would not sound foolish, or tasteless, or just plain gross. She thought of the night Grace told them that she and Bob had "done it." Grace shared no details; her wide-eyed excitement, her sheer joy, said it all. Amelia knew that Lance did not love her. Oh, she guessed he liked her. Certainly he wanted her sexually. How could she find the words to tell Grace how she yearned for him, after all he had done and said, and not be utterly humiliated?

"Where's Hannah?" Amelia walked to the window.

"In Asheville."

"She won't be back soon?"

"No. Wayne drove her. They were going to drop off plants at a retail nursery and run some errands. He wanted to go to Calabash West for a fried fish dinner."

With Grace's bandanna, Amelia wiped the mist off of a section of the windowpane and peered out. "Look. Hannah's rosebushes are sitting in puddles of water."

Another swipe of the bandanna cleared a larger patch of pane. Grace peered out. "I'm glad I don't have to be out in this weather. Any colder, this rain will turn to snow and ice. What a mess the roads will be. Look at that river running down our driveway. I bet the stream's overflowing."

"Let's look, shall we?" Amelia asked, relieved to think and talk about something other than Lance, and at the same time annoyed with herself for not having taken Grace into her confidence.

Minutes later, they stood shoulder to shoulder at Grace's half-opened bedroom window watching in astonishment and growing alarm as their stream, a raging river now, spilled over its banks, splayed across the grass, and slipped in and out of the swale twenty feet from the house.

"Will the house flood?" Amelia tugged at the end of her scarf so hard, Grace worried she would hinder her breathing. Reaching for Amelia's hand, she took it in her own and held it firmly.

"No, Amelia. We're a good three, three and a half feet off the ground. Cove Road would have to flood first and the front lawn, the driveway, the roses would have to already be underwater. What worries me are those villas on the river in Loring Valley." She looked away, pensive. "Bob says they've anchored the condos into bedrock, but I don't know. What if the hill behind gives way? He's up there alone. I wish he hadn't moved out of Russell's house so soon."

"Oh, Grace." Amelia flopped into Grace's rocking chair and hid her face in her palms. "I'm so miserable."

"Why, Amelia?" Grace asked just as the fist of a thunderbolt smashed into the night. Grace shuddered, tore her mind from Bob, and turned to face Amelia.

"I want to sleep with Lance," Amelia whispered. "I know it seems vain, or silly, or adolescent, but I want to experience sex with a skilled lover. It was so indifferent with Thomas." Rain pelted like gravel on the tin roof of the farmhouse. Amelia's words were washed away. Grace had not heard her.

Amelia drew a deep breath. Reprieved. "Is it hail?" she asked more loudly, pointing up with a finger.

"I don't think so, just heavy rain."

"I've never heard it this loud." Amelia's grim visage spoke of depression. As much as Grace wanted to be attentive to her friend, she couldn't help but think anxious thoughts about Bob. "I'm worried about Bob in that condo, on that mountainside. I need to phone him."

The phone, when she picked it up, was dead. Grace stifled rising anxiety. "Amelia. Let's go down. I'll make tea."

Without a word, Amelia followed Grace downstairs and into the kitchen. "I've got to find out if Bob's all right," Grace said.

"How?" Amelia asked, then cowered as an explosion of thunder rattled the house.

Grace didn't know. Outside the windows, lightning speared a leaden sky. Grace flinched. Amelia screamed and covered her eyes. The lights faltered, blinked, and went out; the soft hum of the refrigerator ceased. Under the kettle, gas flames leaped gaily.

"I don't remember anyone predicting this storm," Grace said. She turned on another of the stove's burners, then began to rummage through drawers and cabinets. "Where does Hannah keep the battery weather radio? Ah, here's a flashlight. I'm going to run up to her room, see if it's there." She dug out several candles and holders and lit them. One she set in the sink, the other in a glass platter. "You okay here?"

Amelia lifted a hand. "Okay."

The radio sat on Hannah's bedside table. Grace pressed the on button. A man's voice broke through the crackle. "A storm has dipped into the Carolinas from West Virginia bringing wind gusts to eighty miles an hour. Roads are slick and dangerous, particularly at higher elevations. Sam's Gap reports ice. Accidents have been reported. Traffic is at a standstill. Rain, turning to sleet and snow flurries, is predicted into tomorrow morning. Listeners are advised to remain indoors."

Were Hannah and Wayne driving in this weather? Even in Wayne's four-wheel-drive truck it could be dangerous. Picking up the radio, Grace started from the room, then stopped. How incongruous on a night like this, to see, on a stand near a window, Hannah's Christmas cactus blooming brilliant red.

Grace started downstairs with the radio, thinking how different Amelia and Hannah were. Hannah kept no secrets from Grace, nor she from Hannah. And yet how hard it had been for Amelia to speak of her desire. Grace, like Hannah, wished that Amelia would dump Lance, only she was less verbal about it. Relationships between men and women were more complicated than relationships between women. Involvement and intimacy between women could lead to deep friendship. Sleep with a man, and everything changed. Live with him, and a kind of ownership set in.

"Let there be spaces in your togetherness," Kahlil Gibran had written. Having had more than her share of togetherness with Ted, she agreed with Gibran. Easy to fall into old patterns. Their generation, hers, and Hannah's, and Amelia's, had been programmed to please, to be caretakers. How easy to consign one's life to a man, as she, as they all had done when they were young. And the problem was ongoing. Here it was 1998, with woman's lib and feminism all around, and still Amelia would never go to a movie with a woman in the evening, or have lunch in a restaurant alone.

"I prefer an escort. I feel more comfortable," Amelia had said on more than one occasion. "Otherwise, I think people are staring at me, wondering why I'm alone, if something's wrong with me."

Another clap of thunder sent Grace scurrying downstairs to Amelia. Again she tried the phone. Dead. Was the hill behind Bob's condo stable? Was Loring Valley flooding? She thought of Tyler, Russell, and Emily. Hopefully they were sleeping through this. No way to find out, no way to know. It would be a long night, and where was Hannah?

32

Have Him Checked Out

Gusts of wind pummeled the farmhouse with the ferocity of a sledgehammer. The rain, at times a fairy's laugh tinkling on the roof, more often the drumming of a giant's fingers, never ceased.

Grace had lit candles, which now flickered under glass covers on the mantel, and on every table in the living room, casting light insufficient to read or sew by, yet enough to render a measure of comfort. "It's coming down even harder now." Grace beckoned Amelia to the living room window. "You can't see Maxwell's house, barns, outbuilding, not even the windmill. Lurina would call this rain a goose drownder. Lord, I hope she's all right."

Amelia averted her eyes. "I don't care what it's called. I don't want to look."

Grace felt an urge to go out onto the porch, to stand as witness to the wind and rain. She started toward the front door. Amelia's plaintive cry brought her back to the living room. "Grace, Grace, please don't go out. It's freezing out there." She was at the window now. "It's turning to sleet."

For a moment, Grace leaned against the front door, then in consideration of Amelia, she walked back into the living room.

"I'm scared." Amelia stretched out on the couch and spread a fleece throw across her legs. "Since we've been in Covington, there hasn't been a storm like this."

Cocking her head, Grace listened carefully to a new sound. "It's hail."

"Oh, Grace, it's going to snow and freeze. Sounds like buckets of stones, big, the kind that can smash windshields and windows," Amelia wailed. "I wish Mike were here."

"Mike, not Lance?"

"Mike. He's reliable. I trust Mike." Amelia looked at Grace sheepishly. They were cocooned, she and Grace, in this room, in this house with a fire in the hearth and candlelight to hide her blushes. If ever there was a time to confide in Grace, this was it. *"Mon ami,"* Amelia began in a low, confidential voice.

Grace leaned toward her.

"Can you guess why I'm still seeing Lance?"

"No guessing game now." Grace shook her head.

Tugging the fleece with her, Amelia squirreled down the length of couch until she sat across from Grace. This time she wanted to be heard. "Because, he's like poison oak in my brain."

"Poison oak?"

"Like an itch I can't reach, that won't go away. Lance stirs passion in me that I thought was dead. When he touches me, I feel, well, that if I were a tree, I'd blossom. Even his voice moves me. I like to hear him talk, laugh." She tossed her head. "I dream I'm in bed with him." Amelia waited a moment, unsure how to continue, how much to say without revealing all of the self she concealed beneath a thick veneer of propriety. "Would it be wonderful like I imagine?" Her hand touched her neck.

"When you love someone, and he loves you, being overweight like me . . ." She pinched her middle. ". . . or having scars doesn't matter."

"But do I love him, or is my body off on some wild, irrational adventure and my mind locked away in a drawer? I'm afraid. I don't know if he loves me. He flatters me. I'm intoxicated, giddy with his words, his touch, and I'm frightened, Grace. A little fellow like Tyler does something so brave, and I'm afraid to go to bed with Lance."

Grace was uncertain how to respond. Amelia had bared her soul, and Grace, who did not trust Lance any more than Hannah did, feared that he could easily crush Amelia's fragile self-esteem. Her mind shifted to those early days with Bob. She'd met him in June, run away to Roger and Charles in July, and when she returned in early August, she and Bob had come together, a perfect fit like adjoining pieces of a jigsaw puzzle.

For many minutes, they were silent, lost in their private musings, only to be jolted when a thud caused the living room walls to shiver. Amelia looked about the room with terrified eyes.

"What was that?" Grace hastened to the window.

Amelia's hands fluttered, waving Grace back. "Don't go near the window. The glass might shatter. Stay here by me, Grace."

But Grace was already leaning against the pane, her hands framing her face and eyes. A stab of lightning momentarily illumined the porch. "The wind's blown one of our rockers smack against the house." Another lightning flash. Grace gasped to see the cracked gliders, the split seat and back of the rocker. One of the huge clay pots had toppled to its side and ruptured. Soil spewed across the wooden boards of the porch floor like a trail of ants. Aghast, she pulled back from the window, her stomach churning, her legs unsteady. Fear settled in her gut. She wanted Bob, Hannah.

Walking to the table, Grace lifted the phone from its cradle. Still dead. When she turned on their weather radio again, a man's indifferent voice droned. It was a stranger's voice, with an accent, Dutch or German perhaps, not the voice of any of their regular television weathermen. Without a hint of concern, the foreign voice presented the startling facts of destruction and danger. Anger flared in Grace. From what snug, safe post was he reporting this news?

"Wind gusts up to eighty miles an hour have overturned cars, felled trees, lifted roofs. Those in cars should take shelter near buildings and switch on their blinkers. Patrolling police cars and road crews will find you," he said. "Do not attempt to drive. Many roads are flooded. Bridges are icy. A twelve-car pileup on 19–23 in Madison County has shut the left lane of that highway. Another wreck is slowing traffic on 240 at Exit 8. Current temperature in Asheville is twenty-three degrees, and lower in the northern counties of Madison, Avery, and Mitchell. Snow is already a foot deep in Avery and Mitchell Counties." The voice went on to give temperatures and projected snowfall for Charlotte, two hours down the mountain, and Greensboro, and Raleigh farther to the east.

This afternoon, when Hannah and Wayne left for Asheville, the sky had been slightly overcast with sunshine breaking through. On the morning news the weatherman had announced that the weather was about to take a dramatic turn and suggested that people stay tuned for further news. Grace had not done so. Had Hannah? Had Bob? Bob would have been here at the hint of serious weather. Grace wondered if Molly was over at her mother's, if Pastor Johnson was alone in the rectory of his little church, and was Lurina's house leaking? Thank God, their own roof was new and holding firm.

Amelia was crying, her shoulders shaking. She lifted her head and blew her nose. "I wish Mike were here."

"Let's hope Mike's out of this storm," Grace said. She sat next to Amelia on the couch. "We're safe. This is a sturdy house. It's seen many storms in its day."

"The stress of life wears people out, don't you think, Grace? Maybe houses wear out from storms battering them."

"Our house is fine." If Amelia were not with her at home, Grace would have taken her car, and rain or not, headed for Lurina's, at least to bring her here.

"But people, Grace." Grace felt the urgent squeeze of Amelia's fingers on her hand. "Don't you think stress wears us down, and after a time we lose our ability to cope?"

Grace pondered that. "Seems to me when we're young, say in our thirties and forties, and something bad happens, we handle it and grow stronger from it, learn we can rise above the punches life throws us. But as time goes by and stress piles on stress, then I think some mechanism inside of us breaks down, like a light dims."

"Lance makes me nervous and my stomach knots. I can't think straight." Amelia's voice dropped. "If I sleep with Lance, what happens the morning after? What if he loses interest? I'll be devastated, feel cheap, used, ashamed."

"Seems to me you know what you need to do then," Grace replied. "Have you talked about HIV testing?"

"Heaven, no. Did you with Bob?"

"We did, and each of us had tests."

Amelia stared at Grace. "How did you ever have the nerve to broach the subject?"

"I told him about Charles and Roger, then segued into talking about us." Amelia raised an eyebrow, and Grace nodded.

"It's so hard."

Grace said no more, and after a while Amelia's face grew soft, her eyes dreamy. "When I was young every new city we traveled to, Thomas and I, every party we attended, even the fearful beauty of an active volcano, stirred my blood, triggered all my senses. Then, over time the excitement dimmed, and I grieved the loss of my passion, my exuberance. I convinced myself that passion belonged to the young. I got used to that. Then Lance came along." She stopped, looked down, then up into Grace's eyes. "There's a kind of passion when I lose myself in photography, but it's softer, more subdued, more grounded, and that's been fine for a long time." Amelia's face, her voice changed, softened. "With Lance, I'm hardly grounded. It's rather extraordinary. I soar, feel totally alive, and out-of-my-mind aroused."

Grace, asked to describe her relationship with Bob, would recount that theirs was not fire and ice: rather it was soft like cotton candy, sweet, comfortable, and safe. "I can't tell you what to do, Amelia. Is he pressuring you to have sex with him, or are you pressuring yourself?"

"He wants us to make love," Amelia whispered. "He said recently that if we were young, we'd have been in the sack long ago."

"Probably. But you have the advantage of maturity."

"It doesn't feel mature the way I respond to him," Amelia whimpered.

"Perhaps if you trusted him, felt safe with him."

"He's going off any day now. Won't be back until some time after mid-January."

"So he won't be here for Christmas. Maybe that's for the best. He doesn't like any of us much I don't think. He'll hate hearing Russell and Emily's plans for an early-June wedding, and he certainly wouldn't appreciate Tyler being the center of attention." Grace paused. "Why do you think Lance is so secretive about his goings and comings?"

Amelia bit her lip. "I don't know."

The candles in the living room suddenly flickered as if struck by a breeze.

"I just can't help wondering what he's hiding."

Amelia bridled. It was fine for her to criticize Lance, but not Grace, and especially not Hannah.

The lights flickered on, and off, and on again. "Oh, thank heaven," Amelia said. "I hate being in the dark. The house gets so cold. Even with the fireplace and this fleece coverlet, I can't stay warm. Even the toilet seat turns to a chunk of ice."

A shadow from the doorway drew their attention. They had not heard the front door open or close. Hannah stood looking at them. Snow capped her coat at the shoulders and further whitened her hair. Water beaded her face and oozed from her shoes. "Have Lance checked out," she said bluntly.

Amelia gasped. "How long have you been standing there?"

"Long enough." She did not wait for a reply, but was already peeling off her coat and turning away. "I'm going up to change." Her Rockport oxfords squeaked as she walked to the stairs and mounted them.

"I'm so ashamed."

"Listen to yourself. You've just told me you don't trust Lance. Neither does Hannah. You actually agree. Maybe it's not such a bad idea to check him out."

"How?"

"Come on, let's go ask her."

"Harold Tate has a friend who's a private investigator. He should be able to check Lance's comings and goings and his background in no time," Hannah said as she attacked her dripping hair with a towel. "Got this wet just going from Wayne's truck to our porch."

"It seems dishonest, checking on someone behind their back."

"In today's world, Amelia, you can't be too careful." Unselfconsciously, Hannah loosened her robe, and the others turned to give her privacy while she dressed.

Grace changed the subject. "Did you have trouble getting home? Did you get stuck behind that twelve-car pileup?"

Hannah pulled a blue sweatshirt over her head and hugged herself. "Feels good, warm," she said. "Wasn't raining when we dropped off the plants. They took all the anthuriums and gardenias, and they ordered more. Went for an early dinner, and when we came out it was pouring. Never did our errands. Had a time of it coming home. Sat nearly two hours, a crash, three cars at the Weaverville exit. We heard about a big pileup on the radio, between Mars Hill and the turnoff to Burnsville. At Mars Hill we got behind a DOT plow and sand truck."

Hannah ran a comb through her wet hair, sweeping it back from her face and flat against her head. It looked darker and made her face seem larger and more square. Grace wanted to blow-dry Hannah's hair and fluff it out softly about her face. "Truck plowed and sanded; we followed, drove right along. Icy spots and snow on the road from Mars Hill to Covington. Elk Road's snow-covered, but not icy. I invited Wayne to stay the night, but he's gone to Miss Lurina's."

"I'm so relieved," Grace said.

Hannah sat on the side of her bed and began to pull on socks. "Polar fleece, the warmest. Ordered them from L. L. Bean." She didn't say that she had bought two pairs of the same socks for Grace and for Amelia. They were wrapped and tucked under the tree. "I've got news. Wayne says Lurina insists she and Old Man live in her house. Old Man says the sound of the traffic on Elk Road's 'like near to kill him.' "

"That's one obstacle. Any others?"

"Yep." A teasing smile played about the corners of Hannah's mouth.

"Okay, what?"

"Burial. They agree that 'properly married folk should be properly buried next to one another.' Old Man's hell-bent on burial with his kin in their family graveyard. Lurina has her place next to some aunt in the family cemetery up on her hillside. Lots of arguments about which graveyard is taken care of best, and who's left in the family to tend it, and on and on. They're going to have cemetery visitations, and Wayne says they want you and I to judge which cemetery is kept up the best. That one, I assume, will become the site for the two of them."

"Heaven help us," Grace said. "And we're in the middle of that?"

"I feel left out," Amelia said.

"Price of spending too much time with Lance." Hannah laughed, put her hand about Amelia's neck, and pulled her down gently to sit beside her on the edge of the bed.

"Can I come with you guys?" Amelia asked, smiling and relaxed, just like the old Amelia. "I don't want to be left out of all this good stuff, and I know Mike would love to come too. Please?" She looked to Grace. "A matron of honor can surely ask a favor."

The prospect of the four of them as Lurina's representatives accompanied by a brigade of Reynoldses struck them as funny, and

221

they flung themselves back on Hannah's big bed and giggled like girls. "I can see it," Grace said. She sat up, crossed her arms over her chest, held her back stiff, her eyes straight ahead. "We walk solemnly around the graveyard. The relatives stand off a bit to the side, arms folded across their chests, hats on, Sunday best."

Amelia leaned on her side and propped her chin on the back of her hand. "I'll wear my straw hat with the cherries on it. What do I care if it's winter?"

"Welcome back, Amelia," Hannah said.

Any reply of Amelia's was drowned in a paroxysm of thunder that sent her burying her head under a pillow, at which point Grace tickled her, and they were laughing again. It was the sharp, unexpected ring of the phone that brought an end to their hilarity.

33

The Night of the Big Storm

Bob's voice was frantic. "Are you all right? I've been worried sick."

"I'm fine. We're all here, and we're fine. Where are you?" Grace asked.

"At my apartment. I was just about to leave for the tearoom when the rain started. My god, it was a deluge. The confounded hill across the road tumbled down, mud, rocks, huge rocks blocking the entire road."

"Are you all right?" Grace asked.

"I'm fine, there's just water everywhere, the front yard's a pond; it's oozing under my door. Lucky I was here. I plugged the front door with towels, and that stopped the mud at least. The phone went out for a while. I couldn't call you."

Grace repeated Bob's news to the ladies, who listened, appalled. "Are you all right?" Grace repeated.

"Yes, just shaken to hell. Never seen anything like this. I thought the whole blasted hill was coming down. One huge boulder just missed, or it would have walloped one hell of a hole in my apartment. I'm going to take pictures for the insurance company. Might be of use to Hannah later on."

"I worried so. Thank God you're safe," Grace said. "I love you, Bob."

"I love you too, sweetheart. It's snowing, now. I'm afraid I'm stuck up here. As soon as the road's open, I'll be over."

She craned her neck to look outside. "Snowing here, too."

"What about the villas? Ask him," Hannah said.

"How about the villas? Did Little River flood?"

"Yes. Looks like a lot of damage down there. Can't see how much. I thought I'd stuck my binoculars in a box, but I can't find them. Emily's with Russell and Tyler. She's staying there, you know, taking care of Tyler. What about your stream?"

"It's over its banks, but so far it's running off toward Cove Road. Don't you try to come off that hill until it gets cleared, promise me."

"I won't, don't worry."

"Have you food? Heat?"

"My electric stayed on. Yours?"

"Out for several hours. We had candles. It's on again now."

"I have food: tuna, canned soup, couple of frozen dinners. I'll be fine. We can talk by phone. Take care of yourself. When you can, check the tearoom."

"I will. I'll call you."

"Darn shame a storm like this just before Christmas," he said before hanging up.

"We have a week. I'm sure the roads will be cleared by then."

The night of the big storm, right after Bob called, Maxwell appeared in a poncho and high rubber boots with an unexpected and much appreciated container of Anna's vegetable soup. He stayed on to chat with Hannah after the others slipped off to bed.

"How are you doing, Max?" Hannah asked. He was a tall man, broad shouldered, and he filled the armchair in the living room. His long legs stretched out and under the coffee table.

"I'm missin' Bella somethin' awful," he said. "Anna cooks, and I hardly eat."

"You're not used to eating alone. Would you come over and eat with us sometime?"

"Thanks. That's a great kindness. I will if I'm not too busy. We've had damage to the barn. Lost about a hundred bales of hay."

"You have to eat." They let it drop then and spoke of the storm, and about Zachary. "Boy's good with the herd, and he's got a talent for paintin', like his Mamma. In January he'll be starting college at Clemson University down in South Carolina. He hasn't a clue what he wants to be when he grows up."

"He's so young. He'll find his way. These days young folk take longer to find themselves." She thought of her daughter, Laura, in Maine, mate and companion to a charter boat captain, and soon to sail for the Caribbean. He was so much older than her daughter, and Laura with a degree in computers. Well, you never knew where life would lead, or what might capture your interest. Laura loved the sea. Hannah couldn't fault her for following her passions. Plants were Hannah's passion. She made a mental note to phone Laura, to wish her *bon voyage,* as Amelia would say.

Max's voice startled her. "You're a comfort, Hannah. No wonder Bella liked you so well. She spoke of you every day, and looked forward to your visits."

"Wish we'd met sooner."

"Your visits eased her time, and her passin'," Max said. "She never stopped talkin' how you made it so she could plant daffodils one last time." His eyes misted and he looked away. "That woman loved the earth." They were silent a long time. She thought he would leave. Then he asked, "How you doin' with Anson's land?"

She sat up straighter. "It's a hard thing to come out of nowhere and try to interest people in shelling out money to conserve land, especially since Masterson's tract is scheduled for a park. We created the Cove Road Preserve Coalition, and it's turning out to be only a handful of people. Haven't been able to interest folks from Asheville or even here in Madison County. I've been in contact with land trusts and foundations. I'm waiting. Never give up hope."

"I'd sure hate to see Cove Road go the way of Loring Valley," Max said. He leaned toward her, and his legs slipped even further under the coffee table, causing Hannah to think, He's quite an imposing man, in a good way. She was sorry that they didn't have a chair in this room large enough to accommodate him comfortably.

Max was saying, "Some folks think you have a lot of nerve tryin' to stop a man from doin' what he chooses to do with his own land."

His words startled her. Of course some folks on Cove Road would be angry. Some of her neighbors agreed with her, but as Harold Tate had said, "Sorry, Hannah, I'm with you in spirit, but I can't go against my kin." She felt a stir of fear. "Are you giving me a warning?"

Max cracked his big knuckles. "You go on with this, Hannah, I worry what might happen. Bella was concerned too. Could change things for you ladies."

"Change things, how?"

"I've seen folks shun a person, harass a person, even threaten a person, or worse, till they drove them out."

Had they shunned Maxwell and Bella? Hannah wondered. Probably yes, for the Maxwells, although they were Southerners, were outlanders from Atlanta. "All of that?" Hannah asked.

"Yes, ma'am, all of that."

"You think I should sit back and watch another mess like Loring Valley happen, and not even try to stop it? Just when we may have found a way to stop Anson?"

"You found a way?" Max asked, his brows knitting.

"We found a graveyard. Maybe it's over a hundred years old. If I could just interest some government agency into checking it out, it would at least buy time."

Max let out an audible groan. "I'm not goin' to ask you who 'we is,' and as for the government, don't go threatening government around these parts. They're an independent lot." He heaved up from the chair and towered over Hannah. The room filled with his presence. He smiled. "Be careful, Hannah."

That night, as the storm raged on, Tyler lay in bed, his chest bandaged to hold his ribs secure, and shivered. Thunder scared him; lightning terrified him. Thinking of his mother, how she would come to his room if there was a storm, and climb into bed with him, and hold him, and sing to him, made him cry.

Slowly, for his ribs hurt if he joggled them, Tyler slipped from his bed. Without the thunder, the house was silent. Emily was sleeping in Grandpa's old room. He wished Grandpa was here. Holding one hand to his ribs, and the other to the wall of the hallway, Tyler moved along. He opened his father's bedroom door. Snores greeted him. Tyler's heart fell. How could Dad sleep through thunder that shook the house and such harsh, crackling lightning?

Tyler shut his father's door, and stood for a moment, unresolved whether to return to his room or see if Emily was asleep in her room down the hall. Ear-piercing thunder decided for him, and he moved toward Emily's door as fast as his injuries permitted. Light under the door gave him the courage to knock.

A small voice said, "Come in." Emily sat bolt upright in bed, the covers held high about her shoulders. Her table lamp glowed, and a book, unopened, lay beside her on the bed.

Tyler stood in the open doorway, uncertain, feeling small and alone. "Tyler. Once again you've come to my rescue. I'm scared. Will you stay with me?"

Tyler's shoulders lifted. He smiled, moved a bit too fast, winced, held his ribs with both hands, and walked to the bed.

"Climb up. Take it slow now. Easy. There we are. Lean up against these pillows." She shared her pillows. And with a sigh of relief, Tyler settled alongside her.

She told him stories then, about being a little girl and her father taking her rowing on a big lake in Central Park, and moving to Florida and the beach, and how she made sand castles with her dad.

"We were going to go to Florida on vacation, to Disney World. That must have . . ." He stopped abruptly, remembering.

She knew. Amy had been killed. "Would you like to go to Disney World?"

He nodded.

"We'll ask your dad, okay?"

"Sure."

Another clap of thunder brought their shoulders together, and when the lightning made the room glow as if a flashbulb had gone off, Emily grasped Tyler's hand.

She's as scared as I am, he thought, and felt suddenly less afraid, and older, and protective.

"Tyler," Emily said softly. "I'm glad you came in here tonight. I was really scared. You're very brave, and this is the second time you've really helped me. Thank you." She bent and kissed his forehead gently. Another clap of thunder was a good excuse for holding her hand tight.

The first big storm of the season left Loring Valley a shambles, with owners threatening lawsuits against the developers, who threatened lawsuits against the builders, who questioned county inspectors.

On the hillsides, snow and ice, mud and rocks closed every loop of Loring Valley Road, isolating condominium owners for days. Little River raged. Boulders along its banks were flung across lawns, onto patios, and through glass-sliding doors into the living rooms and bedrooms of villas. All the villas, and most of the condominiums, were severely damaged by mud and water: carpets destroyed, wood floors buckled, drywall soggy and blistered, appliances ruined, furniture waterlogged. In one villa the mud was so high and caked so hard that firemen had to use their hoses to wash it inside and out. In another villa, the damage was so widespread that an owner, when he opened his oven, was aghast to see a cake of mud filling all the space.

The morning after the storm, plows cleared Elk Road, Cove Road, and the flat area of Loring Valley Road, and departed leaving muddy deposits a foot or more high piled along the roadsides. The piles of ice and snow mixed with mud, dirt, and twigs would take many days to melt.

The tearoom, happily, was untouched by rain, snow, or wind. Grace tacked up a sign: WILL REOPEN AFTER CHRISTMAS. HAPPY HOLIDAYS TO ALL.

The Hammers, on their cruise, missed the storm, and returned after New Year's to soggy, mildewed, and smelly carpets, water-stained walls, gobs of mud, as well as to the news that Emily had returned, and that she and Russell would be getting married. Ginger walked into her dank-smelling, mud-smeared villa and stormed out.

"Bad things certainly all come at once. It's just too much. I'm going to my sister in New York. Don't call me until this place is totally refurbished."

On the way to the airport Ginger kept up a running diatribe about Emily and Russell and Tyler. "All that education we gave Emily, and she's throwing it away to live in the boonies. And that child of his. He hardly said a word when we had them over for dinner that time. Depressed would you say? They ought to take him to a therapist. I say that the cards are stacked against Emily. I can see it all now. She gives up a lucrative law practice, moves here, her income goes down, she's got this depressed child to deal with . . ."

"Ginger. Stop this. Bob tells me Tyler's not depressed," her husband tried to calm her. "He's shy and uncertain about what's happening with his father and our daughter. He's a child. He's lost his mother. He's probably scared to death to even think of his father remarrying."

Ginger waved his words away. "Know where it all leads? Right to divorce court. Let's hope she doesn't rush to have a baby. God, imagine that, Martin."

And when he pecked her cheek good-bye before she boarded the plane, she admonished him. "Now you try to talk sense into Emily and if you can't do that, I know how soft you are with her, then you just tell her to do nothing, absolutely nothing, don't set a date, don't make any arrangements until I get back."

And she was gone down the tunnel into the belly of the plane.

The devastation wrought by the storm in Loring Valley left Hannah feeling vindicated. Now, she thought, Jake Anson surely won't sell his land to the Bracken and Woodward Corporation.

But as she was to learn, with environmental issues you never relax or let down your guard. The despoilers, as she had come to think of land developers, would slip away like dogs with tails between their legs, and return snarling.

34

Two Family Cemeteries

During the busy and frustrating week after the storm, Amelia hired Ray Lambert, a private detective, to check on Lance. "I'm sure you won't find anything serious or bad," she said. "But my friends insist I do this." Then she settled down to wait.

Wayne called to set a date, four days before Christmas, for the inspection of the Masterson's and Reynolds' family cemeteries.

Lingering patches of snow on pastures, and snowcaps on the higher mountains, were all that remained of the storm on the day the ladies and Mike sat in Lurina's house anticipating the arrival of the Reynolds clan. "How many graves are there?" Grace asked Lurina.

"Ain't never counted. Some's got wood markers, some stone. Pa's is carved outta marble."

Station wagons and pickups lumbered across the bridge. Engines were shut off. No one came to the house, or blew a horn.

"Joseph Elisha's kin, five cars parked in a row like peas in a shell," Lurina muttered as she peeked through the window. "Grace, come take a gander at this mess a folks." She shuffled away from the window, and sat stiffly in a firm, ladder-backed chair near the door. She wiped her brow with her sleeve. "Y'all git out there, Grace, and take 'em up." Lurina licked her lips again and again. "We got us a fine cemetery. Ain't nobody goes there dumpin' fast-food cups, an' trash like that."

Mike was thrilled to be included. He walked alongside Amelia as they reached the end of the pasture and started up into thick pine woods. Ten unsmiling men and women, dressed in their church clothes and good black shoes, trudged after them. Light barely filtered between close stands of pines. Accumulations of forest debris carpeted the forest floor, making walking difficult. To avoid falling or twisting an ankle, it was essential to look down, and to concentrate on every step.

Grace grasped Hannah's arm, and Mike helped Amelia untangle her coat when it fastened on twigs and low scraggly bark. Just when they thought they were lost, they stepped from the pines into a clearing. Marked by a sagging split rail fence of indeterminate age, the cemetery was almost a square. Behind them, Grace heard contemptuous comments and whispers as she stepped over a rotting branch and pointed out to Hannah where pine needles hid dips and humps in the earth. "Hannah, do you want to wait here?" Grace asked.

"I'll watch my step." Hannah circled the fallen branch and plodded on, glad for the long underwear under her thick khaki pants, and the fleece socks inside her high-top walking shoes.

A man behind them tripped and cursed.

A woman chided him. "Ain't proper cursin' on the Lord's day."

"I coulda been home watchin' the game, 'stead of this," the man replied.

Weeds competed with dry brown grass and patches of snow in all the spaces between the three dozen or so graves. Some had wooden crosses so weather-beaten that the names of the departed were barely visible, if at all.

"Pour l'amour de Dieu," Amelia said. "What a mess. Miss Lurina certainly hasn't been up here in years."

"I wonder if she'll believe it when we tell her how bad it is," Hannah said.

Grace knelt at a grave site and brushed away fallen pine needles that clung to the headstone. "Emma Masterson Green," she said, sitting back on her haunches.

Several of the Reynoldses gathered about her. Some bent to look. Two men removed their jackets and found places to sit on a fallen log and talked football. A short tubby man with a light beard leaned against a high gravestone and chewed on a bit of a twig. In an effort to protect their clothing, most of the five women stood with their hands crossed over their bosoms.

"Who's she?" someone asked, pointing to the stone that Grace cleaned with her bandanna.

"Lurina's, Aunt Emma." Grace related the story Lurina had told her.

"Hot grease," a woman said. "Some of those old-time ways could kill you for sure."

"Lurina loved her aunt. Intended to be buried alongside her." On her knees now, Grace shoved aside a layer of pine needles mixed with prickly pinecones, some small as a walnut, others the size of a small orange. Mike squatted alongside her and helped, as did a woman of middle years whose round wire-rim eyeglasses mimicked the shape of her benign face.

"I'm Mary Reynolds Kelly," she said. "Old Man's my great cousin on my mother's side."

"I'm Grace Singleton. Pleased to meet you." Together they cleared the earth where Lurina expected to be buried, a small space for a small woman, with no space below, above, or alongside for another grave to accommodate a husband. And it would fall to Grace to explain this, as well as the condition of the Masterson cemetery, to Lurina.

Grace hunkered on the edge of Aunt Emma's grave. The picture of Lurina's aunt had shown a small, diffident woman. Gazing at Emma's name and the dates carved deep into the solid gray stone, Grace wondered what would happen to this graveyard when the land was turned over to the park service. Would they build a low stone wall about the place and clean it? Would they set out markers telling the history of the family, the second pioneer family to settle in what would become Covington? Would they cordon it off from visitors? Or would they let it deteriorate? They couldn't do that, however, if this cemetery proved to be over a hundred years old.

Springing up, Grace went from marker to marker. Hannah had told her that ruins of buildings and graves over a hundred years old would be considered historic and might be set aside, sometimes restored and preserved. "Find a grave dating from 1897 or before," she said.

Mike found it. "Look," he said, waving at Grace. He cocked his head and squinted at the numbers and letters barely distinguishable on the cracked and weathered wood. "December 21, 1897–December 30, 1897. Over a hundred years."

"Thanks, Mike," Grace said. "A baby. It lived less then a month." What was she doing? She had no input into what the park service did or did not do with Masterson land, and this graveyard was small and remote, with no descendants to question what the new owners did. Tears filled Grace's eyes. Blinking, she looked around at the barks of trees while she regained her composure.

Later that afternoon, the Reynolds clan led Grace, Hannah, Amelia, and Mike under the stone archway, which proclaimed REYNOLDS CEMETERY. Gravestones: white and gray, tall and short, ornate and simple and all clean, stepped one below the other like ripples approaching shore. Cut low, the grass was soft as a carpet to walk on. Since the cemetery, without the shade of trees, faced south, the snow had melted. Fresh plastic daisies, roses, forget-me-nots, violets burgeoning from vases decorated every grave. To one side of the cemetery stood a long covered picnic area filled with tables and benches. All of the benches had been freshened with dark green paint.

Mary Reynolds Kelly moved close to Hannah. She spoke with pride. "Come September, our family gathers from here and yonder. We clean up the place, put new flowers and all. Then we have a mighty fine picnic. Last gathering Old Man roasted us a right good pig. We had us a fine dinner."

Last year in September, the ladies' apple orchard had burned, and Wayne brought Hannah here and insisted that she accept the gift of sapling apple trees he raised, and then he had offered to help her replant her orchard. Hannah had seen, but not been on, the grounds of this cemetery, and Old Man had told her of a gathering that had just taken place. Now, Hannah looked carefully at the graves and noted that the flowers were too bright to have been placed here in September, not with all the rain and snow they had had. It appeared that the Reynolds family had spruced up the cemetery especially for this occasion, which seemed a bit unfair to Lurina, yet, it would take more than a few flowers and some paint to transform the Masterson cemetery from shabby to well groomed.

"It's a lovely spot, Wayne," Hannah said to the young man standing beside her. She favored this site. Old Man had told her that his parents had died in a fire shortly after he himself had become a husband. Old Man related how scared he had been when he became responsible for rebuilding the farmhouse and outbuildings, working the farm, making a living, and being freshly married, the babies coming one after the next.

"I done it. The Lord don't give a man more'n he can manage," Old Man had said. Then he had pointed to the mountains. "Tennessee. Kin live over yonder."

Hannah's eyes had followed the humps and dips of tall hills. "Over which mountain?"

Old Man waved an arm. "Over yonder, stand atop of that there mountain, and you can spit in Tennessee."

Now, Hannah met the relatives from Tennessee, since five of those family members were hosting this visit to their graveyard that afternoon: Mary Kelly and her husband, Ted, and Wanda and Wilma, Old Man's nieces, who were twin sisters as well as spinster ladies from Johnson City, Tennessee. These four drove across the mountain every third Sunday of the month, weather permitting, to visit Old Man. There was also Wayne's second cousin on his father's side, Freddie Reynolds, a blacksmith living over in Barnardsville. He was the short tubby man who had leaned on the tombstone in Lurina's family's cemetery and chewed on a piece of twig.

Wayne was saying, "Old Man says the dead need a right pretty view, since they can't get up an' go no place."

"View of pastures and meadows filled with wildflowers in spring-time. Wouldn't mind being buried here myself," Hannah replied.

Wayne looked thoughtful. "Where they gonna lay you to rest, Miss Hannah?"

She shrugged, sliced the air with her palm. "Who knows. Probably be cremated and buried under a rosebush."

"Tain't fittin', Miss Hannah. You need a proper restin' place."

Old Man leaned against a tall, double marble stone topped by a small angel that seemed to perch on Old Man's shoulder. "This here's Pa and Ma. Right good folks, they was. Passed in a fire, just after the cows was taken to market. Fire started in the barn, burnt the hog pens, an' the house. Doc said they passed in their sleep, never felt a thing." He moved on, naming relatives, telling how they'd died, one from a ruptured appendix, and too far to get him to a doctor, another from heat stroke, another stomped by a bull. Old Man shook his head. "Never get you between a bull and cow come matin' time."

Finally it was over. When Old Man bade them good-bye, he took

Grace's arm. "Now, Miss Grace, I'm dependin' on you to tell Lurina what y'all done seen. Tell her she'd be right happy to lie a-restin' in this here pretty place."

Grace had an idea. "Pictures," she said. "Amelia, do you have your camera?"

"It's in the car, why?"

"If I show Lurina both cemeteries, it may be easier."

"I have my camera, also," Mike said, and he and Amelia walked down the hill to the car and returned with their equipment. How nice, Grace thought, to see Mike and Amelia working together again. Lance's absence was a blessing, affording Amelia time to mend fences with Mike, to realize how stress-free she was without Lance Lundquist. And yet, Grace also understood Amelia's attraction to Lance.

The following afternoon, Grace sat with Lurina at her kitchen table and spread out two rows of four-by-six snapshots on the green plastic tablecloth. The floor of the kitchen was also green, a mottled, speckled linoleum worn through in spots, worn dull in others. There was no mothball scent today, only the smell of onions mingled with burnt toast and another odor that Grace could not identify, perhaps overcooked greens of some kind. An odd combination, Grace thought, but refrained from asking. Lurina, she knew, planned none of her meals, but ate instead from a stack of frozen dinners in her freezer. Sometimes she cooked greens, or whatever struck her appetite at the moment, anytime of the day or night. And why not? She lived alone. Her time belonged exclusively to her. Would she cook when she married Old Man, or would he adapt her eating habits? Grace reminded herself that it was not her problem.

"These pictures on the top here were taken in the Masterson cemetery," Grace said softly. "And these"—she tapped the bottom row of photographs—"were taken in the Reynolds cemetery."

"Who took 'em?" Lurina asked, pulling back.

"Amelia and Mike."

Lurina snorted, then selected pictures from her family cemetery, and from Old Man's. One by one, she brought the snapshots inches from her face, and her eyes disappeared as she squinted. "Humph," she said several times.

236

"Your cemetery must have been a pretty place, surrounded by the woods, so peaceful," Grace said.

Lurina turned testy. "And who's sayin' it ain't?"

The question took Grace aback. The difference between the two cemeteries was unequivocal. In the Masterson cemetery wooden markers slanted, weeds abounded, fallen branches lay on graves like downed spars on storm-battered ships. Grace spoke candidly. "There was a time when you were able to keep up your family's cemetery, but not in the last year or so, right?"

"I ain't what I used to be," she admitted grudgingly. Then Lurina turned petulant, like a child, shoving away the pictures, jumbling them together. Holding her arms jammed tight against her rib cage, she clenched her fists in front of her. "If Joseph Elisha be a proper gentleman, he'd send Wayne to fix it right pretty like it used to be."

"The Reynolds cemetery looks down on the pasture. In the spring you can see flowers on the hillsides and along the stream. It's a lovely site. Maybe if you saw it, you'd like it."

Lurina's jaw quivered. "What'd Pa think, me buryin' someplace else?"

Grace slid her hand across the table close to Lurina's arm. "Your pa loved you, Lurina. He'd be pleased you're marrying Old Man, and not being alone at this time of your life. You'd be a Reynolds, and properly buried alongside your husband."

Lurina pulled her arm away from Grace's hand. "It ain't right, a Masterson buried outta her own property."

Grace fixed her eyes on Lurina's. "When you're gone, strangers will tromp your woods, people will picnic and camp out. They'll find your cemetery." A plan had been swirling in Grace's mind. She had lain awake last night imagining the park service declaring the cemetery a historic site, and restoring it, protecting it with a low stone wall. She imagined Lurina sitting on her porch relating stories about the deaths of her ancestors to someone assigned by the park service, and later the park service engraving condensed versions of those stories on markers set alongside the appropriate graves: *Emma Masterson Green, died of blood poisoning from a wound treated with hot bacon grease,* or, *As told to his beloved daughter, Lurina, patriarch Grover Masterson on the day of his passing witnessed the light of the Lord in his window.* The old cemetery would take on a life of its own. People would visit. The departed would come alive for them, and be remembered.

Slowly, and in great detail, Grace outlined for Lurina her dreams for the cemetery. "Other folks will want that kind of information about their ancestors acknowledged in their cemeteries, the same as in yours. They'll tell their stories, and write them on signs. The deceased will be remembered vividly, not just a date of birth, death, and their name. And you will be remembered as the one who started the whole thing."

Lurina buried her face in her hands. Her long white braid, thin at the end, hung over her shoulder and curled on the green tablecloth like a white snake in the grass. "And I ain't gonna be there for them to read 'bout," she muttered, and Grace knew the battle was over.

"Maybe the Reynolds family'll do the same. What if they took the idea from you? Your stone could read, *Lurina Masterson Reynolds, former owner of Masterson Park, bride at eighty-one, good shot with a shotgun, good friend,* whatever words you might like."

Lurina's face grew contemplative. "It'd say how I passed."

"Of course, and whatever else you want to say about your life. You could pick the words." Such a weird conversation of dying and burial, as casual as making a shopping list for groceries.

"I hear tell folks put agreements on paper when they gets married. We could do that, about what's goin' on my stone?"

"I'm sure you could."

Both palms struck the green plastic tablecloth simultaneously. "Done, then," she said.

Grace reached for Lurina's hands and squeezed them, and Lurina looked pleased. Now only the problem of where they would live remained, or so Grace thought.

35

'Twas the Night Before Christmas

An infinite blue sky and brilliant sunshine lent no warmth to the day before Christmas. Sweet sounds, Christmas carols being rehearsed, floated from Cove Road Church. This evening, carolers—women and girls in long bright woolen dresses, and boys and men in thick jackets—would traverse the road bringing Christmas cheer. All along Cove Road, homes wore icicle necklaces of light that brightened the nights. Up and down Cove Road, windows glistened with colored lights, including the ladies' porch. Hannah had climbed a ladder held by Grace, and Amelia handed up strands of colored lights that Hannah tacked to the fretwork of their porch. In Maxwell's front yard, a magnificent fir, a great pyramid of white light, shimmered in the cold winter's nights.

Christmas Day, Hannah insisted, was a day to rest and relax; their Christmas meal would be served tonight, Christmas Eve. A twenty-four-pound turkey was basted and in the oven, the sweet potato casserole made and set aside to be heated later, and fresh buns waited to be popped into the oven. Hannah and Amelia, with Grace looking on, sat at a cluttered dining room table wrapping the last of their Christmas gifts. Hannah's boxes, all but two, rose in neat stacks from the floor beside her chair. Amelia deftly tied the fancy bow on the last of hers.

"Put your finger here, will you, Grace." Amelia nodded at the ribbon.

Grace placed her finger on the knot, then eased her finger from under Amelia's glorious big bow. "You make wonderful bows, Amelia. Makes me think of Christmases past. My mother made bows and I'd hold the knot for her." Memories flooded back. "When I was young, holiday meals were such a trial. My grandparents came, my aunt and uncle, four cousins. We crammed shoulder to shoulder at the table. My father insisted on carving the turkey while he lectured us kids about cleaning our plates because there were starving children in Europe. By the time my mother got everything on each plate and served us all, the food was cold. Cold mashed potatoes taste gobby."

"Is that a word?"

"Why not?" Grace shrugged. "It's what they tasted like."

Amelia set aside the long narrow box with the new bow. "Done." She rubbed her hands together.

"What memories do holiday meals evoke for you, Amelia?" Grace asked.

Amelia closed her eyes for a moment. "Holidays were wonderful. We went to Aunt Clea's home, or my grandparents'. There were always friends as well as family, and the table was beautiful, candles, flowers. Aunt Clea gave me her Spode dishes. There was always someone to help in the kitchen, and both my grandmother and Aunt Clea served family-style, huge platters and bowls at both ends of the table, with the ham or turkey already sliced. The food was never cold. Every plate and bowl sat on a trivet of some kind, yes, that's it, silver trivets that were like pockets filled with hot water." She laughed. "What about holiday meals at your home when you were young, Hannah?"

Melancholy curtained Hannah's face. "Tension. Can't remember the food, or if it was hot or cold. My father, before he walked out on us, drank heavily, especially on holidays. We never knew if, or when, he'd explode, so we ate in silence and quickly." She shook her head. "I shortchanged my daughters. Bill drank too, as you know. Our holidays were perfunctory, to be gotten through as quickly as possible. I guess I didn't know any other way." She brightened. "Best holidays are now, with you both, and our friends. I appreciate the pizzazz and enthusiasm you bring to all the holidays."

"Well," Grace said, "let's clear this table and get the leaves in. Time to set it for dinner. How about using the rose tablecloth under a lace cloth. It'll give a warm glow and set off Amelia's Spode china. By the way . . ." She stopped, opening the buffet drawer where the table-cloths were. "Let's put Tyler at the head of the table. He'll be so excited when he sees the ribbon with the medal we had inscribed for him. You want to slip it over his head, Hannah? Amelia?"

"We think you should do it," Amelia said.

They tidied up snippets of red, white, and green ribbon, and left-over scraps of Christmas paper. Then Hannah and Amelia carried their packages to the living room and arranged them under the tree alongside Grace's. There were piles of boxes dropped off by Mike and the Richardsons, and a large one from Wayne, Old Man, and Lurina.

That evening, Max was the last to arrive, and he followed the carolers up the drive to the front porch and stood behind them as they sang "O Little Town of Bethlehem," "Silent Night," "Hark, the Herald Angels Sing," and ended with "Jolly Old St. Nicholas." They did not depart empty-handed; Grace presented Claudia's daughter, Paulette, with a round hatbox tin all wrapped in red and green paper and tied with one of Amelia's huge red bows. It was filled with Christmas tree and angel-shaped sugar cookies that Tyler had carefully stamped out that morning.

When Max entered the house, he propped a bulky, rectangular package wrapped in blue and silver paper along the wall next to the tree. Apple cider whetted their appetites for dinner, and within a half hour they were all seated at the dining room table. A new Orien-tal rug anchored the table. The room floated in soft candlelight re-flecting off the rosy wallpaper. For a centerpiece Hannah had placed a long, low bowl overflowing with fragrant white camellias.

Then the feast began. Besides the magnificent golden turkey and stuffing, there were mashed white potatoes as well as a candied sweet potato casserole, green beans slathered with toasted almonds, creamed peas and onions, and fresh baked buns.

Tyler sat straight and proud and beamed from the head of the table. Emily sat to his right, his father to his left. He had examined everything under Granny Grace's tree, had seen and handled a big box wrapped in paper dotted with snowmen and tagged with his name from Emily and Dad. A computer. He had overheard them talking about it.

They ate quietly for a time, concentrating on the food. Christmas music from a cassette played low in the background. Max turned to Hannah on his left and said softly, "I've an idea I'd like to discuss with you sometime, about Jake Anson's land."

She nodded. Across the table and down a ways, Wayne thought she was nodding at him. He waved his fork and smiled. At least she'd gotten him to take off his hat at meals.

After they had all had second helpings and were nearly finished eating, Max tapped the side of his wineglass with his dessert fork and lifted it to Hannah. The ruby wine sloshed in the fine crystal goblet, Grace's contribution to their fine dining. His nose was red. Maybe he had been crying at home for Bella, this first Christmas without her. "To Hannah," Max said, "a woman of determination and courage." Everyone sipped their wine. He raised his glass again, and to Grace. "Grace. Thank you for a magnificent supper."

Moving her lips slightly and smiling, Grace thanked Max. Bob squeezed her hand. This was what holidays should be like, bountiful with food, a sense of great goodwill, laughter, everyone flushed and happy and delighted to be together.

Mike toasted Amelia, "My dear friend, and magnificent photographer." They drank again.

Bob raised his glass. "To marriage, Lurina and Joseph Elisha, and Russell and Emily." Everyone cheered.

Then Grace rose. "And a toast to the boy of the hour, our hero, Tyler."

Everyone clapped, then sipped their drinks. Grace walked over to the buffet table. Tucked among the Vienna cake and the cookies was a long, narrow jewelry box. She stood behind Tyler and opened it, then placed the wide green and red ribbon around his neck. On the end hung a round, important-looking medal. "Read what it says, Tyler."

Tyler turned it over and read slowly. "Tyler Richardson. His brave act stopped a robbery and caught a thief. Bravo!"

"And won the heart of a maiden." Emily squeezed his hand.

Tyler's face turned beet red and tears formed in the corners of his eyes, but he did not cry. He stood and bowed, then he flung his arms about Grace and went from person to person at the table hugging

242

and kissing everyone. "Can we open presents before dessert?" he asked.

"We certainly can," Bob said rising. "Come along, all of you. Leave the table, Grace. We'll all help later."

As sedate as dinner had been, the opening of the gifts was tumultuous with much laughter, exclamations of delight, thank-yous and oohing, and aahing especially over Tyler's computer. Hannah had given him a monitor and Grace and Bob's gift to Tyler was a printer.

Other gifts were opened then. Upon unwrapping Hannah's gifts Amelia and Grace slipped off their shoes and donned their new fleece socks. Grace presented Bob with a loose, wobbly package of bathroom towels and new sheets for his apartment, and he gave her a gold charm bracelet from which dangled a farmhouse, a big cookie, a teapot, a children's book, and a heart with their names inscribed.

There was not a dry eye except Tyler's when Old Man presented Lurina with a brand-new Bible, for keeping a record of their life together. She gave him a framed photo of herself when she was young, and bright eyed, and laughing, and several plaid flannel shirts Grace had bought at her request. "Get 'em real bright now, red, blue, green." When Old Man held his new shirts to his chest, everyone said he looked splendid, and Lurina beamed.

The mystery box from Lurina, Wayne, and Old Man contained a portable electric keyboard. "One of you is gonna have to learn to play the weddin' march," Lurina informed them. She and Old Man sat side by side, holding hands, and grinning ear to ear.

Finally all that was left was the big package Max had brought. Slipping a pocketknife from his pants pocket, he sliced the silver and blue covering away and removed three canvases. Hannah gasped. "Oh, Max, Bella's paintings."

"You planting your front yard." He leaned toward Hannah. "Bella inserted a yellow daffodil here in the corner, and signed it along the stem."

Tears filled Hannah's eyes as she touched the edge of the canvas. *For Hannah with love, Bella Maxwell.* "It's wonderful," she said. "How incredibly kind of Bella."

"She had me bring it downstairs to her bed so she could put in the daffodil and sign it." There were tears in Max's voice. He cleared

243

his throat. "She wanted you to have it." He removed the other two canvases and presented them to Grace and Amelia. Bella's signature was tiny and in the corner. "Bella had so hoped to sit and have tea on your porch with you ladies."

Amelia struggled for words. "I never met her, and she did this for me?" She held the painting up and studied it. "I remember this day. I was certain I'd never master the technical aspects of photography, and you, Hannah, urged me not to give up." She held the painting at arm's length. "I hung my straw hat with the berries on it outside on the wall of the house across from the stream, and shot pictures of it."

The others nodded.

"It's a lovely painting," Grace said. "See how the trees bend toward the stream. The water sparkles, and you sitting there eyes glued to your camera. Bella didn't know us then, yet she did these paintings. Remarkable."

"She watched you every single day from her bed," Max said. "I wish I'd done something about getting you over to meet her sooner."

Grace's painting depicted the three ladies in their rockers on a porch dripping with flowers. Grace's heart swelled. How very good it was to be here in this house, in this room with these people. She was lost in these thoughts when Mike stood and clapped his hands for attention.

"I have a surprise for you all. If I may." He opened the new keyboard. "I was privy to this gift, and I've been taking lessons." Moving quickly among them, he handed out song sheets. "Let's sing, shall we? 'Frosty the Snow Man,' then 'Jingle Bells.'" Mike cracked his knuckles. His fingers tickled the keys, and then the music swelled and he played and they sang way past Tyler's bedtime, and Old Man's bedtime, and Lurina's bedtime. They sang and rocked from side to side, and held hands and sat in a circle as they welcomed Christmas Day with soaring spirits.

36

The Painful Truth About Lance

Lance returned to Covington on January 16. A miffed Amelia, still waiting anxiously for word from the detective she'd hired, watched from her bedroom window as Lance slammed his car door and started up the walk. She took a deep breath. In his weeks away he had not phoned, or sent a card, and not having a gift from him under their tree had humiliated her. With a new resolve, she had resumed her old life photographing, and spending time with Mike, Hannah, and Grace.

Lance looked up, saw her at her window, smiled and waved, and that simple gesture set butterflies skittering inside of her. She brought clenched fists against her thighs. Why had he come back? She leaned against her dresser. God, she was glad to see him.

And then, as January rolled into February, and there was still no word from the investigator, Amelia set aside her doubts about Lance, and fell back into the old pattern of acquiescing to him. More and more, as she acceded to Lance's wishes, she made excuses to Mike, and quite often left her camera at home. Ashamed that she had confessed her passion for Lance, Amelia avoided Grace's eyes when they were together.

And then one evening after a fine dinner followed by hours of glorious dancing, she and Lance returned to his apartment, which miraculously, was one of two apartments that had been relatively unaffected by water or mud from the storm.

The lights were turned low. Soft music, Benny Goodman perhaps, floated from every corner of the room, yet she saw no speakers. "Where's the music coming from?"

"They're behind the pictures." He lifted one of the two new, stark black-and-white line drawings from the wall. Behind the drawing was a long, flat speaker.

"Clever," Amelia said, thinking how like him to hide the speakers, as he hid his own life.

All else about Lance's apartment screamed temporary and eluded warmth: bare white walls, uncarpeted wood floors, minimal leather furniture, and not a vase of flowers, a book, a photograph, or even a magazine. Amelia never felt comfortable here.

Lance slipped his arm about her waist, drew her down onto the couch, and kissed her repeatedly, first softly, then more urgently. "Amelia."

"Yes?" It was more a groan than a word.

"We're good together, don't you think?"

She nodded.

"So what's the problem. Why can't you just let yourself go, enjoy yourself, enjoy us?"

"I do enjoy us."

"Let's go to bed, darling." He was up off the couch then and reaching for her hands. Against the stark white wall, he loomed dark and somewhat sinister.

Heart racing, quivering, Amelia lay there. She did not raise her hands to meet his. "I can't do that."

"Why can't you?"

"Do you love me, Lance?" She held her breath.

"Do you love me, Amelia?" His lips curled in a wry smile.

She pulled the edges of her blouse together, and rebuttoned the tiny pearl buttons he had undone. God, his hand had felt good on her breast. Keep a clear head, she urged the part of herself that longed to give in to him. Wait for the report from Detective Lambert. It would probably be fine, but still something urged she ought to wait.

"I asked you first, Lance, do you love me?"

He remained silent, turned, and strode to the window. "It's starting to snow."

Slipping from the couch, Amelia was on her feet in a moment. "Take me home, Lance, before I get stuck up here."

He whirled, his eyes gray and stormy. "Stuck? With me?" His eyes frightened her. Why had she come here tonight? Stupid!

It happened so fast. Lance grabbed her, and in a flash she found herself on the couch again with his weight bearing her deep into the cushions. "I'm crazy for you. You tease me and leave me," he murmured. His hands worked at the scarf, to undo it. "What do I care about a few scars. You're a lovely woman." He kissed her neck above the scarf.

Afraid as she was, he stirred passion in her. It muddled her thinking. Why was she making all this fuss? What would be so terrible if she went to bed with him? It's not the scars, she reminded herself. You don't trust him. She grasped this thought and held on to it, determined not to go to bed with a man possessed of so many secrets.

Her hands pushed at his chest, and he raised his head and peered at her with lust-filled eyes. "It's not about scars, Lance. It's about trust. Where do you go each month? I know nothing about you, Lance. Tell me, please."

He eased his weight a bit. "What you see is what you get, Amelia. I thought you understood that."

"I try to understand, but I don't." Her voice cracked. Suddenly she knew she had to get out of here, get away from him. But how? Bob's condo wasn't far, just up around the curve. Grace was there, she knew that. She could walk. No, she couldn't, not on snowy, slippery roads, not in confounded high heels, and certainly not barefoot.

A crooked smile settled on Lance's face. "You know how much I want you, Amelia." His powerful arms crushed her beneath him. Against her thigh, his erection pressed for satisfaction. His mouth clamped over hers, and his lips, which she had enjoyed kissing and being kissed by, were now hard and insistent. He breathed scotch. Suddenly, his kiss repulsed her. Twisting her head away, she gasped for breath. Wiggling one hand free, Amelia pushed against his chest, but it was like pushing granite.

Oh, God, Amelia prayed silently, help me. Somewhere in the recesses of her mind, beyond the shock, and confusion, and deep regret, she determined to fight him, or try to. Could she bring her knee to his crotch as she'd seen done in movies? But it was impossible to move. His tugging at her clothes grew more urgent. Lance grunted

247

something she did not understand, and pinioned both her arms. Under the steamy heat of his passion, Amelia whimpered and lay there helplessly compressed by the weight and strength of him. Amelia closed tear-filled eyes. This was not what she had dreamed. This was horrible.

And then she bit him. Her teeth clamped down like a vise on his tongue, and he screamed. The way he rolled off of her told her she had a chance. In a second she was up and heading for the door. Amelia yanked it open. Barefoot and without a coat, Amelia darted out into the cold night, into the road, and almost into the path of an oncoming car.

The driver slammed on his brakes. The car skidded sideways and stopped. By some miracle Bob and Grace were in the car. "My God, Amelia," Grace shouted, and tearing open the door ran to Amelia, who, having used every ounce of energy, simply stood there weeping. By the time Lance appeared in his doorway screaming, "Amelia, get back here," she was safe in Bob's car, and as they rounded the hairpin curve, they could still hear Lance cursing her. Covering her ears Amelia curled up in the backseat and cried.

At the farmhouse, Bob carried Amelia upstairs to her bedroom and laid her gently on her bed. Grace and Hannah undressed her.

"He would have hurt me," Amelia sobbed. "Oh Grace, if you and Bob hadn't come."

"Thank God, Bob was just taking me home."

Hannah put cold compresses on Amelia's bruised arms, and Grace stayed with her all night and most of the next day. Twice before, she and Hannah had tended Amelia and nursed her physically and emotionally back to health: after she had been lost in Pisgah Forest and rescued, and again when Amelia, out shooting pictures, was caught in a renegade snowstorm and her car slid into a ditch. She had been rescued by the highway patrol moments prior to collapsing into a snowbank. As Amelia herself had said recently, major stress upon major stress left a person more vulnerable and less resilient.

"Lights. Please turn on more lights," Amelia requested. She curled into a ball and stared at nothing. She would not look at Grace or Hannah, and absolutely refused to see Mike. It was odd, wanting to hide from them all, yet needing so much light.

Amelia stayed in her room most of the time for almost a week. It was only when Hannah informed her that Detective Lambert had completed his investigation of Lance and was waiting in the living room that Amelia made it downstairs and collapsed onto the sofa. If she had had major surgery, she could not have seemed more exhausted.

The detective, a straight shooter as Harold had said he was, was of medium height, with sandy hair peeping from his Sherlock Holmes cap, and rumpled clothing. He stood stiffly throughout his report, and though he averted his eyes from Amelia, he spared them nothing. "Lance Lundquist's a scam artist," he declared flatly. "He preys on women, older widows, for their money."

"Why Amelia? She's not rich," Grace asked.

"He also preys on attractive ladies. They're his dessert, a reward you might say for being with women he doesn't like except for their money." He flipped a page of his report. "He's got a wife in Texas."

Amelia gasped.

"That's where he goes every month. They're in this scam together. Everything's in her name. Probably got a stash of cash and jewelry in the Bahamas. He's got two ex-wives who have lawsuits against him for back alimony, to which he pleads poverty. He's got one son who's in jail in Nevada for grand larceny. Gambling casino had him locked up."

His words jumbled in Amelia's brain as she struggled to control her trembling and hold back the tears that pressed behind her eyes. Standing behind Amelia's chair, Grace rested firm hands on her friend's shoulders. "It's going to be all right, Amelia. It's going to be all right."

Amelia shook her head. It would never ever be all right.

Hannah paced. "The bastard. How can we get him?"

"I doubt he's still around," Grace said.

"Right. But you could file charges with the sheriff's office," Lambert said.

"What will I do?" Amelia whispered. It was all she could do just to sit in the room and listen to the report. She didn't want to, or to otherwise embarrass or further humiliate herself in front of Lambert.

"Chalk it up to experience, ma'am, and get on with your life,"

Lambert said bluntly. "The longer you agonize over him, the more he's won."

"The bastard attacked Amelia," Hannah said.

"Visible injuries?" the detective asked.

"A few bruises on her arms, a sprained wrist."

"These guys are slick. They don't leave marks that can't be attributed to a fall or hitting an arm against some piece of furniture. It's his word against hers." He nodded toward Amelia, then shifted his eyes quickly away.

"Damn it, I hate the bastard." Hannah quivered with rage.

"I bet," Grace said, "if we went to his apartment right now, it'd be empty. We drove off, and, I'm sure he wasn't far behind us making his getaway."

Please God Grace is right, Amelia prayed silently, and he's gone, that I'll never have to see him again.

The detective looked contrite, sorry to have been the bearer of such news. "I'm sorry," he said, extending his hand to give Amelia the full written report.

"I'll take it," Hannah said.

Lambert slung on his coat, tipped his Sherlock Holmes cap, and moments later was gone.

With vacant eyes Amelia looked from Hannah to Grace. "Fool. I'm such a fool. How could I have trusted him? The signs were all there." Her eyes found Hannah's. "You warned me."

"It's over. Come. You need to rest." They led her upstairs to her room and Amelia collapsed onto her bed, where she slept for the next fifteen hours. It would be the deepest sleep she would have in many months.

37

The Wedding Dress

"It's for an older lady," Grace explained.

"How old?" the miniskirted salesgirl asked.

"Does it matter how old?" Grace was becoming irritated.

"It would help me find the right dress," the girl said. Grace noted the swelling in the pocket of her jaw. It couldn't be chewing tobacco; it must be gum.

"The bride-to-be is eighty-one years old."

The girl began to laugh. She cackled, and leaned against the wall clutching her stomach. Grace walked briskly from the store. The booth she found had a phone book hanging from a chain and stank of cheap perfume and cigarettes. Grace left the door open as she braced the heavy book on her hip. Two other wedding shops were listed; neither was far away.

Her walk took her past the civic center. For a moment Grace stopped to admire the charming, cast-bronze figures on the sidewalk—a tribute to Asheville's long tradition of folk music, and part of its urban trail—two adults dancing, a young girl clapping to a fiddler, and a banjo player. Overhead, the marquee advertised an upcoming Asheville Symphony concert, a gun and rifle show, an ice hockey match, and a country music program.

Grace scanned Ellie's Bridal Shop for an older saleswoman and saw a middle-aged woman, tall, with dark curly hair.

"My friend is an older lady being married for the first time. I'm shopping for a wedding gown for her. I have her measurements."

"How sweet," the saleswoman said. "I'm always pleased when someone older marries. I'm fifty-four. Gives me hope."

"She may be a size six. She'd like a dress that's high at the neck with long sleeves."

"We can handle that. We may have to order the size. Do you wish to try on the gowns yourself?"

"Oh, heaven, no. We're quite a different size and shape. May I see what you have with a high neck and long sleeves?"

"Step back here with me, please." Silently, over thick mauve carpeting, the saleswoman led Grace across one room, and through another, and offered her a seat on a tufted circular couch in the center of a salon lined with mirrors.

Soft elevator music drifted from hidden speakers, and Grace relaxed. From the bowels of the shop the saleswoman wheeled a rack of wedding gowns and began to rifle through the dresses.

Uncertain of wedding shop etiquette, Grace fought the urge to get up and look for herself. Sitting quietly, she fingered the clasp on her purse and worried that the woman would not find a suitable gown for Lurina. But soon she was holding out to Grace a long-sleeved satin gown that rose without a break to a high V at the throat. The dress zipped down the back.

Grace drew a breath. "That's lovely." Soft to the touch and a beautiful sheen, how could Lurina not love this gown? "I'll need to take it with me to show to my friend. I'll be glad to leave a deposit, or the full price of the gown if you'd prefer, but if she doesn't like it, I'll have to return it."

"I'm sorry. We don't let our gowns out of the shop to be tried on."

"It isn't possible for her to come."

"I'm sorry, then." She began to replace the gown among the others on the rack.

"Are you the manager?" Grace asked. Be polite but insistent, she told herself, but being insistent wasn't easy for her. She should have asked Hannah, or even Amelia to come with her.

"I am the manager."

"Are you the owner, also?"

"No. Mrs. Lerner owns the shop, but she's not here."

"Does she live in town?" Grace asked, trembling inside.

"Well, yes, she does, but I'm telling you, it's against store policy." The saleswoman pushed the rack of wedding gowns back through a curtained doorway, and returned rubbing her hands as if she had just washed them and had used a hot blower that left them damp.

Grace sat properly on the tufted sofa, knees together, shoulders back, purse clasped tightly in her lap. Her throat could not have been drier if she'd awakened from sleep and been breathing through her mouth.

"Would you be kind enough to phone and ask Mrs. Lerner if I might have a word with her, or make an appointment to see her another day, soon? I do like the gown, and I think my friend will also, but you never know, when you're shopping for someone else."

Unsmiling, the saleswoman walked briskly to the front of the store and reached behind the high marble-topped counter for the phone. She turned her back to Grace, who heard not a word being said. Then the woman swung about and looked at Grace. "Mrs. Lerner wants to know who you are, and who you're buying a gown for."

Grace lifted her chin and took the extended phone. "Hello, Mrs. Lerner. My name is Mrs. Grace Singleton. The gown is for Miss Lurina Masterson. We live in Covington in Madison County, and I own a tearoom there. The bride-to-be, Lurina Masterson, is an elderly lady, also from Covington. She's quite frail, and doesn't leave her home much."

Out in the street, beyond the wedding dresses displayed in the window, Grace could see traffic backed up and pedestrians crossing between the cars.

The owner's voice was kind, well modulated, and definitely northern. "I can see your problem. How old is the lady?"

"Quite old as a matter of fact, and she's never been married. It's a major happening. Two elderly people from local families."

"Sounds wonderful," Ellie Lerner said. "Tell you what. You choose two or three gowns that you think might work, and I'll bring them out myself. We can see what your friend likes and order in her size."

Grace felt the tension drain from her body. In fact she felt weak-kneed. "You'll bring them yourself? How very kind of you. Thank you so much."

"Give my saleslady directions, and a phone number. Put her on now, will you?"

A moment later the saleswoman hung up, all smiles, and they returned to the rack to select the three dresses that Ellie Lerner would bring with her to Covington.

✺

On February 21, 1999, Ellie Lerner's blue Buick sedan crossed the old wooden bridge and pulled to a stop at the farmhouse. Grace, Hannah, a silent and withdrawn Amelia, and Mike waited with Lurina on the porch. Grace ran down to welcome her. Ellie Lerner exited her car, and circled for a view of the land, the hills, the old farmhouse, the women, and Mike on the porch. "A well-kept secret, this Covington. Amazing, out of a storybook."

"Thank you so much for coming. Lurina Masterson is the one in the rocker on the porch." Grace did not point. "The other ladies are my housemates, Hannah and Amelia. Mike is Amelia's friend. Lurina's all nerves."

"The other ladies are your housemates, you say?"

Grace nodded.

"Sometime, I'd like to hear how you ladies met, and what brought you to Covington. I'm widowed. My husband died shortly after we moved here and opened the shop."

"I'm sorry," Grace said.

"It was hard, still is," Ellie said. "My kids live in New York and California. Sometimes I wonder why I stay here."

Carefully, they lifted three plastic bags containing the gowns from the back of the car. Ellie moved gracefully up the steps, all smiles. "You must be Lurina Masterson. I am Eleanor Lerner, Ellie. I'm so pleased to meet you, and delighted for the opportunity to show you our gowns."

Introductions and pleasantries exchanged, they stepped inside. Grace held Lurina's arm and felt her shaking. Mike helped Ellie carry the gowns, and they spread the plastic bags across the Victorian sofa. Slim and well dressed in a simple gray pantsuit with an aquamarine silk ascot hanging across her shoulders and down almost to her waist, Ellie took a minute to brush auburn hair back from her oval face. Wide blue eyes took in the people, the house, everything. Her smile was sunshine. Grace liked her.

The living room of Lurina's farmhouse had been given a face-lift. Earlier, Hannah had polished all the heavy wood furniture: the tabletops, the arms of chairs, the carved umbrella stand, everything but the double-barrel shotgun. The mahogany sideboard glowed. Antique Tiffany table lamps sparkled. A pot of water with a dash of vanilla and cinnamon simmered on a low fire in the kitchen, filling the house with the faint hint of baking.

With her long braid wound three times about her head and pinned securely, Lurina glowed. The flowered dress Grace had helped her select for this occasion smelled slightly of cedar, but Grace had dabbed a touch of her own light, fruity toilet water behind Lurina's ears and on the inside of her wrists.

The wedding dresses slipped easily from their plastic bags. Ellie held up the dress Grace had liked at first sight. "Amazingly, I had this in your size, six. Someone ordered it, and the wedding was canceled." Ellie lifted the dress and turned it round and round so that Lurina could see the back, and the way the skirt swirled.

The sleeves on the second dress were scalloped and trimmed in lace, and the neckline came to just below the neck with a binding of lace, and a lace bodice over satin. The Queen Anne collar on the third gown caused Lurina to laugh. "I seen a picture of an old-time queen dressed like that," she said.

"It's called a Queen Anne collar," Ellie said. "Some people like it very much."

"Too fancy for me," Lurina said. Lurina chose the gown that was Grace's favorite. "I likes the smooth feel of it." She ran her fingertips tentatively along the satin, mumbling to herself, nodding her head, smiling.

"Come on, Lurina, let's try it on," Grace said. They went into the dining room and shut the door.

The dress fit perfectly. Mike brought the standing mirror down from upstairs and tipped it so Lurina could see all of herself. Her eyes grew wide, the largest Grace had ever seen them. "This ain't Lurina," she whispered. "It's somebody's fairy godmother."

"It's lovely on you," Ellie said.

Lurina changed back into her clothes, and they hung the dress on the dining room door. "I want to keep it right here with me," Lurina said.

"Well, since it is your size, that'll be just fine. If I'd had to order it, it would have taken weeks until you could have had it."

"I got one room with a window air conditioner. Pa's room. Don't go in there much, but it'll keep the dress fresh and nice, won't it?"

"It will indeed."

"Should I hang it with cedar or mothballs?"

"Neither. Just in the closet."

Hannah and Amelia had prepared cookies and lemonade. Mike passed the lemonade in gold-rimmed tumblers that Hannah had unearthed from an old pie safe in the kitchen. Ellie asked Lurina about the one-room schoolhouse she had attended so long ago. She asked how many students there were, and was duly impressed when Lurina said she was marrying an old schoolmate. Grace appreciated the fact that Ellie spoke to Lurina without talking down to her, as so many folks did with older people. Grace wanted to hug her for her kindness and attention to her friend.

Ellie chatted easily, asking when Covington was first settled, and by whom, and what did the settlers do? She wanted to see Cove Road and the ladies' farmhouse. She was interested in P. J. Prancer's hardware store. "When my grandparents emigrated from Lithuania in the 1880s, they had a small general store in New Jersey. My father was born in the apartment they lived in above the store."

Grace thought of her own grandparents, from Holland, traveling steerage on a ship to join cousins already farming in Canton, Ohio. Amazing country this America. She could think of no country where immigrants from so many diverse and distant nations had come together voluntarily, and in peace, to create a nation.

"Grandpa Luke," Lurina was saying, "his pa and ma done took the fever and died, so he hitched up a mule and come by hisself from flatland down east of Raleigh. Covingtons were already here. Grandpa Luke staked out this land, a good piece apart. Good neighbors oughta be far off enough so as they can't see their neighbors' laundry."

Lurina related only one brief death story, about a drunken McCorkle who had tumbled off a bridge into a gully. "A goose drownder killed him, sure 'nuff."

Grace whispered to Ellie, "Flash flood. He drowned."

Amelia brightened momentarily, when she heard that Ellie enjoyed the theater.

Finally, Ellie said, "I've loved every minute of this afternoon, and I'm so happy you found a gown you like, Miss Lurina, but I must go now."

Lurina started to push herself from her chair. "You come back and see me, now."

"Please, don't get up on my account, I can show myself out," Ellie said. "I'd love to come back." She looked at Grace and smiled.

Mike carried the other two gowns to her car, and they stood in a row like telephone poles, and waved from the porch until the Buick turned onto Elk Road and disappeared toward Mars Hill.

38

Television Arrives on the Scene

Early the next morning, a highly agitated Lurina phoned Grace. "They want to put Joseph Elisha and me on some fancy television show. You talk to 'em, Grace. You tell 'em no."

"Who wants to do this?"

"Don't know the name. Some connivin' woman from New York."

Grace wondered if Lurina had dreamed this. Then Grace recalled Amelia saying the wedding would make a great story for a television magazine show.

"Did they leave a phone number?" she asked Lurina. But who had notified them, Grace wondered, and was it local or national television? Everyone in their small community knew about Lurina and Old Man's upcoming wedding. Anyone could have made that call.

Lurina's voice, raised in agitation, struck her eardrum. "I hung up on 'em right quick."

Hours later, Lurina phoned Grace again. "Woman called again. Name of Jill. She must of thought I was stupid, kept trying to tell me my weddin' was some important story, people all over the country'd be interested. I just kept sayin' 'No' but that woman, she wouldn't shut her mouth, so I hung up."

"Did you get a number?" Grace asked.

"What for?"

She had barely hung up from Lurina when the phone rang again. Grace was busy getting ready to go to the theater in Virginia with

Bob. But, these days, Amelia answered no phones, and Hannah was out in the greenhouse with Wayne, Grace picked up the receiver. A woman's voice asked, "Is this Grace Singleton?"

"Yes, and who am I speaking to?"

"Jill Moran. Our network loved the story about Ms. Masterson and Mr. Reynolds getting married. It's a marvelous story, so encouraging to folks who consider their lives over because they're of a certain age."

"These folks here live quiet, private lives," Grace said. "They don't want to be interviewed by anyone, and they don't want to be on television."

"So many people are hesitant, nervous at first, until we talk to them," Jill said. "I assure you, Mrs. Singleton, we'd do nothing, absolutely nothing to embarrass the couple."

Unrelenting woman, Grace thought, realizing that she had no power to stop them from coming to Covington. What happens when they get here's another story, she thought, and said into the phone, "I'm sorry, but Miss Masterson is adamant. She's not interested in the publicity."

Grace hung up. Her face flushed and the pulse at her temples throbbed. Who in heaven's name had created this problem? Who had called a national television show? "Amelia," she called, sticking her head out of her bedroom door. "Where are you?"

"Here, in my room."

"Can you come to my room, please?" Grace felt the anxiety of time pressure building in her. Bob would be here any minute now. They were driving to the Barton Theater in Abingdon, Virginia, two and a half hours north and east of Mars Hill, and they both hated being late for anything.

Amelia's depression was evident in her dull eyes, the faded muu-muu she wore, and her snail-like walk. "What is it?" she asked, holding the railing.

"Did you call a national television show about Lurina and Old Man?"

"Goodness, no. We decided against that, remember?"

"Well, someone did. Lurina had a call, and now they've called me."

Amelia didn't care. Nothing interested her these days.

"Some TV out of New York's hell-bent on sending someone down here to interview whomever will talk to them."

"So what? You don't *have* to talk to them."

"That's right." She studied Amelia's face for a clue and found only blandness and indifference. "And, you didn't call them?"

Amelia stared at Grace. "I certainly did not. I'm not a liar."

"Please, Amelia," Grace said. "I'm sorry. I know you're not a liar. I'm agitated. The woman on the phone would not be put off, and Lurina's incredibly upset. Bob will be here any minute now to get me." Turning to her mirror, Grace snapped on a pair of silver clip earrings and dabbed on lipstick. She was ready now.

"Who was on the phone and would not be put off?" Hannah asked from the doorway.

Amelia shrugged, stepped behind Hannah, and headed down the hall toward her own room.

When Grace told Hannah about the calls, Hannah rubbed her forehead. "It's always something, isn't it?"

The television van arrived on a Tuesday. Lurina heard the tires and met them on her front porch, shotgun raised. Immediately they turned and rumbled back across the bridge. In hours everyone in Covington knew. Phones hummed. People were excited. Most were more than willing to be interviewed.

The van ended up at Grace and Bob's tearoom. Jill was pleasant enough, thirty-something, with shoulder-length honey-colored hair parted in the center. Grace watched Jill switch from one pair of glasses for reading, then back to another pair for distance, and wondered why she didn't get bifocals.

"It's too good a story to let go." Jill looked at them earnestly through her wire-rim distance glasses while nibbling the temple of her tortoiseshell reading glasses. "Everyone loves it at the office. So often stories come in about crime, kidnappings, things like that. People gobble up a sweet story with a happy ending, and this is one of them." She shook her head, swept her long hair behind her ears. "Good stories are hard to get, folks involved are private, don't want their lives disturbed, and I do understand that. So often, it's the weirdos that want publicity."

"Would the old girl have shot us?" the young man accompanying Jill asked.

"Her name is Miss Lurina Masterson."

"Would Miss Masterson have shot us?"

"She's a mean shot," Grace lied, crossing her fingers behind her.

"This is what we'd like to do," Jill explained. On went the reading glasses. She bent over a sheet of paper on the table and made a few notes, then the wire-rim glasses were on, followed by the tortoiseshell glasses again. She looked intently from Grace to Bob. "Interview the groom, then Miss Masterson, then both of them. I'd prefer the interviews take place where they live, but we can do them anywhere, actually. Here, perhaps?"

"Lurina and Old Man don't want publicity," Grace said.

"Old Man? Is that what he's called? Isn't his name Joseph Elisha? Why is he called Old Man?" Jill leaned forward, eyes flashing with interest.

✦

Dissuading Jill proved impossible. The next day the van squirreled its way to the mountain fastness of Old Man and Wayne and found them digging silt out of trenches along their roadway. As neither was aware of the hullabaloo in Covington, the Reynolds men gave the occupants of the van a country welcome, and invited them for lemonade and Grace's sugar cookies. Jill, as Wayne later told Hannah, was slow talkin' for a Yankee, and real nice. Wayne showed them the Reynolds Cemetery, and told how Lurina had objected, then agreed, to rest next to Old Man, come the time. He gave them the wedding date. He told Jill how it was to be a fancy wedding with Lurina wearing a white satin gown, and how he would take Old Man to Asheville to buy a suit. They visited for over an hour, and Old Man invited them to come back real soon.

✦

The following day dawned cloudy, a perfect day for working in the greenhouse. Wayne went on and on telling Hannah about Jill. "Raised up on a farm, but she's been a city gal too long, I reckon, 'cause she stepped right in the stream crossin' it to see the piglets from Old Man's prize sow."

Hannah's mouth fell open. "They found you way out there. Don't you know who they are?"

"Sure. They're from New York, and they do a weekly nighttime show on TV. They want to tell all about Old Man and Miss Lurina marryin' up after all these years." He smiled sheepishly. "Course they're wantin' to make it like Old Man and Lurina been boyfriend and girlfriend way back, which ain't so. Guess it can't harm no one."

Hannah shoveled soil into a container so fiercely that it spilled over the edge of the container. "Old Man agree to that?"

"Didn't agree or disagree. He's gotta ponder things awhile."

"I can't believe you, Wayne." She waved the shovel at him. "You should have told Old Man to talk to Lurina first. She's very upset and doesn't want to be on television. Took her shotgun to them when they crossed her bridge."

He laughed. "Old Miss Lurina's a pistol, ain't she? Shotgun's empty. Don't even know how to load it. Besides ain't you noticed, Miss Hannah, Miss Lurina always says no to everything first. You gotta talk her into it."

"That's true," Hannah said. "But she seems adamant about not making a spectacle of herself on television."

"We could all be on television, Miss Hannah: me, and you, and Miss Grace, and Miss Amelia. Good publicity for the tearoom, Jill says, and for this plant business, and they'd hang Miss Amelia's pictures so's folks all over America could see 'em."

"A nice tidy package."

"Seems like a mighty fine idea to me."

"They did a good selling job with you, Wayne. If they do this show, then the entire United States will know about Covington. Lord, it will change, guaranteed. Talk about development." She shook the container to settle the soil, and remained silent a moment or two. "Guess it's just that I like things the way they are, Wayne. I've lived through too much change, too much progress in my lifetime." Hannah scooped out a handful of soil, inserted a small plant, and pressed hard about its roots. "Peaceful here, not crime-ridden, no traffic to speak of yet, and lots of decent people."

"Poor folks too, Miss Hannah, back up in the hills, and uneducated," Wayne said.

Hannah looked at him. She had never thought of Wayne as being either personally ambitious or socially aware. She began watering the little plant, and spilled water on her shoes as she considered how to respond. "What do you want to do with your life, Wayne?"

Reaching for another plastic container high on a shelf, Wayne said, "Used to think I didn't want much, wife maybe, kids one of these days. Double-wide manufactured home to put us in."

Hannah recalled visiting in Wayne's single mobile home and being impressed it was so spick-and-span.

"And now?" She took the container from him. When she met Wayne he held no steady job, sported a variety of young ladies, and tore about the place in an old truck.

"You ladies got me thinkin' about my life. Miss Amelia's off takin' pictures, and Miss Grace has her a right pretty tearoom." He waved his arms. "You and this here greenhouse. Sellin' it to me sure settled me down. Now Old Man's gettin' married. Probably move into Miss Lurina's place, if she don't mind the pigs. He ain't gonna give up his pigs no how. Used to be, I just went along. Like you say, things change, Miss Hannah. Guess that's life. That's what Old Man says. One thing, I'm sure gonna miss Old Man up the mountain."

For an instant, Hannah felt an urge to pitch the plant she was working on to the floor and stamp on it. She had read recently about how in quantum physics, the observer changed the observed. This principle applied to people. Anthropologists, as observers of indigenous peoples, were also observed by those people, and both were changed. People rejected cities, relocated in rural areas or on island paradises, and wittingly or unwittingly they introduced the trappings of the culture they held in disdain. Everyone, observer and observee, newcomer and old-timer, everyone was affected, everyone changed. Were there pristine places left? Even remote and inhospitable islands like the Galápagos drew thousands of tourists a year, trampling vegetation, perhaps dropping candy wrappers or film wrappers when guides were not looking. And here was Wayne explaining how she and her friends had influenced him and changed his view of things.

Thinking of this, Max's words of caution plagued her. Had she, by persisting in opposing Jake Anson, invited the ire of the community on herself, on Amelia and Grace? What right had she to attempt to impose her values on Anson? In these mountains, a man reigned supreme over his land, free to hold or dispose of it as he chose. Yet, she realized, she was getting in deeper all the time, haranguing folks, agitating Anson, and others. When she had last chatted with Max, he suggested that before she reveal information about an old graveyard, she contact an attorney. Already this matter, with phone calls, and flyers and petitions and posters, had cost her several hundred dollars.

"You done with that plant, Miss Hannah?" Wayne asked, and Hannah's mind flip-flopped back into the greenhouse. He relieved her of the pot and placed it on one of the shelves.

That very afternoon, Hannah put in a call to Laura. The phone in the bait and supply shop on the dock rang. This was the only way to contact her daughter. They radioed messages to boats anchored out in the harbor. In Hannah's mind the dock at Rockport, the boats, many of them fishing vessels, smelled of salt and fish. She pictured weathered gray docks, small skiffs tied to piers, stacked lobster pots, tourists posing for pictures or holding high the day's biggest catch. And back from the shore, Victorian houses with their widow's walks, perched on hillsides and converted now to bed and breakfasts, inns, restaurants, or shops catering to the tourist trade.

Captain Marvin and Laura hosted day passengers along the Maine coast as far north as Penobscot Bay and Mount Desert Island, or on whale-watching excursions. Laura crewed and cooked for their guests. Laura a cook, imagine. Laura refused to boil an egg when she lived at home. When the phone rang a half hour later, it surprised Hannah to hear her daughter's voice.

"I just walked into the store," she said. "Ron said you'd called. How are you? Anything wrong?"

"No, everything's fine, they've even predicted an early spring, which is great." Hannah's heart raced. So much she wanted to say. In the background on Laura's end she heard muffled voices, a door slam. "Can you speak louder?" Laura asked.

"How was Christmas?"

"Quiet. We went to friends' over in Camden, not far. Yours?"

"Pleasant. Your sister tells me you're going to the Caribbean. When?"

"I was going to phone you, Mother. The ketch is in dry dock. Soon as she comes off, we'll provision and take off."

"What island are you going to?"

"American and British Virgins. Once we get there, we'll see where we want to be."

"It's supposed to be beautiful down there," Hannah said, skirting her real reasons for calling Laura: to wish her well, to say she understood her wanderlust, her attachment to Marvin. The words stuck in Hannah's throat. On Laura's end of the line it sounded as if someone were pouring nails onto a metal scale to measure them. Did they sell nails in a bait shop?

"Do they sell nails there?" Hannah asked, feeling stupid.

"No." Laura's voice sounded puzzled. Then she said, "Oh, what you hear are weights. Someone's buying weights to use in fishing." Then silence. Hannah shifted from one leg to the other.

"Laura," she began.

"Yes, Mother, what is it?"

Hannah heard the tinge of impatience in Laura's voice, and she reacted with her own measure of irritation. Why was there never a time or place where Laura could talk to her without Hannah feeling rushed?

Hannah tried to picture Laura as she was today. Business suit discarded for jeans, cotton shirt, sneakers. Hannah closed her eyes for a moment. Where Miranda was tall like herself, Laura was of middle height, and firm and round, never skinny. Pretty, prettier than Miranda, with blue almond-shaped eyes and high cheekbones inherited from a distant ancestor, eyes old beyond their years, yet when Laura laughed, they twinkled like those of a happy little girl filled with trust, and hopeful. Did they still shine like that? Hannah wondered. Had Laura's smooth olive skin grown darker in the sun? Was it blotched or wrinkled from years of wind, and sea, and salt air? A cheerleader and dancer, Laura had developed strong, muscular, legs, perfect for working on the boat, she imagined.

"A ketch is a boat, Mother," Laura had once explained. "A boat is not necessarily a ketch. A boat could be a yacht, or a trawler, many things. Please call the *Maribow* a ketch."

Marvin's ketch was sixty feet long with four sails: a mainsail, a smaller back sail Laura called a mizzen, and two smaller sails in front, a jib and a foresail. In the library, Hannah had located a book on boating and found a picture of a ketch, so she knew where the sails were positioned, although she had no concept of their use.

Hannah cleared her throat. "Want to wish you good luck, girl. Safe passage. Send postcards." She wanted more than postcards. "Send me an address so I can write to you."

"You never write, Mother," her daughter said.

266

"Miracles happen." Hannah laughed somewhat self-consciously.

"I'll be in touch. Bye now."

"Laura."

"What?"

"I, I . . ." She couldn't get "I love you" out. "My best to Captain Marvin, and you take care of yourself." They hung up. Hannah stood there with her hand on the phone thinking about Laura. Laura, had been so angry, petulant, and defiant as a teenager. Hannah had suspected Laura was sexually active at fourteen, but chose to ignore her suspicions. If asked, would Laura have admitted it? Probably not, only taken umbrage at the question. How did a mother ask a teenage daughter such a question, anyhow? How come, Hannah thought, she had no trouble questioning others or holding her own in an argument, but with Laura, her tongue twisted and curled. She would write to her daughter as soon as Laura sent an address.

This resolved, Hannah walked into the foyer and took her coat from the rack. She'd drive over to the tearoom. If Grace had time they'd sit and have a cup of tea. If not she'd visit with her in the kitchen, tell her about the television crew's courting of the Reynolds, and that she had spoken, finally, to Laura.

39

Lurina Does It Her Way

Then, as suddenly as they had come, the television van with Jill Moran and its crew disappeared. Rumors circulated. Timmy, the clerk at P. J. Prancer's, whispered to everyone, "I heard they got them a better story down in Atlanta."

Buddy, at the gas station, told his customers, "Old Miss Lurina and Old Man weren't a good enough story for national TV."

And one of the Herrill cousins said, "They ain't the best TV show anyhow."

And after a week or ten days, disappointment gave way to resignation, and the rumors subsided.

Spring lay upon the land. In a glory of white, the Bradford pear trees burst into bloom. Rows of Bradford pears at the Asheville Mall resembled the bouffant skirts of wedding dresses held high on lollipop sticks. Forsythia bloomed brilliant yellow, and red bud trees blossomed a glory of pink. On Cove Road, houses swam in seas of white and yellow daffodils. It was, everyone declared, the most glorious March in recent memory.

The tearoom opened each day to waiting crowds. Grace and Bob found themselves with time for little else but work. Lurina called Grace every day, and seemed to need reassurance that all was well and would be well. One afternoon when she phoned Grace at the tearoom, Lurina's voice was teary. "I ain't gonna do it, Grace."

"Do what, Lurina?" Grace shoved a tray of pastries into the oven.

"Marry me up with Joseph Elisha."

"Now, Lurina, you've got normal jitters. Every bride goes through this before her wedding."

"Ain't jitters. It's all those nosy TV people hangin' about just the other side of my land, out of range of my shotgun."

"You mean they're back? Bob," she called, "Lurina says the TV people are back."

"They been sweet-talkin' Joseph Elisha to where he thinks we oughta let 'em take our pictures and all. I don't want to be on no television show, Grace." Lurina began to weep in earnest.

That was a Monday. On Wednesday morning the phone woke Grace. "Get Bob, and get you over here before noon today," Lurina said.

Grace faced a long day at the tearoom. She sighed. "What's the matter?"

"Just you come, and bring Hannah, and Amelia too, and that nice fellow, Amelia's friend, Mike, but no one else, you hearin' me, no one else." She was whispering as if there were spying ears and eyes all about her.

"Is there someone with you? Why are you whispering?"

"Them Yankee TV folks campin' out real close to the bridge."

"They can't hear you from out there."

"You never know about folks like that with all their fancy contraptions."

For a moment, Grace wondered if Jill's crew had managed to bug Lurina's house. She shook her head. Lurina was paranoid, and she was making Grace paranoid.

Lurina whispered, "Joseph Elisha and me's gonna get us married today."

"What? Today?" Grace sat up and swung her legs to the floor.

"Sure 'nuff. Pastor Johnson's comin'. Don't you tell no one now, Grace. You're my matron of honor, so wear your fancy dress, and come on over."

They would have either to call and have Sybil, their new waitress, come in and pick up the keys and open the tearoom or put a sign on the door saying they were closed. Her usual equanimity was fast fading, and Grace found herself struggling against irritation and the sense of having been put upon. She had spent hours organizing this wedding, shopping for the wedding dress, arranging for flowers, food. The wedding date was set for July 1 with a reception at the tearoom. Invitations, one hundred of them addressed by herself, Amelia, and Hannah at their kitchen table, had been mailed to everyone in Covington, and the Reynolds clan in Tennessee, Georgia, South Carolina, and Alabama.

Grace calmed herself. It took several minutes for her mind to process the change and its ramifications. After all, who wouldn't be nervous getting married for the first time at eighty-one? Lurina's entire life would change. And it occurred to Grace that perhaps this was Lurina's way of avoiding a big church wedding and all the people staring at her as she walked down the aisle. "You're upset, that's all," Grace said.

"Sure am. Don't want no television people hangin' about my weddin'."

Grace would have liked to give a good dressing down to whomever it was that had phoned these people in the first place. She resented Jill's persistence, and the way locals reacted, as if they dreamed of being on television themselves. Now, she would have to cancel the flowers for the church, cancel the food ordered for the reception, and the invitations. Grace was beginning to get a headache. How do you cancel invitations? Send out un-invitations.

LURINA MASTERSON AND JOSEPH ELISHA REYNOLDS
REQUEST THAT YOU NOT ATTEND THEIR WEDDING ON JULY 1.
TO AVOID UNWANTED PUBLICITY, THEY WERE MARRIED AT HOME
IN A PRIVATE CEREMONY ON MARCH 13.

People had enjoyed the TV crew. Having them about was exciting for them. Many of the younger residents of Cove Road had visited, and chatted, and brought them cakes, casseroles, and pies. Jill and her crew pandered to their egos, took their pictures with crew members, handed out T-shirts and caps. Brenda had explained that having the crew there enlivened Covington and lent an air of excitement and mystery to most folks' lives.

Suddenly it seemed funny. Grace giggled, covering her mouth so that Lurina would not hear, but the old lady was gifted with sharp hearing.

"You laughin' at me, Grace?"

"No. With you, Lurina. I'm laughing with you. Just thinking how you'll fool Jill and her people."

Lurina laughed. "It's a fine day for a weddin', Grace, wouldn't you say? All them redbuds out back bloomin' and all." Her voice grew serious, lost its conspiratorial whisper. "Ask Hannah to pick me some redbud branches to fix up the place, well, you know, cheerful-like." Then, as if she spotted prying eyes peering through her window, she whispered into the phone. "Don't say nothin' 'bout this to no one else, Grace, you hear me? That gown we bought is sure heavy, hard for me to put on by myself. Come an' help me dress, will you?"

"You're wearing your wedding gown at home?"

"Sure 'nuff. Amelia can take our picture."

What would people think? Say? Grace gathered her wits about her and pushed away such concerns. Who cared what people thought or said? Lurina was a character. Few of her neighbors had paid her much attention in years. "We'll be there, Lurina," she said.

Lurina's voice on the phone turned contrite. "You ain't mad at me, are you, Grace? You've been to so much trouble for me and all."

"No, I'm, not mad. I understand the pressure you're under. You just go ahead and do it your way, Lurina."

When Grace hung up, she phoned Bob and relayed the news. "Well," he said, after thinking about it for a moment, "you've got to hand it to her. Rugged determinism's alive and well in Covington."

Hannah was shocked at the news that Lurina and Old Man were getting married in her house, at noon, that very day.

"She wants us to be there. She's asked if you'd cut redbud branches from her trees behind the house to decorate the parlor." Grace stopped to catch her breath.

"She's doing what?" Amelia poked her head into the room. Even in this awful post-Lance period, no matter how her heart ached, immediately on getting out of bed and before opening her window shades or using the bathroom, Amelia brushed her hair and put on makeup.

Once, recently, Grace, whose every mood was reflected on her face, asked Amelia how she could look so good and feel so bad.

Amelia had tossed her head. "Habit. Training. Mother said you always put on your best face. No one likes a crybaby or a whiner." What choice did she have? Her heart ached, as if someone had died. Not someone, something: hope. Still, as much as Amelia wanted to lie down and die, she knew that she must take one step at a time, one day at a time. Hadn't she survived hell before? "Oh, God," Amelia asked God when she lay in bed at night, "why so much pain again?"

Mike had suggested another photography book. The focus on people this time, perhaps, and in black and white.

"No," she yelled at him, then regretting it, said, "maybe later." Enthusiasm for photography seemed also to have been laid to rest, yet Amelia still loaded her camera and shot pictures, pictures without heart.

Grace studied Amelia's face. Behind the makeup, Grace could make out the tiny lines about her drooping mouth, the pain in her friend's eyes, yet Amelia never uttered one word about Lance. This is not good, Grace thought, not good at all. Lance had humiliated and crushed Amelia. It was impossible for her to brush it away this soon. Her heart went out to her friend. It was easy to ignore someone's pain when they went to such lengths to mask it. It would take time and patience to pry Amelia's suffering into the light of day. Grace experienced a pang of guilt, for she had no time at the moment to stop and ask, and listen to her friend. Like tumbleweed, her own life careened along: the cemetery visits, the wedding dress, Lurina's wedding plans, the tearoom, squeezing out one morning a week for the children at Caster Elementary. It dismayed her that she, and Hannah, and Amelia had not shared a good old-fashioned tea and a relaxed chat at home in months. Hannah came to the tearoom some afternoons, and if there was an empty table and it was slow, they sat awhile, had tea, and chatted; but there were distractions, and it wasn't the same. As a result of choices made, her life lacked cohesion and calm, and Grace did not like it. With all she had on her mind, it was a relief, this change in Lurina's wedding plans. It would be done with, and she would have time to sit and talk to Bob about how she really felt about the tearoom, about how at night she lay awake regretting having gone into business at all.

273

Cars driving across the wooden bridge to Lurina's farmhouse an hour before noon must have alerted the television crew camping at the edge of her property. Three young men in jeans and jackets scrambled to set up tripods and trained their incredibly long lenses on the cars, on the house. As they crossed the bridge, Grace looked away. Amelia, however, waved at the crew, raising Grace's suspicion again that Amelia had made the original call. Hannah, who was driving, ignored them.

"They're just doing their jobs," Amelia said, "and their being here has livened up Covington."

Hannah bridled. "Livened it up for whom?" She too was suspicious that it was Amelia who had tipped them off.

"You think Lurina should let them film her wedding, probe into her life, blast it all over this country?"

The instant they pulled up behind the house, Hannah tromped off to cut redbud branches, and Grace hastened inside. She shoved the sherbet for the punch into the freezer, and set the ginger ale and grape juice alongside the cut glass punch bowl Lurina had set out on the kitchen table. Minutes later, Mike breezed in, all smiles, eager to help, and when Hannah appeared with her arms loaded with branches of pink blossoms, he and Amelia took them and started into the living room to decorate.

Wearing a blue-and-white-checked housedress, Lurina shuffled into the kitchen. "Grace, help me get dressed. I see Wayne's truck comin' over the bridge. They're bringin' Pastor Johnson."

As Grace helped Lurina up the stairs, Lurina whispered, "After the weddin' Old Man and me, we gonna live here."

They moved along the narrow hallway. "What about his pigs?" Grace asked.

"We gonna get us a pen and a shed for them out by that old fallin'-down barn," Lurina said. Grace nodded. One more problem solved.

Lurina opened the door into a large front bedroom with a high ceiling and an enormous four-poster bed, whose heavily scrolled and scalloped headboard spoke of another era. "Ma and Pa's bed," Lurina said. With its bare wood floor and dark high chests placed like sentinels along walls, even the floral wallpaper failed to warm or tie together the cavernous room. "I don't sleep here," Lurina said. "This is where Pa passed away. Some days, lately, I come an' sit by that there window and study those folks over yonder, make sure none of 'em get on my land." She yanked down the shade. "See whatcha can now, city boys."

The bridal gown, its smooth satin glowing, sprawled across the bed like a lovely woman. "You ready?" Grace asked.

"Ready as I'm gonna be." Slowly, Lurina shed her housedress and stood there shivering in her cotton slip. She raised skinny arms and slid them into the wedding gown until all Grace could see of her were her hands and fingers. Grace held the neck of the dress wide, trying not to disturb Lurina's crown of braid. It settled in heavy folds about the tiny woman. And when Lurina studied herself in the standing mirror, she laughed with pleasure and preened. "Not half bad, eh? I look so good, maybe I shoulda let them boys over there make a picture."

What's she going to do, change her mind now? Grace thought. After all this?

"Let's get us down," Lurina said, suddenly flustered. "Gotta talk to Joseph Elisha."

Downstairs, Amelia and Mike had transformed the living room into a floral bower. Sprays of redbud were arranged in containers along the walls and behind the table that would be used as an altar. The men had rearranged the dark, antique furnishings to create an aisle through the parlor.

Getting Lurina downstairs was a feat. Hannah helped, holding the gown high in the back, while Grace went in front to make certain Lurina did not trip.

Soon after, the Johnson City twin sisters, Wilma and Wanda, dressed in silk prints and high-heeled shoes, arrived to represent the Reynolds clan. In their new blue suits, Wayne and Old Man appeared stiff and uneasy. Old Man's black shoes shined and squeaked when he walked, and it was obvious that they pinched his feet. Wayne had brought a cassette player, and now he tested a cassette tape of John Denver singing "Country Roads." Then he put on "Annie's Song."

Lurina and Old Man retired to a corner of the room and within moments were deep in a conversation remarkable for much flailing of hands, nodding, and shaking of heads.

"We ready?" Pastor Johnson asked. He stood by the altar/table, Bible in hand, dressed in black and smiling benignly. One thing

Grace had learned about Pastor Johnson. He never took sides. He was everybody's friend.

Almost reluctantly, the wedding couple moved away from one another, Old Man to join Bob beside the pastor, Lurina to take Wayne's arm in the dining room. Grace had changed into a light blue, ankle-length skirt and tunic top in which she felt slim and trim, and now she stood in the dining room doorway ready, as matron of honor, to lead the way for the bride. Mike handed Grace a nosegay of pink flowers.

Hannah pushed the button on Wayne's cassette player. John Denver began singing "Annie's Song," and Grace started to move forward. Two steps into the living room she felt a hand on her shoulder pulling her back. What now? Grace turned and stared into the face of the bride-to-be.

"Joseph Elisha's right. This here dress is too pretty to hide." She nudged Wayne's arm. "Get you out there, Wayne boy, and invite those picture takers in."

Grace's mouth fell open. Unbelievable! After all the protestation, Lurina was inviting the television crew to film her wedding at home.

"Let 'em all watch it on television," Lurina said to Grace. Then, lifting the skirt of her gown, Lurina plopped into a dining room chair to wait.

Lurina hadn't much formal education, but she's clever and sly as an old fox, Grace thought. Probably had it planned this way all the time, and then, briefly, it crossed her mind that perhaps Lurina herself had been the one to alert the TV people in the first place.

✻

Smiling and looking satisfied, Old Man stood slightly apart from Pastor Johnson looking as if he were about to burst out of his new suit. Unconcerned with the confusion Lurina had caused, he smiled benignly at Hannah, Amelia, Mike, Bob. Old Man liked Jill. She had continued to visit him with her crew, and had endeared herself to him. He called her a "good old country gal" and plied her with blackberry wine. In fact, Old Man had already been thoroughly interviewed and filmed by Jill and her crew. He was pleased at the turn of events, and that they would be married by a "right proper preacher" even if the event took place in Lurina's ancestral home, and Lurina was a sight to see all fancied up in a white satin, wedding dress with

276

her friends about her. He trusted Jill and her crew, and was delighted that Lurina had changed her mind. He'd had some part in that, he thought smugly.

Just then the back door slammed, and footsteps hurried. With a bang and a bustle, three cameramen dashed in, and after Jill had asked Hannah where the bride and groom would walk into the room, they positioned their lights and tripods. Lights glared, hot and much too bright for eyes. Jill said, "I don't usually do this, but . . ." Cosmetic pouch in hand, she dabbed rouge on the bride's cheeks, powdered Old Man's forehead, dabbed at Pastor Johnson's nose, and Grace's chin. "Don't want glare bouncing off your chin," Jill said, smiling at Grace. "Ready, now," she said. "Let's have a wedding."

Hannah punched the go button on the cassette player. John Denver's voice filled the room. A cameraman used the quick release on his tripod and slung the camera over his shoulder. Wayne being too tall and Lurina too short to fit arm in arm, simply held hands. Grace slowed her walk, and Lurina followed, looking this way and that, smiling at Jill, whom she had so belligerently turned away.

Of course "Annie's Song," although sentimental and lovely, lacked traditional tempo for the walk down the aisle, so Grace tried to block it out and counted aloud, "Step one, two, three; step, one, two, three." And so it was, that in Lurina's front parlor, brightened now by flowering sprays of pink, and under the glare and heat of television lights and cameras whirring, Lurina Masterson said "I do" to Joseph Elisha Reynolds. And when Pastor Johnson said, "I proclaim you man and wife," Lurina puckered her lips and Old Man puckered his, and they kissed the way a ten-year-old boy and girl might kiss. Everyone in the room clapped, then hugged one another. Bob helped Grace make the punch, adding a half bottle of Old Man's blackberry wine, and everyone present toasted the couple. Lurina and Old Man, lead actors in this drama, stood arm in arm and accepted the accolades.

"Will you still have a reception?" Jill asked Lurina later.

"Grace, get on over here, girl." Lurina waved Grace close. Perspiration beaded the old lady's forehead, but her face glowed with excitement. "Can we have a reception over at your tearoom come Sunday after church?"

"Why, I imagine so," Grace said, wondering if she could have it catered on such short notice, or try to do it all herself. She lifted her shoulders. One way or the other, with help from Bob and her friends, they could do it themselves, if need be. "Yes," she said, "Sunday, after church. We'll let the neighbors know by word of mouth. Wonder if they'll still come."

Jill laughed. "They'll come all right. They wouldn't miss the opportunity to possibly be on television."

"All of them on television?" Grace asked.

Just then, Bob walked over to them. "Madison County's known for its fiddlers and really great old folk songs," he said to Jill.

Jill turned to Wayne. "Could we get some folks to play and sing sometime before Sunday?" She turned to Grace by way of explanation. "We'll film it ahead, get as many of the folks in as possible, even just as audience, and I'll use whatever I can when we put the piece together. What I can't use will still be on a video I'll have made, and I'll send copies to all of you."

Grace found herself suddenly caught up in the whole affair. "Velma Herrill tells scary ghost stories."

"Great. Can you get her, Wayne?" Jill asked. Wayne was obviously her point man with the community, and from the way he smiled and nodded it was clear he didn't mind it one little bit.

Grace stood back and could not help admiring Jill's persistence. After the first days, Jill had taken a low-key approach, befriended Old Man, wooed the community, and her patience had paid off. Who could fault her for doing her job? Grace could see where it might be a good story. And she could see how Jill would tell it in a way that was not exploitative of Lurina, but sensitive, and without a trace of mockery.

🌰

The remainder of the week vanished in a whirlwind of placating phone calls, and preparations for the reception. On Sunday, everyone came, filling the tearoom and its porch and parking lot. So many toasts were offered that Grace thought they would never get to the food. But they did. Two brawls took place in the parking lot between cousins, before their families shuffled them off. Another day or so, Grace thought, and life will settle back to normal, that is until time for Russell and Emily's wedding and reception.

She did not, however, factor Ginger into the equation. Ginger stomped in from New York, angry at her sister, angry at Martin for not having the villa in what she considered mint condition, although

Grace thought Martin was doing a great job getting drywall replaced and painted, buying new appliances and furnishings. Ginger settled into a suite at a motel in Asheville, and popped in and out of Covington. She glommed on to Grace at the reception.

"This thing with Emily and Russell, how do you feel about it?" she asked.

"What thing?"

"You know. They're getting married. I can't get a date out of Emily. Has she told you?"

"You know as much as I do," Grace lied.

"Well, here they are now." Ginger careened through the crowd toward her daughter and Russell, who had just walked in. Minutes later she was back. "Well, let me be the first to tell you. Emily says they've set a date, June fourth. How in God's name will we ever put together a wedding in such a short time? The gown alone, why if we picked it out tomorrow, it wouldn't arrive by then." And with that she was off, flagging down Martin.

When Grace had a chance and could speak alone and quietly to Russell, she told him about Roger and Charles's offer to do their wedding. "They made this offer a while ago, but I didn't want to bring it up until you had actually set the date," Grace explained.

"Wow, would that be great." He waved for Emily, who was ladling punch for Tyler, to come to his side, and told her about the offer.

"Really, Grace? That's incredible, and so kind of them. It is short notice, we know that, but we hoped to avoid a long, drawn-out thing with my mother." She shrugged.

"Ah, yes, your mother."

Russell rolled his eyes. Grace noticed that Emily looked suddenly morose. "She's going to drive me crazy about a dress. Already she's yelling at me that I'll never be able to get one on such short notice."

40

A Time for Resolutions

After the final cleanup on the Monday following the reception, Grace and Bob sat on his porch enjoying the view. Whispers of a late-afternoon sun warmed their outstretched feet. "I'm absolutely worn out," Grace said.

"Me too."

"Bob, I've been wanting to say something for a long time."

"So have I, darling."

"You go first."

"Ladies first."

Grace sipped iced tea and wiggled her toes. Here goes, she thought. "I hate to admit this, but our tearoom is wearing me out. I haven't time to think. I've neglected . . ."

Bob lifted his hand. "It's a lot of work, and it's certainly time-consuming. I'm feeling about the same way."

"You are?" She searched his face to assure herself that he was not just trying to please her.

"I find I'm often too tired to play a round of golf with Martin, and I enjoy Martin's company."

"What shall we do, then?"

"What would you like to do?"

She grated her teeth slowly over her lower lip and fiddled with the end of the bandanna tucked into the waistband of her skirt.

"Sell it?" he asked.

She reflected for a moment on his tone of voice, trying to identify any trace of disappointment, uncertainty, relief. "Truthfully?" Grace swallowed. "Yes, I'd like us to sell it."

Bob leaned toward her, and kissed her cheek. "Don't look so apologetic. You're right. We need to sell it." He grew pragmatic. "We've done well. It's a nice little business for someone with the time and energy."

She rubbed the sole of one foot against the other. "You're sure? Be honest with me, Bob."

"I am, darling. It's a lot for me, too. What say we put the tearoom up for sale?"

"Oh, yes." Grace frowned. "Are you doing this for me?"

"For you, and for me. We've done good, Grace. You've been incredible, all that baking, and tired as you might be, you're always gracious to everyone. The tearoom's a success. We've even got Sybil trained."

"You think she'd stay?"

"Might."

Somewhere, a crow cawed, and was joined by another. Maybe they're chatting about important crow matters, Grace speculated.

Bob rose, and she moved to do so also, but he waved a hand and said, "No, I'm just going in to get us blankets."

Grace settled back on the lounge, feeling in her heart that they were making the right decision. Bob needed more time for his interests. He was still teaching, and that took hours of preparation. And his golf. She was glad he had found a friend in Martin Hammer. A shame Ginger wasn't a softer, gentler person. She was sure going to make Emily nuts before that wedding was over. Then, a warm, languid contentment spread over Grace, a contentment enhanced when Bob lowered a blanket across her lap and tucked it about her hips. He nurtured her. She was so lucky.

"How long do you think it'll take to sell?" she asked.

"Couple of months."

As they sat there in the quiet evening, Amelia came to mind. "I'm worried about Amelia. She acts as if nothing's happened."

"It's done with, what do you want her to do?"

"Oh, you men, that's how you handle things, is it?" Reaching out she twined her fingers through Bob's. "We women process differently from you men. This whole affair's eating at Amelia's gut, and she won't talk about it. I'll have to make time, be with her until she opens up. In time, she'll open up to me, you know."

"Up and at it then, woman."

Later, when they went to bed after lovemaking, which, as ever, left Grace amazed at its gentleness and pleasure, Grace lay in the dark listening to Bob's light snore, and thinking about Amelia, worrying about her. Then her mind drifted to what Max had said about folks being angry with Hannah for trying to stop Anson from selling his land. They had helped Hannah with posters and flyers, but most of what Hannah did was on the computer now. Hannah, she knew, had given up on land trusts and gone on to contact foundations that might fund this kind of project, to no avail. When Grace asked how things were progressing, a disappointed Hannah would shrug wearily and repeat the same old refrain. "When they find out about the Masterson land earmarked as a park, they lose interest."

Grace was exhausted, yet tonight she couldn't get Amelia or Hannah out of her mind. Well, Grace thought, turning over and closing her eyes, so long as you love someone, you worry about them, and you feel a portion of their pain and loss. Still, as much as Grace would have liked to be sound asleep, she knew that she would rather love and care than the alternative, a detached unconcern and loneliness.

The next day found Grace and Amelia alone in the kitchen, Grace having wooed Amelia there under the pretext of sampling a new cookie recipe she had baked. Neither liked the cookie.

"Too much of an anise taste," Amelia said, and Grace knew she was right.

"You must talk to me," Grace said. "What's going on with you?"

Amelia pushed her chair from the table.

"Stay. Sit." Like an obedient pet, Amelia sank into a chair at the kitchen table.

"Why are you doing this, Grace?"

"Look at you. You don't even hate ladybugs anymore. Those that are still in this house are falling from the ceilings and dying. Look. Here's one right now on the table, and you haven't skinned up your nose. That tells me you're in trouble."

Amelia squinted at the desiccated ladybug as if she had never seen one. "I am not in trouble. Ladybugs just don't bother me anymore."

"I don't believe that for a minute. You're completely distracted about everything. You don't remember anything, you forget to give phone messages. This isn't like you."

Amelia sighed. "I'm busy. I have my work."

"Remember how you'd buried all the pain of Caroline's and Thomas's deaths? Remember when you told us, out there, under the oak? And what a catharsis it was for you and a source of bonding for us all?"

Amelia sighed. Her eyes misted. "I remember. But this is different, no one's died."

"Many things have died: your dreams, your zest for life, your enthusiasm for your work." She almost added, "your self-esteem," but didn't.

Amelia shrugged. "How important, really, are any of those things?"

Grace placed her hands over Amelia's and felt how cold and clammy they were. "Amelia, Lance was a scoundrel and smooth and slippery as ice. He could have fooled anyone."

"But he didn't fool everyone, not Hannah, not you. Ginger maybe, but she's a bit of a fluff," she gasped. "So what am I, a piece of fluff? God help me." Amelia's shoulders heaved. Tears tracked a path down her cheeks. "What a fool I am. I'm so ashamed." Grace let her cry, occasionally patting her arm, once running her fingers lightly across Amelia's fine white hair.

"He may be gone, but every miserable moment you endure, every sleepless night, is one-up for him, the bastard," Grace said.

Amelia whispered, "I think I loved him."

"You think?"

"I'm confused. It's muddled in my brain. I can't think clearly. I just hurt, here." One hand found its way to her stomach. Amelia wiped her eyes with the sleeve of her shirt. "I hurt Mike. I had no time for you or Hannah. I've been a lousy friend. I hate myself."

"What makes someone a friend is time and understanding. What happened to you was horrible. It would make anyone miserable. That's the beauty of our sharing this house and our lives. Everything one of us does affects the others, and we're committed to supporting one another. Hannah and I love you, and Mike loves you. We want to hear you fussing about ladybugs, and hear you go tearing out of the house to a photography shoot, and see more of your wonderful photographs." Grace straightened her shoulders. She felt as if she were having no impact at all on Amelia. "Your life is so much more than having a man, Amelia," she said firmly.

"You're so wise, Grace."

"I'm not wise, just practical, and I love you."

"You've managed to have Bob and not neglect us."

"Part of that's Bob. He understands what we have here. He values our friendships, and he's pleased that you and Hannah are willing to include him in some parts of your lives."

"Bob must think I'm a tramp. He can't possibly respect me anymore. I can't look him in the face."

"Bob hates how Lance treated you. He'd like to strangle the man. He just wants you to be happy."

"Really?"

"Really." Grace nodded. "Think about it, Amelia. We've all done something, just in this last year and a half, that we regretted and felt ashamed of: I overreacted, behaved like a perfect ninny running away that time after Tyler's party, remember? I assumed things. I didn't even wait to talk to you or to Bob. I was a complete idiot. I was mortified at the immature way I acted."

Amelia's huge blue eyes grew wider.

"Didn't you tell me you thought that Hannah overreacted, was quite immature when Sammy smashed the car? Remember how she demanded that Miranda come the very next day to get them. She didn't care if they were in pain, and all bandaged up, or that the Gracious Entertainment Shop was about to have its grand opening. Later she was appalled that she had demanded such an unreasonable thing from Miranda. She was certain she'd permanently damaged their relationship, remember?" Grace reached over and with a corner of her bandanna wiped a tear from Amelia's cheek.

Amelia nodded.

"So you see, my friend, life's like that, up, down, we're wise one minute, foolish the next. You didn't love Lance, Amelia. You told me that."

No one spoke for a long moment. Then Amelia asked. "I did? When?"

"That day in December, when we had the storm. We were in the living room."

Amelia bit the corner of her lip. "I did, didn't I?"

"You knew, but who wouldn't be swept away by all that excitement.

How many women our age get to be sixteen, and swept off their feet? Regardless of how Lance turned out, it was a glorious time for you." Grace reached for Amelia's hand and held it. "Some day, months from now, I'll see you sitting there grinning to yourself, your eyes dreamy, and I'll think, she's sixteen again."

Amelia smiled. "Sixteen again!" Her eyes brightened and she looked down at the ladybug expiring near the cookie plate. "Ugh!" she said, "nasty thing." With one quick twist of her wrist, Amelia swept the little creature to the floor. "Get you with my vacuum, later."

The following morning when Grace went to the box at the edge of their lawn for their newspaper, a sign had been taped to the box. Lowercase letters cut from newspaper read "yankee go home." Grace snatched it off, and raced back to the house.

"What is it, Grace? Seen a ghost?" Hannah was still in bed, propped up, writing a letter, or trying to write a letter to Laura, whose card and P.O. box address arrived yesterday postmarked from St. John in the American Virgin Islands. *Dear Laura,* was as far as she had gotten.

"This." Grace held the paper in front of her. "Yankee, not Yankees. It's directed at you, isn't it?"

Wearily Hannah set the letter board and her pen aside. "Max warned me. What am I to do, Grace? I'm stymied. The U.S Fish and Wildlife Service won't trespass on Anson's land without a permit. We have no way to identify any endangered species if it were there."

"I feel awful not being more help to you. You need a lot of support from the community, petitions everyone signs, letters to the county commissioners and the mayor."

"None of which is going to happen, I'm afraid." For a moment her fists tightened, then Hannah drew her knees to her chest and held them hard. "I'm totally discouraged. Most frustrating battle I've ever fought. Years ago I helped stop a dump going in close to a residential neighborhood. Another time we closed a plant polluting groundwater. With all we know about our environment these days you'd think there'd be more interest."

"Environmental degradation's always driven by greed," Grace said soberly. She flopped on Hannah's bed and tucked her feet under her.

286

There was a sudden scramble and a thud from inside the wall behind Hannah's bed. "What's that?" Grace asked.

"You won't believe it, but Harold thinks it's a possum."

"What? How did it get inside your wall?" So many things, small things, big things happening in their home and she, Grace, run ragged and out of touch because of the tearoom. Not for much longer, though.

Hannah shrugged. "Sometimes they do."

"How do you get them out?"

"Traps, I hear, lure them out." She lifted one shoulder slightly and tilted her head. "What do I care about a little possum inside the wall?"

Grace shrugged. "When Maxwell came over that night after the storm, what did he say exactly?"

"Let me think. He said that I have to remember that this is a very independent, conservative area, and I am beginning to represent everything they resent and resist: government, zoning, whatever they perceive as infringement on their rights as landowners."

"All you're trying to do is prevent Cove Road from turning into one big development," Grace said. The possum in the wall scrambled again, as if for a foothold. "I think that would drive me nuts."

"What am I going to do, Grace? We so much wanted to be a part of this community, now see what I've gotten us into."

Grace thought a moment, then said, "I've come to agree with you and Amelia that we'll never really be a part of this community. Maybe it would be like that anywhere in the country, in a small town where people have lived for an eternity. I'm ashamed to admit that I don't recall ever making friends with anyone new who moved into Dentry. We're outsiders here and probably always will be. The best we can hope for is pleasant tolerance."

"Maybe not even that anymore. They applauded me at the church hall when I spoke, but when they got home people talked it over, while I went charging off calling this government agency, that funding source. I turned them off good. It was a mistake telling anyone anything." Hannah paused and looked over at the window. "Look at my Christmas cactus. It's still in bloom. Pretty, isn't it?"

"Very," Grace said, quiet now, giving Hannah time to collect her thoughts. After a time, Hannah threw up her arms. "I give up. We can all just sit back now and wait to see what happens." But the pain in Hannah's eyes was evident.

"It'll change everything on Cove Road. What will we do?" Grace asked, horrified at the prospect.

For a moment, Hannah closed her eyes. "We could sell this place, buy something where everything we can see belongs to us. By the way," Hannah said, "can you believe the map of Covington came yesterday by UPS, fifty copies."

"Show me," Grace said.

"Over there, those gray tubes."

Grace jumped off the bed, picked up one of the five long tubes, opened it, unrolled one of the maps, and spread it out on Hannah's bed. Hannah held two ends flat, Grace the other two. "I told him not to make it exact. I wanted it to be fluid, informal."

"It's very good," Grace said. "I like the way he marked each homestead on Cove Road with our names, and look, he's even got Lurina's family cemetery up behind her house, and her old barn. Lord, that wasn't used in years until Old Man and his pigs." She continued to study the map, then looked up at Hannah. "It doesn't show all the condos covering the hills in Loring Valley." Grace chuckled. "Guess that's what not being exact means."

"I'm not sure it matters. It's the concept that counts." Hannah released her ends of the map and it curled, then Grace let go of her end. "Guess there's no need for a map now," Hannah said.

"Of course there is. It's a fine map, and there are no maps of this specific area. The chamber of commerce in both Madison and Buncombe Counties will surely want to buy it."

Hannah rolled up the map. Then Grace said to Hannah, "We've decided, Bob and I, that the tearoom is too much for us."

"You're selling the tearoom?" Hannah was astonished.

"Yes. We both feel it takes too much time and creates too much pressure for us." Grace curled up on the bed. "It was a nice adventure, a side trip you might say, and instructive." Suddenly she sat upright on the bed and covered her ears. "You're going to try to get that possum out of your wall, aren't you?"

But Hannah was concentrating on different matters, and as if she had not heard Grace, moments later she was back to talking about Anson's land. "So, you think that I ought to just drop the whole land thing, including the cemetery Wayne found?" Hannah pounded her mattress with her fist, and clenched her teeth. "Damn, I hate to give up."

Grace touched Hannah's foot. "I hate for you to have to give up."

"What's better? Walking away from it, or having us all shunned by our neighbors?"

Grace slumped. "But Hannah, you realize that if you do back off, the folks who put that sign on our mailbox will strut about feeling they've won. Question is, can you handle that?"

Hannah nodded. "I'm weary of the whole thing."

"Come on," Grace said. "Get dressed in grungies. Let's pile on the layers and go outside and do some planting. You can show me how to divide daylilies."

"I usually divide daylilies in the fall." Hannah pushed off her covers.

"So what? If you can live with a possum in your wall, we can divide daylilies in the spring."

41

Family Matters

Dear Laura,
   Your postcard came today. I was happy to hear you'd arrived safely, and no hurricane barring your path.

Hannah crumpled the sheet of writing paper and tossed it into the wastebasket, where it joined a growing mound of crumpled paper. Hurricanes. What was wrong with her? This was April. No hurricanes until summer. Her mind wandered. Across the way, at Maxwell's, dogwoods bloomed above glorious clusters of salmon-colored azaleas.
   Why was this letter to Laura so hard? After all, it was merely to wish her well, to open some small communication between them. Probably, Laura's response would be another postcard, perhaps from another island they had visited.

Dear Laura,
   Spring this year is especially early and glorious.

A vision of palm trees and beaches came to mind. How did anyone prepare gourmet meals in the small galley of a moving ketch? She could not imagine doing so, yet Laura did.
   What is it like living on a boat? Change that to ketch. Why was it so hard to remember to make that distinction? Hannah had never asked her daughter anything about her life with Marvin. Suddenly

she wanted to know everything. Was he an educated man? How long had he been a sea captain? She bent to her writing again.

The tropics must be quite a change after Maine.

Hannah read the three lines. Trite. Stupid, but a start. She did not crumple the paper.

Stay in touch.

Inside her head, Hannah heard words she wanted to say and couldn't. I'm so sorry for not being more a part of your life, sorry for my hardheadedness when you needed understanding and acceptance. Forgive me. Instead she ended her letter with, *Enjoy the islands. Love, Mom.*

She held up the letter. No, it was a note, not a letter. Pitiful that this was all she could say to her child. Her instinct was to rip it to shreds, but instead, Hannah folded it, slipped it into an envelope, addressed it, and stamped it.

✒

Laura's reply came ten days later. A letter, this time, written, as Laura said, by the light of a full moon on the foredeck of the *Maribow*. The *Maribow*. Hannah had always thought of it as Marvin's boat . . . Marvin's ketch. She'd simply asked the man at the bait store to send a message to Captain Marvin's boat. They must have laughed at her in that bait shop.

> *In your wildest imagination, Mother, you can't picture how beautiful it is here. All about me are islands, dark crested in the moonlight, rising from a shimmering golden sea, and by day these islands, large and small, become emeralds floating on blue velvet. Nights are magical. Breezes rippling across my skin soothe me. The salt air is sweet, not hard and coarse as it is off the coast of Maine. We're anchored out off the reef at Trunk Bay on the north side of St. John. This week we're hosting three guests, all divers, who enjoy exploring the underwater trail here. I don't dive. Being underwater scares me, too frighteningly quiet.*

Sitting alone on the porch, Hannah closed her eyes. How had she failed to miss the poetry in Laura's soul? Tears slipped from below closed lids and slid slowly down her cheeks.

You may worry that Marvin is so much older than I am.

How much older? Ten years, fifteen? Hannah wasn't sure.

But he's hale and hearty, comes from long-lived people. I've learned so much from him: how to sail, to fish. Why, Mother, I could make my living lobstering if I had to.

And then the letter ended abruptly with, *Gotta go now. Wind's picking up. People stirring. Love, Laura.*

Love, Laura. Hannah read the words again and again. *Love, Laura.*

Laura had been a swift, easy birth, and she had loved her, but Miranda was a jealous older sibling, and as an infant and toddler, Laura had been so good-natured that Hannah's energy and attention funneled into placating her demanding firstborn. Hannah sat back. A good letter, open and more sharing than anything she could have written.

That evening Roger phoned Grace.

"Had a call from Russell and his Emily. She sounds charming. She explained about having to make concessions to her mother, sounds like a tiger, so they're going to have the wedding in a church in Asheville, but they were thrilled about our doing the reception. We'll throw them the most gorgeous reception. We've rented a U-Haul van, and we'll arrive in Covington by May eighteenth. That leaves us only two weeks or so. I need you to send me a phone book with the yellow pages. I could hunt on the Internet, but that would mean no personal contact with the vendors. We prefer to chat with the people we're going to work with. We'd like to make a lot of arrangements ahead of time."

Charles picked up their extension. "Mother Singleton, how are you?"

"Just fine, Charles, how about you?"

"Excited to be seeing you. Tell me, what's this Ginger like?"

"Difficult at best."

"We'll handle her," Roger said.

"Do me a favor, will you?" Charles asked. "Make us a little sketch of the yard, where the house is, the big oak, the stream, and if you could put some dimensions on it, distance of stream from the house, distance from the road to the porch of the house."

"We'll send it to you by the end of the week, okay?"

"Include it with the yellow pages, Mother."

Moments later they hung up.

Grace sat there, looking out at the big oak, remembering how she and Hannah and Amelia had sat under that oak their first day in Covington, before even going into the house. That day, Amelia had told them about her nine-year-old daughter contracting a rare disease in India, and how she had died in her arms on the plane back to the States, and a year later, losing Thomas in a car accident. In those moments, as Amelia opened her heart to them, she ceased being a pretty face with a mysterious past but became real to them and lovable.

Outside on the lawn, one rabbit, and then another, scampered by. They were cute, but prolific, and Hannah had had to wire-cage the vegetable patch, but not before the critters devoured most of the curly lettuce leaves the ladies expected to have for salads. The rabbits disappeared into bushes at the edge of the lawn, and Grace's mind drifted to Emily and her mother.

Russell had told her that the two women had had a drag-down fight, during which Ginger screamed and yelled about Emily giving up her practice in Florida, the dress, what it should look like, and that they would never find one and have it delivered by June 4. She had demanded that they defer the wedding to some time later in the year, or even next year.

"I was proud of Emily," Russell said. "She may be a size six, but she's tough. She gave it right back to Ginger. In the end we agreed to a small church wedding, and we got the reception. Emily will deal with getting a wedding dress, somewhere, herself, without Ginger's interference and criticism."

When would Emily find time to get a dress? Grace wondered. She was back and forth to Florida: a case to wind up, a court appearance, closing on the sale of her practice. As Grace watched two more rabbits scurry across the yard, she remembered Lurina's lovely gown, now stored upstairs in Grace's closet. Hadn't Russell mentioned that Emily was a size six?

42

A Walk in the Woods

Amelia still rose each morning with the weight of a wrecking ball on her heart. Following her talk with Grace, she began to focus, not on the shame and disappointment of her relationship with Lance Lundquist, but, as Grace suggested, on the fact that it had been a glorious fling with youth. Reluctantly at first, Amelia conceded to herself that although she missed the excitement and the dancing, she relished not having to meet someone else's deadlines. Still, there were moments when she lowered her camera and stared at nothing while feelings of regret, and loss, and humiliation rendered her immobile. Sometimes she cried. Then, she shook herself mentally, picked up her equipment, and proceeded with the task at hand.

April had flounced in with a flush of green, followed by dogwood and azaleas, and in May came the laurels, which the locals called ivy, and the rhododendron, which they called laurel. On a fine May day, something, Amelia knew not what, drew her to the woods behind their farmhouse. She carried no camera, and her arms swung free at her sides as she negotiated the narrow path to the top of the hill.

Between the pines, an unfamiliar glow caused her to stop. Amelia turned off the path. Carefully, for there were branches lying on the ground and a mat of rotting pine needles and dead leaves disguising hollows, Amelia rounded a thicket of rhododendrons. They were tall and impenetrable with dark, glossy leaves, and fecund buds primed for blossoming. How had she never noticed them before in her walks?

Amelia sought to mark the spot in her mind, some fallen tree, or bent branch, something she would recognize and be able to lead her friends back to, in June, when the rhododendrons exploded into flower.

Nothing seemed familiar. Was she lost in her own woods? Through the trees, the angle of the sun glittered on the metal roof of their farmhouse. She was further north from where she, or she and Hannah and Grace, usually walked.

A fallen tree trunk offered Amelia a place to sit, and in a little while, her breathing slowed, and she relaxed. The woods, in this place, were mainly pine. Perky gray squirrels leaped from one stiff, needled branch to another. Ants marched along the rough, scaly bark of a tree, toting bits of white. Somewhere a bird chirped. In the highest canopy, sunlight engaged pine needles in a shimmering dance.

Closing her eyes, Amelia listened: a snap of twigs in the underbrush, birdsong, soughing wind. A lightness came over her, and then a sense that she was floating. The farmhouse came into full view now, and the tops of trees, acres of them, and Cove Road all around to the top of Snowman's Cap. Harold Tate's truck drove slowly along the road. Maxwell, hands shoved into deep pockets, stood talking to Jose outside his red barn. Amelia waved. He looked up, but apparently did not see her. A horse and its colt stood near a fence. The horse lifted its head and snorted. Its long tawny mane fluttered in the breeze. How enchanting it was to drift like this over her world. Drift? The thought stunned her. Amelia opened her eyes. Her feet were firmly planted on dry pine needles. The breeze had diminished. It was so still that she heard, not only her breath, in and out, in and out, but her own heartbeat. Overwhelmed, yet oddly serene, Amelia sat silent for a long, long time remembering the time in Pisgah Forest, when she thought she was going to die, and she had floated briefly over her prone body. At the time, she had confided in Mike, who told her it sounded to him like an OBE.

"What's that?" she'd asked.

"An out-of-body experience." He had explained to her that this was not such an uncommon phenomenon. "There's a man, Robert Monroe, in Virginia who has a center where he teaches people how to go out of body."

"Who would want to learn that?" she'd asked.

"You know Dr. Elisabeth Kübler-Ross, who wrote *On Death and Dying*?"

"Yes. Someone gave it to me after Thomas died, but I couldn't bear to read it."

"Well, Dr. Kübler-Ross went there to learn. She thought it would be wonderful for paraplegics and bedridden people to be able to leave their bodies, get out a bit, you know."

It seemed a joke, then. Now, she wasn't so sure, having enjoyed the sensation of weightlessness, and the wider perspective it offered.

For a time, Amelia kept secret her OBE. It seemed sacred, special. If she told Hannah, Hannah would listen and say nothing, but she knew that Hannah was contemptuous of other worldly matters. Grace would be open-minded, but cautious. But as the days passed and she hashed it over and over in her mind, it was too much for Amelia to suppress. She phoned Mike, met him for lunch in Weaverville, and told him about her rather marvelous experience. But before she did, Amelia apologized for her behavior during the Lance time. "I'm truly sorry for treating you as I did. An apology hardly seems enough. Can you ever forgive me, Mike? I am so sorry."

"Way I see it," he replied, "you were temporarily out of your mind." He took her hands. "Of course I forgive you. I'm just glad it's over. You're going to be fine."

She lifted his hand to her lips and kissed it. "My dear, dear friend. I do love you." Then she told him about floating over Cove Road.

"Incredible," he said, looking at her with wide and admiring eyes. "That's twice. You're lucky. I've always wanted to go out of body. Never have, though."

They talked a bit about Robert Monroe's place in Virginia, and Amelia decided she'd take out-of-body experiences as they came, and not go seeking them. She didn't know why, but the experience changed her perspective about Lance and their relationship. The awful pain in her heart on awakening each morning diminished day by day. The knot in her stomach loosened, and she could eat, wanted to eat again. She felt peaceful more often, even if only for a minute, and with every passing day, Amelia grew more certain that her life was larger and wider then she had ever imagined.

Once again, Amelia became engrossed in photography, this time focusing on Madison County. She photographed an old man, nearly ninety, fiddling and singing ballads brought by ancestors from Scotland and Ireland. She photographed towns: Hot Springs deep in the valley along the French Broad River, once the mecca of the rich, and now making a comeback with new upgraded hot spring baths. Mars Hill, home to Mars Hill College, absorbed many hours, and she shot ten rolls of film there. But she spent the most time in Marshall, the county seat. The town had a long and picturesque history, and seemed stuck in time, wedged as it was between steep cliffs and the French Broad River. A school was built on an island in the river, and she attended picnics and other events at a park near the school.

Amelia also wandered the countryside, where she photographed wood cabins tucked into thickets or perched on slopes. The holes in her Nikes widened as she scrambled down gravel-strewn hillsides to caves reputed to hold treasure, and she cooled her feet in creeks with names like Spillcorn, Shut-In, and Crooked Branch. Amelia thrilled to the sight of hawks soaring from four-thousand-foot peaks, and remembered her OBE. Would it ever happen again? she wondered, and hoped it would.

At first, still recovering from Lance, she pushed herself, and her work began to consume her thoughts and her time. Sunburned, blistered, and peeling, she began to relish every minute spent photographing. *From Such a County* would be the name of her second book of photographs. She liked the way it sounded. She had taken the words from a delightful and informative book borrowed from the library titled *The Kingdom of Madison,* by Manly Wade Wellman. And healing came. Lance and his hold on her, once gargantuan, diminished, until it devolved into a blip rather than a blurring smear on the screen of her life.

43

When the Unexpected Happens

No sooner was the tearoom offered for sale than three buyers materialized, two of them residents of Loring Valley, one from out of state. The bidding was on. An excited realtor called in a new figure every day. Although their bid was several thousand dollars lower than the highest, Bob and Grace decided to sell to Mary and Jim Amsterdam, new residents of Loring Valley. Grace liked the woman's eyes. "Honest eyes, a good face," she declared.

Bob laughed. "Hardly a reason to sell to someone."

But the Amsterdams' credit proved sound, and once the papers were signed and the closing date set for May 29, Bob surprised Grace with tickets to *Ragtime*, onstage in Charlotte, a two-hour drive down the mountain.

After hours of anguished discussions with Grace and Amelia, who both refused to advise her, Hannah stopped pursuing the business of dating the old cemetery Wayne had found on Jake Anson's land. It was just as well, for the next day Harold dropped by to talk about the possum, to warn Hannah that if she didn't get it out, it might have babies in her wall.

"And then there'll be more noise. The smell'll drive you out if any of them die in there," he said. Harold urged her to call animal protection, and have them come and set traps. Finally she agreed. He lingered, working the rim of his hat round and round in his hands. "Hannah, Brenda and I like you ladies right much. I'm not one to interfere, but you best hear me now. Heaven and hell workin' together aren't gonna stop Anson sellin'. Once he makes his mind to something, no stoppin' him." He hesitated, took a few short steps back from her. "Bracken and Woodward got a bad name after what happened in Loring Valley this winter. They're pullin' out. Deal's off for now."

Hannah's eyes lit up.

"Hold it," Harold said, "don't go gettin' all excited. Anson's gonna sell, just a matter of when and to whom."

Hannah's spirits sank. Still, it bought time. With Bracken and Woodward pulling out, maybe there would be no buyer for years and years. She felt better, and for the next few days Hannah hit the plant nurseries and returned with flats and more flats of annuals, and perennials. It felt good to plunge into something over which she had control.

Then Charles called to talk to her.

"We want to create an entry into the space where we'll have the reception. What would you say's the distance between the big oak and the end of the porch?"

"Fifteen, twenty feet."

"Could you get Wayne to build an arbor between the two? If it's too wide a span, could you set a post in the center? After the posts are up, cover the ends with lattice, also across the top."

"I imagine we could do that."

She heard the smack of a kiss on the phone. "Hannah. You're a darling. I knew we could count on you."

So Wayne, with a helper, set about to build the arbor, eight feet and a post and another eight feet wide and post but not to the porch, only to the end of her flower bed beside the porch. And then she helped Wayne and his helper paint the latticework white.

❦

It came as a surprise when George Maxwell strolled over one afternoon while Hannah was on her knees at work on her new perennial bed. She didn't hear him, and it was not until he stooped and tapped her on the back that she was aware of his presence.

"You lose yourself in gardenin', don't you?" He asked. "Same as

300

Bella. I could talk to her, and she'd shake her head, and never know what I'd said."

Squatting beside Hannah, Max punched out the small plants from the flat and handed them to her. Taking them, she set them into the earth. They worked like this for a time, in silence, until the flat was empty. Hannah looked up at him as if surprised to see him.

"I know that look." Max laughed. "Seen it a hundred times on Bella's face."

"Thanks for the help," she said. She smiled then, and for a few minutes they sat on the grass saying nothing before Hannah was suddenly aware of the wet patches on her knees, the straggles of hair in her eyes, and the perspiration glistening on her face.

"A pleasure. Reminds me of old times with my Bella." He sighed and his dark eyes, usually serious, twinkled. "I've good news, Hannah. But first, let me help you up." He offered her hand. She accepted his help. "Here, let's sit on the steps over there."

Tall as she was, he was a good seven inches taller, and they sat on the same step and looked across at his house and windmill across the way. "Bella loved the land, like you do, Hannah. She considered Jake Anson a coarse, ignorant man, and when she heard about his sellin' out she was so upset I had to call the doctor, I was so frightened for her. One of the things she said to me in those last days was, 'Don't let Anson destroy this valley, Max.'"

"What are you saying?" Hannah managed. Their eyes met and held a moment. His closeness, the very smell of him disturbed her. He was Bella's husband. She shifted away from him.

"Bella inherited money which we never used, never had to. It doubled and more than tripled these last few years. Bella wanted the money used for educational purposes. Knowing how she felt about Anson and that land, I decided to do something about it."

Hannah gasped. Her hand flew to her mouth. Inside her chest her heart began to race.

"So, I hired a consultant, a park designer from Atlanta. I brought him on here. Anson chased us off a time or two with that old shotgun of his. But that was when he thought he had a deal with those developers. When that fell through, he changed his tune darn quick. "Hank Baines, that's the fellow's name, and I tromped that land up and down, and he came up with a plan that I feel would please Bella."

The fingers of Hannah's right hand clutched the post of the steps.

Max had hired a man who designed parks. It made sense; it made no sense.

Max took a deep breath and continued. "Hank Baines came up with a plan I think you'll like. If you like it, I know Bella'd like it. We'll turn part of it into livin' history museums goin' back to the time when the Indians lived here, how they hunted, lived, used, and preserved the land. Then we'll move on to white settlers, and how they lived, tools, furnishin's, how they used, and abused, the land, from simple farmin' to ruthless tree cuttin'. Your cemetery'll be preserved as part of that, and we'll put in a miniature dairy farm, with calves that kids can pet, and cows, and a milkin' barn. Like it so far, Hannah?" He grinned.

His smile warmed his face and warmed her heart. She could hardly believe this was true. She had let it go, given up, accepted defeat, and now this. "I like it a lot, Max."

"You're gonna like this next part even more. What do you think about gardens where children could come to learn about gardenin', and soil, and conservation. Every schoolkid in Madison County, and Buncombe County too, could come. And whatever other kinds of gardens you want to have." He drew himself up, squared his shoulders, and his dark eyes looked deep into Hannah's blue eyes. "And Bella and me, we'd like you, Hannah Parrish, to be the director of gardens, or whatever name suits you, of that section of this park, with a salary, of course, ma'am. What do you say, Hannah?"

Hannah could hardly take a breath. Her mind zoomed from Indian tents to log cabins to a sawmill to rows of green beans tied to poles in a children's garden. "What about traffic and crowds coming to the park?"

He shook his head. "Hank's got parkin' lots hidden behind screens of trees. Gotta give a little, Hannah, to get a lot."

She nodded. He was right of course. Her spirit soared. Never, ever, in her entire life, no one had ever given her a more precious gift. How could she thank Max? Her eyes brimmed as she said, "It's an honor for me to be part of such a wonderful and exciting new venture. Thank you." Her hands clasped over his. "Thank you."

"A deal, then. More details later." Putting his arm about her shoulder, Max gave her a quick squeeze, rose, and strode across their lawn, across Cove Road, and up his driveway until he disappeared into his and Bella's house.

Hannah sat for a long time. Tears dried on her cheeks. Almost a stranger, George Maxwell, yet he and even Bella, in death, had performed a miracle.

✦

For days after her talk with Max, Hannah's head spun as she fashioned a series of walled gardens: a children's garden, an herb garden, a water garden, a Japanese garden, an English cottage garden, a shade garden, and on and on. She planned and dreamed as she helped paint the wedding-reception trellis that Wayne and his helper built, and while she worked on her own summer garden, amending soil with peat moss, manure, perlite. Her brain buzzed with ideas as she set out the small plants: petunias, verbenas, coneflowers, veronicas, coreopsis, columbines. She imagined children planting and later harvesting the seeds of sunflowers. As she lay out her English garden of mixed annuals and perennials, she visualized children picking the green beans they had planted from inside a wooden frame on which the beans grew. She saw a maze through a small patch of corn, and saw them pressing, drying, arranging flowers grown by their own hands.

Hannah shared the news with Miranda on the phone. "Most amazing thing's happened. Land on Cove Road soon to become a living history museum, plus a series of different gardens, including a children's garden, that I am to be in charge of." She ran off the list of gardens she planned.

"Why, it sounds like you'll be creating wonderful gardens in Covington. I'm thrilled for you, Mother."

44

Roger and Charles Plan a Reception

On May 17, Roger and Charles arrived exhausted. They slept until noon the following day and came down to the kitchen bubbling with talk of Miranda, and the business, and Philip, who worked at the shop every holiday and loved the business, which delighted Hannah. They talked about Branston, how it was growing, the new developments, how builders were tearing down older homes to build huge new homes, mega-malls, and soon a civic center. "If we keep growing like this, we'll soon be a suburb of Philadelphia," Roger said. It was clear by his voice and the way his eyes flashed that Roger considered this a great idea.

After lunch, Charles, Roger, Grace, and Hannah walked about the land.

"You've done a great job building and painting this arbor. It's going to be absolutely gorgeous when we get the vines and roses on it," Charles said. They rounded a corner of the house. "We'll set up tents alongside the stream, and tables. Won't that be nice? Feasting to the sound of a babbling brook."

"Definitely an evening reception, for the lights," Roger said, "hundreds of tiny lights in the trees."

"Just back here, or will you also decorate the great oak in front?" Grace asked.

"The great oak?" Roger turned to look at it. He stood with his hand on his chin for a minute, then asked, "What do you think Charles?"

"I think it merits decorating." They walked back to the oak and circled about it. "It's definitely a great oak," Charles said. "You know." He took Grace's arm, and they walked for a while together. "Sometimes simple is best. Lights, and more lights, and white tablecloths, and china, and bold dashes of color in the flowers." He stopped and considered the east wall of the house. Would you let us paint those yellow shutters the color of the flowers we'll use? The yellow adds such a jarring note."

Grace looked over at Hannah. "Why not? We'll run it by Amelia. If it's okay with her, it's okay with us."

"We'll repaint them yellow later if you want," Charles said. "I'd also like to run tubs of pink peonies along the bottom of the wall. That okay?"

"Surely."

"How many people will there be?" Roger asked.

"The guest list keeps growing," Grace replied. "Ginger insisted on sending invitations to all the people who live in the villas. Fourteen of them said yes, even though they don't even know the Hammers."

"You'd think they'd have had the wit to RSVP no," Hannah said.

"Then there are a few business friends of Russell's, and of course most of the people on Cove Road are coming, and Mike of course, I just got P. J. Prancer, who said yes. Ginger's sister and family, that's four, are coming in from New York, and Emily has three friends coming up from Florida. Tyler asked four of his friends. I'd figure on about seventy-five. I'll have an exact count for you in a day or two."

Roger made rapid notes. "Figure on ten tables of ten, in case there are extras."

After a flurry of measurement taking, phone orders, and confirmations, Charles was free for the afternoon to accompany Amelia on a photo shoot. Charles liked spending time with Amelia. While they were gone, Roger and Grace visited Bob at his condo, where Roger stood on the balcony and raved about the view.

"We ought to buy a place here," Roger said.

Grace thought of hillsides sliding away and ice-slicked roads.

"We had a hell of a time with slides and mud and water in December, but you can see they're building retaining walls and seeding the hillsides. The loose stuff probably came off the first time. Couple of condos weren't touched at all."

Like Lance's place, Grace thought, and grimaced.

"You might want to stop at the office and inquire," Bob said, re-filling Roger's wineglass.

"Lovely, just lovely. I'll bring Charles over. If he likes it, we'll talk to them at the office here, and then we'll call Miranda and Paul." He turned to his mother. "We'd buy it in the name of the business, you see, Mother. That way they'd come for several weeks a year to see Hannah, and we'd come and see you and Amelia."

Grace knew Roger quietly preferred Amelia to Hannah. Charles especially enjoyed her company, and during their brief times together often spoke of their travels, referring to Europe as the Continent. Roger said they liked to include Amelia because she had no family. Grace smiled at her son. "It would be nice seeing you more often."

A crisis broke one week before the wedding. Emily arrived at the farmhouse in tears and found the women sitting out on their porch. "Mom was right about one thing. I went to every bridal shop in this city, even your friend Mrs. Lerner's, Grace. I thought I could find one that I could buy off the rack, but no, it has to be ordered." With her anxious eyes and frown, she looked as she felt, distraught. "What am I going to do?" The corners of her lips quivered. "I'm down to one week. One week. What do I do, get married in a suit?"

"I'm shocked you're having so much trouble finding a dress. What size are you?" Amelia asked.

"Size six."

How do I suggest Lurina's gown? Grace wondered. I can't. Emily would never consider wearing Lurina's fifteen-minutes-of-fame wedding gown.

After the wedding, Lurina had said, "You can take the dress back now, Grace. I ain't gonna use it no more."

"A store won't take back used wedding dresses."

"Then you just take it along to someplace like Salvation Army and let 'em give it to some girl who can't afford a dress."

But Grace hadn't the heart to just give the lovely dress away, so after being dry-cleaned and bagged, the dress hung in Grace's closet.

It was Amelia who saved the day. "J'ai une idée. Grace, don't you have a brand-new, gorgeous, expensive wedding gown in your closet in a size six?"

"You do?" Emily looked puzzled. "Why?"

"It's Lurina Masterson's gown. It's lovely. She wanted to be married in something special."

"Grace picked it out for her," Amelia said.

Emily drew back. "But she's eighty years old."

"Eighty-one, to be exact. It's a stunning gown, however old she is, and it should be worn by a young and beautiful bride. Lurina was proud as punch walking across her front parlor in it, and that's all the wear it's had. Within twenty minutes it was off of her," Hannah said.

"Just take a peek at it, Emily," urged Amelia.

"Someone's used wedding gown?" Emily shook her head, then her eyes flared. A mischievous look rollicked across her face. "Mom would croak over that." She grinned. "I'll look at it, if I may, Grace?"

From the moment the gown slipped over Emily's head, it was clear that, even without a décolleté neckline, it was perfect, molding softly about her breasts and tiny waist. She loved it.

"On you it's a vision of grace and beauty." Amelia clapped her hands.

Emily turned round and round trying to see it all in Grace's over-the-dresser mirror. "Have you a full-length mirror?"

"Back of my door." Hannah led the way from Grace's room to hers.

"It's wonderful. You picked it out, Grace? I absolutely love it." Emily gave Grace a hug. "Thank you for showing it to me. Can I buy it from Miss Lurina?"

"No, you cannot," Grace said, and as she saw the disappointment in Emily's face, she hastened to add, "My dear, you can have it. Lurina's wedding gift to you, you might say."

"Really? May I wear it, really?"

Grace nodded. Emily's eyes danced, her smile that of a gleeful child, and like a gleeful child she hugged Grace hard. "Thank you, Grace. Thank you so much."

"Thanks, Amelia. I wouldn't have had the nerve to even suggest it. And look at you, Emily, so beautiful. Why, it's perfect on you."

A scramble within the wall of Hannah's room distracted them all. "What is that?" Emily asked.

"A possum friend of Hannah's," Grace said. "What are you going to do about that creature?" she asked Hannah.

"*Mon Dieu.* Can it get through the walls to my room, do you think? This is worse than ladybugs." Amelia shuddered.

308

"I called the people Harold suggested. They're coming tomorrow with special traps."

The thing in the wall scuttled about as if it were stuck and trying to free itself.

"How can you stand that? I'm getting out of here," Amelia said.

Emily turned around one last time and followed them back to Grace's room, where they helped her remove the dress. "I love it," she kept repeating. "Russell's going to love it and Tyler too."

"Do you want to take the gown now?" Grace asked.

Emily tilted her head and considered this, then she shook her head. "I'd like to dress here. I can't bear my mother trying to interfere in this. After the wedding, she'll have plenty to say, I'm sure."

Not long after that, on a quiet afternoon, after the lights had been strung and the shutters repainted a lovely soft rose, Roger and Charles visited Grace in her bedroom. She was resting, propped up in bed reading. Roger plunked his tall frame into her rocker by the window, and Charles sat beside her on her bed, his shoulder touching hers, his back against the wrought-iron headboard. "With all the reading you do in bed, Mother Singleton, why'd you choose a wrought-iron headboard?"

"It was me being impetuous. I wanted something pretty and different, I imagine. Everything in my life had been so staid, I thought wrought-iron would be fun. But, you're right. I stuff a half dozen pillows, at least, behind me to get comfortable. One of these years I'll change it." She wanted to spend some time alone with Charles. Alone, they could really talk. He would share bits of gossip about a customer, or tell her stories from his own life, or about the dogs, both friendly and unfriendly, that they encountered on their daily walks, or about a new restaurant they had been to, or about his health. She wanted to talk to him about the tearoom, to explain why she had gone into it, and why they were selling it. He would understand the stress, the responsibility, the time pressure of a business, especially one having to do with food services.

Roger squirmed in the rocker and extended his legs. Long legs needed a long chair seat, and her rocker's seat was short and low to the ground. Grace considered her son. Where had Roger gotten his height from? Ted had not been much taller than herself, and none of their parents had been more than five feet ten inches tall. Roger was six feet and more, and handsomer than any of his forebears. A wonder.

The rocker creaked. Roger pushed up and out of it. "I can't sit here," he said. "Coming, Charles?"

Alongside Charles's leg, Grace tapped her hand. A quick look urged him to sit awhile and chat. "I'm going to visit with your Mum a bit." Charles waved Roger from the room, turned, and took Grace's hand in both of his. "Now, Mother Singleton, we can have a bit of a chat, what say? Why, for goodness sake, are you selling that absolutely beautiful tearoom? I adore tearooms. Granny had a tearoom once. Smaller than yours, tucked away on a little twisting street." He squiggled his hand through the air. "No money in it, what with her regulars, and how they'd sit and gab for hours over a cup of tea, then go off for a quick fish and chips. She had to give it up eventually. Got to be too much for the old girl. Why'd you go off it?"

"Same reason as your grandmother. It got to be too much. It consumed our time. I found myself constantly on the run, playing catch-up. I was hardly able to get to the school where I'd been tutoring children. I just couldn't give that up, Charles. It's an important part of my life. Then, we were open until five o'clock, so I couldn't even have tea with Hannah and Amelia in the afternoons anymore. I missed that. And Bob likes to golf, and he has his teaching. I guess we got overly excited initially, and didn't think clearly."

"I understand." Charles pushed up higher on the bed, then rummaged behind him to readjust the pillows. "You must get a solid headboard."

She nodded, settled herself the best she could, for she had given him another one of her pillows. She told him how the tearoom consumed their lives, then related the hullabaloo caused by the TV people, and about Lurina's wedding, and her inviting the crew in when she'd protested against them from the beginning.

"Is it possible Lurina phoned them in the first place?"

Grace had considered and rejected this idea. "She wouldn't."

He laughed. "Well. She certainly sounds like a character, and feisty, as you say yourself. So, why not, then? Maybe the idea caught her fancy but the reality was overwhelming."

"Should I ask her?"

"Think she'd admit it?" Charles asked. He was silent a moment, then he laughed. "Grace, why not let it be the great mystery of Covington?"

She patted his arm. "Now, my dear, tell me how you really are," Grace said. "What are those dark circles under your eyes all about?"

He sighed. "I get so knackered some days. I go home for a rest at noon. Miranda can tell how I'm feeling. She pushes me out the door."

"And Roger?"

Charles heaved a deep sigh. "Dear Roger. It's hard on him. I haven't the stamina I used to have. We adored traveling, Grace." His laugh held a bitter edge. "How do you Americans say? Johnny-on-the-spot, suitcase packed, ready to hit the road." His eyes grew dreamy. "The adventure of it all: Morocco, Bengal, Nepal, Israel. Where haven't we been?" He looked at her. "It's different now."

"My goodness, Charles, you're working six or seven days a week, what would you expect?"

"Even without the business, I've lost interest in traveling. It's hard on me, uncomfortable, waits in airports, long flights, cramped seats. My ankles swell. Takes me days to recover from jet lag." He grimaced. "I've lost enthusiasm for the whole thing."

"I'm less enthusiastic about things, myself. More even keeled actually," Grace said. "That's part of getting older, maybe, for some people, and it's all right. I'm still very much alive and enjoying my life, my friends, my family."

Charles coughed, swung his feet over the side of the bed, and sat up straight. "I find that personal comfort's more a priority, my own bed and pillow, food that won't upset my stomach."

"I know what you mean." Silence came easily and comfortably to them, then Charles said, "I better go find Roger," and he stood and smoothed his trousers. Grace also rose.

"Tell me Charles, how's the T cell count?"

"Amazingly good. Ta! Ta! I'm a lucky one, wouldn't you say?"

"I'm very glad."

He hooked his arm around hers as they headed for the door. "Maybe I'm just working too hard." He laughed. "Well you know, how can you not with a new business?" At the door, he stopped and turned to look at her. "There are other things."

"What things?"

He did not answer for a long time. It was so still in her room that Grace could hear the humming of the battery in her bedside clock.

She did not press him. Charles sighed, and said, "It's a marker, you see, our daily walks. Used to be able to go three miles a day. Then it was two, then one. Now I make it around our block. Roger slows down for me, but he's like a dog straining at a leash. I say, toddle off, Roger, get a good run, but he won't." Charles's eyes clouded. "Roger's getting restless." He turned to her. "I can feel it." His chin quivered. Then his face tightened. Charles fastened his eyes on some spot on the far wall. "I'm scared to death he'll leave me." He hit the wall with his palm. "There. I've said it."

Grace stood next to him silent, aching for him.

"After all," Charles went on, "I contracted this horrible disease through no fault of Roger's, and it's changed not just my life, but his too. He's a young man." He stifled a moan. "Maybe it's age. I'm older than he is."

Pity for this man she cared about like a son filled Grace's heart. "Charles," she whispered, "I don't believe Roger's going to leave you. He loves you."

"Did love me," Charles said.

"Roger's loyal. You have a life, a business, friends together."

Charles shook his head. "Not many friends. Miranda and Paul, that's all."

"One true friend is better than many shallow ones."

"Miranda and Paul have kids, a life, they're busy. Roger and I don't talk like we used to, now, it's mostly about business."

"That's how it is when you're in business together." The house was very quiet. Grace wanted to weep. Charles's pain filled her as if it were her own. Taking his hand Grace held it tight. "Dear Charles," she said softly, "whatever life brings, please know that you're not alone. I'm here. I love you as if you were my own son. You are my son, never doubt that."

Like a wounded child, Charles buried his face in his hands. His shoulders heaved. Grace put her arms about him and he succumbed to wrenching sobs. She held him until his sobs subsided. "Thank you, love," he said. "I think I need to freshen up before we go down," and he headed for the bathroom.

She could hear Roger calling from the side yard. "Charles, let's get going. We're going to meet with the caterers."

Grace replied to her son from her window, "Charles is in the bathroom. He'll be right down."

A moment later Charles came from the bathroom, looking some-what better, but with his eyes still puffy, and ran down the stairs.

✳

Grace stood alone in her room in the silent house. Where was every-one? She ached for Charles and Roger. She couldn't imagine Roger walking out on Charles, but you never know. Roger was approaching those middle years, that crazy mixed-up time of life.

At that age, she recalled, Ted had dipped into their savings and bought a speedboat. He'd spent every Sunday of a long and worri-some summer careening across Lake Bixby looking as if he'd capsize any second. By winter he'd lost interest and sold the boat. But he'd given her months of aggravation and anxiety.

✳

That day, Ginger called, her voice cold. "What the hell have you done?" she demanded.

Grace set down the onion. She turned off the fire under the pot of stew on the stove. "What do you mean?"

"I mean, Grace Singleton, that ghastly dress."

Grace picked up the knife and stared at the onion. The phone sat in the crook of her neck. She hardly cared if it clattered to the floor. "You've seen the dress?"

"Don't have to. If it suited an old lady, it won't suit my daughter."

"It's a lovely gown, expensive. Lurina spent twenty minutes in it. It's been in my closet ever since."

"You planning to wear it too?"

Grace bridled at the sneer in Ginger's voice. The knife came down hard, lopping the onion in two. One half of the onion gyrated on the cutting board, then lurched to the floor. Grace stared at it.

"I'm in charge of this wedding, the dress, the music," Ginger was saying. "What right have you . . ."

"Something's burning in the oven, Ginger. Have to go now." Grace hung up. Hadn't Emily wanted to shock her the day of the wedding? Oh well, maybe her mother had aggravated her to the point where she simply had blurted it out.

Within seconds the phone rang again. Sticking her fingers in her ears, Grace hastened outside and walked away from the house. Wed-dings made people irrational. Ginger, of course, was like this much of the time. Grace had tried to like her. She and Bob had gone for dinner with them several times. Ginger invariably found fault with the food, the service, the lighting, the seats. Too hard, too soft, too low, too high. Nothing pleased her. Just the other day, they had even gone on a picnic to Hot Springs with Russell and Tyler and Emily. That had been ghastly.

Ginger had worn slacks and a long-sleeved shirt, a hat, and dark glasses, yet even after smearing her face with a thick white lotion she continued to swat flies no one else could see or feel. And, she called Tyler boy. "Come here, boy. Get my bag from the car, boy."

How had a mild-mannered man like Martin Hammer ever fallen in love with and married such a woman? What kind of mother had she been to Emily, and how had Emily turned out to be such a sweet, kindhearted young woman? Grace wondered. She looked at Martin sitting at a table, deep into a checkers game with Bob and undisturbed with anything else going on. Men had a way of being tunnel-visioned, shutting out all they chose not to see or hear or feel. For a moment she wished that her antennae were not always alert to everything going on around her.

Grace turned away from the men, and concentrated on Emily and Russell and Tyler, who were throwing a ball to one another. Tyler was happy. Emily was seeing an attorney in Mars Hill about joining his practice. They would sell Russell's house and buy a larger home closer to Mars Hill. A new school for Tyler. Grace worried about that. But then, she worried too much.

"Throw me the ball, Emily," Tyler called.

Emily threw, Tyler missed, then flopped onto the grass laughing. Emily ran to him, flopped beside him, and tickled him. Obviously she cared a great deal for the child. Now he would have a new house, a new mother, and a new school. It would probably all work out just fine for Tyler. It was Grace who would miss his bright little face, his quick hug in the hall when she went to Caster Elementary. Grace smiled. She'd come to love so many people since moving to Covington.

Ginger's crabby voice interrupted Grace's musing. "I haven't seen it."

"Seen what?" Grace asked, pulling her shoulders erect.

"The gown, the old woman's wedding gown. First she tells me she's wearing a hand-me-down, and then she refuses to let me see

314

it. I know about these things. It's probably horrible." She nodded toward Emily. "Stubborn like her father, they can do such mean things to a person."

"Oh," Grace said, trying to see it from Ginger's perspective and failing to do so.

The smell of Ginger's heavy perfume wrapped itself about Grace. Grace sneezed, and turned away. This was the last, the absolute last time she would allow herself to be talked into any event with Ginger, after the wedding.

"Tell you what." Ginger sidled over to Grace on the wooden bench. "I'll come over. You show me the dress." Her long face widened a bit with her toothy smile.

"I can't do that," Grace said.

Ginger drew back. Her voice rose. "And why not?"

"I promised your daughter no one would see it until she wears it down the aisle."

"And." Ginger pulled back. "I suppose you promised your son and his, his . . ." She waved her hand in dismissal of Charles. ". . . not to tell what they're doing for the reception?"

"My son's name is Roger, and Charles is like a son to me." Grace swung her legs from under the bench and left the table to join the others in their game of catch.

45

Ripples

The week prior to the wedding saw the closing on the sale of the tearoom, and a series of parties in honor of Russell and Emily. The Tates threw a backyard barbecue, for which Old Man roasted a pig. Ginger and Martin hosted a formal luncheon at the Grove Park Inn in Asheville for family only, which of course included, at Emily's insistence, Hannah and Amelia and Mike. Bob had the family in for cocktails at his apartment. He refused to let Grace cook for this event, and had it catered.

And finally the day arrived. On June 4 at ten in the morning, a radiant Emily walked down the aisle of the church in Asheville on her father's arm, looking exquisite in Lurina's satin wedding dress. Ginger sniffled softly from the front pew.

"Where'd she get that real pretty weddin' dress, Grace?" Lurina, sitting next to Grace, asked.

"It's your dress, Lurina, don't you recognize it?"

"You don't say? We'll if that ain't somethin.' She sure makes a pretty bride."

Tyler bore the ring on a blue velvet cushion. He glanced at Grace as he passed and winked at her. Grace winked back. Tyler had grown up so much since she had first met him. She was so proud of him.

The wedding was lovely, the church a bower of flowers, the music traditional, the service short, with the vows written by Russell and Emily. There was no "obey" in their choice of words. Grace liked that. She hoped a new generation would find more happiness in a married life that stressed cooperation.

✤

The reception that evening was perfect. The music was soft, the weather delightful with clear skies and a cool soft breeze. The buffet was bountiful and scrumptious. Tiny white lights on every tree limb gave the illusion of a fairyland. Charles had selected deep pink peonies for table decorations, and painted the windows the exact color of the peonies. Amazingly, the dance floor spanned the stream. Romantic, she thought, a very lovely touch. Grace counted eighty-seven guests.

✤

Talk of this wedding, and the reception, would continue for weeks after the bride and groom departed for a honeymoon on the coast of Maine.

"Never seen a bride pretty like that Hammer girl," P. J. Prancer reported to his staff at the hardware store.

"Food at that reception. Lord, I never did see so much food, delicious food," Pastor Johnson reported to all who asked, and those who didn't.

"The flowers in that church. Gorgeous. They must have emptied every flower shop in Madison and Buncombe Counties too," Brenda said to Velma Herrill.

Lurina's wedding dress, worn by Emily, caused the biggest stir. "Imagine, wearing a used wedding dress." This from Alma Craine, gossiping with someone at the newly opened beauty salon on Elk Road.

Someone shopping in Prancer's remarked, "Miss Lurina's dress? What's the matter, she couldn't afford her own dress?"

The woman spoke so loudly that P. J. Prancer must have heard her, for he exited his glass-front office, a rare occurrence, and confronted her. "Listen up, Agnes," he said. "Can't imagine Ole Miss Lurina even getting married in it. It sure looked elegant on that young woman. Like it was made for her. Doubt the old lady ever wore it, marrying like she did at home. Probably she gave it to Emily. Mighty nice gift that was, I'd say."

And the rumor became fact, that Lurina had never worn that dress, and had gifted it instead to Emily.

They spoke of Grace's wedding cake: "Where'd she get a recipe like that with all them colored layers?" and "That Grace sure can bake up a good cake."

"How about those fellows who put on the party?"

"You mean Grace's son, and who's that other fellow?" A raised eyebrow. "His partner? Well, they sure did put on one beautiful reception."

"And everybody dressed up so nice and actin' so friendly."

"I liked the music. Good dancin' music."

"Did you hear they put the dance floor over the stream? Good thing nobody fell off. Who but some Yankee would of thought of that?"

And so it went, on and on for days, and into weeks, until the topic of chat shifted to the other big news on Cove Road.

"What you think about what Maxwell's done? Why'd he want to make a park outta Jake's land?"

"I hear tell he's gonna do what they call a livin' museum. Folks dress up in old-time clothes, and use old tools and stuff."

"I got lots of rusty old tools if he wants them."

"Well, it sure beats houses all over the land."

"I hear tell Hannah's gonna run a part of the place, something about gardenin' and kids. That ought to keep the old busybody busy."

This brought laughter. Someone else said, "Ah, she ain't so bad, just wanted the land preserved, that's all."

"Why'd Maxwell do it, do you think? For that Hannah woman?"

"Naw. It's gonna be named after his wife, in her memory, like some folks might put up a statue."

"Hope things quiet down in Covington soon. We've had 'bout enough excitement round these parts to last a hundred years: television people, Lurina marryin' Old Man, big fancy weddin', Maxwell buying Jake's land."

And so it went, friends gossiping, neighbors gossiping, people being people.

✤

But that night after the wedding and the reception, after the ladies, and Charles, Roger, Mike, and Bob doffed their formal clothes and

319

put on grungies, they all collapsed on the front porch. The men settled on the steps. The ladies rocked. Stars ravaged the sky.

Roger and Charles had packed their van earlier, and would leave tomorrow. Local vendors would be by to collect tables, tablecloths, chairs, the dance floor, and the table settings. "Well," Grace said. "I'm sorry to see you two go."

"All's well that end's well," Roger quoted the Bard.

"Yes indeed. It was one amazing week," Amelia said. "So many parties. I'm quite worn out."

"Well done, boys." Hannah, closest to the steps, leaned over and patted Charles's shoulder. "Tell Miranda, I send my love. Tell her to come see us soon."

Charles's hand reached back, and closed over Hannah's. "I certainly will. And since Miranda and Paul liked the idea of a condo in Loring Valley, we'll all be seeing much more of you all."

"Which pleases me mightily," Hannah replied, choosing to ignore the fact of its being in Loring Valley. She could tolerate that better, now that she knew the Anson land was secure for generations to come.

Then Charles's face lit in a wide grim. He turned to Grace. "I asked Miss Lurina if she was the one who called the television people."

"What did she say?" Grace was all ears.

"Sly old bird. She said, 'That's for me to know, and for you to find out.' I still think she did it."

"I thought this was to be the great unsolved mystery of Covington." They laughed good-naturedly. A short while later, Grace pointed to the heavens. "Look at those stars. That's one of the things I love here, we can see the stars, and now there'll be no light pollution on Cove Road to destroy it."

"My goodness," Amelia exclaimed suddenly, brushing her lap vigorously. "Will they never go away, these confounded ladybugs?"

"There can hardly be but a few stragglers these days," Hannah said.

"But there are more of them every year."

"You're going to have to find a way to live with them, Amelia."

"Like you lived with the possum in your wall? Never."

"My possum's gone, lured out, trapped, and taken away."

Grace smiled. Her eyes met Bob's. It didn't get much better than tonight.

While the reception was going on, Jill had left a long message on the answering machine. Lurina and Old Man's story would air in early August. She would let them know the exact date and time. Grace knew that on that night, everyone in Covington would forgo sports programs. Yes, indeed, she thought, the good folks of Covington will certainly have plenty to gossip about for a long while to come.

46

Among Friends in Covington

And so, with the tearoom sold, and the wedding and reception behind them, the ladies gathered, again, on their front porch at four in the late afternoon on a sunny June day, for a good, old-fashioned tea. Grace spread a lace runner over the table, and Hannah carried the silver tray from the house through the door that Amelia held open for her.

Once seated, Amelia said, "So much has happened in eight months." Her eyes clouded. For a moment she fell silent, remembering Lance, then she smiled, and her whole face brightened. "Mother used to use an old cliché, *What happens happens for the best*. I think I'm starting to believe that. Everywhere I go these days, people are kind, they tell me stories about Madison County, and most of them let me photograph them. I even asked Miss Lurina and Old Man. She was a bit resistant, but I think that's how she is at first to anything new. Old Man thought it was a great idea, right from the start, even said I should put their photo right on the cover of my next book. Should they be sitting on her porch holding hands, do you think?"

"You'll figure it out," Grace said.

"How lucky I am that Mike and my friendship survived Lance Lundquist." She could say his name now. "You're right, Grace, time and events, the vicissitudes of life, they do indeed test friendships.

Mike's and my friendship's stronger now than ever. In fact, everything about my life is better."

Hannah rested her head back on the rocker. "I sure learned plenty trying to get funding for Jake's land. Met some nice people, and look how it turned out. Answer lay right here in our own backyard."

"And all because of Bella Maxwell," Grace said.

"I miss Bella," Hannah said. "She was a very special woman. I'm sorry she never made it over for tea." She changed the subject. "What do you think about leaving that wedding arbor where it is, as entrance to the backyard, and planting roses on it, sort of like the entrance to a secret garden? There's a climber rose called Old Fashioned Bella. It's a medium rose color."

"A kind of memorial to Bella?" Grace asked.

Hannah nodded, "I'd liked to plant it so that it will grow over the arbor. I'll always think of it, then, as Bella's arbor."

Grace twisted her head toward the arbor, still adorned with silk roses, and greenery. "It's beautiful, isn't it, all those pink roses, even if they aren't real?"

"How about painting all the windows that nice soft rose color?" Amelia had never liked the yellow window shutters.

The others agreed. Then Hannah touched Grace's arm. "Wedding cake was the best."

"Did we save some, freeze some of it so we could have it another day?" Amelia asked.

"There's plenty in the freezer." Grace smiled. "So many people have asked for the recipe."

"Best cake I ever ate—moist, delicious." Hannah rocked back hard. She felt magnanimous and satisfied.

"Will you type the recipe for me, Hannah, so I can make copies?"

"Of course, I will," her friend replied.

Their talk turned to the tearoom. "Selling the tearoom was as good for Bob as for me. There's a time for everything." She knew it seemed irrational to some people, that she and Bob had opened a business, and so quickly sold it. But Grace was certain that life flowed best when one listened to one's instincts rather than to the opinions of others. They had learned much about themselves and one another during this venture. Each had a clearer vision of how they wanted to live life and use time. Nothing had been lost. They had even made a small profit on the sale.

"Bob seems quite content." Amelia leaned over and poured them a second cup of tea.

"He is," Grace said, smiling. "And I am too."

"Remember when we first moved here, how quickly tea in the afternoons became a ritual for us?" Amelia asked.

Hannah smiled at her. "And I sure did miss it there for a while."

"We've got to watch that our lives don't get so jumbled or confused that we lose sight of what's important," Grace said.

Hannah stopped her chair from rocking. "I wonder, if we did it today, is there anything different any of you would add to our time capsule. It's over a year since we buried it."

"I'd laminate and put the Vienna cake recipe in it."

"I'd add a photograph of our wonderful farmhouse taken from the top of Windy Hill, up there behind our house. I'd show the mountains beyond in drifts as they look in the evening most days."

"I'd add the map of Covington."

At that moment, one moving van, and then another, rumbled by. "That must be the Ansons moving," Hannah said.

For a time it was quiet on Cove Road, and on the porch, and then Molly Tate Lund's car went by, and they waved to one another. "It's wonderful," Grace said, "to be among friends here in Covington."

Grace's Multicolored Vienna Cake

Using three, nine-inch cake pans, this recipe will make one three-layer cake.

1 cup (2 sticks) unsalted butter, softened	3 level teaspoons baking powder
2 cups sugar	1 cup milk
4 large eggs at room temperature	1 teaspoon vanilla extract
1½ cups self-rising flour	Red, yellow, and green food coloring
1¼ cups all-purpose flour	

Preheat oven to 350°. Grease and lightly flour three cake pans and line the bottoms with rounds of wax paper.

In large bowl, with an electric mixer on medium speed, cream butter until smooth. Add sugar gradually and beat until fluffy, about 3 minutes. Add eggs one at a time, beating well after each addition. Combine the flour and baking powder in a separate bowl, then add to batter slowly, in four parts, alternating with milk and vanilla extract. Beat well after each addition.

Divide the batter into three small bowls and add the food coloring—two or three drops at the most—green to one bowl, yellow to another, and red to the third. You will have pale yellow, pinkish, and light green batters. Pour the batters into three different baking pans. Bake for 20 or 25 minutes. Watch carefully, and test with knife tip or toothpick for doneness. Be sure layers are baked through.

Let the layers of the cake cool in their pans for ten minutes, then remove and finish cooling on racks. When completely cooled, spread a thin layer of strawberry or apricot jam on top of the first and second layers as well as a thin layer of the frosting on top of the jam. Stack the layers, and frost the top and sides with cream cheese frosting. Keep cake in a cool place before serving

Cream Cheese Frosting

2 (eight-ounce) packages cream cheese, slightly softened and cut into small pieces.
½ cup (1 stick) unsalted butter, softened slightly and cut into small pieces
1½ teaspoons vanilla extract
5 cups sifted confectioners' sugar

Makes enough frosting for a three-layer cake.

In a medium-size bowl, with an electric mixer on medium speed, beat the cream cheese and butter until smooth, about 3 minutes. Add vanilla extract. Gradually add sugar and beat well until mixed and of a consistency to spread easily.

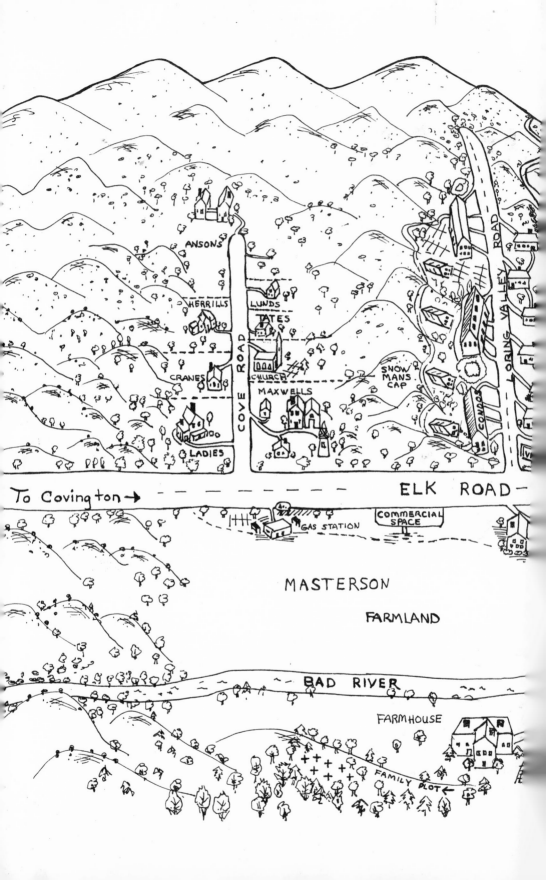